THE SHELTERING TREE

J.R. LAWRIE

Carnation Books

ISBN (ebook): 978-1-948272-49-0

ISBN (print): 978-1-948272-50-6

Published 2021 by Carnation Books

CarnationBooks.com

contact@carnationbooks.com

Seattle, WA, USA

For Rachel,
who loved it the most.
(Happy birthday.)

Friendship is a sheltering tree.

- Samuel Taylor Coleridge, Youth and Age

Chapter 1

"Six o'clock, sir," Juliet announced, striding into Alastair's office with his dress uniform draped over her arm. She'd already changed into her usual little black dress, chandelier earrings sparkling in the overhead lights. "I'm sorry to cut in on your fun, but it's time."

Alastair smiled in surrender, folding shut the lengthy counter-terrorism report he'd been reading. After three years of evening events together, she had the procedures running like clockwork and the timings down to a tee. If the need ever arose, she could probably prepare him for a function in his sleep.

It was only a pity he couldn't attend them in his sleep as well.

"Time waits for no man," he supposed, standing reluctantly from his desk. Juliet transferred the heavy uniform with care into his arms. "Refresh the details of this evening for me, will you? I'll admit they've been pushed to the back of my mind."

Juliet produced a fresh black tie as if by magic, and added it on top.

"Small charity of the year," she said. "Formal dinner—it's beef wellington, don't get excited—and then you'll present the award on behalf of the Metropolitan Police Service to this year's charity. Your speech is on cards in your top pocket. Brief and breezy. I've marked all the witticisms in orange. And before you ask, sir. No. I don't know what you would do without me either."

Amused, Alastair laid his uniform over the back of his chair. "I hope I never have to find out," he said. "Who is this year's winner?"

"The Fieldhouse Foundation," she replied, scooping up his outgoing post from its tray on his desk. "They're quite a new charity, but they've done a lot of good work with disadvantaged young people across London. They seem to focus on outreach to those teenagers at risk of falling into gangs."

"Ah. Yes, excellent. Very commendable." Alastair flipped up his shirt collar. "'Fieldhouse' in honour of—?"

Juliet blinked, pausing as she shuffled through his letters.

"Oh, no," she said, realising. "No, nobody died. The charity was set up by a Mr Jay Fieldhouse. He's their chief executive. I expect he'll be there."

All very standard, Alastair noted to himself, loosening his tie. *Nothing out of the ordinary.* These occasions formed a vital part of his role, but they could drain his energy into the dirt at times. He wasn't a particularly social creature by nature, his successes in the field born of practice rather than talent. From what he was hearing, tonight had every chance of remaining uneventful, and he was glad of it. With luck, he might even be in bed by midnight.

"Arrival for seven o'clock, is it?" he checked, giving up his tie to Juliet's waiting hands.

She tossed it over her shoulder. "Arrival for seven," she said, striding away towards the door. "Champagne and schmoozing. I'm sure you know the drill." The black sequins on her heels flashed with each step. "Dinner starts at half past. Oh, and the events team have handled the seating plan, so just prepare yourself."

Alastair's gaze snapped up from his cufflinks. "Who am I seated with?"

By way of response, a feline smirk came his way from the door.

Alastair groaned.

"Again?" he said. "Must they do this to me on *every* occasion?"

"She's a pillar of the community, sir—and a baroness to boot. They can hardly stick her at the back by the fire exit."

"May *I* please sit by the fire exit?" Alastair sighed. He dropped his cufflinks into his desk drawer with a clatter. "At least it would provide me with some means of escape. The woman has no shame, Juliet. She definitely squeezed my knee at the Lord Mayor's Banquet last November. The audacity."

"Are you certain it was her? Those tables were very cramped."

"It was her or the foreign secretary. And I hardly think he's the type."

Juliet swallowed a smile, reforming her expression into its usual faultless composure. Her heart-shaped face, pixie cheeks and delicate mouth had been crowned by Mother Nature with a pair of enormous brown eyes, almost cartoonish in their scale. The first five minutes of her interview, three years ago now, had locked her forever in Alastair's mind as a girl in her earliest twenties, young enough to be his daughter. In truth, she'd be turning thirty-three in spring. There was nothing doll-like nor dainty about Juliet. Those around her forgot it at their peril.

"Perhaps Lady Ingham just needs a stronger hint," she suggested mildly. "She clearly missed the memo about your disinterest in the charms of the fairer sex. Drop something into wider conversation. Make it obvious."

Alastair snorted. "Not exactly appropriate," he said. "Not exactly relevant, either. The charms of either sex would be wasted on me these days."

He began to unbutton his shirt.

"Besides," he said, working through the fastenings, "I don't think there's any hint in the world that would work. If I had a gentleman in a rainbow thong sprawled across my lap all evening, she'd just assume we have an eccentric new deputy commissioner. Nothing will keep the bloody woman from pawing at me."

Chuckling, Juliet reached for the door handle. "It's the aiguillettes, I think. They're like cat toys."

"They're a menace," Alastair said, "is what they are. If she reaches any higher than my knee this time, I shall throttle her with them."

"Very good, sir. I have your dress shoes at my desk and Larry should be here with the car in twenty minutes. Don't be long."

"Lady Ingham," Alastair said, forcing himself to smile as she breezed across the lobby towards him. "What a pleasant surprise."

"Commissioner," she crooned, beaming. Though it pained Alastair to acknowledge it, Selena Ingham was precisely the kind of woman he'd once been expected to marry. He assumed she'd had the brick-red blusher sprayed on at some point during the mid-eighties, then kept it in place all this time with collateral applications of L'Oreal Elnett. If Princess Diana had survived to discover orthopaedic shoes and grow a menopausal moustache, the two women might have been mistaken for each other at parties.

As she hauled him into an embrace, her enormous jade earrings pressed painfully against Alastair's cheekbone, squashing his smile out of shape.

"The pleasure's *all* mine," she husked in his ear.

Quite certain that he'd never offered her any, Alastair patted her once—and once only—on the back.

"How are you?" he asked, attempting to let go.

Lady Ingham held on around his shoulders, forcing him to stay just as he was, his face half-buried in her fluffy white cape. "All the better for seeing you," she said, then sealed his fate with her bell-like laugh. "I *do* hope we're seated together at dinner."

"Aheh," Alastair said, inwardly ruing the day he ever joined the Metropolitan Police Service. "Yes, let's hope."

As she finally released him, Lady Ingham winked.

"You know," she said in a stage whisper, "it's *three years* this month since Melvyn died. The time has *flown.*"

"Has it?" Alastair said, doggedly maintaining his smile. He could feel Juliet's amused gaze trained squarely on the back of his head.

"How strange. For me, it seems like yesterday. Three years. What a thought."

He turned to the next person in his welcome party, shooting out a hand for them to rescue him.

"Good evening—Alastair Harding. Lovely to meet you."

He was introduced one by one to various people from the charity, fresh-faced young professionals with unpracticed handshakes. They all smiled and gave him a nervous bob, as if he were visiting royalty. He often wished he could come to these events in ordinary formal-wear. The fussiness of his uniform never failed to unsettle people, though it did mean he'd now become an expert in soothing quips. One of the young men had accidentally matched the pattern of his tie to the very busy floral carpet underfoot, which provided a nice platform for some gentle humour. They all broke into relieved giggles as Alastair joked with them, promising he'd prepared an extremely short speech.

He took the gentleman last in line to be Fieldhouse himself, greeting the man with a two-handed shake and a broad smile—though this turned out to be one of the charity's trustees. He seemed pleasant enough and was happy to talk. Alastair accompanied him through to the function room, where they spent a few minutes chatting over champagne, discussing the charity's upcoming projects. As the space around them slowly filled with well-dressed people, Alastair kept one eye on the crowd, looking out for unfamiliar gentlemen of authority. He suspected the PR team would want pictures of him talking with Fieldhouse. It was usually their top priority at these events. In fact, it was curious not to have been nudged together already.

The signal for dinner was given before he'd had a chance to check with anyone.

"You're up by the stage," Juliet told him, walking him casually towards his table as the rest of the room took their seats. "The events team put you next to Ingham. I've had a sly word with the caterers and they swapped her place with Fieldhouse. Let's hope he's a little less handsy."

"Thank Christ," Alastair murmured. "Remind me in the morning you're due a pay rise. Are we even sure Fieldhouse is here? I haven't been introduced."

"Well, there's somebody sitting in his chair." Juliet tipped her head towards the table. "Shall I do the honours?"

Surprised, Alastair followed her gaze.

The table nearest the stage had gained a single occupant, a man sitting alone with his back towards the crowd. From this angle, Alastair could see very little of the mysterious Mr Fieldhouse: a dark navy blazer with sleeves rolled back from the wrist, hair midway from brown to black, short at the sides and dishevelled on top. His apparently casual posture was undercut by a touch of tension in the line of his shoulders. The fingertips of his right hand drummed a tiny, unconscious rhythm on the tablecloth, as if he were trying to reassure himself.

Alastair watched the motion, intrigued.

"Not necessary," he said to Juliet, giving her a brief smile. "I'm sure I can manage."

She bowed her head. "Of course, sir. Enjoy your dinner."

Alastair made his way between the tables, giving a genial nod to every glance that came in his direction. He recognised many of the faces. These events tended to attract a certain subset of society, well-heeled Londoners who liked to lend their support to charitable endeavours. The charities changed, and the venue, and the food, but the list of VIPs rarely varied.

As he finally reached his seat, Alastair put his hand on the back of Fieldhouse's chair.

"Mr Fieldhouse," he said, preparing his warmest smile. "I'm sorry to have missed you so far. I'm—"

Lord.

Fieldhouse was a sight for the weary soul. Big, broad-shouldered and gorgeously modern, he could have made a fair career modelling jeans. From the back, his dark hair had put Alastair in mind of brown eyes. In fact they were a mossy shade of green, as bright as polished brass. A touch of boyishness lent warmth to his features, though he couldn't be any younger than forty. Perhaps only a decade separated the two of them in age. He kept his stubble shaped and well-tended, just on the right side of scruffy, and a bump in his nose suggested he'd broken it in the past. It only added to his charm. Such startling good looks fully excused the lack of a tie.

As he registered Alastair's dress uniform, Fieldhouse broke into an awkward but honest smile. He rose at once from his chair.

"Sir Alastair," he said, putting out his hand. "Hi. Pleased to meet you."

Composing himself with a breath, Alastair accepted the handshake.

"Alastair," he said, clasping Fieldhouse by the palm. "Please don't bother with the 'sir'. They can insist upon the ceremonial dress, but I'm allowed to leave the title at home."

Fieldhouse's smile became a tentative grin. "Alastair," he said, flushing. "Great."

They resumed their seats together, shuffling themselves in.

"You can probably just call me Jay," Fieldhouse added. "I, ah... I only ever get Mr Fieldhouse at the bank."

Alastair unfolded his napkin, offering a smile. "It's difficult balancing these events," he said. "Formality might be traditional, but it isn't necessarily welcoming."

Jay huffed. "Well, we're honoured to be here. It's very kind of you. Very unexpected. Still pinching myself a bit, if I'm honest."

Even his accent was magnetic—a sort of moderated northern, consciously smartened up in the presence of a police official.

"The honour's all ours," Alastair said, hoping he'd get the chance to hear that voice untempered and untidied, honest rather than clean. The glass of red wine sitting by Jay's elbow would hopefully help. "It's only right that your good work be celebrated..."

Other guests began to join their table, checking the name cards to locate their seats. Beneath his surface of calm, Alastair found himself flustered, startled out of his routine by this unexpected surge of attraction. It didn't happen often. Even as a younger man, he hadn't been prone to sparks and fireworks. He'd almost forgotten what it felt like to take a shine to someone.

After a long career built on moderating his responses, he could trust his own face to keep the feeling away from view. It still took him a moment to decide what 'ordinary behaviour' would now involve.

"I've just been talking with some of your people," he said, falling back on one of the standard threads of conversation he'd picked up many years ago. Socialising with strangers was like gymnastics—well rehearsed movements, performed as smoothly in sequence as possible. It usually felt a little more fluid than this. "The passion within your organisation speaks for itself. I understand you're still a fairly new charity?"

"Pretty new," Jay replied, still flushing, though his smile seemed to be coming more easily. "We registered... wow, actually about seven years ago now. That's gone by quick. But yeah, on the grand scale of things."

"Where were you before then?" Alastair asked.

"Up near Leeds."

"Still in the charitable sector, or—?"

"Youth support worker," Jay said, taking a drink. He swallowed and put the glass down. "Tell the truth, I didn't know a thing about charities until I started one. But the universe sent the right people my way, and I've done what I can to support them, hear their feedback, get them what they need so they can work their magic. And now... yeah," he concluded, dropping his gaze with a half-laugh and a grin. "Fancy dinner with the police commissioner. Who knew?"

Alastair's heart thumped. He was used to sharing these evenings with pretentious brown-nosers who'd been preparing their small talk for weeks in advance of meeting him. He'd never encountered such a reluctant chief executive before.

That bashful grin was extremely refreshing.

"Your role seems very similar to mine," he said, prompting a dubious lift of one eyebrow. "Helping the right people to achieve their best, I mean."

"Pretty sure there's a bit more to yours," Jay said. "Top copper in England."

"Well, my authority's largely limited to London. I'm... *technically* the highest-ranking officer, but no man is an island."

"Don't your lot guard the queen?"

"Ah—well, yes, protection of the royal family does fall under my jurisdiction."

"Thought so," Jay said, smirking behind his wine glass. "I googled you this afternoon. You meet the home secretary every week. And you've got..."

He gestured at Alastair's chest.

"Silver bits," he said. "Special magic ropes you have to wear. You're on Wikipedia. Don't sit there and tell me you're not a big cheese."

Alastair wasn't sure when it was he'd started smiling. He found himself helpless to stop.

"I didn't even know I had a Wikipedia page," he said. "I hope it was enlightening."

"Oh, yeah. Picture of you on a horse with a big plumed helmet. It's a belter."

"You wanted to know what you were letting yourself in for, did you?"

Jay's expression warped with amusement. "Exactly," he said. "Mandatory hobnobbing at some swish function all night? Needed ideas for stuff to talk to you about."

Something inside Alastair's chest seemed to bubble and dance, something which felt lighter than air. It warmed his blood and made him brave.

He leant a little closer, and was granted Jay's ear.

"Whatever ideas you came up with," he said in it, his voice low, "please forget them. I *hate* hobnobbing. Normal conversation for once would be bliss."

A flash of delight filled Jay's eyes. "Think I can manage that," he said, grinning. He searched Alastair's gaze from up close, as playful as a puppy with a stolen sock. "Does the Met commissioner drink wine?"

"In moderation," Alastair said. "Until he's given his speech, at which point he can drink however much he likes."

Pleased, Jay reached for the bottles at the centre of the table.

"Let's get you started," he said, picking one up. "Huh. Turns out this *is* my kind of evening."

Dinner unfolded as both a wonderful and vexing experience. Even before the soup bowls had been cleared, Alastair became aware of two wildly conflicting priorities. The first was his professional obligation to act as something of a host, guiding the wider conversation of the table through a series of polite and pleasant topics; the second, and far more appealing, was to talk privately with the man just beside him.

Lady Ingham, relegated several seats to Alastair's left and out of flirtatious touching range, seemed to be compensating for the distance by launching conversation topics like cannon balls. Every time Alastair attempted to withdraw from wider chat, hoping for a moment or two with Jay, she let fly another subject at a volume he couldn't ignore.

"Dear Alastair, do tell everyone that *terribly* funny story about the protester at the Boat Race a few years ago. It's such a *scream* when you tell it."

"Well, Alastair of course knew my late husband *very* well—didn't you, Alastair? They were at Oxford together. Yes, he and Melvyn were terribly close..."

"Alastair, darling, what exactly is this nonsense I was reading in the paper about stamp duty on second homes?"

Ever patient, Alastair responded to her prompting and retold her favourite anecdotes on demand, relieved that the Fieldhouse guests sharing their table were pleasant enough not to mind.

Their chief executive, for his part, seemed happy to observe the conversation. He followed every word of it, often smiling at salient points made by his people, or else huffing in wordless amusement, though he contributed very few thoughts of his own. This reticence was apparently normal in him; his team seemed quite at ease. When he did speak, it almost always led to laughter from his people. The younger members in particular looked towards him as they ventured their opinions, their eyes bright, and Alastair caught one or two reassuring winks being given in response. This might not be Jay Fieldhouse's natural environment, but his people were clearly *his* people.

Halfway through the main course, with Lady Ingham midway through some lengthy monologue on the importance of grammar schools, Alastair discreetly inclined his head towards his right.

Jay took a measured sip of wine, regarding Alastair with amusement over the rim.

"What's your speech about?" he asked, his voice soft. This was a private conversation.

Alastair's stomach squirmed. He wished he knew what it was about those impish green eyes that captivated him so completely. He couldn't remember when somebody had last looked at him that way. Not within a decade, at least.

"I haven't a clue," he said, provoking a delighted laugh. The freeness of it made him smile. "But I'm sure it'll be one of my best."

"Do you make a lot of speeches?"

"Hardly a day goes by when I don't."

"All blurs together after a while, I suppose." Jay took another drink of wine, rather more slowly than necessary. The subdued lighting had swollen his pupils. "You're not like I thought you would be," he said.

"No?" Alastair asked, his tone as mild as he could make it. *God help me. Those eyes.* "Dare I ask what you were expecting?"

Jay grinned rather guiltily. He licked the smile off his face, sweeping his tongue over his lower lip, then straightened his expression into something more serious.

"Don't think I anticipated the sense of humour," he said. He leant forwards in his chair, retrieved the bottle of wine they were sharing, and topped up Alastair's glass. "When they told me I'd be at the commissioner's table... I don't know. I'm some stray from the backstreets. I don't have much worth saying to the rich and the beautiful."

Before Alastair could respond, a voice rang out from across the table.

"Mr Fieldhouse!" Lady Ingham called, flattening nearby conversations into the dust.

Jay shot Alastair a brief and conspiratorial glance, his smile twitching at its edges. If they weren't so well-placed within Lady Ingham's eyeline, Alastair suspected he might have been treated to one of those winks. Even the thought made his stomach swoop.

Jay turned in his seat to face Lady Ingham, his expression polite and accommodating.

"Do forgive me butting in," she beamed, batting her eyelashes at them both. "I don't think we've been introduced—Lady Selena Ingham—your head of finance here was just telling me that you cap your salary to the London average. Is that *true?*"

Jay's head of finance gave him a look of sound regret over her shoulder, mouthing the words: *I'm sorry.*

Jay's smile stayed true, his eyes as bright as ever. "You're correct, Lady Ingham," he said. "I didn't set out to make money."

Alastair drew a breath, preparing to coast the conversation away from personal finances and onto something a little lighter.

"But doesn't that make it terribly difficult to live?" Lady Ingham demanded before he could speak. "The London average *can't* be particularly roomy. How on earth do you support a family on it?"

"I'm not married," Jay said. "No family to support. But if I was, I'd be doing it the same as anyone e—"

"Now that I *cannot* believe," Lady Ingham cut across him, laughing. She looked to the other ladies for support. "A handsome man like yourself, and *no wife yet?* Why ever not?"

Jay pulled the corner of his lip between his teeth. "Well, I'm gay," he said. "That probably hasn't helped."

As the Fieldhouse team tidied their expressions and busied themselves with their food, Alastair very carefully loosened his grip upon his wine glass. Lady Ingham took a moment to reboot her brain.

"How lovely," she said at last.

Out of her sight, one of the Fieldhouse team choked in silence on her wine, reaching hurriedly for a napkin. Her chief executive cast the girl a sparkling glance, making no comment.

"What a surprise, I mean," Lady Ingham went on, forcefully resurrecting her smile. "You really don't seem the type."

Alastair's mouth beat his brain to the goal.

"We rarely do, Selena," he said, lifted his glass of wine, and took a sip.

How she reacted, he would never know. The whole of his attention was focused on the silent and invisible shift which took place at his right hand side—a stirring in the ether, a recognition.

Perfectly composed, Alastair set down his wine.

"I have to admit," he said, addressing the table at large, "I'm not usually too thrilled by the prospect of beef wellington, but this is actually very nice. Maybe I've judged it too harshly in the past."

As the table flowered into relieved discussion on the merits of beef wellington, Alastair sat back and simply listened, drinking his wine.

The silence on his right seemed to gather close around him.

He extended his own in return, wondering.

With his audience relaxed, well-fed, and in the cosier stages of intoxication, Alastair's after-dinner speech gave itself. His attention strayed once or twice to the front table, where a smile awaited his gaze, green eyes glittering with interest. While it was enough to cause a lift in Alastair's pulse, it didn't disrupt his train of thought. He was almost sorry to finish speaking so soon.

He presented the award to the group of delighted young people accepting on behalf of the Fieldhouse Foundation, thanked everyone for coming, and invited them to enjoy the rest of the evening in the bar.

As the PR team ushered necessary people into the lobby for photographs, Alastair noted the absence of a particular face among them.

He beckoned Juliet from the crowd.

"I need you to do something for me," he said as soon as she reached him.

She pulled her phone from her clutch bag in readiness. "Of course."

"Find Fieldhouse before he vanishes," Alastair said. "He seems deathly allergic to publicity. But I need you to give him my card."

If it struck her as an unusual request, it didn't show. She nodded, put away her phone, and slipped back into the function room without a word.

A few minutes elapsed, in which Alastair tried to focus on the photographs and not on the strange jumping in his chest. He didn't know what he hoped to gain from Fieldhouse having his details. He didn't know what he was offering or requesting. *A valuable professional connection,* he tried to tell himself, then despaired a little at his own transparency. The truth was that any kind of contact would do. If he could simply establish a link for now, he could work out what to do with it later.

Juliet reappeared behind the photographers, lingering just within his eyeline.

Alastair gestured her over between shots.

"Did you find him?" he asked in undertones, as the PR officer rearranged the people on either side of the award plaque. "Did you give him the card?"

"No, sir," she murmured.

Alastair's heart fell. "Has he alr—"

"He says you can give him one yourself," she finished coolly. "He's waiting in the bar for you."

Oh.

Alastair cleared his throat, keeping one eye on the PR team. "Good," he said. "He had some interesting thoughts on our recent community engagement initiatives. I'd like to hear more."

Juliet smiled.

"Very good, sir," she said. "You'll be remaining here for a while, then?"

"Yes. Likely not for long, but... well, there's no reason for you to hang around. You're welcome to head off."

"Are you certain?"

"Yes, of course. If you just let the driver know I'll need—"

"I shall. May I ask for some small reassurance that you'll stick to your pre-agreed security restrictions?"

Alastair's cheek twitched. He wasn't meant to stay overnight at an unauthorised address; the suggestion that such a thing might be on the cards was ridiculous.

"As my personal assistant," he reminded her quietly, "my security isn't strictly among your responsibilities."

Juliet hummed. "You're quite right," she said. "All the same, I'm going to take that as a yes."

As the photographer gestured for Alastair to rejoin the shot, Juliet gave a small bow.

"Have a good evening," she said, turning elegantly on her heel. She was gone into the crowd before Alastair could look for her, leaving only an indistinct whisper of perfume in her wake. She would breeze back into existence at half past eight tomorrow morning, as faithful and loyal as a shadow. Until that moment, he was alone—and at liberty to spend his time however he wished.

He smiled for the glare of the camera, trying to ignore the restless prickling in his blood.

What on earth am I even expecting? he thought. He took a measured breath, relaxing out his jaw. The camera flashed. *We'll have a drink and a conversation. That's all.*

I'm not expecting anything.

Chapter 2

THOUGH JAY LONGED FOR A BEER, HE ORDERED A GLASS OF LEMONADE and drank it slowly, sitting in a corner and reading emails on his phone. He didn't *feel* drunk, and he wasn't anywhere near his usual limit, but he wanted to keep an eye on his intake of liquid courage. He'd been cheeky enough already, close to ordering the head of the London police to come and have a drink with him. More alcohol wasn't the way to do this.

Jesus, he thought, shivering a little as he scrolled. *When did I grow a pair of balls this big? What's even going through my head?*

This entire year had been insane, ever since they'd been shortlisted for the award. *The Metropolitan Police Service's small charity of the year.* It still wrecked Jay's head. Even being in the running had brought the world to their door. It wasn't his place to start limiting things, dragging them back out of the sky just to soothe his own fear of heights. He owed it to everyone else to let the good times roll. All the same, he would be glad when this spike flattened out.

Clearly, it was giving him grandiose ideas about his station.

Jay gulped back another few mouthfuls of his lemonade, letting it cool some of the heat in his face.

Just a drink, he told himself, flicking through messages he'd already read. *Just have a laugh, have a chat. Seems like a nice guy. Not a huge issue.*

He wished he could kid himself that this was about the charity, making connections. Anyone who saw them chatting would assume so—and maybe that *was* what they'd talk about. Maybe this was all just a great opportunity for business, and he'd seen things in those gorgeous, serious eyes that just weren't there.

Damn, though. Sir Alastair Harding, commissioner of the Met.

It seemed wrong somehow, aching in his trousers for someone who'd been knighted by the queen. People like that were meant to be admired, not fancied. They weren't supposed to really register on the radar.

But Alastair registered loud and clear.

It had been a while since anybody had. Jay hadn't really looked for anything since rolling up in London a decade ago. He'd stumbled into a few depressing one-night stands here and there, trying to scratch an itch he couldn't reach on his own. Crawling from a stranger's flat before dawn had never actually scratched it, only dampened his appetite for next time. The years had slipped by, eaten up by more important things.

This felt very different, though.

Just see where it goes, Jay told himself, finishing the last of his lemonade. He started up another email to keep his head busy. *Stop getting ahead of myself.*

As he hit send, he glanced towards the entrance and caught a sight he wouldn't soon forget. Alastair was strolling down the carpeted steps into the bar, impossible to miss in his uniform. The single-breasted black overcoat made his figure so crisp and lean it almost hurt to behold. The silver ceremonial cords were a little over the top, but the insignia on his epaulettes gleamed as he passed beneath the lights—and Jay couldn't tear his eyes away.

Alastair scanned the crowd, his head upright and his expression tense, somewhere between hope and nerves.

Fuck, Jay thought, sucking in a breath. *I can handle this.* He gave a wave to catch Alastair's eye and attempted to smile like this was normal, like he chatted up police commissioners every other night.

Spotting him, Alastair relaxed in an instant. The tension seemed to flood from his face, replacing him at once with a man who seemed much younger, happy and bright-eyed just to see Jay. He gestured that he'd be a minute, then headed across to the bar, sliding a slim black wallet from inside his overcoat.

As Alastair ordered and paid for two drinks, Jay gave in and let himself look. He wouldn't have described Alastair with a word like 'pretty'; he was far too serious and upright for that. His cheeks were slightly hollow, his mouth a little flat, and his eyebrows naturally huddled close to each other in a searching sort of pre-frown—but he wore the subtle indications of his age like he'd earned them, and the sureness of it grasped Jay by the heart. Alastair had a face for dry humour, clever and cutting, and clearly he knew it. Jay liked those kinds of people. He loved the thrill of coaxing them to let go and laugh, loved seeing them undone. Though Alastair's accent hailed from the Home Counties, his name and his colouring suggested a drop of Scotland in his blood. The copper in his hair had probably gotten him bullied as a child. It would have done at Jay's school.

Alastair presented it the same way he presented the rest of himself, wholly oblivious to any idea he might be a catch.

When he finally joined Jay at the table, he brought two glasses of whisky with him.

"Highland Park," he said, setting one down in front of Jay. "Eighteen years old. You strike me as a whisky man."

Jay gave him a grin, hoping the lights were low enough to hide the pink in his face.

"You got me," he admitted. "Eighteen years old, huh? You don't mess around."

"As a rule," Alastair said, settling into the plush leather seat beside Jay. He crossed one leg over the other and relaxed, lifting his tumbler to his mouth. "You're not one for publicity, are you?"

Jay tried a small laugh, unsettled that it had been spotted so quickly. He was usually better at concealing it—then, he thought, it was a police officer's job to notice the unusual. He shouldn't really be surprised.

"Never liked cameras," he said, watching Alastair drink. "Just not my thing."

"Most chief executives jump into press photographs uninvited," Alastair said. "Peeling them away from the camera is the problem."

"Yeah, well... I'm not much of a chief executive. I've asked them three times to call me a founder or something, but they said it wouldn't properly reflect my role. It's the charity I want in the papers, not me."

"Quite refreshing of you."

"You think?" Jay took a sip of scotch, unprepared. He swallowed with a helpless shiver. "Shine a light," he breathed as the burn oozed its way down his throat.

Alastair smiled, delighted. "You approve?"

"Jesus, yeah. That's amazing."

"Mm. It's very drinkable. If anything, I've started us off too ambitious."

"Fine by me," Jay said. "I've got no problem with ambitious." He took a second sip, shivering again. "Just don't let me get wasted, will you? I don't want to embarrass myself. Way too easily done."

Alastair huffed, his gaze rather soft. "You're safe in my hands," he promised. "I don't make alcoholic mistakes."

Jay's stomach tugged. He couldn't think of anywhere he'd rather be right now than in Alastair's hands, and he doubted it would be a mistake to end up there, alcoholic or otherwise.

"Nice to talk," he said. "Just the two of us, I mean."

"Mm, it is." Alastair gave him a pained smile. "I can't apologise enough for Lady Ingham. She's something of a throwback."

"It's alright," Jay said, amused. "Think she learned something."

"All the same, I hope you weren't embarrassed."

"Nah, it's fine. Never kept it from my team. She didn't like us chatting, did she? Couldn't share ten words without her leaping in."

"She, ah... tends to monopolise my attention at these events," Alastair said. "I think she's had her eye on me for a starring role in Melvyn

II, the sequel." Some secretive amusement tightened his mouth. "I'll admit something to you, on the promise that you repeat it to no one as long as you live."

Grinning already, Jay crossed his legs towards Alastair, resting his arm along the back of their seat. "Go on."

Alastair's eyes glittered. "My assistant made a last minute amendment to the seating plan," he said. "She thought you might make better company for me."

Jay laughed aloud, throwing back his head.

"I *thought* there'd been a shift!" he said. "On the stuff they sent out, it said I'd be sitting next to Gary. That's fantastic. Wow. Well, I hope you're going to tell your assistant she was right."

"I am," Alastair said, taking a sip of his drink. "It's rare for her to be wrong, but she excelled herself on this occasion."

Something squeezed behind Jay's ribs.

"Almost sounds like you're taken with me," he said, hardly daring to believe his own mouth. He smiled, resting his head upon one hand. "Do you not meet many scruffs from up north?"

Alastair looked as if he wanted to smirk, casting his eyes away across the room. The corners of his mouth curved upwards. "Not enough of them, clearly."

Jesus, Jay thought, his pulse a little dizzy. *The things I'd let you do to me.*

"I don't meet many police commissioners," he said. "Guess it's a good thing we ran into each other."

"Mm." Alastair swirled his whisky, eyeing Jay with some pleased, unspoken thought. "How do you spend your time outside of work?"

Jay laughed a little, unsure how to put this without sounding like a tragic bastard.

"Fill it up with more work, to be honest," he said. "Sort of job where there's always something to do. When I'm ill, I watch a bit of telly..." Suspecting he should brighten things up a little, he added, "I keep thinking about taking the weekend off somewhere. Get some clean air in my lungs. It's tough just to set a date and do it, though."

"I understand," Alastair said. "I think it's part and parcel of being single. There's no one to encourage you to make plans, and so the plans go unmade."

Jay attempted a casual tone. "You're single too, then?"

Alastair nodded. "Wedded to my work."

We know that one. Jay offered out the edge of his glass. Alastair tapped it with his own, and they drank.

"What would you do with your time?" Jay asked, brushing a hand back through his hair. "If you weren't in the police, I mean. If you woke up and everything was different."

Alastair thought about it for a moment, intrigued. He readjusted his legs, angling a little more towards Jay.

"I don't know," he said. "I joined the force as a young man, and that's where I've stayed. It's hard to imagine any other life." He smiled, watching Jay drink. "What about you?"

"If I woke up and everything was different?"

"Mm."

Jay had thought about this many times before, often late at night when his cluttered flat was too quiet to sleep. He didn't know if the answer made him happy, but it seemed like the only answer possible.

"Probably just start again," he said, tipping back his whisky. It spilled like fire through his chest, rich as rubies. A short cough cleared the smoke. "Build it all back up, brick by brick."

Alastair seemed to like it. His blue-grey eyes regained their glitter, glancing just once at Jay's mouth.

"We both seem very secure in our life choices," he remarked.

Jay smiled. "Only get one life," he said. "Might as well make your choices like you mean them. Another whisky, is it? I'll get this round."

"So... first gay commissioner," Jay said. "How did that come about?"

Alastair took a moment to structure his answer, visibly putting it all in order.

"I suppose I began at the beginning," he said. "I joined the force as a constable in the early eighties, then slowly and painfully climbed my way up. I've worked in various territorial districts, kept moving, taken opportunities as they arose. A lot of work, a little luck. Here I am."

"Wow, so... you literally went from nothing right up to the big job? Climbed the whole bloody ladder?"

"Mm."

"Is that normal?"

"For the Metropolitan commissioner? Yes, since the seventies."

"Huh," Jay said. "I'd have thought there'd be more... you know, skulduggery. Friends in high places pulling you up."

"You'd be surprised," Alastair replied, smiling as he sipped his whisky. "The police force has made great efforts to modernise in recent history. It's better for everyone if senior officers are chosen for their experience, not their connections."

"Hence why... well, you're openly gay and you still got there. Right to the top."

"I, ah... I've not been *wide* openly gay, to coin a phrase. I've never worked to conceal it, but I've not had a partner while I've been in London. Means it's all a little irrelevant, really. I'm not certain it's even known outside of Scotland Yard."

"It's not on Wikipedia," Jay admitted. He wondered briefly what counted as a partner, and how long Alastair had been in London. He supposed that managing the forces of law and order across the entire metropolis couldn't leave a lot of time for dating. "Do you ever get any trouble for it? Homophobia, I mean."

The corner of Alastair's mouth turned upwards. "How long do you have?"

"Jesus. That bad?"

"In the early days, it was." Alastair took a drink, cleaning his expression. "Things have come on a great deal," he said. "I'm sure you'll know this yourself. There was a time a chief executive of anything would be expected to have a charming wife and two exquisitely polite children standing beside him. The world is changing."

Jay offered out the edge of his glass.

"Progress," he suggested.

Alastair hummed. "To progress," he said, meeting Jay's glass with a tap. "Long may she reign."

They drank together, throwing back the last of their whisky.

As they put down their glasses, Jay bundled up his courage.

"Must take a lot of sacrifice," he said. "Doing what you do, I mean."

Alastair hummed. "We can't have everything in life."

Jay wondered how long this had been a personal motto. "Do you get to see family much? Friends?"

"I, ah... I'm a little thin on the ground when it comes to family. Always have been. I was a long-awaited only child, then my father died when I was a young man. My mother took it very badly, never quite recovered her confidence. She passed away not long after I became a chief constable. Breast cancer."

"Oh, damn. I'm sorry. That must have been hard."

"Quite alright. She wasn't overly thrilled that I'd become a policeman. Even less pleased that I was advancing my way through the ranks."

Jay blinked, trying and failing to make sense of that. "Really?"

Alastair took in his surprise with a smile, his gaze a little rueful. "She came from money," he explained. "Believed the profession was beneath me. In her eyes, having a policeman for a son was only one step up from having a criminal."

Helpless, Jay let out a laugh. Nearby heads twitched around at its volume; he ignored them, too delighted to care. "Your mum didn't know that many criminals, did she?"

"She did not," Alastair said, amusement dancing in his gaze. "What about you? Do you get home to family that often?"

Ha.

"Nah, not often," Jay said. He covered his flush with a smile, scratching the back of his neck. "These days there's just me, really."

Alastair's gaze gentled. "Oh?"

"My family wasn't all that close. Just one of those things." The quiet stretched a little, thick with things unsaid. Awkward, Jay filled it. "Never a lot of money around. What there was, my dad drank.

Mum used to bray him for it. Bray us too, if we ever looked at her wrong."

He shrugged, hoping this was easier to hear than it was to say.

"Should've left about a decade before I did," he admitted. "I stuck it out hoping things would just magically be different one day. But they're all pretty set in their ways, and I wanted something more out of life... so I sort of said goodbye. Headed out on my own."

"That can't have been easy," Alastair murmured, watching Jay with quiet sympathy. "I'm very sorry."

Jay pulled a smile together. "Don't be," he said. "Been happier since I came down here. And I doubt they're missing me all that much."

Alastair's gaze warmed. "Happier with friends?"

Jay kept his smile in place.

"Sure," he said, broadening it, hoping this was how people with legions of glamorous London friends tended to smile. "The family you pick for yourself, right? Life's too short to spend it with the wrong people."

"Yes. Well said."

"So long as you're alright in your own company, then..."

"Then what else matters?"

"Exactly." Jay reached instinctively for his glass, finding it empty. "Ah, bollocks. Nothing to toast with, but... well, let's call it toasted. Do you fancy another drink?"

Alastair pushed back his sleeve, checking the face of an expensive-looking watch.

"Given that it's a week night..." he said.

Jay's heart gave a nervous tug. *Don't run off,* he begged in silence. *Not yet. Hardly got to know you.*

"I suppose just one more won't hurt," Alastair finished. The muscles in Jay's shoulders eased, unwinding with quiet relief. He hadn't realised that he'd clenched them. Alastair reached inside his jacket. "My round, I think?"

Though the room began to empty at around ten, it was midnight before Jay realised the staff were discreetly cleaning tables. A handful of determined drinkers remained; he and Alastair seemed the only two still capable of conversation. Alcohol fuzzed in Jay's lips and his fingers, curling across the back of his neck, all over his skin beneath his clothes. It made him feel warm.

"Do these fancy shindigs of yours have a scheduled end time?" he asked, finishing his Glenallachie.

Alastair huffed.

"I've never been around to see it before," he said. He drew a hazy breath, rubbing the side of his neck. "We might have to leave fairly soon."

With effort, Jay rescued his eyes from the lazy circling of those elegant fingers.

"Yeah?" he said, looking up into Alastair's face. Alastair's pupils had broadened so much they obscured the colour of his eyes. "Shame. I've had a nice time talking."

"Mm," Alastair said. "So have I."

Jay pulled at the corner of his lip, hoping a joke might ease the intensity.

"Suppose I should have spent at least a minute or two talking business," he said.

Humour flickered through Alastair's eyes. "We can talk business some other time. I've enjoyed just connecting."

Fuck. The warm ache in Jay's stomach seemed to deepen, burning. *Let's go somewhere. Connect some more.*

"My team'll think I was sweet-talking you into helping us," he said, trying a laugh as he scruffed a hand through his hair. "Don't know how I'll explain that we just got a bit pissed."

"I'm not certain I'm pissed, in fact."

"Well... I mean, that you said the word *pissed* to me is a pretty reasonable indicator."

"You're capable of the word *indicator,*" Alastair pointed out, his mouth curving. "Perhaps we should take our average and conclude that we're fine."

Damn, I want you.

Jay ran his tongue between his lips, catching a faint flash of whisky that he'd missed. He stole a glance around the rest of the bar, making sure this conversation was genuinely private. If this went wrong, he didn't want any witnesses.

"Hey," he murmured, leaning nearer. Alastair watched with quiet interest, sipping from the tumbler in his hand. Jay eased one arm along the back of the bench behind him. "Listen... I, erm... I'm probably about to shoot my whole organisation in the head and wreck my future in this town forever. But let's go for it."

Alastair waited, watching Jay's eyes.

Jay braced himself with a breath.

"I don't meet men like you all that often," he said. "I can't believe I'm doing this, but... do you fancy coming back to mine? For a drink, I mean." He paused, reading Alastair's face. "Maybe breakfast, too."

Alastair's expression opened. It took him several seconds to speak, looking at Jay as if he couldn't quite believe it.

"And... for—?" he checked.

Nodding, Jay bit his lip. "If you want. My flat's a bit small, but... well, the bed's nice and big. Room for two."

As awkwardness entered Alastair's gaze, Jay's heart shrank to half its size. *Shit.*

"I have to be careful where I spend the night," Alastair said hesitantly. "I'm supposed to stick to pre-authorised places only. For my security."

"Oh, right," Jay said, attempting to join the dots.

Alastair's throat muscles worked. "You'd... have to come to me. To my flat."

Oh. Jay's stomach tightened up behind his ribs. *Oh. Okay.*

"Not a problem," he said quickly. "That's fine. I mean, if you'd be happy with that."

Alastair flushed.

"I'd be happy with that," he said. His eyes flicked down to Jay's mouth almost guiltily, as if he couldn't help himself. The colour deepened in his cheeks. "I'd like you to."

"Alright. Erm, how far's—?"

"I have a driver. He can collect us from here."

Jesus. "Alright," Jay said again, watching Alastair retrieve a mobile phone from inside his jacket. His fingers shook a little on the screen. "If you're sure."

Alastair opened up his text messages.

"I'm sure," he said, typing quickly. "He probably isn't far away. He might only be a minute or two."

Holy shit, Jay thought, wild. *Is this happening? I think this is actually happening.*

"Shall we go wait out front?" he asked. Humour offered itself to his scrambling mind. "Sure I can keep an eye on you 'til the car gets here."

Chapter 3

THE MOST INTENSELY SILENT CAR RIDE OF JAY'S LIFE TOOK THEM TO THE heart of Kensington. From the moment they set off, he hardly took a breath. Alastair sat beside him in the back seat, apparently answering messages on his phone, though a flush remained high in his cheeks. Jay doubted many actual replies were being sent. He couldn't stop wondering if the driver could feel this strangling silence, too. Maybe this happened often enough that the guy knew the drill—a thought which left Jay fluttery and unsettled, but not one fraction less willing to be here.

Alastair didn't offer even a moment of eye contact until the car rounded the corner of a street called Observatory Gardens, at which point there came a wordless sideways glance.

This is us, it seemed to say.

Jay shifted and reached for his seatbelt. He tried to project an air of cool as he unclipped it, hoping he looked like this sort of thing happened to him all the time. Maybe twenty years ago, sex had been meaningless and easy to acquire—but not these days. He'd left that sort of cockiness behind him, along with all the rest. Casual sex didn't feel half as casual as he remembered.

They came to a stop outside one of the pretty porticoed townhouses. All the ground floor windows in the street were ringed with a curious white-and-red striped brickwork, the sort of whimsical rich people architecture that just didn't seem to exist outside of London. There were tiny potted trees beside each door. This neighbourhood was immaculate.

What the hell am I doing here? Jay thought with a lurch of his pulse, keeping his face clean and under control.

"Thank you, Larry," Alastair said, opening up his door. Jay took his lead. "That's all for the night."

The driver gave a nod. "Very good, sir."

Interested, Jay kept one eye on the car as Alastair led him up the steps. The driver didn't pull away until they'd been safely buzzed inside, with the front door closing behind them.

Jesus. Is someone running security checks on me right now?

It was better not to think about it, though the possibility twisted at Jay's already frayed nerves. He shoved the thought aside, telling himself he wasn't committing any crime here. He was a private citizen, and this was private.

He followed Alastair quietly past the front desk, offering the concierge what he hoped was a steady smile. *Like I'm just here for business,* he thought, hands in his pockets, shoulders loose. *Like it's one in the afternoon, not one in the morning. Like I'm here for any reason except ripping him right out of that uniform.*

Alastair keyed them through a door into a ground floor flat, switched on the lights, and locked the door at once behind them. As he attended to a flashing security panel on the wall, Jay took a discreet and careful glance around. Through open double doors, he could see most of an elegant lounge-cum-kitchen, decked out in modern monochrome and gleaming stainless steel. The suede leather sofas seemed to beckon him to kick off his shoes and come sprawl on them. Alastair had proper art on the walls. All his house plants were healthy, there were oranges in a bowl on the table, and he had a reed diffuser on the mantelpiece. This was a *nice* flat.

A cordial bleep sounded from the security system, all problems taken care of. Alastair folded shut the panel.

As they turned to each other in the silence, Jay found himself moved by the sudden touch of nerves in Alastair's eyes.

You don't do this often either, Jay realised. He searched Alastair's face, his pulse picking up. *You do speeches and dinners and schmoozing, don't you? You do them like you were born for it. But not this.*

Jay's stomach tightened.

It's alright, posh thing. I've got us.

He stepped forwards slowly, calmly, letting Alastair register his approach. Alastair's gaze flickered. As Jay backed him up against the wall, his expression opened and colour bloomed across his face, flooding out his authority—no longer the police commissioner, now just a normal warm-blooded human who'd brought a pretty stranger home for sex. His back arched.

"Jesus, you're lovely," Jay breathed, pressing him tight against the wall. The helpless look on his face was a memory Jay would treasure, too gorgeous ever to let himself forget. "Just look at you..."

Alastair's arms nervously encircled his shoulders, holding onto him as if uncertain this was real.

Jay took Alastair's jaw into his hands and laid their foreheads together, holding for a moment, sharing their fractured breath as they paused here on the threshold.

"I don't mind what we do," he murmured. Alastair trembled, listening. "I just want to make you moan. I want to run my mouth over all of you. And I want you to think about me tomorrow."

Alastair audibly swallowed, curling his fingers in the back of Jay's hair.

"You've already achieved that last one," he whispered. "I assure you."

Jay smiled, settling their noses side by side.

"That's good to hear," he said as Alastair breathed in. "Let's give you a little more to think about, mm?"

He kept this first kiss soft and slow, a demonstration of his gentleness. He didn't plan to rush a moment of whatever was about to happen, and he wanted Alastair to know it. As their tongues brushed gently between their lips, Alastair gave a shudder and let out some small, breathy sound, already overcome. Flattered, Jay smiled against his mouth. He stroked a hand up into Alastair's hair, taking hold, and let their second kiss grow a little hungrier, a little dirtier, with just a touch more stubble and scotch. Alastair's arms drew tight around Jay's back. He opened his lips to the coaxing sweep of Jay's tongue, then with a shaky breath took all of it, clinging to Jay as a subtle shift in the air tipped them from kissing into sex.

Feels nice, pretty? Jay wished he had another mouth. He wanted to whisper in Alastair's ear as they kissed, tell him how good he looked arching back against the wall like that, how perfect he sounded trying to gasp around Jay's tongue. As Alastair's fingers pressed into his shoulder blades, Jay rolled his hips forwards in a promise of what was to come, grinding them together. It won him a shocked little whimper, half-swallowed. Repeating it, setting up a lazy rhythm, turned the whimper into moans. *That's it, beautiful. There you go. Open up for me.*

They stayed by the door, tongue-fucking and stroking until Alastair's sounds grew too appetizing to resist. Jay broke the kiss by catching Alastair's lower lip between his teeth, giving it a hungry tug.

"Where's your bedroom, sweetheart?" he asked.

Alastair shuddered, his cheeks stained red. "Upstairs," he whispered. His pupils were gigantic, deep and soft, his gaze locked tight in Jay's own. "Just off the lounge."

"Mm?" Catching hold of his hand, Jay tangled their fingers. "Want to show me?"

Alastair nodded, then nervously pulled him by the hand.

It was a cosy white nest of a bedroom, hidden away up a half-flight of steps. The octagonal, low-ceilinged space had room for little more than the bed and a nightstand, though closed doors along one wall suggested a bathroom and a closet. There weren't many trinkets or personal touches to be seen. The nightstand held a water glass and a lamp, but not a photograph; the black-and-white panorama of a mountain peak, framed above the bed, had most likely come with the flat. Something about the bed itself—snowy white covers neatly pulled smooth, tucked in nice and tight around each edge—called to a very animal and restless part of Jay's soul, the side of him that could never leave ice cubes in a glass uncrunched. He loved that Alastair had tidied it so carefully. It was going to look amazing, pulled apart and thrown all over.

Alastair turned towards Jay, embarrassed, drawing a breath to begin some sort of apology. Before he could say a single word, Jay knocked him back into the middle of the bed. He crawled on top of Alastair's body, leant down and claimed his mouth, kissing him hard as he gasped.

Removing the uniform was an adventure in itself; even the buttons seemed to have buttons. Jay worked his way through them one by one, so eager to unwrap this unexpected gift from the universe that he almost forgot about his own clothes. He spent a long time still fully dressed, his suit getting more and more crumpled as Alastair's hands scrunched and hauled at the fabric, his whole body trembling beneath Jay's attentions. Jay had never found the texture of someone's skin so rewarding before. He'd never felt someone grip onto him like they'd waited for his touch all their life. Beneath the buttons and the power, Alastair was as naked and warm as anybody else on earth, blushing all over and scattered with toffee-coloured freckles, and Jay would sooner have died than left a single one of them unkissed.

"Jay—"

It was the first time Alastair had spoken his name, and the fragility in it nearly killed Jay. Alastair whimpered it as if unsure he had the right, and yet with a need which pulled Jay's stomach into knots.

"I'm here," Jay breathed against his inner thigh, kissing the rosy pink mark he'd just made. He didn't know why *I'm here* came as the instinctive response, or why it didn't feel stupid a moment later. Where else would he be? He'd not exactly gone far. And yet it felt so natural in his mouth that it ached, and it tightened Alastair's hands upon his shoulders. Jay looked up to meet his shy and sparkling gaze, a little bit in love with the nervousness he found there. "You alright, beautiful? Something I can change for you?"

Alastair's fingers flexed; he seemed comforted by the eye contact. Blushing harder, he tugged a little at the shoulder of Jay's jacket.

Jay stroked his open mouth against Alastair's thigh. "Off?" he said.

Alastair's shaky nod in response raised heat from the pit of Jay's stomach. At a dinner table, decked out in his dress uniform, Alastair was the king of clever conversation. Naked, spread out underneath Jay, he was suddenly lost for words—and it was glorious.

"You want to step things up a little?" Jay hummed, flashing his tongue along the crease of Alastair's thigh.

Alastair's gaze flickered.

"Jay," he begged, sinking his teeth into his lower lip. Jay didn't need a second plea.

They grappled him free from his jacket and trousers, tossed the fabric out of bed to join Alastair's uniform, then returned to rough kissing, panting with their chests pressed together through the thin white cotton of Jay's shirt. Jay toed his socks off as they kissed, drinking Alastair's whimpers from his mouth. Alastair seemed almost hungry to keep on kissing him, desperate for just a little more of his skin. His fingers worked their way through Jay's shirt buttons, easing open one and then the next. When enough of them had come apart, Jay shivered and reluctantly pulled away from their kiss, reaching down to haul the shirt over his head.

As the fabric came loose, Alastair let out an odd breath.

"Oh," he said, the sound shocked and shapeless.

Concerned, Jay dropped his shirt off the bed.

"You okay?" he asked, panting—then realised Alastair was staring at his chest. Alastair's eyes had gone wide, his mouth slightly open, his hands suddenly tight on Jay's forearms. "Oh, you... you mean my ink?"

Alastair said nothing, his stare roaming in astonishment over the spread of Jay's tattoos.

Flushing, Jay tried a smile. "Suppose I've got a few more than most," he said. He wondered why his heart was suddenly hammering, why he felt ten times more naked in an instant. "I, erm... I forget that people can't see them when I'm dressed."

Alastair visibly swallowed. His eyes skimmed over the roaring lion which covered most of Jay's left shoulder, then across the thick tangle of black roses and playing cards spanning his pectorals, catching at last on the lines of Gothic lettering along his collarbones. He looked as if he'd never seen anything like it in his life.

"Are you okay with them?" Jay checked, suddenly wondering if he was about to be thrown out into the street. "It's... I-I get them all done at decent places. And I get regular checks, if you're worrying about... you know, needles..."

Alastair drew a breath, looking up into Jay's eyes.

"They're magnificent," he breathed. His throat muscles worked, squeezing tight. "Really, Jay. They're beautiful."

Relief surged through Jay's veins.

"Jesus," he whispered, breaking into a grin. "Thank fuck for that. You scared me."

"I'm sorry," Alastair let out in a rush, his expression desperate. "I didn't mean to worry you. I just didn't expect you to have... I-I think they're wonderful. Truly."

Jay's heart seemed to squirm.

"Yeah?" he said. He held still as Alastair reached out both hands to touch the designs, laying his fingertips very carefully against the skin —as if he expected them to feel raised or still wet somehow, as if the ink would come away on his hands. "Touch them all you want," Jay said, his pulse skipping. "I'm glad you're good with them."

For a few moments there was quiet, their breath slow and settling as Alastair gently studied the designs.

"Why playing cards?" he asked, looking up.

Jay grinned a little. "Bit pretentious. Don't think badly of me."

"Go on," Alastair said, pink-cheeked. "Please. I'm curious."

"Sort of... play-the-hand-you're-dealt kind of thing. Possibility. Making the most of what you get." Glancing down, Jay watched as Alastair stroked his fingers over the king of diamonds. "Tattooist said her granny used to tell the future with playing cards. Lay them out on a white cloth when the moon was up, take them all as omens. I made her promise only to give me good ones."

Alastair's mouth twitched with humour. "And do they work?"

Unable to help himself, Jay winked. "Yep. I'm *definitely* about to get lucky."

"Scoundrel," Alastair said, his smile creeping into a grin. "Come here this instant."

They fought their way under the covers together, squirming and kissing as Jay wriggled free from his boxer shorts. Before they'd even hit the floor, Alastair rolled Jay over onto his back.

"Lie back," he breathed, cupped Jay's jaw in both hands, and kissed him soundly. Jay shivered, arching up in hope. "I'm out of practice," Alastair said against his mouth, stealing one last heated kiss. "Be patient with me."

"Out of practice at what?" Jay asked.

As Alastair began to wind down his body, sweeping long licks across his tattoos, realisation dawned. Jay let his head fall back into the pillows.

"Oh," he said, and bit into his lip. *"That."*

Alastair eased his way ever lower, following the lines of Jay's body to where his cock now stood as erect as a flagpole, damp at the tip and aching for attention. As Alastair nuzzled against the shaft, teasing with his nose and the heat of his breath, Jay dug his fingers quietly into the mattress. He pushed down the covers, wanting to watch.

"You take all the time you need," he groaned, letting out a breath. "Don't worry about me. I'm a patient man."

Alastair chuckled, painting a first soft lick against the underside.

"You're big, aren't you?" he murmured, swelling Jay's ego beautifully. "Shame I'm not used to taking."

Been a while? Jay wondered. He watched as Alastair lapped and kissed at his cock. *Or just not usually your thing?*

"Looks like you'll have to be nice to me," he said. "Maybe I'll take one for the team."

"Mm?" Alastair lifted his gaze, holding Jay's eyes as he swept his tongue in a swirl around the crown. He looked so much better all ruffled and undone. All the seriousness had gone from his face, replaced by something far softer and more human. The careless scrunch of his hair made him seem younger; the colour in his face brought out its copper glow. "That would be very kind of you."

Shivering, Jay wrapped a hopeful hand around the back of his neck.

"Don't tease me," he begged in a whisper. "Please."

Alastair hummed. "As you like," he said, sliding Jay gently into his mouth.

Oh, fuck. Filling his lungs with a breath, Jay relaxed out his jaw and closed his eyes. *God, yes.* He'd always loved this. Alastair's quiet hums made it all so much better. The strands of his hair rumpled between Jay's fingers, cool to the touch and so soft that it felt almost slippery. He didn't seem to be trying to get Jay off—instead just exploring him, learning him. He moved his mouth back and forth with perfect slowness, a long and lazy glide that caused a swoop in Jay's stomach every time Alastair reached the tip. He varied his lips with his tongue, drawing patterns and little stripes, moving so slowly that Jay's thoughts began to drift to beautiful places. He'd not had anything inside him but toys for several years now. He used them fairly often, though.

Watching Alastair lie back and enjoy that might be nice.

Watch you moan, Jay thought, looking down. He shuddered as he tightened his grip on Alastair's shoulder, his cock throbbing at the thought, warmth washing over his face. *Rock up into me. Get what you need.*

He let Alastair suck him, getting hotter and more restless as the minutes passed, and he realised that his thoughts, all the teasing, were psyching him up for sex. He wanted it—and with every passing second, he was starting to need it.

"Hey," he breathed at last, and gave a gentle tug to the back of Alastair's hair. "H-hey... you'd better get up here."

Alastair lifted his head, sliding Jay's cock from his mouth with a last wet lick.

"Are you certain?" he asked, thick-throated.

Shivering, Jay tipped his head back into the pillow. "Al, if you're not inside me in the next five minutes, I'm going to fucking explode."

Alastair's pupils blew. He crawled his way back up Jay's body, kissed him hard, then reached towards the nightstand.

By the time any semblance of thought returned, it was long past two in the morning.

Exhausted, every nerve still echoing, his entire body now filmed with sweat, Jay let himself slump forwards against Alastair's chest. His muscles seemed to melt as he collapsed. They were no use to him now, broken. He laid his cheek against Alastair's collarbones and simply breathed, listening to Alastair's heart hammer out the last of his orgasm.

"Holy shit," Jay whispered, helplessly giving one last moan. It shook its way free from his throat, drawn out by another pounding aftershock. All his insides were throbbing, stretched and slick and hot. He'd not come so hard in years. "Oh, holy fuck..."

Shaky fingertips brushed between his shoulder blades; it felt like a question. Stirring, Jay lifted his head.

Alastair gazed at him from the pillow, flushed and dark-eyed, his hair now a riot of tufts and flicks.

Jay's heart kicked against his ribs.

"Hi," he rumbled, breaking into a grin.

Alastair's chest seemed to swell. "Hello," he murmured, breathless.

Jay lowered his mouth to the freckles strewn across the top of Alastair's chest, touching them with tired and tender kisses.

"Was that alright?" he asked. "Not too much?"

Alastair shivered in response.

"Not at all," he whispered. "You're... God almighty, Jay..."

Jay grinned, glad to hear it. "You're God almighty, too," he said. "Fuck me up... I don't remember the last time I wanted someone in me so badly. You're something else."

Alastair's expression worked with bright-eyed humour.

"It's been a while for me," he admitted, watching Jay kiss the steady rise and fall of his stomach. "Any of this. I'm... well, it's difficult.

Finding time to... to meet people safely, and then to build something to the point of... it's been a few years."

Jay knew that feeling. He rested his chin on Alastair's sternum, looking upwards.

"I couldn't tell," he promised.

Alastair huffed. "I'm desperately out of practice."

"Nah. News to me." Jay smiled, nuzzling the tip of his nose against Alastair's heart. "I'll be grinning like the Cheshire cat all tomorrow."

Alastair's gaze grew soft. "Ridiculous man."

Jay placed another kiss upon his chest, wondering if he actually understood that he was gorgeous. "Guilty as charged," he said. "Lock me up."

As Alastair smiled, drawing a deep and contented breath, Jay decided to take a risk. Chances like this didn't come along often. If the answer was an awkward no, he'd still be glad that he asked.

"Hey," he said. "I... I get that you're important."

Alastair's right eyebrow lifted, curious.

Jay steeled his nerves, hoping this didn't go south.

"But if you ever... you know," he said. "We both work a lot. I don't have a clue exactly what you go through week by week. But I know it gets stressful, people relying on you. We could blow off steam together, maybe."

He glanced with hope at Alastair's mouth.

"Be friends," he said. "Help each other out."

Alastair seemed to take a moment to work out what he was saying, reading Jay's face with care for extra clues.

"You're suggesting some sort of arrangement between us?" he checked.

Jay smiled, trying to keep this light. "Sure," he said with a shrug. "Something easy. Casual. Just whenever." He brushed his fingertips through the mess he'd just made on Alastair's lower stomach, supposing it wouldn't hurt to be clear. "Good sex is hard to find."

Alastair's pupils widened.

"I think that might be nice," he said. He took a second to phrase something, sliding the words through his mouth. "I should probably be honest with you up front. I don't know much about the etiquette of these things. You might have to enlighten me."

"No worries," Jay said with a smile, trying not to look too relieved. "It's our thing, sunshine. We can always decide on the etiquette as we go."

He curled his fingers around Alastair's hip, leaning forwards to nuzzle at his nose.

"How about we start simple?" he suggested. "If you find yourself with an empty evening and you fancy some company... text me. How's that sound?"

Alastair's breath seemed to catch. "That simple?"

Jay grinned, liking this more and more with every second. "Things are better simple," he said. "Life's complicated enough on its own."

Alastair gave a huff.

"That's true enough," he said. His eyes shone, enjoying something in Jay's expression. "In this arrangement of ours... would it be alright if I now kissed you?"

Jay's heart seemed to hop a little, fluttering. Lying here naked, covered in each other, the gentle propriety seemed adorable.

"I don't do things by halves," he said. "Especially sex. When we're in bed together I'm yours, all of me. So don't hold back, posh thing. Kiss me all you want."

Alastair's mouth curved. "Do you realise just how charming you are? Part of me suspects you do."

Grinning, Jay cosied a little closer.

"Changes day to day," he said, stealing a tiny kiss. He slipped his arm around Alastair's middle. "Feeling pretty sparkly right now."

Alastair's chest heaved. As their lips pushed together, Jay held on tight and rolled over onto his back, pulling Alastair eagerly on top of him. Alastair's tongue eased its way between his lips, coaxing him to open up.

Shivering with happiness, Jay let him in and kissed him back.

Chapter 4

On ordinary mornings, Alastair usually woke a few moments before his alarm. He'd kept himself to a six o'clock start for most of his adult life. His mind and body had become so accustomed to the pattern that the alarm clock itself was redundant, a ceremonial habit kept up for the sake of tradition.

This was not an ordinary morning.

The bleeping from the bedside wrenched him back into being, piercing its way through his sore and shrunken skull. He winced, groping blindly towards the noise. It took several undignified slaps to find the button and snap it down.

Sweet Christ.

Every single cell inside his head seemed to be pounding. His tongue had grown moss overnight. Even with the bleeping switched off, the silence rang in his ears and his brain whimpered back from his skull to get away from it. Laying both hands across his face, Alastair took a moment to castigate himself. This was not dignified. Drinking his way into a hangover was not the behaviour of a servant of the crown, and it was not going to happen again. If he suffered today, then so be it. He deserved it.

Taking a deep breath, he pushed back the sheets. A shower would be the first step in cleaning up this mess. After that, an extremely black coffee.

As he sat up in bed, Alastair discovered he hadn't been occupying it alone.

Oh—

Oh, God...

The awards dinner. The hotel bar.

Jay.

He was still fast asleep, settled on his stomach and with his face nuzzled deeply into the pillow. Even the alarm hadn't disturbed him. He looked as peaceful as a lamb, if a lamb could also be the extremely attractive chief executive of a small London charity. Lying on his front, his gallery of tattoos was only half-visible. Feathered wings, inked in extraordinary detail, spread outwards from the centre of his back, up to his shoulders and then onto his upper arms. Alastair's memory gave a dizzy pulse, throwing up details of the designs across Jay's chest—Latin script, the ace of hearts, black roses. He remembered digging his fingers into them, kissing them and licking them. If there had remained any doubt in the matter, the deep pink love bite at the side of Jay's neck would have confirmed it.

They very definitely had sex last night.

From the ache in Alastair's lower back, they'd had rather a lot of it.

Over the course of twenty minutes in the shower, leaning against the frosted glass wall for support, Alastair recovered the rest of his memories. The details were enough to make him flush even now. He let the water slide soothingly over his head as he recalled the wide variety of playful positions and the creative language, Jay's enthusiastic exploration of every single part of Alastair's body. They hadn't held back from each other. They'd had sex like they meant it.

And agreed to do all of it again in the future.

Oh, lord.

Alastair washed himself clean, towelled dry, and very gingerly managed to shave, all the while attempting to rehearse what on earth he was going to say. So much depended on Jay's reaction upon waking up. Some awkwardness was inevitable. That went without saying, but whether Jay would recall their post-coital conversation or not was anybody's guess. He might be horrified to have slept with Alastair even once, let alone to have made some arrangement to repeat the incident.

This is a mess of my own making, Alastair sternly told his reflection in the mirror, patting his face dry. *I've only got myself to blame. If he sprints from the flat within five minutes, then... Well, lesson learned.*

He tightened the sash on his dressing gown and drew himself a steadying breath.

Coffee, he thought. *Coffee, then awkward conversation.*

Opening the bathroom door, he found that the bedside lamp had been switched on. In the pool of peach-gold light was Jay, still naked, still gorgeous, still settled on his stomach with the covers pushed down around his waist, but now awake.

As Alastair appeared, his bright green eyes took on a glitter.

Alastair's heart seemed to whimper. *Christ, but you're beautiful.* Before he could arrange his face into something that felt more polite, Jay stretched beneath the sheets and gave a sleepy smile.

"Are you going to be all awkward with me?" he asked.

Alastair inhaled without a sound. "Not unless you'd want that."

Jay's smile grew, his eyes aglow. "Life's too short," he said. "How's your head? You a bit sore?"

"Somewhat," Alastair admitted. He became aware he was still hovering at a distance, and cautiously came a little closer. "I hope you're not too..."

Jay snorted with amusement.

"Takes more than a couple whiskies," he rumbled, stretching again, and shifted enough to make space on the edge of the bed. He patted the empty spot within the sheets. "Hey."

Ignoring the renewed heat in his face, Alastair came over. As he took a cautious seat, Jay shifted to sit up beside him. He brushed a hand against Alastair's back, up to his neck and then hooked a gentle finger beneath his chin, coaxing his face to turn.

The kiss washed Alastair with equal waves of longing and relief, calming him even as it thrilled him.

"Do you remember?" Jay asked against his lips, his voice soft. "What we talked about, I mean?"

Briefly incapable of speech, Alastair could only nod. His eyes stayed closed.

"You know I meant it, right?" Jay stroked another gentle kiss against his mouth, their lips catching. "No pressure. But I'm here, if you ever want some fun. Just drop me a text."

Sex with a modern Adonis, Alastair thought, unable to suppress his shiver. *A single text away.*

"Thank you," he said quietly, letting out his nerves on his breath. "I'd like that. Seeing you again, that is. I enjoyed this."

He felt Jay smile. "There. Sorted." He nudged the side of his nose against Alastair's, playfulness entering his voice. "You know the best cure for a hangover?"

Alka-Seltzer would probably be a start. "Suggestions welcome," Alastair said, hoping this wouldn't involve raw egg. He knew a number of senior detectives who swore by it, but he'd never been inclined to try it.

Jay kissed him slowly. The sly flash of his tongue between Alastair's lips vanished all thoughts of cold egg yolk at once, replacing them with far more appealing possibilities.

"Hangover sex," Jay murmured, lying back in bed. He pushed the sheets down past his waist, offering himself to Alastair's eyes: stomach muscles, black ink roses, his heavy cock half hard already. As heat bloomed through Alastair's abdomen, Jay grinned and gave a stretch. "Come here, posh thing. Let me set you up for the day."

Oh, God.

Swallowing, Alastair reached for the sash of his dressing gown.

In for a penny.

He left not long after eight, kissing Alastair goodbye beside the half-open door.

"I'm sorry I can't stay longer," he said. He slid a business card into the top pocket of Alastair's dressing gown, tucking it down safely. "Just can't remember if I've got a clean suit at the office or not. Better if I head home and change."

Alastair's heart seemed to thump against the card, relieved by the gesture. "I understand," he said. "I wouldn't want you to attract uncomfortable questions."

Jay smiled, pulling at his lip.

"Have a good week, yeah?" he said. He let go and stepped out into the hall, his eyes still on Alastair. "Don't be a stranger. This was fun."

"It was," Alastair agreed. His pulse was skipping and skittering, not wanting Jay to leave. "Do text. Whenever you..."

Jay winked. "I will, sunshine. Promise. 'Bye."

Alastair watched him go along the hallway. As Jay passed out of sight, he sucked in a silent breath and closed the door, determined not to take this for more than it was. Getting fluttery over possibilities would end in tears, and the right thing to do was what he'd always done: proceed calmly and steadily through the steps of daily life, focus on his work, and take the rest as it came.

All the same, he had a smile on his face as he got dressed.

He made himself some breakfast, brushed his teeth, and on the dot of half past eight he left his flat. A pleasant day seemed in progress, the air crisp and the early autumn colours rich. The leaves were holding well; winter seemed just as distant as it had in summer.

The car was already cruising up to the kerb.

"Good morning," Juliet said as he got in, her smile rather chirpier than usual. "How are you?"

"Good morning," Alastair returned, occupying himself at once with his seat belt. He'd checked his reflection thoroughly before leaving the house, fully aware that he'd be scrutinised. "A little tired, but still in one piece. Nothing that caffeine won't fix."

"Successful night?" she asked.

"Mm, very." Supposing some further detail was warranted, Alastair added, "Mr Fieldhouse is very interesting. I must make sure to pass his details onto the right people."

The car set off with a jolt, easing on its way towards Scotland Yard.

As they turned onto Hornton Street, Juliet recrossed her legs at the knee. "When did he leave?"

Alastair kept his eyes straight forwards, his expression as neutral as a freshly-plastered wall. "About thirty minutes ago."

She chuckled in the back of her throat. "You hound," she said. "I didn't realise you'd be strengthening our links with local charitable organisations so personally this year."

"Yes, well... 'lead from the front'."

"I hope the lack of sleep was worth it?"

"It was." Alastair retrieved his phone from inside his jacket, opening up his emails. "When on earth did men become so attentive in bed? I assume this is a recent development."

"Fairly," Juliet said. "Ever since rechargeable vibrators hit the market, they've had to up their game."

Alastair huffed, supposing it was his own fault for asking.

She cast him a rather proud smile. "This isn't like you," she remarked, her eyes bright. "I've never known you to have overnight company, not once in three years. What's different about Jay Fieldhouse?"

"It's been longer than that, I assure you. And believe me that I'm just as surprised."

"Something special about him?"

"Mm." Alastair took a breath, attempting with all his might not to flush. "There were tattoos. A number of them."

"My, my."

"More generally, he's... very friendly, and very charming. It's not often someone takes an interest in charming me. The dress uniform might as well come with a chastity belt sewn in, but it didn't seem to bother him in the least."

Juliet's eyes sparkled. "Are you going to see him again?"

Dear God, I hope so. "He's left me with his contact details."

"Has he really? That's a very good sign."

Alastair's stomach stirred. He'd suspected it might be, but with a tragic lack of experience in these things, he hadn't fully dared to hope. He couldn't actually pinpoint in his memory when he'd last woken up in someone else's company. At the very least it was before he'd transferred to London, and he didn't recall anything happening when he was in the upper ranks at Thames Valley.

The truth was that the higher he'd been promoted, the more removed from ordinary socialising he'd become.

Most officers of his rank would have acquired a spouse and a family somewhere along the way. Those domestic ties would tether them like kites to the world of real people, no matter how high upon the breeze they sailed. In his thirties, while all his colleagues had been cheerfully dating and marrying, Alastair had been taking pains to keep his aberrant sexuality to himself. He'd put his head down and worked, painfully familiar with the suspicions that encircled an officer attracted to other men. Even now, the memories ached. He'd attempted to be candid as a young constable—some lofty belief that his own quiet dignity would dismantle his brother officers' dark assumptions about public toilets, drug-fuelled breakdowns, and suicides in sex clubs. They'd simply papered the stereotypes across him, altering what they knew of him to make the patterns fit. No one had asked about his weekends, fearing what sordid sort of things he might have been up to. When he'd had the audacity to flag up a small flaw in another constable's paperwork, a nasty rumour had quickly burned its way through the station. Too many people were all too willing to believe that he'd been caught up in the raid in Vauxhall two weekends prior, only spared the disgrace of dismissal because he was the governor's star boy.

By the time the governor himself took Alastair aside, begging him to consider his future, the concern felt so rare and so comforting that Alastair had caved. He'd never intended it to be a proud crusade; sex was not the hill he wanted to die on. He'd agreed to be transferred, start again somewhere new, and though the humiliation of it all had burned within his blood, he'd considered it a lucky escape.

Only the millennium had changed things. The end of Section 28 had caused a shift within the police force, a sudden interest in being seen as modern-thinking and progressive. Alastair had decided to accept the forward surge in his career as long overdue reparations, rolling over and allowing them to rub his belly however much they wished. If he'd benefited from the swing in attitudes, it was fair payment for all the years of additional work they'd had from him—years he might otherwise have spent distracted by family, children, and a home.

He didn't regret his choices. Every late night and every weekend spent at his desk had paved his way here to this car, this role, these heights of responsibility. In the grand scheme of things, sex had seemed an easy sacrifice.

Then again, at the time, no one had been having sex with him like Jay just had. Certainly no one had been leaving him their phone number, telling him not to be a stranger.

If they had, things might have turned out rather differently.

Straightening his back, Alastair guided his thoughts with a firm and practiced hand away from the shadows. There was little to be gained in raking over the ashes of the past. He'd already learned every lesson that he could.

"We shall see," he concluded simply. "If I'm asleep by two o'clock, I have only myself to blame."

Juliet smiled, still terribly pleased.

"Well, sir," she said, "I'm very glad for you. Congratulations on your highly successful night of networking."

Alastair coughed. "Yes, ah... thank you. Charity of the year indeed. How's our schedule looking for today? Did you rearrange CTC to ten o'clock or eleven?"

Jesus. Sneaking in late.

Jay took the back stairs up to his office, hoping that no one had noticed his absence. Their corner of the car park had seemed a little sparse today. It looked like several people were still sleeping off the drink. Traffic had added half an hour to his journey, and the wreck of his hair meant he'd needed a shower before he changed.

At least I'm not rocking up in last night's suit, he told himself, unlocking his office. *Smelling of whisky and sex.*

Jay slipped inside, dropped his bag beneath his desk and fished his laptop out, opening it quickly.

There, he thought, putting it down on his desk. *Been here all along. Model boss.*

As his daily glut of emails rolled in, he took himself to the kitchen and made a coffee to settle his head. It was hard to think of anything but Alastair. Two rounds of sex and four hours of sleep had scrambled Jay's brain into mush, and all he wanted to do was switch off, lie down somewhere quiet and dark, and remember. Every time he rested his weight too much on one side, a twinge from below reminded him that last night he'd been railed until his throat went dry with groaning. He had a feeling he wouldn't get much work done today.

In a way, he was lucky that everyone else had been out last night as well. Nobody would be firing on all cylinders. He could blend in, blame any distraction on the drink.

Back in his office, Jay scrolled dimly through this month's accounts for ten minutes, struggling to keep his focus for more than one column. He drank his coffee, sent two emails, then started wondering how much was being achieved in the police commissioner's office. He hoped it wasn't much. He ended up half hard at the memory of Alastair's hands clenched in his hair, that Saville Row uniform discarded in a heap beside the bed.

Damn, how soon can I see you again? You'd better not pull a vanishing act on me...

A knock on the door jolted Jay out of his daze. As he looked up from his laptop, Connor gave him a genial wave through the glass. His big grin, brick-red pompadour and checked salmon suit made him look as fresh-faced as the day he was born, though his eyes had their usual *we-were-wasted-last-night* sparkle. He'd described himself in his interview as a pointy-shoed marketing twat, but the best of them

—and as soon as Jay had finished laughing, he'd given Connor the job. He'd never had cause to regret it.

Grinning, Jay beckoned him through the door.

"Morning," Connor said, strolling inside with his hands held at ease in his pockets. Where on earth he'd bought the suit, Jay couldn't imagine. Only a man who tweeted for a living could pull off such a lawless sense of style. "Came to offer you a coffee, but it looks you've beaten me to it... how'd things go with the commissioner?"

Jay coughed into his coffee and put it down before he could spill it.

"Fine," he said. "Yeah, yeah, all great. Really good. Really nice guy."

"You were on fire with the schmoozing," Connor said, arching an impressed ginger eyebrow. "How late did you stay? He was still eating out of your hand when I left."

Jay rubbed the side of his neck, offering a sheepish grin. "Midnight-ish? Something like that?"

"All good things?"

"Oh, all good things. Hundred per cent. Playing it slow, taking it easy, but... yeah. Think it'll be good for us."

Connor's eyes danced.

"Great," he said. "Promo materials have arrived for the new campaign. Left you one of everything in your pigeon hole. Distribution should be finalised by Friday, then the social media kicks off in a couple of weeks."

"You star," Jay said. "Tell your team well done from me. They're knocking it out of the park this year."

"Aren't they? We've had some great coverage from last night, by the way. Near the front in most of the nationals. I'll do you a round-up of highlights."

"Sure. Glad to hear it. Just, ah... just keep an eye on the coverage for me, will you? Make sure my ugly mug's not in it."

Connor nodded, his smile clean and easy. "Always do."

Returning the smile, Jay reached for his coffee. "You're a diamond, mate."

"Not a problem," Connor said. "By the way, there was somebody looking for you earlier. Left a card at reception and asked if you could give her a ring."

Frowning, Jay took a sip of coffee.

"What sort of woman?" he asked. "Was she selling something?"

Connor shrugged. "Pretty ordinary. Average height, average build... brown sort of hair. Just a normal woman. I don't know if she was selling anything, but she was from your neck of the woods."

Jay hesitated. "Up north, you mean?"

"Caught a few sounds as I was passing." Connor winked. "Them flat Mancunian vowels of yours," he said, mimicking the accent. "I'd recognise 'em anywhere."

Jay took care to keep his eyes on Connor's face and his expression locked into calm.

"Right," he said, his tone steady, even as his heart crammed up into his throat. "Thanks. I'll ask at the desk when I next go down."

"Alright. I'll let you get on, then. Unless you're ready for another coffee?"

"Oh—no, erm... no thanks. I'm fine."

"You sure?"

"Yep," Jay said, forcing himself to smile through the waves of hot and cold now pouring down the back of his neck. He turned his attention back to the accounts with a click. "Thanks, mate."

Connor doffed an invisible hat and took his leave, his pointy-toed leather brogues tapping down the hallway as he went.

Jay waited until his footsteps were gone, barely breathing, then reached beneath his desk to scramble his phone from inside his bag, trying not to fumble. He'd been on his last scraps of battery when he left Alastair. He'd called a taxi without checking through his messages, then grabbed a charger as he left his flat, intending to top it up when he got here.

As he scrolled through his notifications, his heart pounding, three calls from an unknown number flashed up before Jay's eyes.

"Shit," he whispered. He swallowed, his fingers shaking, then opened up his contacts. "Shit, shit—"

He found the right entry—Kim, no surname—hit call and pressed the phone against his ear.

"Pick up," he muttered, staring through the glass door of his office into the corridor outside, his heart now banging in his ears. "Pick up. Pick the fuck up right now."

After three more rings, there came a gentle click. The line opened and nobody spoke.

"It's Jay," he told the waiting silence, gripping the edge of his desk. "Did you call here looking for me?"

She drew a gentle breath, then answered with regret.

"Hello, Jay," she murmured. "Can we meet somewhere for coffee?"

Shit.

No.

Please, God, no.

"Depends," Jay said, swallowing again. "Are you about to ruin my life?"

"I don't think so," she said. "But I'd really like to talk. I'll make my way back to your office."

"No. No, Jesus, don't come here. I'll..." *God, please. Don't do this to me now.* "Can you meet me at Kings Cross? There's a Caffe Nero in the concourse. I'll see you there."

It killed Jay how ordinary she was.

He knew it was an advantage for her to be that way. It always seemed so wrong, though. The first time they'd met, he'd expected her to show up with jet black hair, leather trousers and mirrored sunglasses, flash some top secret ID badge at him then start issuing commands that must be followed without question. If his life was going to be blown into pieces, it made sense in his head for someone dark and dramatic to come and do it.

But she was just some gentle woman in a belted green mac, mid-height, mid-fifties, as mild as mid-June. He didn't know her real name. The only name he knew it couldn't be was Kim, and that was because she'd asked him to call her that.

She was already outside Caffe Nero when he arrived, waiting quite calmly with a couple of shopping bags beside her. She smiled as she spotted him coming; she held onto his gaze until he reached her.

"Are you moving me?" he asked, so worked up from his taxi ride here that the words burst out of him at once. "Have I got a problem?"

"No," Kim said, looking up at him. "No, there's no suggestion of a problem. Not yet. And I'm not here to move you, Jay."

"Then what the hell are you doing here?" Jay demanded. "What's going on?"

"Have you noticed anything strange in the last few weeks? Anything that's given you cause for concern?"

"No. No, not at all. Everything's been fine." Memories of last night flashed through Jay's mind: the award, his team all beaming from the stage at him, their faces bright with what they'd achieved. His heart clenched. "Everything's been pretty bloody perfect," he bit out, "and I really, *really* need it to stay that way."

Kim nodded gently. "I'm largely here to ask you to be vigilant. If you've not noticed anything troubling, then that's an extremely good sign."

Jay's jaw set.

"Something's changed," he said. He searched her eyes, his heart pounding. "You wouldn't be here otherwise. What the hell has changed? Please just tell me."

Kim waited to speak until she'd seen him breathe, visibly preparing the words inside her mouth.

"A probation meeting was missed last week," she said. "Attempts have since been made to contact him, and then to trace him. Unfortunately those attempts have been unsuccessful."

Jay's brain crunched through the words, translating. "He's disappeared," he said. "He's... they've lost him. He's gone."

She gave a single, silent nod.

For several seconds, Jay simply looked into her face. He almost wanted to laugh. He didn't know where to begin in responding to that. He had half a mind to simply turn on his heel and walk away from her in silence, make his way down into the underground and throw himself in front of the next tube.

"Six months," he said at last. He dragged in a breath. "Six fucking months and he's vanished."

Kim's expression filled with regret. "I'm told there's every chance he'll still be traced," she said. "We've seen no indication that he's left Manchester."

"But you've no indication he's still there," Jay said. "Have you? If he's disappeared, he's disappeared. He could be on the moon. He could be sitting on my doorstep. Can I—listen, can I just check here—has *every single part* of this country's supposed justice system now let me down?"

"Jay—"

"Because I'm pretty fucking sure it has."

"Jay, this isn't necessarily a—"

"They promised me he'd go away for good," Jay said over her, fierce, "and he didn't. They said that he'd serve the whole length of his sentence, and he didn't. I warned them not to grant him parole, and they gave him it. And now he's gone. And the one person who's going to pay for this fuck-up is *me.* What a fucking surprise."

Kim reached out. She placed both her hands upon his shoulders, sinking him into silence.

"Jay," she murmured. "Please listen to me."

Biting down into his tongue, Jay listened.

"Even though he's absconded," she said, "we have no reason to believe you're in any danger. There's no suggestion your protection's been compromised. He has no idea where you are. He has no way to try and find you. So long as you've been mindful of your own security, and you continue to follow my instructions, I don't believe that you should lose even a moment's sleep. It's just a case of exercising a little extra caution."

Bitter humour rose in the back of Jay's throat.

"Caution," he huffed.

He looked away across the station concourse, pushing his tongue into his cheek.

"Fuck me up," he said. "If you knew what I go through in the name of caution. If you knew how many chances I've had to turn down, just in case it all comes out. If you knew all the things I can't have, just because I—"

Jesus.

Ranting at her wasn't going to change anything.

"Fine," he bit out, swallowing the rest. "Just... fine. I'll be cautious."

"I'm sorry to have to tell you," Kim said, watching him gently. "I wasn't sure whether to contact you at once, or wait a few weeks in case he's found. I hope I made the right choice."

Jay loosened his jaw, still struggling to look at her.

"Better I know," he muttered. "So I can..." He sighed, blowing out the thought. "Keep watch. Keep my eyes open. Can I say something to you? For the record?"

Kim nodded quietly. "Of course you can."

Jay pushed the words around behind his teeth.

"I'd still do what I did," he said at last. "It was the right thing, and I wouldn't go back and change it, even if I could. But Jesus, I wish just one of you had told me the truth."

"The truth?"

"You promised it would guarantee a sentence. The only sentence it guaranteed was mine. I got a life sentence that day. And if I'd known..."

Jay shrugged, numb. *Like it makes any bloody difference.*

"Fuck this shit," he concluded. "Tell them to find him."

"The police are working round the clock."

"Good. I've got people who need me." Jay shifted, pushing his hands into his pockets. "I'm finally doing some good with my life," he grunted. "No offence, but the last thing I need is *you* showing up."

She smiled a little, lowering her gaze. "None taken. I appreciate that you've been doing extremely well for yourself."

"Mm."

"You're probably our greatest success story, you know."

Jay shook his head, not wanting to hear it. They could take it all away from him in a heartbeat. He was renting his whole life by the hour, and the higher he climbed, the harder he would fall. That wasn't any kind of success story.

"My people got some fancy award from Scotland Yard last night," he told her. "Small charity of the year. They worked their arses off for it." His jaw tightened on its own. "Don't let Ian fuck that up for them. They deserve better than that."

"The police are doing everything they can," she promised. "I'll update you as soon as I know anything."

"Fine. Don't turn up at my office again, will you? Ring me."

"I prefer not to leave a paper trail, if that's alright. Digital or otherwise."

"Yeah?" Jay said, shooting a raised eyebrow at her. "I prefer that my employees don't realise I'm in witness protection. It's suspicious enough that I won't let marketing take any photos of me. So just text me a time and we'll meet up here, alright?"

She wanted to argue. He could see it in her eyes.

But with a breath, she patiently relented.

"Very well," she said, sweeping her hair back behind her ear. "I hope that I won't have to contact you, and I hope that you won't have to contact me. If we're lucky, he'll surface very shortly and be returned to serve the rest of his sentence."

Jay snorted. "That joke of a sentence he got," he said. He shook his head, exhaling. "Sorry to get mad at you."

"Not at all."

"Didn't really need this right now. Not your fault, though."

"You have every right to be angry. I'm angry on your behalf."

"Kind of you. It's just... y'know. Things are good at the minute." More memories flashed through Jay's mind: a warm mouth at the side of his neck, Alastair's weight upon his back, their fingers tangled together over his heart. He flushed, loosening his jaw again. "I've got good stuff starting to happen. I don't want to drop it all and run."

"Nobody wants that," Kim said—and in spite of his anger, Jay realised he still trusted her. That instinctive trust had saved his life ten years ago.

He just hoped that it would pay off this time, too.

Kim swept something gently off his shoulder for him, offering up a smile.

"We've never lost someone under our care," she said. "Not once. I'm not willing to let you be the first, Jay."

Jay's heart heaved. "There's more than one kind of loss," he said. "Please, please don't move me. Not unless you know for sure."

"I won't. Not without excellent reason."

"It... it didn't matter, before. Nothing in my life worth taking with me. It matters now."

"Put it from your mind," Kim advised. "Carry on entirely as normal. Just let me know if anything unusual happens, and I'll handle the rest."

She tipped her head towards Caffe Nero.

"Do you have time?" she asked. "Let me buy you a coffee. It's the least I can do."

Jay's veins tightened at the thought. He felt as if he'd now been awake for a week, and it wasn't even noon. *I got laid last night,* he recalled with a flush. *And this morning.* It already seemed like a dream.

Letting out a breath, he gave Kim a grateful look.

"Sure," he murmured. "Coffee'd be great. Thanks."

Chapter 5

HOW TO PHRASE THIS?

Alastair brushed his thumb along the edge of his phone, looking down at the empty message window. The evening's traffic had slowed almost to a standstill. It seemed as if the whole world had stopped for him to make this decision. An unproductive and irritating week had taken its time to pass, and he'd made it through to Friday against all odds. Rain had started up around lunchtime, continuing in droves ever since. Something about its sound, mixed with the bright lights of London in the darkness, had brought a possibility drifting through his mind.

Relaxation, he supposed, listening to the rain drumming against the window. Memories stirred: Jay gently sucking the bite he'd just left at the crook of Alastair's neck, hands stroking over Alastair's stomach, his voice as soft as smoke, murmuring, *"Do you like slow?"*

The low, delighted chuckle at Alastair's eager response.

"Mm. Good. Me too."

Hands fisting in the sheets, hips arching to meet each lazy roll.

Falling apart as Jay took it slow.

The memories hadn't faded. Alastair had worried that they might, but they'd stayed clear and urgent in his mind. He wanted it again, all of it. He wanted other things, too.

He'd spent this week explaining the simplest of concepts to people who still hadn't listened, and next week would entail much of the same. There was nothing he needed more in this moment than for someone to make him gasp and beg.

Help each other out, Jay had said.

Alastair wasn't sure how much explanation was required—how much honesty was too much.

"I've had a long week. I was wondering if maybe you'd like to..."

"Can I see you?"

"I can't stop thinking about you. Are you busy?"

The traffic continued to crawl.

Alastair shifted in the back of the car, longing to loosen his tie just a little. He wanted strong fingers to pull it off for him. He wanted to see it discarded without the slightest care over a lamp, over a chair, onto the floor.

But how to ask?

It was Friday evening. The chances of Jay receiving a better offer were surely increasing by the minute. While Alastair was not a blunt man, nor a reckless one, it wasn't often that he craved something for himself so powerfully. He'd never really longed for company before. His usual weekend comforts comprised a glass of wine and a book—but then, he'd never been offered company so openly, so generously. He didn't want to miss the chance, even if accepting it made him nervous.

Subtly, he thought. *Lead into it. Casual.*

He woke his phone with a short press of his thumbprint on the scanner, returned to the message window, and typed.

> **[AH - 18:54]** *Has your week been as intolerable as mine?*

Determined not to monitor the message like a pining teenage girl, he locked the phone and put it away inside his coat.

The car had advanced all of ten feet when his phone began to vibrate.

Alastair retrieved it, keeping his expression cool. *Incoming call from Jay Fieldhouse.*

With a sweep of his tongue across his teeth, Alastair answered. He took a breath and pressed the phone against his ear.

"Hello," he said, his heart thumping.

Jay's voice curled with a smile. "Hi."

"Bit of a long day... do you mind if I shower?"

Jay walked into the flat as comfortably as if it were his own, pulling off his coat and hanging it on the back of the door, then turning to Alastair with his easy smile.

"Not at all," Alastair said, hoping the disarray of his pulse wasn't evident on his face. "I thought I'd open a bottle of wine."

"Good idea," Jay said, bright-eyed. "Save some for me, yeah?"

Alastair found himself smiling, unable to resist that playful tone. He'd thought about it often. "I make no promises."

Jay winked, twisting open his topmost button.

"Won't be long," he said, heading towards the stairs.

Alastair watched him go. *Heaven help me,* he thought as he locked the door, then attended to the security panel. By the time he'd finished, a few small clunks and a soft, steady hiss within the wall announced hot water entering the pipes. Jay was showering. He was in Alastair's bathroom, naked, rubbing soap across all those glorious tattoos.

Alastair drank his first half-glass of wine fairly swiftly, hoping to settle his nerves. He sat in the lounge to drink a second one more slowly while dealing with his last few work emails. It was hard to put the thought out of his mind: *He's here. He's in my bathroom, washing himself, so he'll feel clean and comfortable in bed with me.* Alastair was suddenly very aware of his own clothing, his skin underneath it.

Unable to concentrate, he downed his glass of wine. He retrieved the bottle from the kitchen, along with another glass, and moved upstairs.

The door to his en suite was still closed, a few wisps of steam gathered around its edges. Alastair removed his waistcoat, hanging it neatly in the wardrobe, then stored his cufflinks in their box on the bedside cabinet. He poured himself another half-glass of wine and sat down on the bed to drink it, ignoring his own reflection in the wardrobe door. This was torture.

A minute or two later, the water cut off. Alastair glanced up as the bathroom door opened, wine glass held to his mouth.

Jay emerged. He wore a towel slung low around his hips but nothing else, his hair slicked back and wet, as dark and glossy as his tattoos. He smiled as he found Alastair waiting for him.

"Stubble or clean-shaven?" he asked, as if he were checking how Alastair liked his steak. The designs on his chest seemed to gleam in the light.

Alastair swept the final drop of wine off his lips. He moved the glass to the bedside, stood up without a word, and crossed to the bathroom door.

As he lowered himself to his knees, Jay audibly breathed in.

The towel was damp and soft against the tip of Alastair's nose. He nuzzled against the fabric until Jay had swelled enough beneath it for him to tease with his mouth, tracing the shape of Jay with his lips, enjoying the restless shifting that it caused. He leant up and kissed the water drops on Jay's stomach, closing his eyes. *Mine for the night,* he told himself, trying to believe it. *Mine to enjoy.* It still seemed a little unreal. He'd never dreamed this would be happening in his fifties—sex was for the young. He'd left all that behind.

And yet here it was again, wrapping a gentle hand around the back of his head.

Carpe diem, he supposed. Gift horses and mouths came to mind.

As he pulled down the front of the towel, freeing Jay's cock from behind the fabric, Jay's fingers flexed hopefully in his hair.

"Fuck," he heard Jay breathe, and glanced up. Jay's delightful green eyes gazed back down, watching intently, his pupils dark and soft. He really was a magnificent-looking man.

Alastair leaned in, wetting his lips. With his eyes on Jay's, he let his tongue paint a lazy stripe from root to tip along the underside, drawing the motion out as long as possible.

Jay flushed, biting down into his lip. *"Fuck,"* he whispered again, and with a shiver took his cock in one hand.

Obediently Alastair parted his lips, sitting still and pliant as he let Jay guide into his mouth. The hopeful little pull on the back of his head made his own cock twitch with longing. He took Jay's hips into his hands and closed his eyes, overwhelmed by the comfort and relief of having his mouth full, a lover's fingers tangled in his hair. Nothing mattered now. He'd been wrong to think he merely wanted this; he *needed* it. Humming softly, he started to suck.

Jay's sounds were sublime—thick-throated groans and heady breaths, with a distinct hitch in volume as Alastair softened his throat and took him in. The hand in Alastair's hair grew restless, agitated. At length it cupped his jaw, wanting to hold him and fuck his mouth. Alastair allowed it, shuddering as Jay's other hand tightened on his shoulder for balance. His short, tentative thrusts deepened gradually into more urgent motions, his moans now breathy and stuttered. Alastair reached around to hold his arse in both hands and steady him, guide the swaying of his hips.

Jay's fingers clenched in his hair. "Fuck—" he choked out.

Alastair moaned in the back of his throat, wanting to soothe him *—I like that, I don't mind—*thick fingers knotted through his hair, shaking and holding him where he was needed*—oh, God...*

"Shit," Jay gasped out, grasping his shoulder hard. "Stop—stop, Al, or I'll come—I'm not kidding—"

Alastair almost wanted it. *Hot. Straight down my throat.* He'd spent the week trying to impose his authority on slack-jawed politicians who couldn't process that he might just know better than them. All he wanted now was to serve someone worthy on his knees and be rewarded.

But then this would be over. Jay would no doubt be enough of a gentleman to reciprocate—hands, mouth—and it would be a heavenly few minutes of relief.

Alastair wanted more than just relief. He wanted closeness. That took time.

As he relaxed his mouth, disengaging with care, Jay let out a deep and shaking breath. His fingers loosened their grip in Alastair's hair. They began to pet instead, apparently calming himself with the comfort of stroking Alastair, and it raised a quizzical smile on Alastair's lips.

He let the smile remain there as he nuzzled Jay's stomach. The laboured rise and fall of his breath was terribly flattering.

"You're way too good at giving head," Jay breathed, half-laughing.

Alastair chuckled, pressing his cheek against Jay's warm skin.

"You're very good at receiving," he said, his voice thick from the stretch of his throat. He glanced up and found Jay's darkened gaze awaiting him, his handsome face flushed with pleasure. Alastair's smile grew. "Haven't even poured you a drink yet. How rude of me."

"Where's your manners?" Jay said, grinning, and cupped his jaw. He stroked his thumb across Alastair's pinkened lips. "Don't they teach you this stuff at Eton? Drink first, *then* blow job."

"I went to Harrow," Alastair told him with amusement, placing a kiss to the pad of his thumb.

"That'll explain it," Jay said. He watched Alastair fondly, his eyes aglitter. "Don't worry, posh thing. You're still the classiest guy who's ever fucked me."

"Mm." Alastair took Jay's thumb inside his mouth for just a moment, curling his tongue around it. Jay's cock twitched against his cheek in response, sending a fresh wave of heat through Alastair's blood. He closed his eyes. "How was your week?"

"Shit," Jay replied in a murmur. "Not sleeping properly. How was yours?"

The honesty seemed to deserve the same in return.

"Over now," Alastair said. "Fortunately." Inhaling, he rubbed his cheek against Jay's stomach. "I think I want you to fuck me, Jay. Not straightaway. After some coaxing perhaps."

Jay's fingers slid back into his hair, taking hold, tipping a shiver down Alastair's spine. When he opened his eyes again, he found Jay smiling down at him, dark-eyed and pleased, just a little possessive.

It was the most singularly affecting look he'd ever received.

"I can do coaxing," Jay said, and pulled gently at Alastair's hair. *Up.*

Alastair obeyed, rising from his knees. Every cell in his body seemed to ache with joy.

"Have you got anywhere to be in the morning?" Jay asked, starting on his shirt buttons.

Alastair flushed. "No."

"Good." Jay gazed at him, his eyes as warm and deep as the bed just behind them. "Let's take our time, hm? No coming 'til midnight."

Oh, God. "That sounds..."

Jay's soft grin went straight to Alastair's cock. He gathered his fingers in the loosened fabric of Alastair's dress shirt, using it to pull him close.

"Kiss me," he said, and as Alastair pushed him back against the door frame, he gasped. "Jesus—Al—"

Whether Alastair was to be granted the latter parts of his name or not, he never found out. The syllables were lost against the gentle strike of his mouth, melted into nothing between their tongues.

The only sounds for some time were hisses and pants, the crumple of fabric and snap of buttons as Jay undressed him. More and more of their skin came together as they kissed. By the time they reached the bed, Alastair no longer cared where Jay ended and he began. They were blurring into one, a haze of hot gasps and rough kisses, hands grasping and skin sliding and sounds so arousing they took Alastair's breath.

Stubble, he thought, cradling the delicious bastard's jaw into his hands. He rasped his thumbs across the tantalising prickle there. *Quite definitely stubble.* He wanted his thighs and his neck to be red and raw by the morning.

Jay wasn't hesitant with his body. He stroked Alastair, gripped him, pulled him close, always moving his hands where they were wanted. It was wildly reassuring; it felt safe to respond in kind. *I want you,* Alastair pleaded without words at Jay's throat, nuzzling along his shoulder, biting as Jay's hands cupped his arse, spreading him, making him moan; *I want you,* as Jay's thick fingers teased him with lazy swirls and tormenting presses, then finally slid into him, breaching, filling; *I want you,* hauled up onto his knees in front of Jay, held back against Jay's chest and locked there with one arm, panting just to cope with the intensity of Jay inside him, so big he couldn't breathe, so perfect he never wanted to be empty again. Jay's other hand curled tight around Alastair's cock, forming a lube-slick sleeve for him. He fucked Alastair through it with short and steady thrusts a little faster than Alastair's breath, over and over. It was too good, too much. It was impossible not to moan.

"Yeah?" Jay breathed in Alastair's ear, tugging at the lobe with his teeth. "Good, beautiful?"

Alastair dug his fingers into Jay's tattooed forearm. He'd lost the power of speech; only whimpers remained in his throat now, pleas, panting as he was held here, kept upright and fucked. At first he'd strained against Jay's hold, but it felt too good when he did. It took him too close to coming. All he could do was relax into the cradle of Jay's arms, gasp out his name, and take.

Take you, he thought, burning up inside. *Full of you—yours—pant for you, moan for you—*

"Nearly there, sweetheart?" Jay flashed his tongue against Alastair's neck and tightened his grasp on his cock. "Going to come all over these pretty sheets for me?"

Oh, God—come—fuck, please—yes—

As Alastair writhed and nodded, panting with the sheer excess of sensation, Jay pressed against his back to lower him forwards, down to the bed on all fours. Alastair arched, lifting his pelvis. Jay's hands rasped down his sides to take hold of him, raising up his hips, then began to fuck him hard and fast. Alastair's moans kicked into cries. In only seconds, the dizzy spikes of pleasure erupted and he was coming, panting and pleading as Jay drove into him, ratchetting the feeling higher and higher still.

Somewhere in the rush, Jay let out a guttural groan. He pushed deep into Alastair's body and held on, one hand tight at his hip, the other wrapped around his shoulder to keep him still. The feeling ripped the breath from Alastair's lungs all over again. He twisted his hands into the sheets and panted, shining in every nerve and every vein. *God, yes. Come in me. Come in me, hold me, keep me...*

In the aftermath, exhausted, Alastair could do nothing but collapse. He sagged down onto the bed as loosely as a ragdoll, flopping to one side in an attempt to avoid the mess he'd just striped across the sheets. There he lay within the wreckage of himself, struggling to catch his breath.

There came a hazy chuckle from nearby.

"Hey," Jay husked, gathering an arm around his body. "Don't lie in the damp. Come up here with me."

He shifted back across the bed to make room, then pulled Alastair gently to lie upon his chest.

"There we go," he murmured, cuddling Alastair close with one arm. He swept back the sweaty red strands of Alastair's hair and placed a kiss upon his forehead, encouraging him to settle. "That's better, mm?"

Something about resting his cheek upon tattoos, listening to the thunder of the heart beneath them, made Alastair feel alive.

"Beast," he breathed, earning himself another laugh.

"Suppose I am." Jay smiled, running his fingertips down Alastair's back. They brushed against his skin as soft and sly as whispered secrets. "You don't have a clue how gorgeous you are, do you? The *noises* you make. Fuck me up."

"Entirely your fault," Alastair said. He stirred just enough to brush his mouth against Jay's chest, still breathless. "You fuck me like I'm half my age, Jay."

Jay huffed. "I live to serve." He craned his head to watch Alastair kiss the rise and fall of his chest, tracing the shining black patterns. "They turn you on a bit, don't they?"

"Mm?"

"My tattoos."

Having spent the entire evening licking and grasping them at every possible opportunity, Alastair supposed he was in no position to deny it.

"My mother crossed the street to avoid men with visible tattoos," he said. "She used to shepherd me behind her skirts before I could see them."

"Yeah?" Jay said. "What would she've thought of you and me?"

Shivering, Alastair swept his tongue across the petals of Jay's largest black rose. "She'd have been utterly appalled."

Jay tipped his head back against the pillow, grinning. "Did she have paintings up in the house?" he asked. "Ornaments?"

"Sailboats and rosy-cheeked Victorian children. Ceramic figurines on every surface."

"They make me laugh, you know—people who spend a fortune on art for the wall, but wouldn't dream of putting it on their skin."

Alastair had never thought of it that way. He smiled a little, tracing his fingertips across the designs. "Do they hurt?"

"Mm hmm. They're meant to."

Jay caught Alastair's fingers, guiding them up to the lion on his left shoulder.

"Took about ten hours," he said, "start to finish. The first two or three hours are easy enough. Gets worse as you go along. I was ripping the arms off the chair by the end of it."

Fascinated, Alastair brushed the lion's teeth with his fingertips. "Is the chest more painful than other places?"

"Some bits of it. Collarbones are agony. The needle's buzzing straight onto bone, nothing padding it, so all the script up here hurt like hell. And here—" Jay moved Alastair's hand to the very side of his chest, tucked up beneath his arm. "—fucking tickles. I smoked an entire packet of cigs to get through those two inches."

Alastair's smile grew, unsure why he found it all so enchanting. "It's worth it, though?"

"God, yeah. Wouldn't mean anything if they hadn't hurt." Jay stretched, folding both his arms behind his head. "Just like everything in life."

"Mm..." Alastair ran his fingers along Jay's lines of Gothic script, trying to read them. The text was bunched and angular, difficult to scan with ease. *"Flectere si nequeo...* Oh, Virgil. It's *The Aeneid,* isn't it?"

Jay laughed aloud. "Are you kidding me? You speak Latin?"

"I had enough of the classics drummed into me to remember some scraps," Alastair said, trying not to flush. "I'm surprised you know *The Aeneid* though. With respect, you don't seem the type."

"I'm not," Jay admitted. "Just thought it was cool when I was twenty. You know that age when you're invincible and you need the whole bloody world to know it?"

Alastair hummed, gazing dimly at the script. *"If I cannot bend the will of heaven,"* he translated, *"I shall move hell."*

"I was a gobby little arsehole. Your mum would've run a hundred miles. Wouldn't blame her for it, either."

Helpless, Alastair smiled. "And yet angel wings."

Jay raised an eyebrow. "Mm?"

"Up here, you're raising hell," Alastair murmured, stroking the script. "On the back, you've gained your wings. Which is more recent?"

As Jay made the connection, he smiled a little. "The wings," he said, his gaze soft. "About a year after I started up the charity."

Alastair's heart stirred. "Heaven bent its will, did it?"

Jay took a moment to respond. He wore a curious look on his face, as if there were things he didn't quite know how to say—things he wished he could. In the end, they slipped away beneath a smile.

"Not really," he said. "I just stopped being a mardy little tosser." He winked.

Amused, Alastair reached up to kiss his nose.

"And have you planned any further works of art?" he asked, as a smirking Jay stroked both hands down his back, pulling Alastair to lie on top of him. "What's your next one going to be?"

"Depends," Jay said. "What's Latin for *I fucked the Met chief?"*

Sated to the bone, kept warm by the heat of Jay's bare body beside him, Alastair slept deeply and peacefully.

He woke to the wet brush of Jay's tongue, teasing his sleepy cock to hardness. As he moaned, shivering, he discovered his left leg had been arranged over Jay's shoulder. Jay's fingers were already between his thighs, toying through the slickness left there from earlier.

"Mm hmm?" Jay hummed against his cock, licking.

Alastair's entire body took flame.

"Christ—" he gasped. He drove his fingers through Jay's hair, shaking. "Yes—" Two fingers pushed into his body, thick and firm, in a single slick stroke. "Oh, fuck, *yes...!*"

When he finally came, it was swearing and arching up from the bed, heaving his breathless gasps into the darkness as he poured himself down Jay's throat.

Lying in his afterglow, dazed and insensible with pleasure, the nuzzle of Jay's cock against his lips sent a shudder through his bones. He relaxed his jaw and opened his mouth, letting the thick head slide against his tongue. Jay knelt over him, gathered him close with a hand around the back of his neck and held him there gently, supporting him. Alastair's pulse leapt.

God, use me. Do it. Have me.

In slow, shaking thrusts, Jay chased what he needed. He panted as he did, gasping out fragments of Alastair's name. Alastair groaned his soft encouragement in response, licking and bobbing, trying to make this something to remember. A restless shift in Jay's voice warned his closeness, a tightening in his fingers which Alastair recognised. *I know you already,* he realised with a shock. *Know your signs. Know your sounds.*

As bitterness hit the back of his throat, he shook and swallowed and simply breathed, so at peace he felt he might evaporate. Jay cradled his head in place, his moans desperate; Alastair licked him slowly back to earth.

Somewhere in the fog of exhaustion, there came a kiss—long and lazy, the taste of Jay shared between their mouths, fond fingers winding through Alastair's hair.

"Couldn't stop myself," Jay whispered. His voice seemed to swirl through Alastair's mind. "You're just so..."

Alastair shivered, staying close for another slow kiss. "Were you lying awake?"

"Not for long. I'm alright."

"If you'd like a hot drink..."

Jay's fingers stirred, curling at the back of Alastair's neck. "Sleep, sweetheart," he said. "I know how to use a kettle."

Nestling against Jay's shoulder, it occurred dimly to Alastair that he'd normally be protective of this space—his home, which no one else ever saw. Juliet knew not to rearrange his desk, his files, or even his pens without asking. He had things very much how he liked them.

Touching his lips to Jay's pulse, Alastair closed his eyes. "Use anything you want," he said. "I don't mind."

Jay's fingers brushed between his shoulders. "Should be alright. Think I'm settling now."

"Is it chronic?"

"Mm?"

"The insomnia."

Jay huffed. "Just recent," he said. "Fine during the day. Then I get my head on the pillow, and start thinking. Daft stuff. Stuff I can't change, especially at two AM."

Alastair knew the feeling all too well. "Has anyone recommended camomile tea?"

"No. Why, does it work?"

"It doesn't. Utter bloody nonsense. I drink gallons of the stuff. It makes no difference."

Jay laughed.

"You lie awake sometimes, do you?" he said. "Suppose... the stresses you're under..."

"Par for the course," Alastair murmured. He never really got the chance to speak about this. All the people he knew were co-workers; the last thing they needed was to hear a senior officer lamenting his lot in life. He wrapped his legs with Jay's beneath the sheets, cuddling closer. "If a police commissioner sleeps well at night, they're probably not doing their job properly."

Jay kissed the top of his head. "You tried tons and tons of sex?" he teased. "I've heard that does the trick."

Alastair smiled, helpless. "Let's see how rested I feel in the morning. Have you ever been told you're a wicked man?"

"Mm. Few times, actually."

"Add my name to that list. You're a scoundrel."

Jay hummed, tilting his mouth to nibble very gently at the shell of Alastair's ear.

"Keep talking," he murmured as Alastair squirmed. "Please. Tell me I'm bad in that posh and pretty voice. Kinda turning me on again."

Grinning in the darkness, Alastair put his arms around Jay's shoulders. "Who paid you to kill me, may I ask? Did they specify you have to do it as slowly and enjoyably as possible? Or did you come up with that part?"

"Voluntary role," Jay said. He stroked a hand down Alastair's side, his eyes flashing. "Took one look at you and thought, this guy needs to ride me 'til his brain explodes. It'll do him a world of good."

"Chivalrous of you."

"Yep. And don't look now, but I'm cooking you breakfast in the morning."

"Excellent. Wearing what? I hope it's not much."

"Just your legs around my waist."

"While cooking?"

"Yep."

"Ambitious of you."

"Isn't it just?" Jay squeezed Alastair's arse with one hand, kissing the corner of his jaw. "You'd better go to sleep soon. Otherwise I'll be mauling you again."

Mm. If I'm lucky.

"Wake me if you'd rather have company," Alastair said. A yawn wracked through his exhausted body, his feet stretching out beneath the sheets. "Thank you for coming over, Jay. You've rescued my week."

He felt Jay smile against his temple. "Thanks for having me, sunshine. You've rescued mine as well."

Sunshine, Alastair noted fondly. He'd caught it several times now. *Rather sweet.* He trailed his fingertips against the back of Jay's shoulder, enjoying the natural pad of muscle there.

"The joy of these arrangements," he supposed.

"Straight to the good stuff?"

"Mm. It's... reassuring, being upfront and honest. I feel very at ease with you."

Jay smiled, brushing back his hair.

"Good to hear," he said. "You chill me out, too. Whenever you want the good stuff, I hope I'm first in line."

[JF - 11:03] *thanks again for an amazing night...*
[JF - 11:03] *looking forward to next time*

[AH - 11:05] *As am I. Very much.*

[JF - 11:11] *and thanks for the send off ;)*

[AH - 11:14] *My pleasure, I assure you.*
[AH - 11:14] *Thank you for breakfast.*

[JF - 11:18] *anytime :)*

[AH - 11:20] *I hope your sleep improves.*

[JF - 11:26] *yeah, me too*
[JF - 11:26] *hope its a better week for you*
[JF - 11:26] *if it isnt...*
[JF - 11:26] *give me a ring ;) x*

Chapter 6

Three weeks later, Jay's Friday started excellently. A decent night's sleep and time for a proper breakfast fooled him into a peppy sort of pre-weekend cheerfulness; the positivity even survived his tube journey. On the short walk to the office, he bought himself a fancy coffee and a sandwich for lunch and was nearly humming by the time he got to work.

He buzzed in through the security gate, rounded the corner towards the familiar entrance, and stopped dead.

Two uniformed police officers were studying the open double doors. The glass was webbed from floor to ceiling with deep, purposeful cracks; five or six attempts had been made to smash through. It was a miracle they hadn't given way. Only something like a hammer could have caused that kind of damage.

As Jay stared, frozen to the spot, a possible explanation pounded through his head.

No, he thought.

No, this... no. There's no way.

In Jay's peripheral vision, someone peeled away from the gaggle of employees watching the police take pictures. Their blurred shape strolled towards him, hands in their pockets.

"Are you alright?" a voice asked.

Jay recognised Connor only dimly. He glanced up, lost, and found a look of sympathy waiting for him.

"Don't worry," Connor said. "It's clearly criminal damage. The insurance'll pay out."

Jay swallowed, trying to string enough words together to form a sentence. "Who—w-when did—"

"Must have been some time in the night," Connor said, shrugging. "The cleaners reported it early this morning. Vandals, maybe? Thieves trying to break in? It's a bit crap that they'd target a charity."

Fuck. Shit.

"Yeah," Jay managed on auto-pilot, staring white-faced at the cracks. "Yeah, it's... it's shit that someone's..."

One of the reception team was informing the police of Jay's arrival, directing them towards him with hand gestures. Jay gripped his coffee cup and tried to breathe, shaping his expression into something a little less scared out of his senses.

"Did we get anyone on CCTV?" he asked, not certain he wanted to know.

"They took out the camera," Connor said, pointing. "Looks like they climbed the gate and smashed it right off the wall. They've taken most of it with them, apparently. Stops the police from being able to recover any footage."

The officers began to walk their way.

"Want me to sit in?" Connor checked carefully. "You've gone as white as a sheet, Jay."

"No." Jay dragged in a breath, then released it without a sound. "No, it's... you're alright. I'll handle it. Thanks."

The police were convinced it was a random act of vandalism. They told Jay over coffee in his office that they'd seen similar things in the area, and that professional thieves would more likely have targeted the lock than the glass. The only CCTV overlooking the scene was the one above the gate; the company's own security fence blocked the view of any other nearby cameras.

"Vandals go in for that," one of the officers assured Jay. "It's textbook. Get a decent cage around your camera, and you shouldn't have any more problems."

Unwilling to give voice to the alternative explanation, Jay let them put 'vandalism' down on the form.

A difficult morning unfolded into a difficult day. Fixing the doors would cost money that the organisation hadn't budgeted for. An insurance claim would take time. Jay spent the entire afternoon developing a joint headache with the finance team, trying to work out how they could conjure an enormous amount of money from thin air. The short answer was: they couldn't, not without cuts. Though it swallowed up Jay's day, it kept him busy. Time to think would mean a chance for his thoughts to stray towards places he couldn't let them go, not until he was alone.

And once he'd told twelve separate people that the police had ruled vandalism, he almost started to believe it himself. This was London, after all. Everything got vandalised eventually. Standing for too long at the bus stop would soon attract someone with a spray can to doodle on you. From the outside, their building looked like all the other offices in the city, and any kid tired of being kicked around by the system would see it as a viable target. Jay might have slung a brick through the windows himself when he was fifteen. These things happened.

It wasn't necessarily connected.

He told Connor to run with vandals on social media, focus on the underlying causes and keep it compassionate. By the end of the day, seven separate news teams had gotten in touch to ask for interviews with the chief executive. All seven had to make do with Connor.

Jay left work via the back exit, his head down and his hood up, and took a different tube route home.

By the time he reached his flat, he was almost too weary to turn the key in the lock.

One of those days, he thought as he let himself in. He snorted to himself in the quiet. *One of those lives.* Even switching on the light seemed like too much. He dropped down onto his sofa in the dark, still wearing his coat and shoes, and let the bulging Sainsburys bag at his side slump over. His head had become some weird combination of screaming alarm bells and swamp, nothing moving, everything panicking. He had to put the milk away. He had to make some food. He needed to psych himself up to do anything other than just lie here like an empty sack, listening to the leaden thump of perpetual R&B coming through the ceiling.

Staring through his empty TV screen, Jay reached vaguely into the bag at his side. He fished out his new pack of Benson and Hedges, wheedled one from the packet and lit it, telling himself this was progress.

As he smoked the cigarette, he thought.

The problem was the gulf between the two possibilities. This thing was either nothing, or an actual threat to his life.

If the latter, it meant Ian had found him. A trail somewhere had been followed, and in spite of all Jay's efforts, his fresh start was about to turn to dust. *Like it never even happened,* he thought miserably, his heart straining as he dragged on his cigarette. *Ten years.* Something about those cracks, splintered into the glass, read as clearly to him as any written message. Jay could still see them now, every jagged line smashed into his memory. *I'm here,* they seemed to say. *I'm at your door.* The thought poured cold down the back of his neck.

Or perhaps it didn't mean a thing, and the police were right.

Part of him wanted to wonder whether Ian would really play games like this. If Ian was now in London, and he'd tracked Jay down to the Fieldhouse Foundation, he could just have easily tracked Jay to his flat. The Ian that Jay knew would have sent someone to crack open his lock in the night, let themselves in and empty Jay's throat across the floor. Messing around with corporate vandalism seemed almost too gentlemanly for him.

Closing his eyes, Jay tipped his weary head back against the couch. He blew smoke into the air as he exhaled, supposing he had no way to figure this out. His focus shouldn't be on whether this was Ian.

What he needed to figure out was whether to tell Kim.

She'd asked to hear about anything strange—but telling her might mean she'd pull the plug. The second she decided that Jay was in danger, life as he knew it would end. He'd be out of this flat within days, out of a job, out of everything. The Protected Persons Service had never lost anybody, but it was because they just didn't fuck around. The best way to keep someone safe was to fling them hundreds of miles away as soon as there was any suggestion of a problem. If they'd handled it once already, why not twice? A lot of people who entered the programme lived rootless, nervous lives, cautious to do anything with their time in case it all had to be abandoned.

Jay had sworn to himself that his life wouldn't be like that. He was going to *live,* and live like he'd always wanted, none of this half-arsed waiting around to die.

And living had been easy when Ian was in prison. There'd been plenty of people still left on the outside, but Ian was the lifeblood, the one with the plans and the grit to get them done. Chopping off the head, the body had fallen. Jay had taken to freedom like a dream.

If Kim heard about today, she'd rightly put an end to it.

As soon as he'd had the thought, Jay questioned it with a frown.

Rightly? he asked himself, leaning aside to knock his ash into this morning's coffee cup. *Would it be, though?* He wasn't certain he could cope with the idea of losing the charity, all his good work, just because a kid hopped over a gate one night to work off some stress. Losing everything but his life should be a last resort—Kim might not understand that. After all, her only job was keeping him alive. If he was still in one piece, she'd achieved all her goals and the UKPPS could carry on saying they'd never lost someone, no matter how miserable and meaningless those new lives were.

If Jay had to give everything up, he wanted it to be for a solid fucking reason.

Right.

He took a breath, flicked his ash, then jammed the cigarette back in his mouth.

No rash reactions, he told himself, working off his coat. *No blowing everything to shit unless I'm certain. It was only two panes of glass. Can't start letting ghosts into my head.*

It was Friday night. If he put his mind to it, he could do a lot this weekend—get this place tidied up, for a start. Do some ironing. Maybe even hit the gym. *Switch my brain back on,* Jay thought, rolling the cigarette against his lip. *Sort myself out.*

Or...

Jay glanced towards his bed, stroking the side of his cigarette.

He wondered how Alastair was.

This flat wasn't the sort of place you brought a guest. It had a grand total of two rooms: a bathroom and a jumbled all-in-one room of everything else, the kitchen at one end and the bed at the other. The couch and the TV filled up the space in the middle. Sir Alastair Harding wouldn't be seen dead here.

Would he?

Jay's cigarette smoked between his fingers, forgotten. He supposed if he was setting up a romantic meal, trying to wine and dine someone, it would be mortifying to have them here. There wasn't room to swing a cat. It looked like cheap student accommodation.

But... well, if it's not about wining and dining...

The thought burned in Jay's chest—his tired old bones, his crap and pointless week, Ian back reigning supreme in his head. He wanted to stop thinking. It would be good to feel skin. He'd love to be naked with someone—with Alastair—those gorgeous moans, his clever gaze turning soft and senseless with pleasure. Alastair was eager and appreciative in bed, and he knew how to make Jay forget.

Biting his lip, Jay slid a hand into his pocket for his phone. He pulled it out, scrolled through his contacts in the dark, and paused before he tapped the name. Alastair might still be at work. Besides, he seemed to prefer texting over calling. He must be more comfortable that way.

Jay keyed the message in, telling himself not to get his hopes up. This was extremely last minute. A yes wasn't guaranteed.

[JF - 20:09] *how was your week? :) x*

He pressed send.

Determined not to sit here on tenterhooks waiting for a reply, Jay forced himself up off the sofa. He hung up his coat and untucked his shirt, put the milk away in the fridge, then set the kettle boiling for a cup of coffee.

As he filled the mug, his phone lit up beside his keys and began to judder across the counter top. *Incoming call from Alastair Harding.*

Dropping the kettle back on its base, Jay grabbed for his phone. He let it ring three more times, nervous not to seem too keen, then lifted it casually to his ear.

"Hi," he answered, hardly daring to hope.

Alastair's voice seemed to stroke across his soul.

"Hello." There came the distinctive click of a lighter, a flash of flame, then a sleek metal snap as it shut. "My week has been extremely dull."

Good.

"Yeah?" Jay said. "Mine too." It hadn't been anything of the sort, but it seemed like things might be about to pick up. Jay found himself rubbing the side of his neck. "Busy weekend planned?"

"Not exactly busy. More of the same, really." Alastair was smoking somewhere. He didn't sound like he was inside, but Jay couldn't hear traffic either. "And yours?"

Get the fuck round here. Make me eat my pillow.

"Nothing on," Jay said. He bit the corner of his lip, deciding just to go for it. "Wondered if you'd wanted to meet up, maybe. Have a drink, order some food. Chill."

Alastair took a slow drag on his cigarette. "When?"

"Now, if you like. I'm free."

"I'm... afraid I'm occupied this evening. I'll be busy for another two hours or so."

"Two hours is fine," Jay said, trying not to sound too relieved. *I can get the place clean in two hours. Change the sheets. Have a shower and a shave.* "Come round to mine. You know I'm not a threat now, right? I'll make you breakfast."

Alastair let out an almost fond huff; Jay had a feeling he'd just made him smile.

"My security's somewhat more official than that," Alastair said. "It's not that I don't trust you, Jay."

"I'll come to you then," Jay said. With every word he spoke, he was realising more and more how much he wanted this. He wanted Alastair pressed against him, moaning softly, that gorgeous neck to run his mouth along and those elegant hands gripping at his body. He needed it. "Shall I meet you at your flat? Ten o'clock?"

Alastair took another drag. "You've caught me out of London," he said. "I'd... like to see you, Jay. Very much. I'm just not sure I can put you through the inconvenience."

Jay hesitated, his heart falling. "How far out of London?"

"An hour. I'm attending a function at a hotel in Berkshire. I'd planned to spend the night here."

Jesus. Let's go for it. "Alone?"

"Mm." Alastair paused. "Though I suppose that part could flex."

Jay breathed in. He prepared the words in his mouth, wishing this didn't make him feel so nervous. He'd been reluctant to want things lately. It felt like tempting fate.

"Could be lonely," he said. "Big hotel bed on your own, I mean. More fun with a friend. Chill you out after your function."

The sound of Alastair's shiver cut his breath.

"I'd like that," Alastair said. He was starting to sound like he did when they were in bed—no more authority, no more fancy words. "I'd like to see you."

Jay squeezed his phone, hoping against hope. "Say the word."

Alastair was silent for a moment, decisions being made. "I'll send a driver," he said. "Can you be ready in twenty minutes?"

Jay's pulse kicked. "Yeah. Sure. What should I—?"

"Whatever you'd need for an overnight stay. I hadn't anticipated needing... certain supplies. If you could bring them with you, it'll spare us an uncomfortable conversation with the desk staff."

Jay was already opening his wardrobe, rummaging through the bottom for a backpack.

"Sure," he said. *The good lube,* he thought. *The tingle stuff.* "Can do."

"You're sure this isn't inconvenient?"

"No, sunshine. Weekend's wide open. It'll be nice to see you."

He could almost hear Alastair's smile.

"I should be able to make my escape by half ten," Alastair said. "I'll leave my room key at reception for you. It's a junior suite in the east wing."

Bloody hell. "East wing. Right."

"Make yourself comfortable. If you want to order room service, feel free. I'll join you as soon as I can."

"Right." As he threw spare boxer shorts into his backpack, Jay smiled into the phone. "Al?"

"Yes?"

"Looking forward to you."

Alastair audibly shivered again. "Likewise." A playful note entered his voice. "A pity you won't be able to make me breakfast, though."

Hnnh. "I'll order it for you."

"Mm. The modern gentlemen."

Jay's smile became a grin. "See you soon, then. Enjoy your function."

"I shall try," Alastair murmured, and hung up.

Twenty minutes later, a Mercedes S-class in silver eased up to the kerb outside Jay's flat. The driver got out and held the door for him, then needed no instructions as to where they were going. Jay stashed his backpack in the footwell, relaxed back into the leather seat, and breathed. He had a feeling he was about to have his mind blown.

With every mile they drove out of London, the tightness in his chest eased more and more.

No more thinking 'til Monday, he decided, watching the roads roll by. *No more ghosts.*

[JF - 20:45] *so where exactly am I going? x*

It took a few minutes for Alastair to see the text. When he did, he began to reply almost at once.

Jay smiled to himself in the darkness, watching the little bubble bob.

[AH - 20:56] *Cliveden. Once the home of Nancy Astor.*

Utterly oblivious, Jay googled.

"Shine a light," he whispered, scrolling through image search. He snagged one that looked like the hotel's own website and let his jaw drop as he browsed. Out of interest, he navigated his way to the junior suites. The price per night made his kidneys shrink back into his body and whimper; the photographs showed rooms that looked like works of art, king size beds, ornate lamps and oil paintings, baths of marble with vases of fresh white flowers.

His phone buzzed in his hand.

[AH - 21:01] *Meets with your approval?*

[JF - 21:02] *will they even let me through the door?*
[JF - 21:02] *or will I have to be smuggled in through the kitchens*
[JF - 21:02] *up to the commissioners bed x*

[AH - 21:03] *Would be fitting. Cliveden has a history of scandal.*

[JF - 21:04] *just reading about it*
[JF - 21:04] *profumo affair huh?*
[JF - 21:04] *whatll they call ours? ;) x*

[AH - 21:05] *Ours won't bring the government to its knees I hope.*
[AH - 21:05] *Nor are you the mistress of a well known Russian spy.*

[JF - 21:05] *you sure? I might be ;) x*

[AH - 21:06] *Beast. x*

This was all taking an interesting turn—summoned in secret to a posh country hotel at night. It made Jay smile, remembering that he'd imagined Alastair joining him in his poky flat for a takeaway.

[JF - 21:07] *so this function youve ditched so you can text me... x*

[AH - 21:07] *I've earned a cigarette break. You're very kindly entertaining me. x*

[JF - 21:07] *posh evening do?*
[JF - 21:08] *formalwear? x*

[AH - 21:08] *V posh. Not a mini quiche in sight. x*

[JF - 21:09] *you in your uniform? xxx*

[AH - 21:10] *More of a social weekend. Dinner jacket. x*

[JF - 21:10] *you mean a tux? show me :) xxx*

[AH - 21:10] *You'll have the pleasure of a private viewing when I return to the room. x*

[JF - 21:11] *show me now*
[JF - 21:11] *I want a pic xxx*

A couple of minutes went by. Jay watched the other cars driving on the motorway, wondering where they were all going—if any of them were going somewhere as exciting as him. He doubted it.

The message, when it arrived, had a picture attached.

Grinning, Jay opened it at once.

Alastair's expression was almost playfully defiant, one eyebrow slightly arched, his pale blue eyes bright with amusement. He'd slicked back his hair to keep it neat, darkening down its hint of red. Behind him, an enormous marble fountain illuminated a wide open terrace, beyond which the sweeping lawns of a country estate could be seen. They stretched out of sight into the darkness, endless. Stars were visible in the sky.

Jay's stomach ached at the sight of the svelte black jacket and crisp bowtie. They were begging to be hauled off and crumpled. He'd never wanted to spoil something so much in his life.

[AH - 21:14] *Will that sate your rampant appetite for the moment? xx*

[JF - 21:15] *fuckkk xxx*
[JF - 21:15] *I want you xxx*
[JF - 21:15] *want to scruff you up xxx*

[AH - 21:15] *Scruff me up? x*

[JF - 21:15] *wreck you... make a mess of you... xxx*

[AH - 21:16] *Mm. I think I might let you.*

[AH - 21:16] *Something for me to think about while I schmooze.*
[AH - 21:16] *I'll have to head back inside now. xx*

[JF - 21:16] *go shmooze posh thing*
[JF - 21:16] *think about me xxx*

The message was seen; no reply came.

Grinning, Jay pocketed his phone. He sat back in the seat, closed his eyes, and told himself he was more than due a break. If the universe wanted to spoil him, he wasn't going to stop it.

The car eventually pulled off the M40, continuing through the darkness along winding hedge-lined country lanes. They reached the walled outskirts of an estate; Alastair's driver had a discreet word with uniformed security at the gate, showing a piece of ID that Jay didn't get a chance to properly see. They were waved through onto a long straight driveway, carved between an avenue of perfectly matching trees.

The house waiting in the distance took Jay's breath.

He'd never really seen a place like this, not in all his life. London's rich weren't shy about showing off their money, but this place was a whole new level. Royalty probably came here when they fancied a little bit of luxury. Jay immediately wanted to laugh for bringing a backpack with his boxers and a toothbrush—it would be the first backpack through those doors in all of history. This place was unreal.

Jesus, and I'm here for...

The police commissioner's company after hours. Here to make a powerful man feel like an animal again. Here to strip off a tuxedo and a bowtie, and tend to the bare skin underneath it.

Fuck. This is getting fun.

Right now, somewhere in this building, the rich and the powerful were chatting over champagne with Sir Alastair Harding. They were laughing at his witticisms, asking how he'd been.

Meanwhile, his fun for the night was being bowed through the front doors by a uniformed porter, approaching the desk with an old backpack slung over his shoulder and a smile.

"Hi," Jay said to the young woman on duty. He didn't know if you were meant to say *hi* in a place like this. *Good evening* might have been better, but it was a little bit late for that now. "I'm, erm... staying with a friend here tonight. Said there'd be a key at the desk for me."

If she sensed what this was, or what Jay meant by friend, she didn't show it.

"Certainly," she said. "What's your name, please?"

"It's Fieldhouse. Jay. Room's probably under Harding."

She checked a list beneath the desk then smiled.

"Yes, we have a key for Fieldhouse. You're in the Orkney suite." She collected it from the board for him, handing it over. "Would you like a hand with your bags?"

Jay indicated his backpack with a guilty grin.

"Should be fine," he said. "Can you tell I've never been here before?"

Her eyes sparkled. "Then I hope you enjoy your first stay with us, sir. The lift is over there, if you require. Your room's up on the first floor."

"Great. Thanks."

Halfway to the stairs, Jay had a thought.

He returned to the desk.

"Hi, sorry. Me again. Do you have a menu for room service at all? Thanks. Starving."

Alastair's door had his name displayed on a little white card, written out in script with a fountain pen. *Sir Alastair Harding. Orkney Suite.*

Biting his lip, Jay let himself inside.

It looked like his imagining of a duke's bedroom: winged armchairs and an antique bureau, a vast bed with four carved wooden posts, tastefully hideous carpet and floor-to-ceiling windows now tucked away behind heavy curtains of muted dark red velvet. The lamps were all lit, and it was quiet and warm. A glance in the bathroom revealed Alastair's toiletries. An empty leather suitcase peeked from beneath the enormous bed.

Jay's things all fit in a single bedside drawer. He left his backpack in the wardrobe, hung his jacket behind the door, then sprawled out on the couch with the room service menu. *Friday night begins,* he thought, kicking off his shoes. Alongside some rather fancier options, he was delighted to spot fish and chips. He doubted it would come wrapped in newspaper with a wooden fork, but decided to order it anyway. The staff member on the phone told him it would be added to the bill. He supposed Alastair *had* offered—and having seen what Alastair was paying for the room, Jay doubted the cost of an evening meal would make much difference.

The food arrived within fifteen minutes, delivered by a polite young woman who laid everything out for Jay near the fireplace. She turned down the bed, checked if he needed anything else, then wished him a good evening and left.

As he ate, Jay wondered what it was like to work in one of these places. The staff must have seen some jaw-dropping things. Posh people would have dirty laundry like everyone else; if anything, it would look all the dirtier for the whiteness of the sheets.

Alastair couldn't be the first male guest who'd had a friend turn up late at night.

There's probably a prostitute in this building right now, Jay thought. *Shit, there's probably a few.* Posh people more likely called them escorts, but sex for cash could only get so classy. There'd be mistresses and dirty secrets sleeping on every floor of this hotel tonight.

And Jay was one of them.

Probably shouldn't be getting off on that.

As he considered the alternative evening he could be having—Chinese food in front of the TV, kidding himself he'd do the ironing any minute while really just worrying himself to death about Ian—Jay decided he didn't care all that much.

With his plate cleared, he checked the time on his phone: ten past ten. Alastair wouldn't be long.

Long enough for a shower, Jay thought, his stomach tightening. *Might be nice to get clean.* He'd had a long day. Hopefully, there was still a long night ahead.

As he slipped beneath the water, he couldn't help but groan. The spray was powerful enough to dig into his muscles a little, blasting the day's grime off his skin. Squinting, spitting, he groped for one of Alastair's pale green bottles and studied the label at arm's length. *'Scalp revitaliser',* he read. *Known by us commoners as shampoo.* As he lathered it through his hair, a deep breath filled his lungs with the scent and made him smile. This was how Alastair's hair smelled. The shower gel, too, smelled of him. *Penhaligon's,* the label said, flashing Jay not one but two royal coats-of-arms. Soaping it into his skin, shivering, he soaked in the scent of Alastair on the steam and let his last few worries pour away. He'd earned some proper peace. It was a relief even to be out of London.

Drying himself off on the fluffiest towel ever created, Jay considered his clothing strewn about the floor. *Like wrapping a present you're about to hand over,* he thought, and decided to leave it where it was. He gave his hair one last scrub with the towel, threw it over the heated rail, then got into bed.

The thing was as deep and satisfying as a hot bath. Jay sank into it, shuddering, and kicked the covers off to bare his body to the lamp light. He sprawled across the mattress diagonally and stretched, tipping his head back against the pillows, wondering how many thousands of pounds this bed must have cost. Just being in it felt erotic.

No wonder posh people are so over-sexed.

The poor things probably couldn't help it, riddled with lust every time they laid their heads down. Jay wondered how consciously the hotel had picked these beds. Whoever chose them must have known they were good beds to fuck in. Surely they had known. The mattress felt broad and indulgent beneath his back, the covers snowy white and so soft he never wanted to get up again. This bed knew all his secrets. It knew every wicked thing he'd ever done, and it loved him for it. It made him feel like he needed to be fucked—several times, very slowly.

I could be ironing right now, Jay thought. *Staring at the box. Worrying I'm gonna die.* Instead he was here, half-hard just from being in this bed. He closed his eyes, breathing the comfort of it all into his lungs. *Damn, I could almost get used to this.*

A quiet rattling interrupted his thoughts. Realising what it was, Jay smiled and turned his gaze towards the door, watching with hope as it opened.

A discreet sweep of light from the hallway cast Alastair's familiar figure in silhouette, framing the long and tailored lines of his body. Neither the selfie, nor Jay's memories, had done him justice. They hadn't even come close. Every part of him was crisp and clean and composed, every inch of his tuxedo shaped to him, every copper-red hair smoothed back into place. He was as composed and empyrean as a bird of prey, and no less stunning to behold.

He spotted the empty plate beside the fire at once, smiled quietly at its presence, and cast his gaze around the room.

As he found Jay lying in the bed, he stopped, one hand still holding the door. Something flickered across his expression—or more rightly passed beneath it, deeper than the calm which lay like frost over the surface. It looked as if memory had done Jay no justice either.

Jay pressed his teeth with care into the corner of his lip.

"Hi," he said.

Alastair seemed to take a second to reassemble the fragments of his brain. He then realised he was still holding the door, still offering this sight to the corridor behind him, and closed it at once.

In the soft and smoky quiet, he approached the end of the bed. Jay remained as he was and let Alastair's eyes drink their fill, enjoying their slow and silent passage across his skin. He'd never felt this naked in his life. *I will do literally anything you want,* he thought, trying to let it show in his eyes, in the lazy stretch of his back. *There's nothing you can't have from me. Nothing I'll turn down.*

Alastair's eyes finally reached his face; a smile lifted the edge of his mouth.

"You're made yourself at home, I see," he said.

Jesus, Jay thought with a noiseless breath. *Your fucking voice.* "How was your function?"

Alastair raised an eyebrow. "Increasingly difficult to care about."

Jay kindled a smile, fanning out his toes. "Yeah?" he said, and stretched again for Alastair's gaze. "How come?"

"I found myself strangely distracted," Alastair said, reaching up to undo his bowtie. He eased the black silk apart with barely a pull. "Not that you played any part in that, I'm sure."

Jay's cock seemed to ache as he watched Alastair undo the top button of his shirt, leaving the bowtie loose around his neck. Nothing in the world should be this hot. They hadn't even touched yet.

"I've never been fucked by someone wearing a tuxedo," he said.

Alastair raised an eyebrow. "Remiss of you," he said. He undid another button, exposing just the top of his chest hair. "I've never left a party to be scruffed up."

Jay's grin widened. "Does that make me special?"

"I think we can agree you are." Alastair reached for his left cuff, carefully removing the brushed silver stud. "Did you bring—?"

"Mm. In the bedside."

"Good." Some scent in the air seemed to catch Alastair's attention. He tested it lightly with a lift of his head, bemused recognition brightening his smile. "Have you used my shampoo?"

"Getting pretty comfortable, aren't I?" Jay sat up slowly and eased down the bed, kneeling on his haunches as he reached for Alastair's lapels. "Do you regret bringing me yet?"

"Not in the least," Alastair said. As Jay nuzzled along his jaw, he offered his neck to Jay's small, hopeful kisses, busy undoing the other cufflink. "You seemed eager to meet tonight."

Jay nosed beneath the collar of his shirt.

"Crap day," he admitted. He let a chestful of Alastair's scent sweep the thoughts back into the depths where they belonged. "Started thinking about you," he said. "About your body."

Alastair pocketed his cufflinks, then finally put his arms around Jay's waist. "I'd have thought you'd be drowning in offers of company for a Friday night," he said.

Something warm and rather soft stirred behind Jay's ribs. He had a feeling Alastair hadn't even meant it to be flattering; he seemed to be stating a fact, one he assumed Jay would already know. *Like you can't even imagine me lonely,* Jay thought, sliding his hands beneath Alastair's jacket, stroking the silk back of his waistcoat. The thought felt thick inside his throat. *Like that just wouldn't make any sense to you.*

"I'm not, as it happens," he said. It seemed important to say. The little confidence boost of being taken for a stud didn't matter as much as having Alastair know him properly in this moment, see this whole thing for what it was: *I want you as much as you want me.* It was simple and it was good, and not much in life ever was. "For the record, if I'd had other offers, I'd still be here."

Alastair's chest rose up against Jay's. What it was, Jay didn't know —relief, surprise, something else—it didn't matter. Moving Alastair in some way was enough. He brushed his mouth against the crook of Alastair's neck, earning himself a shiver, and let his voice warm Alastair's skin.

"Is that alright?" he said, hoping it was.

Alastair's hands flexed on his back. "Yes," he said, a little strained, gathering Jay in. "It's... yes, that's alright."

Jay leaned in closer, drawing Alastair's scent in through his nose. This was starting to feel like a cuddle, and he didn't think he minded. Alastair's hands weren't rushing to the places he'd thought they might rush; Jay found himself in no hurry to get them moving. Perhaps they'd just done this enough times now to take the scenic route and go slowly. Perhaps it was the thought of the whole night ahead of them, guaranteed, no need to think about goodbye until breakfast. Perhaps it was something else. But simply holding each other, getting comfortable, seemed fine for now.

With a breath, Jay thought briefly of his sorry excuse of a flat—always cluttered, somehow still empty. He'd sat there on the couch a few hours ago and longed for Alastair, wanting him badly enough to risk reaching out. He'd hoped that sex would be enough to stop him thinking.

But even this was working. This gentle nuzzling, breathing. This feeling like he'd arrived somewhere he was needed.

Pressing his lips to Alastair's pulse, Jay whispered the words against his skin.

"Come lie down with me," he said. "We'll do whatever you want. Whatever would feel good right now. Just let me touch you."

Alastair said nothing for a moment, his fingertips gentle on Jay's back. The pattern they were tracing seemed barely there.

"May I kiss you?" he asked.

Jay's heart gave a squeeze. He lifted his head from Alastair's neck and met his eyes, wondering what that expression was—that cautious, soft-eyed weakness.

He tried a smile, brushing his fingers over Alastair's cheek.

"Of course you can," he murmured. "That's what I'm here for."

Alastair's gaze flickered to his lips. "That would... fall within the terms of our agreement?"

Jay let his smile warm.

"Think so," he said softly. "Don't you?" He ran his thumb beneath Alastair's mouth, watching what it did to his expression—the longing that tightened beneath the surface. "Yours for the weekend, sunshine. I want to touch. I want to kiss and fuck. While we're here, I'm yours. Have me."

A possibility occurred.

"Is there something special you want?" Jay asked, reaching up. He stroked his lips against Alastair's mouth and felt a shudder pass through the body in his arms. Alastair kissed him back, his grey eyes flickering shut as if he'd dreamed of it for days. Their tongues brushed gently, sweeping and softening. "Tell me," Jay whispered between kisses, his heart thumping. "I want to give you it."

Alastair took some moments to respond.

"Would you rub my shoulders?" he asked. He hesitated, his lips held a breath away from Jay's. "I need to... settle. Use your mouth on me. I'll do the same for you. Hold me while I drift off, after."

God. Jay cupped Alastair's jaw in his hands, unsure why the realisation affected him so much. Alastair needed this tonight for the same reasons he did. The motions and the details weren't important. What mattered was dropping down beneath the noise. "You had a crap week too," he said.

Alastair held his gaze for a moment, his expression giving nothing away. With a breath, he said, "I'm glad you texted me."

Jay bit his lip. "Work? Just the usual?"

Alastair nodded, tired. His eyes strayed down to Jay's lips, lingering there.

With care, Jay reached for the buttons of his shirt.

"Come here," he whispered, and leant up to rest their cheeks together. His fingers found their way onwards, working through the fastenings on their own. "Let's get you comfy, mm? No more thinking for a while. Just me and you."

Alastair's fingers curled against the small of Jay's back, cradling him close. His nose nudged gently at the side of Jay's. It was a wordless plea. Even now, he didn't quite dare.

Closing his eyes, Jay kissed him slowly. *Yes,* he promised without words, winding the fingers of one hand through Alastair's hair. *Yes, I meant it.*

Shivering, Alastair relaxed into his arms.

Chapter 7

JAY WOKE THE NEXT MORNING TO FIND ALASTAIR LEANING OVER HIM, kissing him. Every muscle in his body ached. Every inch of his skin was hypersensitive, so wrecked and wrung out that even the gentle stroke of Alastair's lips cut his breath. Jay shivered, lifting his face to the kisses, and reached out with hope to pull Alastair's body closer. They couldn't possibly go again, not after last night. But it didn't mean they couldn't try.

As his fingers encountered a buttoned shirt, Jay's heartbeat faltered in confusion.

"I need to show myself at breakfast," Alastair murmured against his lips. "It would be considered very rude if I don't."

Oh. Jay's spirits sank. *All over, already.*

"Oh... right, sure. I get you." He hesitated, wishing they'd had a few minutes to touch and kiss. Last night had turned out to be intense. They'd been awake into the small hours together, having the kind of sex that didn't fit easily into words. Alastair had taken him from behind over the bed, twisting at a handful of his hair. He'd taken Alastair on his back so they could kiss. The night had been a blur of switching from top to bottom without a breath, soothing whichever of them most needed to be fucked in that moment. Jay wouldn't forget it as long as he lived. He'd pretty much passed out at the end, too exhausted and too spent to stay conscious. "Can I, erm... drop the key at reception for you? I kind of need a shower."

Alastair nuzzled against his cheek. "I shouldn't be much more than an hour. I'd... hoped you might be here when I return."

Hope stirred in Jay's chest. "Yeah?"

"After breakfast, I have nothing to occupy me until dinner." Alastair paused, taking another kiss from Jay's mouth. "Maybe you'd be so kind."

"Occupy you, you mean?"

"Mm."

Jay curled his fingers around the lapels of Alastair's jacket. Shivering, he tugged Alastair down into the pillows to kiss.

Their tongues stroked, their mouths soft and open. As Alastair's weight pressed Jay down into the bed, Jay's heart began to thump with urgency. He arched up, his breath already shallowing, and ran his hands with hope down Alastair's back. Alastair's touch roamed his chest like he was mapping Jay, committing him to memory.

At last, with what felt like reluctance, Alastair pulled away.

"Later," he whispered, even as Jay protested and reached for him. He placed two fingers against Jay's mouth. "I can't present myself at breakfast with stubble rash and an erection. Later."

Jay groaned beneath his breath, slain. The man had absolutely no right to talk about erections while standing there and looking like he did, as fresh as a February morning, immaculate in his crisp white shirt and pale grey suit. He looked like snow wouldn't melt if it landed on him.

It only made Jay want to fuck again.

"Fetch me a croissant," he said, sinking back against the pillows.

"I'll have breakfast sent up for you. Sleep now." Alastair placed a kiss between his eyes, light as air. "Restore your strength."

"Enjoy breakfast," Jay said. He caught Alastair by the lapels. "Mnh. One more. Please."

Alastair's eyes flashed, pleased to be wanted. He took hold of Jay's wrists, lifted them either side of his head, and held them there as he leant down for one last kiss.

He was smiling as he let Jay go.

"Sleep," he said, keeping Jay pinned as he rose out of reach. Returned to his proper height, he pressed the back of his hand against his mouth. "Don't leave."

Holy shit. Jay couldn't really tell which side of Alastair aroused him more—the tired and weary soul that he'd freed from a dinner jacket last night, then soothed with sex into small hours, or this delicious bastard right here, rolling off to breakfast with Jay's love bites underneath his suit. Each of them separately had the power to absolutely ruin him. In combination, he didn't stand a chance.

"Not sure I could even make it to the door," he say. "How're you managing?"

Alastair fixed the lapels of his jacket to lay flat again, smoothing the rumples left by Jay's fingers.

"I've had several rounds of practice," he said, "walking with grace after you've spent the night ravishing me. I've gotten rather good at it." He fixed Jay with a wolfish glance, one eyebrow raised. "Now I have to share granola with the country's social elite while attempting not to picture you lying here. Thank you for that."

Jay stretched his toes outside the covers. "Say hi to everybody for me."

Alastair huffed. His smile kindled, smouldered and flared out with a curl.

"I shall," he said.

Helpless, Jay kept his eyes on Alastair until the door slid shut behind him, taking him from view. In his wake, the whole room seemed to heave a sigh.

You were a shadow of yourself last night, Jay thought dazedly. He gazed up at the ceiling, recalling the way Alastair had trembled when Jay first began to move inside him—the way he'd grasped Jay's shoulder and his lower back, gasping—the utter relief which had flooded through his face. *A few hours moaning my name, and now you're a demi-god again.*

Jay shifted onto his side, smiling to himself, and bundled the covers up around his neck.

Now he felt like a stud.

Jay's day began a second time with a tentative knock upon the door. He lifted his head from the pillow, wondering if he'd dreamed the sound.

The door opened a crack, just enough for a peek into the room.

"Room service?" a voice said.

"Oh—yeah, sure." Jay rubbed a hand across his bleary eyes, shifting a little to sit up. "Come on in."

A uniformed young man entered the room with a tray. "Would you like breakfast laid out for you, sir, or in bed?"

When in Rome, Jay thought. "Will you think I'm a lazy bastard if I have it in bed?"

"Not in the least," the young man said, and brought the tray across the room. As he straightened out the covers, Jay wondered what Alastair had said to the staff. To whom had they been asked to bring breakfast? His partner? His friend? The gentleman in his room? It fascinated Jay, though he couldn't put his finger on why.

The young man laid the tray out on the bed.

"Is there anything else I can get for you?" he asked, pouring out Jay's coffee.

Jay found himself marvelling at the friendly smile. *Like I'm not lying here naked under these covers,* he thought. *Like that's not another man's name on the door. Like you haven't noticed the absolute fucking wreck we've made of the bed.*

"Think I'm sorted now," he said, returning the smile. "Thanks."

The young man bowed, the very model of discretion, and excused himself from the room.

In the contented quiet that followed, Jay reached for his cup of coffee. He drank it slowly, letting his thoughts drift. Alastair was downstairs somewhere, networking over croissants with Jay's kisses still painted across his skin. He wondered if any of them could tell. If they could see something different in Alastair this morning—the lines in his face a little easier, his eyes a little brighter. Jay knew this shouldn't be so thrilling.

And yet it was.

Alastair had wanted him to be here for this. He could have told Jay he wasn't available, asked to meet up some other time. Instead he wanted Jay kept secret in his room, sleeping off their night of volcanic sex with the staff on hand to tend to his needs. This felt like spending the weekend in the faraway kingdom of Alastair's world, seeing things that he didn't share with just anyone. London was all of an hour away; it seemed much further.

Must have taken courage to fetch me here, Jay thought, warming his hands on his coffee mug. For all he knew, there could be royalty sitting downstairs right now. Alastair was trusting in his discretion.

He'd rubbed Alastair's back for an eternity last night—laid him down on the bed and melted away all his edges, listening to his moans grow low and soft. It still felt oddly special, being here for that. Getting to share in that.

It was all a little bit magnificent.

Jesus, Jay thought, tingling with the realisation. *I'm a rich man's darling.*

With a long drink of coffee, he rested back and shut his eyes.

Whatever this was, it felt good.

Alastair was among the last to enter the French dining room for breakfast. As he approached his assigned place at one of six circular tables, surrounded on all sides by gilded Rococo panelling, he realised he'd been fundamentally altered overnight. These were the same faces to whom he'd said goodnight less than ten hours ago; they now seemed like the faces of utter strangers. He moved himself on autopilot to his seat, greeting and nodding at those he passed, offering a polite good morning to anyone who smiled his way.

His thoughts were still in his room, where the rest of him wanted to be—leaning low over the bed, murmuring sweet things between kisses.

He'd spent the night inside Jay. He'd swept his tongue across each and every single tattoo, memorised every line of muscle with his fingertips. The two of them had hardly slept, too eager to keep kissing and fucking, wearing each other into weakness. Alastair's thighs and lower back now burned with every movement. He felt as if every set of eyes in this room were flickering towards him, noting his transformed state of being. He must be moving differently, sitting differently, radiating the sort of animal satisfaction which came from fucking someone so hard you were the only thing left in existence for them.

Jay had been pleading with him by the end.

"Fuck, please—please let me come—" Fingers struggling through sweat to keep their grip on Alastair's body. Ragged panting. Crying out as Alastair only drove harder inside him, his perfect face flooding red, his mouth wide, his eyes screwing tight. *"A-Al—shit—"*

Alastair watched, barely conscious, as a waitress poured him his coffee.

"Say hi to everybody for me."

Indiscretion was fitting for Cliveden. It was almost tradition. This was a social weekend, not business, which meant that what Alastair did after hours was his own concern. Whether he spent it in a rowing boat with a flask of tea on the Thames, or writhing in bed beneath an incredibly wicked man, it didn't matter.

If only he could now stop thinking about the wicked man in question—about the precise sounds he made while having his hair gripped; the shift of his back muscles as he braced himself against the headboard, black angel wings and shoulders as solid as a mountain; the restless flash of his ivy-green eyes when something began to feel not just good, not just wonderful, but *perfect.*

Alastair was at breakfast in body only. As his mouth made small talk over grapefruit, he was turning Jay over onto his back, kissing his sleepy mouth, pushing away the covers to slide his hands over endless plains of warm and willing ink-stained skin—following the path of his hands with his mouth—wrapping his lips around Jay's rigid cock, feeling Jay stretch and sigh and thrust up in frustration and *groan...*

"Sir?"

Alastair blinked free of his thoughts, inclining his head over his shoulder to the waitress. "Yes?"

"Would you care for any more toast, sir?"

"Ah. No, thank you."

The waitress nodded, moving on her way. Alastair reached for his coffee, unsurprised to find it going cold.

Over pastries, he was asked by those near him regarding his plans for the day. He told them with suitable regret that something had arisen over night which needed his attention. He received understanding smiles in response. Many of the men and women here were of a class that required no occupation, but it seemed quite right to them that the head of British policing should always be busy. Alastair's dedication to his position rather characterised him in their eyes; he was well known for it. Even the shadow of his duty was unassailable. No doubt they would all picture him in his suite, working in silence at his laptop until dinner.

He'd be doing nothing of the sort. His deputy commissioner would handle any matters of urgency this weekend, with Juliet there to help.

Alastair would be handling Jay.

It was all so *animal.* It left Alastair feeling like he couldn't really hear other voices. As soon as this was over, he'd be with Jay again, touching his skin, the curtains half-closed and the bed a smoking wreck around them. They'd be wrapped around each other, kissing in a fever. He'd have Jay inside him, coaxing him to fall apart. They'd be listening to each other make the most intimate sounds a human could make. He wanted Jay to plead with him.

He was having breakfast at Cliveden with the country's elite, and all he wanted was to abandon them and return to his lover.

The romance of it was rather heady.

Alastair wondered if any of them would believe it. His reputation was staunchly asexual, a man of duty, not pleasure. His uniform preceded him, even when not wearing it. He'd lived his life as a disciple of the mind. This morning, he was a creature of the body. One of two bodies, in fact—joined even now, floors apart. He wasn't truly sitting here, trying to follow some inane conversation. He was still in bed, still inside Jay, watching him pant at the unhurried grinding of their hips, kissing his throat and feeling the muscles clench as he swallowed. Beneath his suit, Alastair's skin burned with the need to be touched.

It was impossible to focus on anything else.

Dear God, he thought with a breath, glancing across the room in a daze. *What has happened to me?*

The answer was simple. Jay Fieldhouse had happened. He was happening still, moment by moment, and he seemed to have only just begun.

With a blink, Alastair realised Viscount Brackley was topping up his coffee cup unasked, obliging him now to stay and drink the thing. Mentally consigning the man to oblivion, Alastair thanked him with a close-lipped smile.

It was twenty minutes more before he could excuse himself. They all wished him a pleasant day as he departed, and looked forward to seeing him at dinner. Alastair did his best to seem gracious, rather than desperate to leave, and wished them the same. He then he made his way quickly to the lift, cramming down the buttons as hard as he could.

As he walked along the corridor to his suite, his pulse began to climb.

Please still be there.

It made no sense that Jay would have gone. The thought was utterly irrational, but it gripped Alastair tight in its claws all the same. He didn't know what to expect any more than he had last night. *God almighty,* he thought, retrieving his key from inside his jacket. *Don't be gone.*

The click of the lock seemed far too loud. He stepped through the door with a whisper-quiet creak, telling himself it didn't matter if Jay had taken off. This was sex, not life and death.

He was still here—somehow even more gloriously *here* than he had been before, perfectly at ease reclining in one of the window seats overlooking the grounds. Naked except for a navy silk robe, he'd made no effort to cover himself with the fabric. The morning sun had draped itself across his body, warming him from chest to thighs, and he was contentedly drinking a coffee. At the sound of the door, he turned his head towards it, his expression opening with hope.

His smile knocked Alastair's heart out of rhythm. It was the warmest and easiest smile he could ever remember receiving, as bright and natural as the sunlight streaming through the glass. Jay had quite possibly been put upon this earth just to smile. He was an artist's study in the wonders that happiness could work upon the human face, and he didn't seem to realise.

It felt like a reward Alastair couldn't possibly have earned. There'd been a mistake somewhere in the system of cosmic remuneration, and he really should let someone know.

With a final sip of coffee, Jay set the cup aside. He slipped down from the window seat and padded over, his bare feet soft upon the carpet. Alastair's pulse quickened oddly. He watched Jay come closer, his face strangely hot, his mouth suddenly unable to speak.

As he reached Alastair, Jay smiled and wrapped both his arms around his waist.

"There you are," he murmured, pulling gently and leaning in.

Alastair's eyes fluttered shut as if on command. Jay's lips pressed to his own, perfectly warm. He tasted of coffee, smoke, and sex, and he kissed Alastair just as he had last night, firm but easy, coaxing Alastair's mouth to open.

Reeling, all too aware of the tremor in his hands, Alastair hugged him close.

"I'm sorry that took so long," he managed between kisses. His breath shortened. "Every time I tried to get away—"

"Shhh." Jay stroked his strong hands down Alastair's back, still brushing his lips with lazy kisses. "It's fine, sunshine. Gave me time to think."

Alastair hesitated. "Think?" he checked. He didn't know why his mind leapt to bad things—then, he supposed Jay was the very definition of too good to be true. He couldn't blame himself for being skittish.

With a hum, Jay took hold of his arse through his trousers and squeezed.

Ah, Alastair realised. *Think.*

Jay rasped his stubble with purpose along Alastair's jaw, taking his time to reach his ear.

"When do I have to give you back?" he asked. He teased his teeth against Alastair's earlobe.

Alastair inhaled, his breath already shortening and his blood full of fire. *Mine,* he thought. *Mine for now.*

"Dinner is at eight," he said. He paused, swallowing as Jay continued to nibble at his ear. "I'll need a while to dress, though. To get ready."

"Don't worry, posh thing. I'll give you time to get all tidy again." Jay's tongue flashed behind Alastair's ear, sending a hot flicker of sensation sizzling straight down his back. "You'll be pretty for your party, I promise."

As he began to undo Alastair's shirt, Alastair let go of all his thoughts.

"Jay," he murmured, overwhelmed. Joy shivered through his senses. "Jay, I..."

"I know," Jay said softly, pulling Alastair closer.

By the time they reached the bed, Alastair had forgotten every person he'd spoken to at breakfast. He'd forgotten every face he'd ever seen. The sensation of Jay's hand in the middle of his shoulders, pressing him face down into the pillows, made him want to stay in this room as long as he lived. Jay's other hands soothed with intent between his thighs, coaxing them to part. He never wanted to see anyone but Jay again, never wanted to be in someone else's company. This felt so easy. It felt so right.

Alastair spread his legs, trembling as Jay's weight rested on his back. Jay nuzzled into the nape of his neck.

"Can I use my mouth on you?" he asked. His fingers brushed between Alastair's legs, teasing his sore and stretched passage. "Here?"

Alastair buried his face in the pillow. His hips lifted up on their own, wanting it too much to wait. "Yes," he whispered, his voice breaking. "Christ, yes. Please."

Jay kissed what felt like a new bite at the side of Alastair's neck, taking hold of a pillow.

"Have you ever come from this?" he asked, relocating it beneath Alastair's hips. His nose trailed between Alastair's shoulder blades. *Where my wings would begin,* Alastair thought in a daze.

"No," he whispered. "No, I..."

Jay huffed, pleased.

"Good," he said. He wound his way down Alastair's back, leaving tender kisses as he went. "Don't have to worry about tipping you over the edge."

As Jay parted Alastair gently with his hands, Alastair twisted his fingers into the pillow and prayed. He thanked God for the day that he'd joined the police. All of it, every argument, every chance in life he'd ever given up, had led him right here to this bed, to this man, and to this perfect, comfortable closeness.

A soft wet stripe slid from his tailbone to his balls, and Alastair stopped thinking at all.

Sex never felt complete without this part—lying back in bed, shiny and exhausted, heartbeats slowing as Alastair stroked Jay's tattoos.

"Why a lion?" he asked, tracing its fangs with his fingers.

Jay smiled, wishing he understood why this made him happy. Alastair's enchantment was enchanting. It was nice to feel fascinating to someone.

"Lions are mint," he said, kissing the top of Alastair's head. "They roar and they've got massive paws. That's why."

Alastair made a noise of dazed amusement against his collarbones. "Why not a wolf? Or a bear, or some other animal... why specifically a lion?"

"I love how much thought you're putting into this."

"Did you *not* put thought into it?"

"Not really," Jay said, smiling. "If you think too long and too hard about what you're going to have, you'll never make the appointment. Always waiting until you've picked something perfect. Better just to book a slot, turn up on the day, look through what they're working on and point at the one you like."

Alastair gazed up from his shoulder, amazed. "Don't you worry you'll choose something you regret?"

Jay's smile widened. "What's to regret? Lions are mint, sunshine. We've covered this."

"But what if... I don't know, what if your thoughts change? What if one day you wake up and realise you are in fact a bear person, not a lion person? What if you have some blinding realisation that you should have had snakes instead of playing cards, geraniums instead of roses? What then?"

"I've got space left. I'll have snakes and geraniums down my legs. Sorted."

"But what about when you've filled your legs?"

"I'll look amazing, won't I? And judging by how much you already love the ones I've got, you'll want to shag me senseless twice an hour. I'll be king of the fucking world."

Chuckling, Alastair hooked one ankle around Jay's. "There's a spirit of *carpe diem* to it," he concluded. "When it comes to tattoos, seize the day. Trust your instincts in the moment."

"There you go," Jay said. "Now you're getting it." He stirred, tilting his head enough to press a small kiss against Alastair's hair. "Suppose making the right decisions is a bit more important in your world."

Alastair huffed. "Not even just making them," he said. "Justifying them. Defending them endlessly, over and over, to people who believe they know better than me." He gave a quiet sigh as he stretched. "Never admitting to doubt," he went on. "Not even the smallest flicker of it, not in any decision I've ever made in my life. If I did, someone would use it against me."

Jay frowned a little. "Make trouble for you, you mean? Give you grief?"

Alastair hummed, brushing his fingers over the patterns on Jay's arm.

"What, just for being honest?" Jay said. "That's a good thing in a leader, isn't it?"

"Not in my field. In admitting an instance of uncertainty, I'd show my true colours for what they are. After all, if I've made one decision with anything less than total conviction, who's to say that my other decisions can be trusted? Have they also been made with the same reckless contempt for proper thought? Perhaps I, as a person, am simply reckless. All the people who support me are reckless. All the people who come from the same stock as me are reckless. It would be foolish to trust another one of us again, given that our careers are always characterised by weakness and irresponsibility. A moment's honesty could shipwreck the careers of the next five gay commissioners to come, before they've even applied for the job."

Jay's heart gave an uncomfortable thud.

"Fuck," he murmured, wishing he could offer some kind of comfort—change that, make it different somehow. He didn't like the thought of Alastair living beneath the tip of a slowly swinging sword. "Yeah, that's... I can see that. I wish I couldn't see it. But I can."

Alastair drew a breath. "Thus the state of the world."

Jay thought about it for a while, gazing up at the ceiling.

"You must end up burying a lot of regrets," he said at last. "Just pushing them out of sight, I mean. Not thinking about it."

"I try not to think about how much I don't think about." Alastair returned his cheek to Jay's shoulder. "Then, I'm sure everybody else is the same. My tenure as commissioner so far has been marked by stability. Steady reform. Nothing too dramatic has happened. If I'm lucky, that will continue."

Jay nodded dimly, stroking the back of his neck. "Why was it you became a police officer?" he asked. "If your mum wasn't keen, I mean. You must've had a good reason to do it anyway."

Alastair lifted his head a little. "You remembered," he said, surprised.

Jay smiled uncertainly. "Yeah," he said. "Why? Should I have tried to forget or something?"

"No, I'm... just rather touched, that's all." Alastair laid his head back down, taking a moment to get comfortable. "Is it tragic that I wanted to do some good with my life?"

"That's not tragic. That's called being a decent person."

"My mother considered herself to be from excellent stock. Her family had quite an old name, even if the pile of old money was starting to dwindle. My father came to the rescue with his brand new money, and lots of it. He was in banking, you see. I remember an evening when I was about thirteen, hovering at the edge of one of their cocktail parties..."

Alastair shook his head a little, his eyes tightening at the edges.

"I found myself watching them with their friends," he said. "For the first time, I saw my parents as if they weren't my parents. I saw them simply as two adults in the company of other adults. I stood listening to them compete with their guests over houses, holidays and cars, and I started to realise that none of the people in that room actually cherished the things they had. It was point-scoring, nothing more. It was a game, all of it, and their so-called friends were actually just fellow competitors. There was no meaning in that room. Nothing real. Then my mother started to explain to them all how well I was doing at school, and I... I suppose I made a realisation that I didn't like. About what I was to my parents. And I suddenly couldn't bear the thought of turning out like them."

Jay made no sound, stroking Alastair's hair without really feeling it. He remembered being thirteen, too. He remembered looking up at his enormous tattooed uncles, their fists as broad as bricks, hoping to God that he *did* turn out like them. It seemed like the only way he would ever survive.

"Were you expected to?" he asked. "Turn out like your parents, I mean. Follow in your dad's footsteps."

"Yes. It was never discussed, of course. Never decided. I just grew up hearing things I would need to know when I joined the bank." Stirring, Alastair laid a quiet kiss on Jay's chest. "My mother expressed once or twice that I killed my father," he said.

Jay's eyebrows shot up on his forehead. "Seriously?"

"Mm. She stopped the day I pointed out that the cigars, the port, and the multiple affairs had probably played some part as well."

"Jesus, I'm sorry. That must've been really shit to hear."

"There's no need to be sorry," Alastair said, half-smiling. "We all arrive in adulthood bruised." He leant a little closer, nudging the side of his nose against Jay's. "From what you've told me, your experiences were worse."

Jay's pulse hitched, wobbling as he tried to find the right facial expression to wear here. This familiar wave of anxiety was never just unnerving. It always sickened him a little too, spreading cold across his skin after the first surge of heat. Its whispering little voice burrowed into his ear, reminding him of the hundred thousand things he couldn't share, the stains he hoped that nobody could see.

"Still," he said, uneasily. "It's crap you went through that, I mean. It's wrong that you weren't treated right. I'm sorry you didn't get what you needed."

"I could say the same to you," Alastair murmured. His expression softened; he held Jay's gaze across the tiny space between them. "It's quite alright, Jay. Don't grieve for me. I'm happy with the choices that I made."

Jay's heart refused to settle as they kissed, continuing to thump out its unrest. He couldn't really stop picturing it—a young Alastair looking around at the adults he knew, searching for some glimpse of his own reflection, finding nothing.

Alastair's hands brushed up his chest, fingers fanning at his shoulders. He gave a softened hum against Jay's mouth.

"What are you thinking?" he asked between kisses. "You're quiet, sweet."

Jay took a breath. Something about the endearment, the first that Alastair had ever picked for him, brought him to a decision. He couldn't share the honest facts; he could maybe share the feelings, though. It seemed like it was safe to do that.

It had been a long time since he'd felt safe.

"Do you ever kinda hate them a little?" he asked.

Alastair reached up to stroke his cheek. "Who?"

"People with families," Jay said. "Happy families, I mean. People who just... you know, had it normal. Christmases and birthdays. Doing stuff at the weekend. Ringing each other up just to talk."

Alastair was quiet for a moment. He read Jay's face, looking into his eyes, and for a moment Jay worried that he'd said too much, cast just a little too much light into the darkness.

Then Alastair's gaze grew gentle, and Jay realised it hadn't been searching him. Alastair had been trying to decide what to show.

"We can't have everything in life," he said.

No, Jay thought, his heart falling still. *No, I guess we can't.*

Alastair shifted, pressing another kiss to his lips. "I think I'm rather ready for a shower," he said. "Aren't you?"

Jay couldn't remember the last time he'd been given such a helpful emergency exit to a conversation. It was kind, and it made him smile in spite of his sadness, strangely moved by Alastair's grace. He pushed the thoughts out of his head, caught hold of Alastair's lips and kissed him properly.

"Problem is," he said as they parted, "if we make ourselves nice and clean, I'll only get you sticky again before long."

Alastair's breath stalled. "Will you now?" he murmured. "Seems like it would be a waste of our time, then."

"Mm. Time we could spend doing other things."

"Oh?"

Jay hummed, sliding a hand down Alastair's body. "Better things."

"Such as?" Alastair asked. As Jay cupped him by the arse, he let out a small gasp which edged into a groan. "You are aware that some of us suffer the curse of a refractory period, aren't you?"

Jay shrugged.

"So you can't come for a little while," he said. "Doesn't mean you can't still enjoy yourself." He licked Alastair's lips. "Doesn't mean we can't still have fun."

Shortly after one o'clock, the Cliveden guest services team received a room service request from the Orkney Suite.

A short but fierce argument broke out at once. Discussion as to who should go went on for several minutes, ended at last by the reluctant acknowledgement that it *was* Katie's birthday tomorrow, and she'd been missed off the rota on the night that Meghan Markle was here.

She could have the honour.

"Really? With the commissioner in the Orkney Suite?"

"Yep. He arrived late last night, and apparently he's *gorgeous.* Green eyes and great big shoulders. He's from somewhere up north. Ellie checked him in."

"Who took him his breakfast?"

"Matthew did. He's not been the same since. He says there were tattoos. Like, *everywhere."*

"God."

"Says the guy was still in bed, not wearing a stitch, and the sheets were a disaster. Clothes all over the floor. They clearly didn't sleep for long."

"I thought Alastair Harding was meant to be stuck-up?"

"He is now," someone said.

Tittering broke out across the kitchen.

With a smirk, Katie's team leader handed her the silver tray. She'd chosen an especially fancy platter, to complement the items requested.

"There you go," she said. "Then get back here with details, young lady. Happy birthday."

Head high, Katie carried the tray from the kitchens. She took the lift in the east wing to the first floor, and carefully tidied away her smile as she approached the door of the Orkney Suite.

With a well-trained expression of neutrality, she knocked.

"Guest services," she called.

It was usually safe to enter a room with food. Most guests, having ordered, would be waiting for it eagerly, and didn't mind if you brought it right in.

The significant delay that followed her knock suggested she'd been wise to stay out here.

The door opened at last, and there he was, the mythical *him* hidden away in the commissioner's suite. Ellie and Matthew had been right. The man was a bona fide feast, broad-chested and cheeky with his hair all soft and scruffy. He'd covered up with one of the hotel's silk robes, but it did nothing to hide the tattoos. The black lines shone beneath his subtle shimmer of sweat. Behind him the room was cloaked in darkness, the sunlight muffled by tightly-drawn curtains.

Seeing Katie and her tray, the commissioner's guest broke into a guilty grin.

"Sorted," he said. He took the jar of honey and the wooden dipper. "Thanks. You're a star."

It was the policy of guest services, on completion of a request, to ask if a guest required anything else they could help with. Katie simply smiled. She had a feeling they were all set.

"You're welcome, sir," she said, folding the tray beneath her arm. She bowed. "Good afternoon."

As Katie re-entered the kitchens, flapping, the platter was whisked at once from her grasp. She was placed into a nearby chair, made comfortable, and all interested parties gathered round.

Her team leader guided a large cup of tea into her hands, smiling.

"Leave nothing out," she said.

Chapter 8

Jay had never seen the appeal of window seats before. He'd never cared much for windows in general, having lived his whole life in places he was happy to shut out. The only view he could enjoy from his flat was the backyard of the Indian restaurant downstairs, where gangs of one-legged pigeons waged constant war on the bin bags, tugging them open in the hunt for discarded naan bread. It wasn't exactly a sight to sit back and behold.

But it turned out that a pretty sunset, a pack of cigarettes, and good company made for a much better experience.

"What was your crap week about?" he asked, tipping back his head against Alastair's shoulder.

Alastair expelled a plume of smoke into the air, perfectly formed.

"Morons," he replied. He returned the cigarette to Jay, their fingers tangling fondly as they passed it. "People who expect miracles, refuse to hear sense, then get upset when everything I said would happen happens."

Jay smiled, taking a drag on the cigarette. He couldn't figure out why he liked the matching robes so much. It felt like he was wrapped up in Alastair's skin somehow, perfectly at peace, the scent of cigarette smoke underlaid by the shared fragrance of Alastair's shower gel. Even after an hour here, they were still too sated to move, a comfortable slump of limbs and skin and navy silk. The ache that had arisen in Jay's lower back was soothed by the warmth of Alastair's body pressed against it. Only tattoo pain ever felt more satisfying than a sex injury.

"Any morons I'd recognise from the telly?" Jay asked, smoke curling from the corners of his mouth.

Alastair chuckled. "If there were, it'd be reckless of me to identify them to you. Taking into account where we are."

"Cliveden?"

"Mm. It has a long and illustrious history of indiscretion... one to which I shan't be contributing."

Jay grinned, stretching. "Worried I'm some cheeky foreign spy?" he said, offering back the cigarette. It was taken out of sight by slender fingers. "Do they often pretend to be Mancs?"

"Not usually. Though my discretion's more for your sake than mine."

"Yeah?"

"The less you know about my work, the safer you'll be." Alastair kissed Jay's shoulder. "The things I deal with can be sensitive. I wouldn't want anything to affect you."

"You're sweet," Jay murmured, touched by the protectiveness. For a moment, he wished he could tell Alastair the truth of it all, show him what exactly had shaped Jay into the man he was. It was so rare to have somebody care about his safety. He didn't quite know how best to seem grateful; in lieu of sentiment, humour rose up. "Sounds like you're a dangerous bloke to go to bed with."

Alastair huffed, amused. He reached up to the narrow gap in the window beside them, flicking their ash out into the breeze.

"No more than any other," he said. He took one more drag, then returned the cigarette to Jay. "In all seriousness, there's no reason for you to worry. People are rarely stupid enough to target senior police officials or their associates. You're not in any danger."

Associate. Jay moved on before he could think about it, not wanting to give it time to settle. It didn't mean anything. A word was just a word.

"Don't worry, sunshine," he said. "I don't frighten easy." He closed his eyes, smiling as Alastair stroked his hair back from his forehead. "I probably wouldn't understand what it is you do all day, even if you told me."

"You do yourself a disservice," Alastair said. "I've seen through the self-deprecating northerner act, I'm afraid. Your company's very well run, you have an excellent memory, and it takes considerable intelligence to be charming."

Jay emptied out his smoke, trying not to laugh. "Don't tell anyone, will you? I've got a reputation to maintain."

Alastair kissed his head again. "Fret not," he said. "Your secret's safe with me." He declined the offered cigarette with a hum. "What caused your terrible week?"

Ah. Jay made his drag a long one, buying himself time to think. A few short coughs stretched it out. He didn't want to lie, but he couldn't exactly tell the truth.

"Kind of a long story," he said at last. "I, erm... I don't know if I should bore you with it."

"Go on," Alastair said, his voice soft. "I don't mind."

Jay took another short drag. He'd never approached this subject with anyone—not once, not even skirted it, not even been tempted to hint. Kim had made sure he was clear on the risks of doing so. Even if he trusted his friends with the truth, they might decide to trust *their* friends. Once it left his mouth, it was free and it could go anywhere it wanted.

But then, Jay supposed he wasn't talking to just anybody right now. Alastair was high-ranking police; confidentiality chains were in place. He'd lose his job if he passed this information on, and from what Jay knew of Alastair, he'd rather die than have that happen.

Realising the pause was getting long, Jay braced himself and pulled the words up into his mouth. It took a second to decide how to frame this, which viewing angle would show enough but not too much.

"Kinda made an enemy," he said. "Ten years ago. Back in

Manchester. He, erm... he was a pretty hard bloke. Police had been after him for years. He headed one of the big gangs where I grew up. Lots of violence."

He rubbed the length of the cigarette, already a little nauseous with how much he hadn't said.

"I told the police about a couple of things I'd seen," he went on. "Felt like the right thing to do. He got sent down in the end, but not for long. Hired some killer lawyer. Evidence went missing. I moved down here. Better safe than sorry. They released him on parole not long ago."

Alastair's fingertips brushed along Jay's hairline, barely there. "Who is this man?"

Jay's throat muscles pulled, making room for the name. He'd not said it aloud in years.

"He's... called Ian Straker." Jay returned the cigarette to his mouth, keeping it there for a moment. "It got in all the papers."

"I think I know the name," Alastair murmured. "I'm not overly familiar with the case, but... and you said he's been given parole?"

Jay's hand threatened to shake. "Fucking joke, really," he said. He dragged on the cigarette, closing his eyes. *Keep this clean. Keep this easy.* "Must have behaved himself inside."

Alastair held something back for a moment, still quietly stroking Jay's forehead. "You're concerned there'll be some sort of retribution?"

"Someone took a hammer to the front doors of our office. Thursday night. Reckon it's... you know, just mindless vandalism. Happens. London. I don't want to think about it too hard, that's all."

Alastair nodded gently. "If you're worried," he said, "there's an organisation called the UK Protected Persons Service. It provides support to people judged to be at risk from this sort of harm."

Oh, Jesus. Jay forced himself not to react, trying to stop his hand from tightening around the cigarette. *If you knew. What would you even say? Would you throw my fucking shoes down the hallway after me?*

He put the cigarette back in his mouth.

"Don't they just move you somewhere new?" he asked. He'd lived beneath that shadow for ten years now, built his life on the slope of that volcano. It was his greatest fear. He produced the words like they meant nothing to him.

"In serious cases," Alastair said, "and when necessary, yes. But they're—"

"I can't do that," Jay said. He blew smoke towards his lap, his insides now writhing like snakes. This was no longer a case of angling the truth, framing it to show the relevant parts. This was actual lying, and he didn't want to lie—not here, not now, not to this man. "Too many people relying on me," he explained vaguely. "I can't run away. I'm... that's not an option."

Alastair took this onboard.

"There'll be other security precautions you can take," he said. "Less drastic steps." He paused, sweeping his fingers over Jay's forehead again, stroking them back into his hair. "Jay?"

Oh, shit. Please. Please don't ask me. "Y-yeah?"

Alastair's free arm gathered close around his chest, holding him. "I don't want to overstep," he said. "But... well, my help would be available if you'd want it."

Jay didn't move, his heart pounding in the silence. *Could you actually keep me safe?* He didn't want to ask. It felt like protection that he didn't deserve. If he took up the offer, it would all have to come out—and that would change things.

"That's... thanks," he said. "You're sweet. I probably just need to learn to relax, to be honest." Recalling the cigarette in his hand, he took a lengthy drag. He closed his eyes to let it do some good. "Not had any other signs he's tracked me down," he said.

"That's positive."

"Don't really know why I'm... hey, I'm sorry. To vent. Seriously, it's... I'm sorry to spew this all over you. I'm just mithering."

"Not at all," Alastair said. "I appreciate now why you're not sleeping."

"Sleep fine when I'm with you." Jay felt his heart kick against his ribs, wishing he hadn't said that so freely. It sounded like too much. He tried to cover it, suspecting he was only making this worse. "Being by myself lets the thoughts in. It's... kind of exhausting, to be honest."

"Mm." Alastair took the cigarette gently from Jay's hand. "I'm sorry you're dealing with this," he said, tapping its ash against the window.

Jay's pulse slugged. *Jesus,* he thought. *I'm such a tosser. Letting you worry about me.*

Fuck me up, if you knew.

"Shit happens," he said, and told himself that was the end of the conversation. He watched a bird crest over the distant river. "Other people have it worse, anyway. Should just pull myself together."

"On the contrary," Alastair said, "I think most would consider your situation to justify a great deal of background anxiety. I certainly do."

Jay huffed.

"You've got proper stress," he said. He turned his head a little, trying to nuzzle Alastair's jaw, but couldn't quite reach him at this angle. "What you do, I mean. Proper power. I'm just..."

"Stop, please," Alastair said, his voice soft. Every cell in Jay's body obeyed, falling still to listen. "In this arrangement, your needs matter as much as mine. That's what I understood, at least. If you're under stress, regardless of the cause, I'd want to know. You don't need to present some false front of stoicism to me, Jay. I'd... hoped we're free of that."

God.

Jay closed his eyes, resting his cheek against Alastair's shoulder. "Alright," he said, taking in a breath. "I'm sorry. I don't get to talk about it much, that's all. I think it's building up a bit."

Alastair quietly passed the cigarette.

"I'm happy to listen," he said, kissing the side of Jay's head. "Sincerely. If there's anything I can do to help you sleep, please tell me."

It was hard to push away the glow of comfort that it caused.

"You're sweet," Jay said again. He smoked for a few moments as they looked out towards the river together, watching the colours deepen in the sky. Darkness wouldn't be far away. "What time is it?"

Alastair stirred, reaching into the pocket of his dressing gown. He checked his phone and sighed.

"Time I should consider getting ready," he said. "Duty calls."

Time I'll have to leave. Jay pressed his cheek against Alastair's shoulder, listening to his heartbeat for a moment. *Damn. Just when we were getting somewhere.*

Alastair gave no sign of moving him.

"Are you back in your tux?" Jay asked, trying to dispel the quiet.

"Mm. Formal dinner."

"Going on late?"

"Fairly late." Alastair drew a long breath, resting his chin on the top of Jay's head. "These weekends always tire me," he said. "I hate them, to be frank. Turning down the invitation isn't an option, but I usually reach Sunday evening without having had a single meaningful conversation in two days. It's a tiresome waste of time."

"You're here tomorrow too, are you? More schmoozing?"

"There's lunch," Alastair said dimly, "then everyone will depart. Feel free to finish the cigarette."

"You sure?"

"Mm."

Jay used the time it took to gather his courage. He leant up and flicked the stub through the open window, telling himself that not asking guaranteed a no. One night here had done him more good than he could have ever dreamed. Two nights felt like it might just change his life.

He shifted in Alastair's arms, turning just enough to reach up and kiss his cheek.

"Hey," he said, as Alastair's arms gathered around his middle. He nuzzled his nose against Alastair's jaw. "Tell me if you want some space. I don't want to outstay my welcome. But... well, if—"

"Stay," Alastair said. He hesitated, placing his hand at the small of Jay's back. "Spend another night here. With me."

Thank fuck.

"You sure?" Jay said. His heart seemed to be beating twice as hard as it should; it felt oddly like a stay of execution. "Promise me I'm not driving you mad."

Alastair huffed. He drew back a little, just enough to study Jay. His expression was unreadable, his eyes more grey than blue in this light. The sunset's orange glow had streaked his hair with strands of fire, so much brighter and thicker without product keeping it flat. He wrapped his fingers around Jay's cheek.

"How would you possibly be irritating me?" he asked, leaning in.

As their lips met, Jay's eyes fell shut on their own. He returned the kiss, unable to hold in a deep shiver of relief. Alastair's kisses felt somehow more precious than his orgasms. Each one seemed to promise something, offer something. Even when the fires of sex were burning low, Alastair wanted to lie close together in the ashes, to talk and kiss and share.

It caused a funny tightness in Jay's throat.

"I know you're important," he said. "I know you're busy." The closeness of their faces turned his voice into a whisper. He let his eyes stay shut, hoping this wasn't too much. "I don't want to join the queue of tedious people you've got to put up with."

Alastair's thumb passed with care beneath Jay's lower lip, tracing its shape.

"You're nothing of the sort," he murmured. "You've been a very pleasant addition to the weekend. By far the best part. I'd love for you to stay another night."

God.

God, this is getting...

Jay kissed him again, buying a few moments to try and calm himself. Alastair's fingers slid up into his hair, stroking it and scrunching it onto end. Little tingles of sensation poured in waves across Jay's scalp, lifting the hair on his neck onto end.

Of course it's getting comfy, he told himself. *Spent a night and a day fucking like animals. How else am I going to be feeling?*

And why wouldn't he want me to stay? Who'd turn down sex like this?

Alastair's hands trailed their way down Jay's back, following the lines of his body through the dressing robe—enjoying him, flexing just gently above his hips. Alastair tended to touch there when Jay was riding him. Jay liked to be held there, guided and shown. *"Please me,"* the grip seemed to say. *"Give to me."*

As their lips came apart, their foreheads stayed together. They shared each other's breath for a moment, and Jay became aware of how comfortable it was to sit like this, not even needing to speak.

His pulse hadn't slowed down at all.

"I don't want to leave you for the evening," Alastair said. He hesitated, nudging Jay's nose. "I feel guilty, keeping you in here without company."

"It's fine. Promise. I'll catch up on sleep." Jay stole a tiny kiss, his eyes still closed. "Erm... if I'm honest, my back hurts a bit. Not as young as I was. Reckon the staff would fetch me up some painkillers?"

Alastair smiled, resting his palm at the base of Jay's tailbone. "I'll ask," he said. A thought seemed to cross his mind. "A massage might be more effective than painkillers."

Jay nearly laughed.

"I'll get one booked when I'm back in London," he said. "Think I'm due a pedicure, too. Thanks for the reminder."

Alastair smirked. The glitter of his eyes evoked a pedigree cat with a feather stick, never too posh to want to play.

"There's a spa on site," he said patiently. Jay's eyebrow quirked. "If you're planning to rest while I'm busy, you might as well rest in professional hands."

"Really?" Jay had never had a massage. He'd grown up in the kind of neighbourhood where massage parlours were blatant fronts for brothels. Most of the ones in London seemed to ply a similar trade. "I mean... are you sure?"

"Mm. It's included in the weekend. And I shan't be making use of it."

Wow. Humour bubbled through Jay's chest. He couldn't keep it in.

"Sending me off to be pampered," he said, grinning. Alastair's mouth curled in response, delighted by the teasing. His eyes flicked down to watch Jay laugh. "Spoiled while you're at dinner. People'll talk, commissioner."

"Unless you're announcing yourself to all and sundry as my guest, you shouldn't attract any attention. And I wouldn't want you to be bored." Alastair smiled, stroking his hands up Jay's sides. "I'll arrange something for you," he said. "Leave it with me."

Is this normal? Jay thought dizzily. *Do all rich people do this for their—?*

His heart heaved. He leant forwards, catching Alastair's lips.

Fuck, I don't care.

Katie rather liked evening functions. They were good money and easy to work, especially after the meal was over. Carrying a tray of champagne around a reception room became oddly relaxing after a while. There were certainly worse ways to earn a living while a student, and the steady trickle of celebrity anecdotes to share with friends made a nice little bonus.

No one especially famous was here this weekend. A few politicians were skulking about, and plenty of people with titles, but nobody worth texting her mum.

The only person who meant much to her tonight was Alastair Harding.

He was doing an admirable job of pretending that he'd not spent the day beneath his insanely attractive boyfriend. Katie supposed a police official of his rank must spend a lot of time with politicians. He'd definitely learned how to lie like one. During the course of the evening, he hadn't seemed particularly absorbed in any of his conversations. People were approaching *him,* never the other way around, and he had a glass of champagne in his hand because it was mandatory, not because he wanted to drink it. He'd kept the same one going all night. While polite to everyone who approached him, he seemed to forget their existence as soon as they walked away. He kept subtly checking his watch.

Wishing the time would go faster, Katie thought. Then, why wouldn't he? She'd wish the time away as well. At least fifteen people had asked her for the story today. She wasn't tired of telling it yet. Whenever she passed Sir Alastair with her champagne tray, she had to fight not to picture it in her mind.

She almost wondered how he'd managed that. He didn't seem

particularly warm or fun-loving, while his boyfriend was a great deal of both.

Opposites attract?

Maybe he softened up when they were alone. Maybe his boyfriend liked being the one person in this world who meant something to him.

It was cute as hell, whatever it was.

Not long after nine o'clock, as a guest picked up the last two glasses of champagne from Katie's tray, she found herself glad of a reason to walk to the kitchens. This party would likely go on until midnight, and it would be nice to check her texts.

She was almost out of the room when she caught the flash of a beckoning hand. She responded through instinct and stepped towards it, even before she recognised Sir Alastair.

"Can I ask you to deliver a message for me?" he said, removing a business card and a silver pen from inside his jacket.

Interesting.

"Yes, sir," Katie said. "Of course."

The card was almost entirely white: on one side his name and title printed in pale grey, *Sir Alastair Harding QPM, Commissioner of Police of the Metropolis;* on the other side, a telephone number and e-mail address. He jotted quickly around his contact details, his eyes low, then handed the card to Katie between his fingertips with the message facing downwards.

"To the spa," he said, "to my... to Jay Fieldhouse. He's having a treatment there. If finished, he'll have returned to the Orkney Suite."

Oh, wow. 'Jay'.

"Of course, sir." Katie placed the card on her tray face down—a discreet promise it would remain so until it reached its recipient—then bowed and left the function suite.

The fastest route to the spa was out of the main entrance, across the courtyard and into the other wing. The cover of the starlit night gave Katie the opportunity to slyly flip the card, squinting down at the cramped handwriting.

Hoping to excuse myself from the endless tedium of
small talk by ten.
Are you being looked after? x

Katie slipped through the door to the spa, biting her lip.

After a moment's delay, a receptionist appeared from the back room. Recognising Katie, her manner relaxed at once.

"Are you working that function?" she asked, leaning against the desk with a grin. "You picked the wrong shift, girl. You wouldn't *believe* the guy we've got in here tonight."

Katie beamed. "I would," she said. "I've got a message from his boyfriend. Where is he?"

Treatment room one was their premium room, usually reserved for brides on the night before their wedding. As Katie slipped in through the door, taking care not to make undue noise, Simon glanced up from his work. He was entirely heterosexual, professional beyond reproach, and clearly had zero awareness of the blessing the universe had given him. He gave Katie an inquiring look, his hands unfaltering in their slow motions along his client's oiled, tattooed back.

"I have a message for Mr Fieldhouse," Katie explained, holding up the tray.

Simon nodded, making no comment, and carried on.

Dazed, Jay Fieldhouse raised his head from the massage bed. His green eyes had gone foggy under Simon's expert care. As they found Katie, recognition flickered across his face and he smiled.

"H'lo," he said to her. "You fetched our room service."

"Good evening, sir. I have a message for you." Katie came over, holding out the tray.

Puzzled, he picked up the card. It seemed to take him a moment to understand what he was seeing. When he did, he grinned and stroked his thumb across the words, as if he couldn't help himself but touch them. Even Sir Alastair's handwriting was precious to him.

Katie couldn't remember ever seeing someone more in love.

"Don't suppose you'd take a reply back for me, would you?" he asked, glancing up.

Without the slightest skip in his focus, Simon slipped a pen from his top pocket and handed it to Katie. She reached inside her jacket for the notepad she used when serving tables, tore a piece of paper from it, then placed it on the tray.

She held the tray steady for Mr Fieldhouse to write, discreetly reading his message upside down.

Like a king. Can't believe this place. Had a swim and
sauna. Now massage. Think my bones have
melted. Should be finished at 10.
Don't expect anything athletic off me later xxx

"Thanks, flower," he said, flipping the card with a wink.

Katie nodded. As she backed out of the room, she watched him lay his handsome head back down, and Simon returned to kneading his lower back.

Jay groaned, shifting.

The door swung neatly shut.

Back in the function suite, Sir Alastair was in reluctant conversation with an MP that Katie half-recognised from the papers. She stayed discreetly nearby, collecting empty glasses while she waited, listening to the commissioner grow increasingly short in his responses. The MP grew increasingly oblivious.

After almost fifteen minutes, Sir Alastair's continued glances in Katie's direction gave her courage.

She approached the two of them with caution.

"Forgive me, Sir Alastair," she murmured. "I have an urgent message for you from reception."

"Ah, yes. Thank you. Do excuse me," Alastair added to the MP, as he indicated for Katie to come with him, "I've been waiting for this. Good evening."

Katie followed him to a corner of the room, glass-faced.

Safely out of earshot, Sir Alastair kept his voice low.

"Thank you." He took the piece of paper from Katie, turning it coolly between his fingers. He read it with an impressive lack of reaction, then retrieved his pen from inside his jacket. "You don't mind?"

"No, sir. Not at all."

Katie kept her eyes to herself as he wrote.

Crossing the car park once more, she took a peek.

Slow and idle will more than suffice.
I'll come to you at ten. x

At last, Alastair thought, opening the glass doors of the Cliveden spa. A clean and subtle perfume whispered beneath his nose, welcoming him inside. Collecting Jay in person was something of a risk, but the weekend's other guests were all very occupied at the party. It had been a long evening with a maddening lack of Jay, and a maddening excess of other people. Alastair was very glad to reach its end.

As he crossed the gleaming white reception area and approached the desk, a young lady appeared from a backroom. She smiled as brightly as if it were mid-morning, not late into the evening.

"Good evening, sir," she said. "Can I help?"

Alastair's brain made a snap decision on how to phrase this.

"My partner is here having a massage," he said. The young woman could hardly be expected to hear *my sexual companion.* "I wondered if he'd finished."

"I think they're nearly done," she said, and indicated the double doors behind her desk. "Do go through, sir. It's the room at the end."

Only as Alastair approached the treatment room did it occur to him he hadn't specified his name, or who he was. He hoped this meant that Jay was the only client of the spa this evening. Otherwise, he might be about to invite himself into someone else's wife's massage.

Before he reached the door, it opened and another member of staff emerged, a gentleman cleaning oil from his hands and forearms with a towel. He gave Alastair a faint, questioning smile—a polite and non-verbal, *can I help?*

"Jay Fieldhouse?" Alastair checked, and received a nod.

"Just grounding," the masseuse said. "Go on in." He held the door for Alastair, admitting him to a candle-lit space where music lulled from unseen speakers. The distinctive aroma of clary sage drifted on the air.

Jay was resting beneath a towel on the massage bed, looking for all the world as if he were asleep.

Alastair stepped inside, closing the door behind him. "Jay?"

A slight stir indicated he'd been heard. "Al'sser?"

Trying not to smile, Alastair approached the table. He moved into Jay's line of sight, and found a pair of dazed green eyes gazing up at him, glittering with warmth. Jay looked as relaxed as if he could be decanted into a travel mug.

"I understand you're grounding," Alastair said, amused.

"Tryin'. Bit floaty." Jay smiled, admiring him in his dinner jacket. "How's s'function?"

The sleepy slur was rather affecting.

"Tiresome," Alastair admitted. He reached out to touch Jay's hair, combing the dark strands gently with his fingertips. Jay's eyes closed in pleasure. "Heavens... you *are* floaty, aren't you? I suspect even slow and idle might have been an ambitious request."

"Nah. S'fine, s'nshine. Juss gimme a minute."

"Have you eaten?"

"Mm." Jay tilted his head to kiss Alastair's fingers. Alastair fanned them out of reach, playful, gliding across Jay's cheek instead. Jay made a little sound of protest. "Cruel," he mumbled. "Teasin' me."

Alastair passed his thumb across Jay's lips. *You are wonderful,* he thought. *Quite, quite wonderful.* Jay licked him gently, humming. Alastair watched, lost in the sight and strangely moved by it: Jay lapping him in affectionate submission, nuzzling his hand as if no other joy existed. Curious, Alastair curled his fingers around Jay's jaw. He eased his thumb inside Jay's mouth; Jay shivered and pliantly lifted his head.

"Fuck my mouth," he whispered, his voice thick. "When r'upstairs. Please."

Alastair drew a soundless breath. He took a moment to cool the surge of heat in his stomach, still cradling Jay's head in one hand.

"That necessitates you getting up the stairs," he said in a murmur. "You currently seem a little incapable."

"S'your fault," Jay protested, his eyes fogged and soft. He kissed Alastair's palm. "Posh massage. Too relaxin'."

If you drop one more 'g', you delectable man, I shan't be held accountable for my actions.

"I hope your back feels better," Alastair said.

Jay's eyes sparkled. "Sweet about me," he said. He stretched a little, inhaling. "S'fine. Feels really good."

"I'm glad." As the masseuse re-entered the room, carrying Jay's clothes, Alastair discreetly let go of his jaw. "You'll sleep well for it, I'm sure."

It felt strange to be dressed. As they made their way across the lobby together, Jay hoped he wouldn't stay dressed for long. His clothing seemed weirdly heavy against his skin. Being this relaxed out in public was bemusing, the air still fragrant and hazy all around him.

Alastair stayed close by his side, scanning their surroundings as he guided Jay discreetly to the lift. The doors slid shut with a ping, leaving the two of them alone again, and Alastair released a small breath.

Slyly, Jay shuffled a little closer.

Alastair wrapped an arm around his waist, smiling, and let him lean. The lift rumbled around them in the quiet.

"Thank you," Jay murmured. "For spoiling me. I feel amazing."

Alastair tilted his head, placing a single kiss on Jay's temple. "You're very welcome."

"Do you have to go for schmoozy breakfast in the morning?"

"No, thank God. Only schmoozy luncheon."

Jay's soul seemed to glow. "Breakfast with me, then. In bed."

"Beast." Alastair lowered his head, nipping at the tip of Jay's ear. The lift bumped to a stop. "I'm sure I can handle such a—"

The doors eased apart. A couple appeared on the other side, waiting for the lift: a balding gentleman in a violet silk shirt, with a glamorous young lady at his side. She was rather taller than him, dressed in very pretty sequinned gold, and giggling fit to burst as he pawed at her.

As they came into view, Alastair stiffened as if he'd been plugged into the mains. He let Jay go at once, straightening up in alarm.

"Clarence," he said.

The balding gentleman froze. He released his hold on his young lady, hitching a panicked smile into place.

"Alastair," he said. The two shot out their hands and shook across the threshold. Jay glanced with curiosity at the blushing young lady, who bit down into her lip and met nobody's gaze. "H-how are you, old boy?" Clarence asked.

"Very well," Alastair said. "Thank you."

Clarence stole a glance towards Jay, swallowing. "I didn't realise you're... familiar with Cliveden," he said.

Jay had heard a few euphemisms in his time, but never that one.

"I'm here at Hortensia Campbell's invite," Alastair said. He allowed something to hang in the air for a second, his stare a little fixed. "Rather kind of her."

Clarence visibly paled. "That's... *this* weekend, is it? Here?"

"Mm." Alastair drew a breath. "Haven't responded to you about the contract renewal in November, have I? I must get round to that."

A negotiation of some kind seemed to be unfolding. Clarence held Alastair's gaze for a second or two, realisation dawning. He then gave a quick nod.

"Yes," he said. "Well, that would be very good of you, old boy. No hurry." He hesitated, glancing at his blushing companion. "We, ah... we should probably be going."

"Mm. Yes, as should we." Alastair placed a hand on Jay's back, nudging him gently but firmly forwards. "Good evening."

Jay waited to speak until the lift doors had closed, carrying the two of them away.

"Was that a bit awkward?" he said, as he and Alastair headed down the corridor.

"A little," Alastair admitted. "That was Clarence Talbot. That was not Clarence Talbot's wife."

Yikes. "Have I just gotten you in trouble?"

Alastair put his arm around Jay's waist again, pulling him close. "No," he murmured. "No, you shouldn't concern yourself. I doubt that he'll say anything. Not if he has any sense."

They reached the door of their suite. Hoping to lift the dampened mood, Jay said, "If he brings it up, tell him that we're cousins."

Alastair shot him an amused glance, fitting the key in the lock. "Nuzzling in a hotel lift is acceptable for cousins?"

"We're a close family," Jay said. "And at least I wasn't wearing gold sequins."

Chuckling, Alastair opened the door.

"Clarence has more to lose," he said. It seemed more a reassurance for Alastair himself than for Jay. "I'm sure my private life will hold little interest for anyone."

The room had been tidied in their absence, the bed re-made with fresh sheets. A small box of chocolates was sitting on the bedside, with a note offering the compliments of the Cliveden guest services team.

Jay picked the box up with a smile.

"This place really *is* swish," he said. "You don't get chocolates at Premier Inn."

Alastair undid his bowtie, surveying the box with amusement. "Very kind of them."

"We must be popular," Jay said as he loosened the ribbon. "Have you been leaving generous tips?"

"No more than my usual," Alastair said. He came over, slipped his arms around Jay's waist from behind, and rested his chin upon Jay's shoulder. "Perhaps guest services are attempting to sate your sweet tooth," he remarked, watching Jay open up the box, "lest you ruin another set of their sheets with honey."

Jay grinned.

"They'll have seen worse." He relaxed back into Alastair's embrace, retrieved the tiny menu from inside and scanned the selection on offer. "Ooh. White praline."

"Mm, that does sound nice."

Jay rolled the chocolate free from its mould. He held it up to his shoulder, prompting a soft snort.

"I do believe that's yours," Alastair said.

Jay grinned. "There's two of them, Al. Get it eaten."

Smirking, Alastair took a bite from the small chocolate heart. His low murmur of enjoyment raised an interested flutter in Jay's stomach.

"Mm. Yes, very nice. You should have the second one immediately."

Jesus, I love the way you put things.

"Come share the rest in bed," Jay said. He tipped his head, pressing his cheek to Alastair's. "Lay me out a trail."

"A trail to where, precisely?"

"From your throat to your cock, love. I'll find my own way from there."

Alastair's breath seemed to catch. "Jay," he said softly.

Jay put the box aside on the bedside table, then turned around in Alastair's arms.

"Still in the mood for slow and idle?" he said. He cupped Alastair's jaw, looking into his eyes. "I wonder how long I can make you wait to come. Bet you it's at least a couple of hours."

Alastair's throat muscles shifted beneath his fingertips. He glanced down at Jay's mouth, his pupils swollen.

"Jay," he said again, lost for words.

Jay pulled him forwards into a kiss.

Not long after midnight, guest services delivered fresh raspberries, whipped cream and a bottle of single malt whiskey to the Orkney Suite. A note returned with the tray, requesting the next morning's breakfast in bed—a *late* breakfast if possible, with coffee for two.

Chapter 9

THE KNOCK CAME NOT LONG BEFORE TEN. ALASTAIR BLINKED, resurfacing from the email half-typed on his screen. Without a sound he put his laptop aside, removed his reading glasses, and slipped out of bed, tying the sash of his dressing robe. The room was still in darkness as he moved towards the door, everything quiet.

Opening it, he discovered the young lady who'd delivered messages for him last night, bearing their breakfast on a large silver tray. Her shiny black hair was tied back into a ponytail this morning, her smile as bright as sunshine on the morning dew. The Cliveden staff were prompt and very pleasant as a rule, outfitted in neat navy waistcoats with name badges, but this young woman seemed to go above and beyond. *Katie Kelshaw,* her badge said. *Guest Services.*

"Good morning, sir," she chirped, holding out the tray. "I have your breakfast for you."

"Ah, yes... thank you," Alastair took the tray from her, wondering if the guest services team had recently been awarded a pay rise. It would explain the remarkable cheerfulness. "I don't suppose I could trouble you for fresh coffee in an hour, could I?"

"Of course," she said, and bobbed. "Enjoy your breakfast."

And off she went.

As Alastair carried the tray towards the bed, its sleeping occupant stirred beneath the sheets.

"Al?"

Something in Alastair's chest responded with a thump. No one had ever taken to shortening his name before. As a child, his mother had been fiercely displeased by any attempt to modify the name she'd picked out for him. She considered pet names in general to be over-familiar and unseemly—then, disapproval had been her standard reaction to most things.

She really would have despised Jay. Denounced him. Wept, wailed, and grieved to anyone who would listen that her son could have so little regard for the effort poured into his upbringing, throwing in his lot with some tattooed Mancunian oik who called him Al.

Setting the tray at the end of the bed, Alastair smoothed the sheets flat around it. He leant down, kissing the bare back of his tattooed Mancunian oik.

"Breakfast," he murmured. Jay's eyelids fluttered, his gaze foggy as he rubbed his sleepy face against the pillow. "Though it possibly counts as more of a brunch now."

Stretching, Jay inclined his head over his shoulder. "Why're you up?" he asked. "S'early."

"Answering some minor emails," Alastair said, fighting a smile. "It's rare for me to sleep late."

"Mhrm." Jay squinted up from the pillow at him, one sleepy green eye just visible. He was almost mouth-watering this morning. His gaze was bright and fond, his dark hair tousled into tufts. The sheets had contrived to drape across his lower back with the sort of masculine grace rarely seen outside classical sculpture. Alastair had the curious need to stroke that perfect shape, contemplate its curve and its texture not only with his eyes but with his hands. "Come lie down," Jay murmured, looking hopeful.

Alastair returned himself obediently to bed, careful not to upset the tray. Jay smiled, shuffled closer, then reached for the sash of Alastair's dressing gown.

"Don't need this," he rumbled, and pressed his wicked mouth to

Alastair's. As they kissed, he untied the fabric sash, easing it carefully apart with his hands. Alastair made no move to stop him. He wanted skin; he wanted closeness. He'd wanted them all morning, and it seemed they were the first things Jay wanted too.

Easing the robe back from Alastair's shoulders, Jay gave a hum of contentment, as if Alastair's body quite rightly belonged against his. Some higher order in the universe had now been restored. They nestled together, naked, sending waves of warmth and relief through Alastair's body. He let himself shiver; Jay hugged him tighter, a sleepy and almost possessive squeeze which Alastair liked far too much.

"Can you reach the tray?" Jay asked, kissing Alastair's shoulder.

Alastair shifted to pull it up the bed, close enough for them to reach. Jay selected a cinnamon pastry from the plate. He tore it carefully into pieces, taking his time, then gathered Alastair close against his chest.

As he fed it to Alastair by hand, he watched Alastair's face, stroking rather fondly beneath his lips—as if he just enjoyed the sight of Alastair eating.

Alastair took piece after piece from his fingers, half-aware of a riot now taking place inside his heart.

Is this normal in this kind of...?

He'd never known this kind of intimacy. Last night he'd fallen asleep in his afterglow, boneless with pleasure and cradled in Jay's arms, their skin still damp from their exertions. He'd woken up this morning still cuddled, glowing with the warmth of nearly ten hours' sleep.

Even lying in silence together felt like a shelter. Jay didn't say a word as he fed Alastair, simply watched him, admiring him, taking pleasure in his pleasure. Alastair had never shared something like this in his life.

He gazed up at Jay without speaking, lost.

If our affair came to light, he thought, watching Jay reach for another pastry, *it would be assumed that I own you in some way. That you amuse me like a pet. Not like this. That you comfort me, settle me. That you feed me things, just for the experience of watching me taste them. That when*

I kiss you, I feel as if absolutely all of my needs are taken care of, and nothing will worry me again.

Not, of course, that I need you.

Not that this is an affair.

They shared the whole of breakfast in comfortable quiet, leaning together to drink their coffee. Finished, Jay moved the tray gently to the floor. He eased himself back into Alastair's arms, nudged him over onto his back, and nuzzled into his throat as he shifted to lie on top.

"How long until your schmoozy lunch?" he murmured, parting Alastair's thighs with his hands.

Alastair's pulse hit the ceiling.

"An hour," he said. "A little less." He grasped Jay's shoulders, colour flooding his face already. *Oh, God. Please.* "I'll need to shower and get dressed, but..."

Jay's fingertips skimmed down between his thighs, slipping behind his sack. Alastair unleashed all his breath in a gasp, his lungs empty in an instant. He wrapped his thighs around Jay's waist, gripping onto his shoulders.

As Jay's fingers began to rub a lazy circle, Alastair's mouth fell open.

"Oh, God—" He felt like touch paper, suddenly struck with a match. Something in him ignited, burning all at once with the need to fuck, to be held open on his back and used in ways his horse-faced mother hadn't even known were possible. Jay wanted him; it was all he needed. "Please—please, I want—"

Jay shivered, shifting his weight to pin Alastair to the bed. "Mm?" He rasped his mouth up the side of Alastair's neck, then grazed over to his ear, his breath hot and his stubble tickling, the contact rough and gentle all at once.

Alastair panted with longing for more of it, prying his fingers into Jay's shoulders.

"Right now?" Jay's fingers pressed as if to push inside him, teasing.

Alastair arched, throwing his head back into the pillow. His voice tore its way from his throat. "Oh, *fuck*—right now—"

Jay reached out towards the bedside for a familiar tube, then popped open the cap with his thumb. "Get me ready for you, gorgeous."

Shaking, Alastair held out both hands. Jay dispensed the clear gel into his palms, too much of it, dripping down through Alastair's fingers onto his stomach, wet and messy. Alastair had never liked messy before. He liked it now. He liked the feel of Jay's thick cock between his palms, hardening as he rubbed and squeezed. He liked the grunt of satisfaction as Jay thrust between his fingers, the restless flashing of those perfect green eyes. He let Alastair slick him until the colour had risen in his face and their breath had grown ragged, the thought of more too much to resist.

Jay shifted, placed his hands under Alastair's thighs and pushed them apart and back. He pinned Alastair open with a hand beneath each knee, crowding him up against the pillows. Alastair swore and clenched his fists in the sheets, panting, panic and animal excitement pounding through his blood as the head of Jay's cock nuzzled into place, blunt and thick.

"Yeah?" Jay breathed against his lips, curled over Alastair. He kissed him with firm, hot strokes of his tongue, raking it between Alastair's lips, no space to do anything but gasp an answer into that devilish mouth: *yes. Yes. God, yes.* The heave of Jay breaching him wrenched a cry from Alastair's throat. He grappled for Jay's biceps and dug in his nails, hard enough to leave half-moon marks. As Jay pushed inside him, slow and firm and unfaltering, he panted and begged; all he could do was grip Jay harder. The stretch stole his breath, sharp, searing, and deliciously good. *Fuck me,* he heard himself pleading. *Make me ache. Make me feel it.*

Jay's first deep thrust sent lightning up his spine.

Alastair filled his lungs, held on tight, and let Jay wreck him.

He kept one hand scrunched deep within Jay's hair, dragging the other over the muscles in his back. The pace picked up. Alastair clawed into Jay's back for more, panting through his teeth and now unleashing an amount of noise which nearby rooms could surely hear. Jay drove into his prostate on every thrust, groaning hot words of praise and encouragement against his neck.

Let them hear, Alastair thought as he panted, wild. *Hear me need this. What you do to me.*

Climax came from nowhere. One moment, he was calling Jay's name and begging for harder; the next, he was writhing in silence with the sudden cascade of relief, arching up from the bed and dragging Jay inside him with his thighs. Alastair sobbed, realising in a rush that Jay's thrusts were suddenly short and slick and urgent, Jay moaning at volume into his neck, heat flooding his insides. They'd come together, finished this with as much of a feverish eruption as they'd started. Shuddering, they sank into a heap.

When Alastair's thoughts managed to reform, he found himself cradled in Jay's arms in the bath.

Damp, gentle fingers stroked through his hair.

"—this afternoon, maybe?" Jay said, placing a kiss against his temple. "If you feel like it."

Alastair shivered, weak. "S-sorry?"

"After your lunch," Jay murmured. "Might be nice. Masseuse was telling me there are different trails through the woods. Says they're gorgeous this time of year... might be fun, you know? Get some fresh air."

He smiled against Alastair's forehead, tightening his hug.

"Stop me savaging you for five minutes," he added.

"A walk?" The prospect felt like a window opening in Alastair's soul. He didn't know why he wanted it so much, but he did. "Yes... yes, I... I'd like that. The woods *are* beautiful."

"You walked in them before?"

"A few times." *Never with company,* Alastair thought. Never with someone at his side. "I'm in ordinary footwear. We might have to..."

"That's alright." Jay reached for a washcloth on the side, dipping it beneath the surface of the steaming hot water. "We can take an easier route. Just stroll."

As the cloth brushed down Alastair's back, his every worry in the world seemed to melt. He groaned a little, shuddering, and pressed his face against Jay's neck.

Jay kissed the side of his head.

"Are you sore?" he said, his voice soft. "Did I get a bit too rough?"

"No," Alastair said, shivering again. "No rougher than I wanted."

Jay took this in, passing the cloth very slowly between his shoulder blades. "You know you can tell me if I get too much?"

Please, Alastair thought. *Please be too much.*

"You're not," he said, closing his eyes. Jay touched a kiss to his temple. "I'm very happy, Jay. With how things are."

Jay's mouth curved. "Good," he said, reaching for the soap. "I'm happy, too."

As Jay washed him, cleaning the sweat from his body, it occurred to Alastair he felt more emotionally affected in this moment than if they'd made love slowly for hours. Rough sex with Jay left him feeling soft and tactile. He wanted to be held. He wanted to talk, to walk, to disappear together into the woods.

I rarely trust like this, he realised. *I'm rarely so... conscious of my skin. So aware of what I feel. So raw.*

The rest of the world never seemed to know how to take him. He spent his life among people who hovered, addressed him with their eyes low and laughed before he'd actually finished his jokes. They never shared a cigarette with him. They never called him Al.

It took a very special man to fuck him like he needed it.

"Can I help you get dressed?" Jay said, slowly pouring water through his hair.

Alastair shuddered, his eyes still closed.

"Yes," he said. "I'd like that."

Halfway through the buttons of Alastair's waistcoat, there came another knock upon their door. Alastair pulled his gaze with reluctance from Jay's smile, turning his head towards the sound.

"Come in," he called.

It opened. Their young lady appeared, bearing a coffee tray.

Alastair had entirely forgotten.

"Ah," he said. "Yes, thank you..." She bobbed and brought the tray towards the fireplace. "I might just have time for a cup," Alastair said, looking back into Jay's eyes. "Will you finish the rest?"

Jay nodded, slipping the final button shut. "Sure, sunshine. I'll find a use for it."

"Order some lunch, won't you?" Alastair murmured. "Don't go hungry."

Jay leant in, placing a kiss on Alastair's cheek. "I won't. South Terrace at two, did you say?"

"Mm. We should be released by then."

The young lady was pouring their coffee for them, her eyes averted. Alastair was almost sure he could see her smiling.

"What is it you're having for lunch?" Jay asked. "Pheasant sandwiches, is it?"

Alastair smiled helplessly. "Pheasant being the staple diet of the upper classes?"

"So I've heard." Jay retrieved Alastair's jacket from the back of a nearby chair, holding it open for him. "I bet you're not allowed to put crisps in a pheasant sandwich," he said, his eyes bright. He smoothed the fabric over Alastair's shoulders. "Probably doesn't fly at the country club."

Alastair lowered his voice, attempting to mask his delight. "Beast."

Grinning, Jay fixed his lapels. "Yep," he said, and kissed Alastair's nose.

The young lady from guest services was laying out their biscuits with great care, ensuring they were all equidistant from each other and pleasingly arranged.

"Do you know what you'd like for lunch?" Alastair asked Jay, prompting.

The young lady, deciding the biscuits were now fine, stood up and awaited instruction.

"Do you guys do sandwiches?" Jay asked her.

"We do, sir," she said. "Pheasant and otherwise."

Jay's grin lit his eyes. "How about ham and cheese?"

She nodded. "Of course. With crisps?"

"Salt and vinegar, thanks. Don't worry about installing them. I'll do that."

"Very good, sir. I won't be long." She headed for the door, prompt and efficient. As it swung shut behind her, Alastair caught the distinct first two steps of a skip, and then she vanished.

Jay's arms slid around his waist. "Tip that girl when we leave, will you? I like her."

"I'm very happy, Jay. With how things are."

Jay flicked the ash from his cigarette, scattering it into the breeze. He was leaning with his forearms on the balustrade of the South Terrace, admiring the view in the white and chilly sunshine. It was beautiful here—the kind of place where you could forget you had work the next day. It was a place where the soul might get comfortable.

And *comfortable,* it was getting.

He'd thought of little else but Alastair since they parted at the door of the suite. Two hours had since gone by, thought by thought and memory by memory—sleeping, curled up close all night; Alastair whimpering his name during sex; resting together in the bath, cradling Alastair's head against his shoulder, stroking his hair with wet fingers.

It was hard to move his mind onto anything else. With every night they spent together, he only wanted Alastair more.

Sir Alastair, Jay thought, dragging on his cigarette. *Commissioner of the Met. Mercedes S-Class, three piece suits.*

Sometimes whimpers and pleads for rough.

The explosive sex wasn't actually the surprising part, even if the memories alone were enough to heat Jay's blood. He'd suspected a full weekend with Alastair might get a little playful.

The real surprise was everything else.

This was their third day together in a row—and it felt just as comfortable and easy as the first. London was long gone. Jay hadn't thought about what awaited him back in the city all day. He and Alastair were alone here in luxury at the edge of the world, no distractions, no worries, and when Alastair was briefly absent, all Jay wanted to think about was him. There was no sense of relief at having a few hours to himself. He didn't want to find some space for a while. The thought of his cramped and cluttered flat didn't bring him any joy. Tonight, trying to get to sleep, he already knew he'd be thinking about Alastair and missing the perfect hours they'd shared, the sleepy peace of their suite, the way Alastair sought his gaze, listened to him fondly as he spoke.

He'd miss the fun of good sex with someone familiar, but he'd miss the company, too.

Could be weeks before we see each other again, Jay thought, gazing numbly at the distant trees. *Depends when he's free. What he wants.*

There was a chance that Jay needed to have a think.

A very hard, very serious think.

Realising his cigarette had burned low, threatening to scorch the ends of his fingers, Jay stubbed it out against the wall and flicked it off the terrace. He started up another, cupping the lighter in his hands and scowling at the breeze.

A voice addressed him from nearby.

"I don't suppose I could trouble you, could I?"

Jay glanced up. He'd been joined on the terrace by a man who could only work in politics—tailored suit and striped blue tie, toupee far too thick to ever pass for natural, and an oddly heavy set of eyebrows and gold-rimmed glasses. Behind them, his eyes were small and amused.

Wary, Jay handed over the lighter. The breeze blustered around them.

"Sure," he said. "Good luck with it."

The politician retrieved a pack of king size Chesterfields from inside his suit, then took his time in extracting one.

"You're new to Cliveden?" he said.

Jay's thoughts had drifted to Alastair again. He retrieved them, taking a drag on his cigarette. "Erm, yeah," he muttered. "Just visiting."

"Easy to be awestruck," the politician remarked, with the idling self-awareness of one who loved the way he sounded while flirting. "You don't seem to be, though."

Jay said nothing, watching the horizon.

"You're a native of the north, by your accent?"

Not sure your type's allowed to talk about natives anymore, mate.

"Yeah," said Jay vaguely, glancing for his lighter—which was still in use. Mr Hairpiece didn't seem to be troubling himself to shield the breeze too diligently.

"What line of work are you in?" the man asked.

Jesus. At what point does this count as a hostage situation? Jay supposed he was coming across as a bit of a challenge—gruff northerner, clueless about how conversation worked. If they weren't somewhere so fancy, he'd have resorted to *'piss off'* by now.

"Charitable sector," he said, trying to square his shoulders. "Working with young people. Do you want to try facing away from the wind with that? You might get somewhere."

"Oh, a youth charity? How fascinating. I imagine that keeps you busy, does it?" The guy smiled, his eyes twinkling. "How long have you been involved in that?"

Jesus Merry Christ, take a hint.

"Too long," Jay said. "Here."

He reached up, attempting to shield the lighter with a hand.

Before he'd thought the gesture through, Mr Hairpiece quickly and sleekly took hold of him, curling a hand around his wrist, helping to hold him steady.

"Aren't you kind?" he soothed. His fingers were cold and insinuating. He dipped the end of the cigarette into the flame, attempting to meet Jay's eyes.

Jay's stomach twisted. *Enough's enough.* He'd have to be rude. He didn't want to get thrown out of here, but he wasn't having this. He braced himself to pull away, but the politician's grip tightened.

A furious voice cut through the air.

"Frederic!"

Relief flooded through Jay's chest. He looked around towards the open double doors as Alastair came striding out onto the terrace, his head high and his silhouette tall and clean in the sunlight. He'd been up to the room to change, and wore no tie beneath his coat.

The sight of him sent Jay's heart thrashing.

"For heaven's sake," Mr Hairpiece muttered beneath his breath, apparently for Jay's entertainment. "No sense of timing..." Releasing Jay's wrist, he assumed a flat and unwelcoming smile. "Alastair," he said in apparent pleasure. "Just heading off, are you?"

Alastair came towards them, perfectly calm, his eyes fixed on Mr Hairpiece.

"Not just yet," he said. "I thought we'd take in the grounds for a few hours. Shame to waste the chance."

The politician gave an awkward laugh. "That's, ah... very nice of you," he said, "but I'm afraid I hadn't planned a stroll. I'm also rather busy. Another time perhaps."

Something in Alastair's targeted stride told Jay what he was about to do. He angled his body just a fraction, opening to the plan.

As Alastair reached them, his arm slipped at once beneath Jay's coat, wrapping tightly around his waist. Jay leant into his side. The gesture couldn't have been more fluid if they'd rehearsed it all morning. They came together in one smooth and easy motion, two jigsaw pieces fitting.

Mr Hairpiece's eyebrows vanished beneath his toupee.

"You've met my Jay, have you?" Alastair enquired, sharp. His arm tightened, his leather gloved fingers curling protectively around Jay's waist. "He always ensures I have my fill of fresh air before we head back. You're indispensable, darling, aren't you?"

Jay's pulse kicked. Holding Mr Hairpiece's shocked stare, he rested his head against Alastair's shoulder.

"I try," he said, placing his cigarette in his mouth.

Alastair's fingers flexed. "Frederic and I were at Harrow together," he explained. He pressed a kiss to the top of Jay's head. "Quite the long-standing association. What's that old saying, Frederic? *'God save me from my friends; I can protect myself from my enemies'.*"

Frederic's mouth twisted. "Mm," he said. "Very droll. I believe my aunt has it on a fridge magnet."

"A lady of great taste," Alastair said.

"As, it seems, are you," Frederic remarked, eyeing Jay. "Hadn't realised you're attached, Alastair. How wonderful."

"Privacy's a jewel," Alastair said. "Don't let us keep you."

With a last darkened glance towards Jay, Frederic—and his hair-piece—slunk off towards the doors.

As he disappeared from view, Alastair released Jay's waist.

"Forgive me," he said at once. "I... may have overreacted."

Jay exhaled in a rush, his heart still beating very hard. "No, don't worry. I'm glad you got here. Any longer and I might have decked him."

"Are you alright?"

"Bloody weirdo. Just wouldn't take a hint."

"Had he been pestering you long?"

"No. No, not long. Still long enough." Jay dragged on his cigarette, suddenly feeling stiff and cold. He missed Alastair's arm around his waist. "Sorry," he mumbled. "Should've just told him to..."

"Men like Frederic exploit their position," Alastair said. His jaw had set and he looked pale. "They realise it's rude not to be accommodating. They use it to their advantage. He's a bloody serpent. I'm sorry I took so long to change."

Jay's heart gripped.

"Hey... hey, don't—it's not your fault." He stepped close, placing his hand on Alastair's arm. "I'm alright. No harm done."

"I'm sorry. Forgive my clumsy handling."

"Don't. It was perfect. He's gone, I didn't have to punch him, and that's all I could ask."

"I just needed to get him away from you. He's been known to be forceful in—"

"Oi..." Jay moved his hand to Alastair's chest, spreading his fingers gently across the fabric of his shirt. He looked into Alastair's eyes, watching them struggle to connect with his, searching for anything else in the world to look at. "What's eating you?"

Alastair's jaw clenched. "I realise I... exaggerated the nature of..."

"It's fine," Jay said. "Can you look at me, please?"

Alastair did, meeting his eyes uneasily.

"I don't mind that you dressed it up," Jay said. "Seriously, Al. My solution to that particular problem would've gotten me hauled off the premises. I'm glad you were here."

Though he didn't speak, Alastair's eyes stayed with Jay's, the discomfort in them softening a little.

"Is he going to cause you problems?" Jay asked.

Alastair's mouth pulled at one edge. "He might make it known that I'm..."

"Yeah?" Jay reached up. He cupped Alastair's face, brushing a thumb against his cheek. "Tell people to mind their own fucking business. Problem solved."

Alastair flushed. He took a moment to speak, visibly preparing and then abandoning several replies.

"I'm sorry that he touched you," he said.

Jay's stomach gave a tug. "I've had worse," he said. He dropped his cigarette to the floor and ground it out beneath his foot, then put both his arms around Alastair's shoulders. "Come here."

Alastair's hands tentatively encircled his back. They lay flat, squeezing Jay, taking some comfort in his closeness.

Jay pressed his cheek against Alastair's, scrunching a hand in the back of his hair.

"Don't worry," he murmured. "Some shitbag grabbed my wrist. That's all. I'm fine, Al. I promise."

Alastair's hands rubbed the material of his shirt. "I think I'm in need of a walk now," he admitted.

Jay hugged him tighter, closing his eyes to the breeze.

"Good job I'm here then," he said. "Come on, sunshine. Let's chill you out."

It was almost half an hour before conversation became easy again. Jay kept a gentle watch as they walked together through the woods, giving Alastair space to think, then drawing him to the surface with casual questions when his thoughts seemed to weigh on him too heavily. Focused on Alastair, he wasn't sure which one of the woodland walks they were actually following. The path was tidy and clear between the trees, with the estate now off to the west. Occasionally they came across other people out on a Sunday walk, families with young children and dogs, couples like them who nodded and said hello as they passed. Jay supposed it didn't matter which path they followed. On a National Trust property, there was only so lost they could get. Someone would find them to sell them a membership before long.

He let the forest lead them where it wanted, side by side beneath the trees as the rhythm of their footsteps carried Alastair through. After a while, as Jay told some absent-minded anecdote about the office, he felt Alastair's hand slip quietly into his own. Jay knotted their fingers together and carried on. Soon, they hadn't encountered any other walkers for a while. How far the woods would lead, he didn't know; it was easy just to wander and to talk, listening to the wind among the leaves. The afternoon sun had painted every tree in gold and copper, the colours so bright they seemed unreal.

At last they came to a fork in the path, split around a beech tree that could have been here for centuries. Their conversation eased to a pause as they approached it, looking up. The tree's great crown was full of sunlight; tiny insects danced against the deepening cornflower sky. Gazing up into its craggy and ancient branches, Jay had the strangest sense of being where he should be, as if every decision in his life had led him here to this moment. Everything was proceeding as it should be.

Alastair's hand tightened gently. Jay turned to look at him, smiling, hoping that his awe was shared. For a moment, the look on Alastair's face made him pause. He wasn't really sure if it was a happy look or not, too full of too many things for him to tell. Alastair was looking at him as if seeing him for the first time, and it left Jay unable to speak.

He held his breath as Alastair studied him, desperate not to shatter this moment.

Alastair's throat muscles worked.

He stepped forwards, backing Jay up against the tree.

As they kissed, Alastair's hands found their way beneath Jay's coat and under his shirt. They pushed with longing across his chest. Jay arched, panting with the shock of cold fingers on his hot skin; Alastair's tongue filled his mouth. He gripped Alastair's hair tight and breathed, the bark firm and rough against his back, sunlight dappling across his eyes. Alastair kissed him like they'd never get another chance. Jay kissed him back until his jaw ached, until he knew beyond doubt that only this place existed anymore. Outside these woods, every clock had come to a stop. Every person stood frozen in time, an illusion waiting to resume. Only Alastair's body, pressing him here against this tree, was really real. Alastair's pulse, quick and hard against his own, was the only other living pulse.

Jay shook, struggling with a feeling he didn't dare to understand.

Alastair whispered against his mouth.

"Stay for dinner." His fingers raked through Jay's hair, begging. "We'll travel back to London tonight. I'll return you to your flat by ten o'clock. I promise."

Don't.

Jay's heart clenched.

Don't give me back, he thought. *Keep me here and kiss me. Keep your arms around me. Tell people we're here all the time. Tell them I look after you. Tell me I know what you need.*

Oh.

Oh, no...

Aching, Jay shut his eyes and swallowed.

"Sure," he whispered. "Dinner. Y-yeah. I'd love to."

Alastair's fingers curled beneath his jaw. They tilted back his head.

"I'd love you to," he breathed, pressing his lips to Jay's.

Chapter 10

"Your couple are in the Astor Grill."

Katie looked up from her sheet of tonight's guests, finding a work friend leaning against her desk. *My couple,* she thought. "Oh?"

"Yep," Priya sighed, sweeping her braid back over her shoulder. "None of us can concentrate."

Katie laid the check-in sheet aside. Some things mattered more. "What're they doing?"

"Don't think they know anyone else is in the room with them. Just gazing at each other over cocktails." Priya rested her chin on one hand. "The hot one—"

"Jay."

"—was feeding the posh one gnocchi across the table. Watching him eat them. Just smiling."

Katie shook her head, lost in wonder. She wished she knew what it was that had first brought them together. She couldn't imagine how someone so serious and someone so playful had found common ground, started dating, fallen in love.

"They've ordered the chateaubriand to share," Priya said. "I think I'm going to die. I had to come out here just to breathe." She eyed

Katie with interest, smiling. "Are they seriously still like that when they're alone? You took their breakfast up, didn't you?"

"They're exactly like that," Katie said. She thought about it, drawing in a sigh. "Actually, you know what? They're more. They're *more* that."

Priya's chest heaved. "Really?"

"Yep. Flirting and kissing." Katie glanced towards the CCTV screen showing the restaurant, wishing the picture wasn't so blurry. "Jay calls him 'sunshine'," she said. "Sir Alastair."

"Ugh, Katie. Just bury me."

"Alright. We'll bury each other."

"What does he actually do, the posh one? Someone said he's high up in the police."

"He's the commissioner."

"What's a commissioner?"

"I'm not a hundred per cent sure," Katie admitted, frowning, "but there are pictures of him on Google, riding a horse through London. With a..." She gestured, trying to recreate the plumed helmet. "I think he's probably pretty well-off."

Priya groaned, rubbing the side of her neck.

"Do you ever wish you could have that?" she said. "Someone rich to come and spoil you and adore you forever? God, and the pair of them look so *good* together. I can't cope."

"Did you know we had a noise complaint from the next room?"

"What?"

"Earlier today. I promised I'd pass it along, but... how do you explain to someone that we can't ask other guests to have sex more quietly please?"

"Oh my God. Stop it."

"I'm serious."

"That's amazing. Are the two of them married?"

"They've got different surnames, but... maybe. I bet they've got a beautiful house." Katie's chest expanded at the thought. "Bet they've got dogs or something. Really cute ones."

"I want to be married like that..." Priya trailed her fingertips along the polished surface of the desk. "I want someone to feed me in a restaurant and call me 'sunshine'."

"They're leaving today," Katie murmured, sad. "We've got their cases in left luggage."

"Leaving after dinner?"

"I guess so. It's been nice this weekend, hasn't it? Seeing a happy couple like that." With a breath Katie reached for her check-in sheet, supposing she'd better get on with some work. "I hope they come back," she said.

As the bill arrived, Alastair slid a debit card from inside his jacket. Jay reached at once for his wallet.

"Can I get this?" he said. "To thank you for..."

Alastair cast him a look of gentle reproach, half-amused and wholly fond. "I owe you thanks for joining me," he said, handing his card to the waiter. "There's no need."

"I saw how much those steaks cost, Alastair. Let me at least cover my share."

"Not at all." Alastair took the card machine as it was handed to him, checking the amount with a quick and easy glance. "I appreciate your company," he said, tapping in his pin.

Jay relented, flushing gratefully, and put his wallet away. *My turn next time* hovered on the tip of his tongue, but he couldn't quite bring himself to say it. It felt too assumptive, too cocky. It seemed safer to be quiet and thankful.

As he finished the dregs of his Woodford Spire, there came a faint ping from nearby. Alastair consulted his phone.

"Our car is here," he said. The waiter returned the card to him with murmured gratitude. "Thank you very much. Are you ready to leave, Jay?"

No, Jay thought. *Not at all.* He could probably sit here for another week and not be ready. It seemed wrong that someone else would be sleeping in their room tonight, someone else's toiletries in the bathroom. It felt so much like theirs that all he wanted was to go back up, cuddle together in the window and smoke.

But that wasn't an option, and grieving it wouldn't make a difference.

Jay plastered on a smile, determined not to wreck these final minutes.

"Sure," he said. "Let's get going."

As they approached the front desk, a familiar face looked up from the CCTV screen.

"Hello, sir," she said, her smile as bright as ever. "Are you here for your luggage?"

"If you wouldn't mind," Alastair said, handing her the key for their suite.

Jay found himself oddly touched that she didn't need his name. She hopped down from her swivel chair and disappeared into a back room, returning a moment later with Alastair's suitcase. Alastair was filling out a feedback form on the desk, occupied.

Jay nipped behind the desk to help her.

"Here, chick," he said with a smile. Her badge read *Katie;* it suited her. "I'll take it. There should be a ratty old backpack, too."

She found it for him and handed it over. "Here you are," she said. As Jay slung it onto his shoulder, she smiled. "Have you and your partner enjoyed your stay?"

Jesus—my—

Jay wasn't sure if Alastair could hear them or not. He didn't want to risk a glance to find out. He couldn't exactly correct her, anyway. *"Oh, no, I'm just his fuck friend."* He'd have to roll with it.

"Yeah," he said gratefully. "Yeah, we have." Pretending it was real, even for a handful of seconds, sent a feeling like sparks skittering through his chest. He knew at once he would remember this moment. "You've been really good to us. Thanks."

Katie twinkled at him, settling back on her chair. "I hope we'll see you again soon."

One hour from now, I'll be alone in my two-roomed flat, ironing, staring at the TV, wondering if this was all a dream.

Jay smiled, hoping it looked stronger than it felt.

"Yeah," he told her. "Yeah, me too."

They carried Alastair's suitcase down the steps to the waiting car, handling its weight between them. Jay found himself awkwardly aware of the quiet, conversation now crowded out by thoughts. He wished he knew what Alastair was thinking—if it was good, bad, or just nothing much at all. He didn't know which of the three would be worse.

"Did you write something nice on the form?" he asked, not wanting to do this in silence.

Alastair gave him a short smile, busy wheeling the suitcase round to the trunk. "I wrote that I hope the management are proud of their front-of-house team," he said. "They made us feel very welcome during the course of our stay."

Did you really put 'us'? Jay wondered. *Did you actually put 'our'?*

Any possible chance of him asking came to an end as Alastair's driver emerged from the front seat. The man nodded to Jay briefly, a polite minimum of acknowledgement, then moved around the car to help Alastair lift his suitcase into the trunk.

Jay hovered uncomfortably, stealing one last glance up at the house's glorious front. He didn't know if he'd ever be back here again. He didn't know if he'd ever be anywhere *like* here, any place in the world half as comfortable and beautiful as this, and he hated himself at once for not simply being grateful.

With his suitcase stowed, Alastair stepped forwards to get the door for Jay. One lock of his coppery hair had come free in the breeze. The clean white light of the overcast sky had turned his eyes an almost arctic blue, and though he was smiling as Jay got into the car, he didn't offer any words.

Last hour together, Jay thought, sitting back in his seat. Alastair got in beside him and shut the door. *Final sixty minutes before the weekend's over.*

It had somehow come about very quickly.

The driver took his seat; Jay's stomach tightened up.

Not even alone anymore, he thought, and suddenly realised he wouldn't get the chance to kiss Alastair goodbye. He didn't know if Alastair would leave the car to see him into his flat, or just politely turn him out onto the pavement. He wished they'd kissed one last time inside the hotel, taken a single minute just to hug.

As a wave of painful, nervous heat swept over Jay's face, he drew a deep breath to try and calm it.

Fuck, I'm in deep. This is big. This is too big.

Shit, shit—

Alastair leant towards his driver, murmuring something just behind the man's ear. The driver gave a cordial nod, started up the engine, then reached for the controls of the radio. After a few taps, a burst of easy music filled the silence.

Alastair settled back in his seat. Eyes forward, quite casual, he laid an arm across Jay's shoulders.

Breaking apart in silence, Jay cuddled into his side. He put his head on Alastair's shoulder and closed his eyes, not wanting to watch the grounds and the house slip away. It seemed better somehow for them just to be gone.

Alastair didn't speak for a song or two, his fingertips quietly stroking through of Jay's hair.

"Thank you for joining me here," he said at last. His voice was barely audible beneath the music. He seemed to pause, weighing his words. "I've very much enjoyed your company."

Jay swallowed, hard.

"Thanks for bringing me," he said. *Come on, idiot. Don't get clingy. You've had your fun.* "Hope I've not been too distracting."

Alastair huffed, placing a single kiss against his head. "I'm glad that you were."

The car seemed suddenly very small. Jay wished he could come up with something casual to say, some cheerful piece of conversation he could offer, as if he was the friend he claimed to be. But all he could think about was how it would feel to walk through the door of his flat

—see the mess, hear the silence. Put his bag down on the floor. Look around and realise he'd been lonely for an entire fucking decade, not even really living his own life. Just borrowing it, ready to hand it all back at a single moment's notice.

Now he'd lived two days at Alastair's side, and he didn't want to be lonely anymore.

Jesus.

Jesus, what... what the actual fuck have I done? Bloody police commissioner. Fancy dinners, evening functions. Work you can't even talk about.

Promised you something casual, and now...

"—give you any trouble," Alastair murmured. Jay made a conscious effort to tune back into the world, lifting his ear to Alastair's voice. "I realise it might be hard to put out of your mind."

"Sorry?" Jay said, unsettled.

"Ian Straker," Alastair replied. Though the name came like a fist to the gut, Jay took it unreacting. That was the last bloody name in the world he wanted to hear. "I know I've said this already, but to reiterate... if I can help, Jay..."

For several seconds Jay floundered, too overwhelmed to think straight, his instincts wrenched in opposite directions.

Tell him, he thought wildly. *Right now, right here, one big breath and get it out. All of it.*

Alastair would understand. He was holding Jay this very second, offering to help, and everybody had a past. They'd spent the last two days as close as two people could ever get, and if Jay couldn't tell him now, he probably never would.

Don't you dare, breathed another voice—sharper, louder. This voice knew loss. It was the voice that kept count of Jay's wounds and wanted him to live at all costs. Though not a gentle voice, it was a loyal one and it loved him fiercely. *You open your mouth, and it's over. All of this will be over. He's offering because he's a good person, too good for you, and if you're stupid enough to get soft, to try showing him the truth, he'll be gone in a fucking instant. And you know he will be. And it'll hurt like all fucking hell. You think he'll put you under police protection just because you've gotten good at sucking his cock? That's not what this is. You'll lose him, and you know we won't cope. So just have some bloody sense and chill.*

The decision happened automatically. It was done before Jay could think twice.

"I'll be alright," he heard his own voice say. He brushed his nose against Alastair's cheek, struggling to understand how he could say this so calmly. He didn't feel like himself any more. "It's a coincidence, that's all. I'm just paranoid, seeing things that aren't there."

Alastair tipped his face, enough to look gently into his eyes. "Are you certain?"

Jay inhaled. He couldn't backtrack now. It was done, and what had happened in the past didn't matter. He'd just have to hope that it was all prepared to stay where it belonged.

"Certain," he said. "Honestly, Al. I just work too much. Need to get myself a life."

Alastair said nothing, stroking the back of Jay's neck. His eyes dipped down to Jay's lips, and for a moment Jay almost had the feeling that he knew, or at the very least sensed there was something going unsaid. It didn't seem to bother him. Perhaps the offer had been simply polite after all. Perhaps he thought Jay could handle himself, or perhaps they weren't close enough for the presence of secrets to bother him.

Then he looked up into Jay's eyes again, and Jay realised it wasn't any of those things. He just respected Jay's silence, regardless of what it hid.

"Keep yourself safe," Alastair said softly. "Won't you?" His fingers stirred through the back of Jay's hair. "Tell me if I can ever help."

Jay's stomach gripped.

"I will," he said.

Jay watched the streets of south London appear as if it was a dream, one he desperately didn't want to have. He tried to anchor himself in thoughts of work in the morning, hoping he had at least one clean shirt in the wardrobe. His kitchen bin probably reeked by now. The ironing pile was no smaller than it had been on Friday. Life was waiting for him, right where he'd left it, and by this time tomorrow he'd be neck-deep again.

He'd never been so sorry to see a Sunday evening.

Alastair had gone quiet in the seat beside him, slightly awkward now reality had returned. He'd pulled his gloves on against the gathering cold, and his features were hard to read in the darkness. He looked as if he was thinking things too complex to be shared. They kept his face blank and his eyes guarded, some tightness in the lines around his mouth.

At last, feeling uncomfortably like a taxi passenger, Jay leant forwards to the driver.

"I'm... just past the lights, thanks. You can drop me by the phone box, if it's easier."

Alastair's driver complied without a word, easing the car to a halt on the corner.

Jay hesitated. He turned his gaze to Alastair in the darkness, utterly lost for what to say.

"Thanks," he tried, "for..."

Alastair nodded, a little guarded. "No need to thank me," he said. "I enjoyed having the time."

And now it's over.

Something in Jay's chest strained. He wanted to kiss Alastair goodbye. This three-day fantasy was now at an end, and he didn't know if he'd ever get the chance to repeat it. This had been fun, but he'd fallen too far.

He looked into Alastair's face, wishing he could put his distress and gratitude into words that felt safe to say. *This was really special. I'm sorry it's over. I'll think about you.*

It seemed too much, and at the same time not enough.

"Text me, yeah?" he said. His voice threatened to shake. He clamped down on it, forcing himself to smile. "Hope work goes easy on you this week."

Alastair gave another nod, lowering his eyes.

Take a hint, dickhead, Jay told himself. *Don't make this weird. It's your own fault. You knew who he was.*

As Jay took hold of the door, Alastair's hand appeared on his arm.

Jay froze.

"I... appreciate this might be too much," Alastair said. The painful silence stretched. "Forgive me, if it is."

Jay searched his face, trying to breathe. "Yeah?"

Alastair's expression didn't move. He regarded Jay with care, as if he were calculating a risk. "If you wanted," he said, "if you've no objection, you could... join me, maybe. For tonight as well. At my flat."

He hesitated, his fingers loosening from Jay's arm.

"If I'm overstepping," he added, "please say."

Jay inhaled, dizzy with the rush of a reprieve. *Jesus. One more night.*

"Can you, erm... can you give me a minute to grab my stuff for the morning?" he asked. "I've got an early start. Won't be able to get back here, to..."

"Yes. Yes, of course. We'll wait."

Holy fuck. "Right," Jay said. "Sorted. I won't be long."

He hurried across the road, unlocked the door and took the stairs three at a time. He'd left his backpack in the trunk of Alastair's car. It didn't matter. Up in his flat, he threw his suit over one arm, grabbed Friday's empty Sainsburys bag from the kitchen counter and scooped a random clutch of toiletries into it. He dug some clean boxer shorts out of his drawer, tossed them in too, and seized his work keys from the bowl.

Halfway down the stairs, he remembered. He ran back up, swearing, to get a shirt.

As Jay let himself back into the car, Alastair looked up from his phone with visible relief. He reached out to take Jay's suit at once, helping him into the back seat with his things.

Like you worried I wouldn't come back, Jay thought, reeling. *Like you thought I'd get up there and bail on you.* He slammed the door, dropped his bag and scooted close along the seat.

He wasn't sure who moved first. All he knew as Alastair kissed him, hands gripping at his hair, was that he'd sleep tonight after all.

He registered the rumble of the engine only dimly, far more focused on the tightness of Alastair's hands beneath his jacket, holding onto his body like releasing it for even a few minutes had been unjust. They curled together as the car set off, still kissing around Jay's laboured breaths. Alastair hushed him, brushed back his hair and pulled him closer, whispering his name as the lights of London swept over them in the dark.

One more night, Jay thought. *Just one more night like it's real, then face it in the morning.*

The lights were off in Alastair's flat. Something about the darkness seemed welcoming, as if the space itself now recognised Jay somehow. It didn't mind that he was here. It was glad. As Alastair locked the door behind him, fumbling with the key, Jay stood close at hand and held his breath, his head full of thoughts he couldn't handle any longer. There would only be one way to drown them out.

The lock clicked. For such a tiny sound, it had the echo of a cannon. Alastair turned to face Jay, his expression invisible in the shadows.

Jay stepped into his body without a word and backed him up against the door.

I want you to miss me, he thought, seizing Alastair's mouth. *To think about me.* Alastair shuddered and pulled Jay closer by the belt, opening his lips to the rake of Jay's tongue. Taking hold of his jaw, Jay tipped his head back and kissed him harder. *I want you to ache when you remember me.*

Kissing turned quickly into touching. As restless moans and rough breath filled the air, more and more fabric found its way to the floor, and more soft, freckled skin was exposed to Jay's mouth and hands. Alastair's body had never felt as good as it did in this moment, arching between Jay and the door. He pushed back against every touch with a gasp, wanting exactly what Jay wanted. His mouth was hot and soft, and so eager to be filled with Jay's tongue it was obscene. He was perfect—and for just a little longer, he was Jay's.

Stumbling, panting, they stripped off each other's underwear. Alastair began to shake as Jay helped him to step from his briefs. Jay straightened and slammed him back against the door, pinned him there and kissed him with ferocity, rubbing every inch of their skin. Alastair's nails scraped his angel wings and Jay hissed against his mouth, groaning out for more.

They stayed as they were until Alastair whimpered, grasping at Jay's hips to temper his rhythm and slow it down. *You're close,* Jay realised with a shiver. *You don't want to be. You want more.* He broke the kiss, bent down and swept Alastair up off his feet. Alastair let out a gasp, but his arms went around Jay's shoulders without hesitation. He clung on, trusting. Kissing him on the cheek, Jay adjusted his hold to keep Alastair comfortable, then carried him upstairs to the bedroom.

Still no lights; they didn't need light for this. Jay knew where the bed was. He knew where Alastair's body was. Nothing else at all could matter. He laid Al gently in the middle of the covers, crawled on top of him and resumed their rough, restless kissing. Jay shivered as Alastair's hands roamed eagerly down his sides. They kept kissing as he stretched Alastair gently with his fingers—teasing him, playing with his prostate until he was struggling to breathe. Shifting to the middle of the bed, Jay dragged him up onto his lap.

They kissed as they fucked, hard and slow, the same aching motion in a cycle. Alastair trembled with each stroke, his arms locked tight around Jay's shoulders. He let Jay lift him, fuck him, pull his hips down harder when he needed it, his gasps and whimpers muffled against Jay's mouth. He rocked perfectly in the rhythm that Jay showed him. Even when Jay knew he must be exhausted, he kept on going, panting, his thighs shaking. He kept fucking himself on Jay's cock and gasping encouragement against Jay's groaning mouth, resisting all offers to stop and change position. He knew Jay was enjoying it this way. He wanted Jay to have it.

Jay couldn't bring himself to resist.

"You're so fucking gorgeous," he heard himself breathe, his whole chest pounding. Alastair moaned against his mouth, slamming himself down faster. "Fuck—fuck, Al—*shit—*"

The muscles in Jay's abdomen clenched. No one else on the planet was getting this right now; no one else could hear Alastair panting like this. His red hair was slick with sweat just so Jay could have what he needed, his face contorted with ecstasy and effort, and no one else got to see it but Jay. The thrill of it all began to sharpen, rioting through Jay's body in white hot waves. He choked out his broken warning, suddenly too close to stop.

Alastair's arms gripped tight around his shoulders. "Yes," he sobbed, dragging his hands through Jay's hair. His fingers scrunched and pulled. "Fuck, yes—*yes, fill me—*"

Jay bucked in desperation, groaning his last into Alastair's mouth. *Please—God, that's—*

Alastair cried out, loud enough to echo. "Fuck, Jay—"

As Jay erupted, flooding Alastair's insides, his groan hitched up into a whine. Shuddering, Alastair took him deep and held on. He stroked Jay's hair through every moment of it, murmuring gentle nothings against his lips and soothing all his ragged gasps with kisses.

The rush of relief after climax seemed to drench Jay from the inside out. All his senses blew wide open as he breathed. Suddenly he could feel the gleaming sweat upon his back again, hear his own heartbeat pounding out the last of it. Every cell in his body begged him to slump back against the pillows and rest. But the press of Alastair's cock against his stomach mattered more.

Gasping, aching, Jay secured his arms round Alastair's waist and tipped them sideways. It took the very last of his strength to push Alastair over onto his back.

"Rest," Alastair gasped. "Rest, Jay... you're—" Jay pushed his thighs apart. "Oh, *God—*"

Jay leant down, still breathing hard, and nuzzled his nose beneath Alastair's balls. Alastair quickly stifled out what sounded like a cry. Shifting, Jay pulled Alastair's legs into place over his shoulders, then reached up to wrap his cock with one hand. He began a loose and easy stroke, dipping his nose lower, then flashed his tongue across Alastair's softened ring of muscle, tasting himself there.

Alastair's back bowed upwards from the bed.

It's alright, Jay murmured in his mind, licking slow stripes with the flat of his tongue as Alastair begged. *Let me make it alright.* He spiralled his tongue round and round, varying his pattern and his speed until Alastair's fingers began to hurt in his hair. His soft and pleading cries were just too perfect; Jay wanted a thousand more. In search of them, he let his tongue nudge its way inside, shallowly at first, then thrusting deeper, licking with gentle swirls. He kept his fist moving around Alastair's cock as he worked, stroking light and loose.

Alastair's thighs soon felt like rock on either side of his head. He couldn't seem to keep his hips still, bucking up in search of tighter stroking, then grinding down for deeper fucking from Jay's tongue. His steady stream of gasped sobs and little twitches were heaven. As he finally hit climax, he let out a cry like a howl. His entire body stiffened, every muscle pulling tight. He dug his nails so deeply into Jay's shoulders that it stung, but the pain was an honour, the scratches a reward for Jay's service. He licked Alastair through it, burning up with pride, stroking his softening cock until he whimpered.

In the panting quiet which followed, Jay lowered Alastair's legs to the bed. They trembled faintly, limp within his hold.

Mine, he thought, kissing Alastair's stomach. It heaved with Alastair's laboured breath, smearing come across Jay's jaw. He swept it from Alastair's skin with his tongue, closing his eyes. *My Al. All mine.*

Alastair shuddered with exhaustion, brushing his fingers through Jay's hair.

I know you're important. Jay breathed in the scent of his sweat, trailing kisses up Alastair's body until he found where his pulse beat the hardest, then laid his forehead there. Alastair's heart drummed back to him, calling. In silence, Jay called back. *I know you don't have time. I know I'd wreck this into pieces if I asked.*

But if you're going to fuck someone, please. Please let it be me.

I'll take anything you'll give me.

I'll give you anything you want.

Chapter 11

Fingertips moved gently over Alastair's cheek, their touch protective as they cupped his jaw. Lips stroked with care against his lips; their slow brush lifted him from his sleep.

"Al?" Jay's voice came soft, little more than a murmur. Alastair felt it as much as he heard it. "You awake, sunshine?"

Alastair shivered, stretching within the sheets, and reached up for a proper kiss.

If every day began like this, he thought. *The two of us, here. Together.* Perhaps the thought should alarm him, or at the very least surprise him, but in this moment all he felt was happiness. Their lips sealed, easy and gentle, and Jay's stubble tickled around his mouth as they kissed. Alastair arched up with hope, his interest kindled by the closeness of Jay's body. *Once more before you leave,* he thought. *Once more, just to feel close to you.*

Jay's nervous murmur of protest stalled his pulse.

"I've... got to go, Al. I'm really sorry."

Alastair opened his eyes. He found Jay fully dressed and leaning over him, already in his coat, his expression heavy with regret. His eyes were rounded, his mouth tense and guilty.

"I've had a call from work," he said. "They've got someone there early to look at the damage, and he's mithering over the costs. It'll affect our insurance. They need me to come and sort it out."

Oh.

"I see," Alastair said, his heart thudding. He drew a short breath, fighting to settle the overpowering surge of distress. "Well... yes, if you..."

"I didn't want to just... you know." Jay seemed to flush. "Couldn't creep out with my shoes in my hand. Not after this weekend."

Postponing the moment of parting hadn't made it any easier. If anything, it had only made things worse.

Alastair reached up, trailing his fingers through the dark brown tufts of Jay's hair one last time.

"Thank you," he said. It took considerable effort to let go. As he slipped his fingers free from Jay's hair, his throat muscles strained and he forced his expression not to shift. "Thank you for... have an excellent week."

I'll think about you. Miss you.

Jay hesitated, still looking down into Alastair's eyes. "I'll text," he promised. "I'll be in touch."

Alastair didn't know what to say. He found himself emptier of words than he'd been in his entire life. All the things he could trust himself to say felt trite and meaningless; all the words he truly meant were far too big to fit through his throat.

From somewhere outside, there came a truculent honk from a waiting car.

Jay's fingers shook against Alastair's jaw, then curled tight. "'Bye, sunshine," he breathed, leaned down, and kissed him fiercely.

Before Alastair could relax enough to feel it, it was over. His chest seemed to cave as Jay pulled back. There was nothing he could do to change this moment. Opportunities to prolong the illusion had run out.

"Goodbye, Jay," he managed.

Jay stepped away from the bed, his expression pale and unreadable. Alastair wanted it to look like longing, so much so that he couldn't trust what he was reading in Jay's eyes. There was guilt, and plenty of it. But what else, he couldn't be certain.

Jay turned, leaving the bedroom without a sound. A minute later, there came the thump of the front door on the floor below, and he was gone.

Wide awake, Alastair lay alone in bed and faced his ceiling.

Monday.

The same faces he'd last seen on Friday. The same problems he'd been dealing with. The same office would be waiting, the same green salad for lunch, the same steady progression from meeting to meeting to meeting.

The only thing which had changed was him.

Somehow he'd have to pretend that things were normal. He'd have to convince himself his life still contained only work, as if he hadn't spent the last three nights as close to another human being as he'd ever been. Closer, even. Closeness of a kind he hadn't realised was attainable.

"I'll text," Jay had said. *"I'll be in touch."*

But when?

Weeks had passed between their previous meetings.

It had only been a matter of moments since Jay left, and already Alastair missed him. Never before had he lain in this bed and felt so keenly, distressingly alone. He almost didn't seem to be present in his own body. Part of him was somewhere in the back of a taxi, trying to follow Jay, wanting to stay with him, sit by him, for no reason other than to be where he was.

Mine, Alastair thought. Pain stung in his chest. *Mine for a while.*

He'd envisioned waking up together. Some time to themselves in the warmth and quiet. Perhaps a shower, gently kissing. Breakfast at the counter. Simple conversation. Some reassurance that the weekend had truly been what it seemed.

As Alastair realised he hadn't hoped for sex this morning, but for affection, the distress grew too sharp to permit. He pushed back the covers, took himself in silence to the bathroom and switched on a scalding hot shower, forcing his thoughts to the day's upcoming schedule.

Entirely my fault, he thought, scrubbing at his skin and his hair. He didn't want to do this gently. He didn't want to feel touch that reminded him of Jay. *Our arrangement was sex. Stress relief. Sex has been had.*

And it's all my fault for forgetting.

Unable to bear the silence, Alastair waited for the car out on the pavement. The cold air numbed a little of the heat left in his face, but couldn't take it away entirely. He'd left this flat for work on a thousand mornings, and never once in his life had he felt so awkward and so visible standing here. His heart didn't seem to be beating properly.

The car arrived as normal at half past eight, coasted to a stop in its usual place, and the door to the backseat popped open. As Juliet appeared, bright-eyed and smiling, Alastair experienced a brief and unsettling rush of resentment towards her. She heralded another stage of his weekend ending, another miserable step away from 'Al' and towards 'sir'. It wasn't in any way her fault, and fast on the heels of his resentment came guilt—but the sight of her distressed him all the same.

"Good morning," she said.

Alastair kept his eyes down and got into the car. He noted with a wary glance that she'd picked one of the cars with a privacy screen; it did not bode well for this journey. He shut the door with a short and blunt slam, fitting his seatbelt without looking at her.

"Thank you, Larry," Juliet said. The driver nodded and the doors locked.

As they set off, she leant forwards to the privacy screen. Alastair watched her close it with an increasing sense of foreboding.

Juliet sat back in her seat, crossing one leg over the other.

"How was Cliveden?" she asked.

Alastair held her gaze, unmoving, and waited for the pretense to be abandoned.

With a faint spark in her eyes, Juliet allowed her smile to finally show itself. "From several sources, actually."

Alastair did not return the expression. He cast a pointed glance towards the back of his driver's head.

"Perish the thought," Juliet tutted. "Our darling Larry? The very soul of discretion. He wouldn't tell me a damned thing this morning, though he did go terribly pink when I asked."

Alastair bit his tongue. "Then from whom did you hear?"

"I decline to name my contacts," she said coolly. "But *they* had it from Clarence Talbot and Frederic Hargreaves."

I will hunt down and throttle the pair of you. Alastair forced his face to retain its neutrality, swishing his tongue through his mouth. He hoped Clarence Talbot's wife knew a very good lawyer; he hoped Frederic Hargreaves enjoyed speeding tickets.

"Cliveden's guest services team were also very helpful," Juliet added, interrupting his thoughts. Alastair fixed her with his stare once more. "I wasn't about to believe the rumours without some impartial confirmation. I called the hotel early this morning, introduced myself as your assistant, and asked if a made-up item of yours had been found in the room. The young lady who answered couldn't find any sign of the item, but was *thrilled* to chat about you and your husband."

She might as well have tipped cold water over Alastair's head. It could not have stung more if she'd presented him with photographs of the two of them, walking hand in hand through the woods. He took a long and very silent breath, telling himself fiercely that she couldn't know the fullness of the situation. It wasn't her fault. It was not Jay's fault. It was solely and entirely his *own* fault, and nobody should suffer for it but him.

"I think we've discussed the boundaries of your professional domain," he said stiffly. "We reached the consensus that they end at my private life."

Juliet flashed him a knowing smile, her kohl-lined eyes bright.

"Unless, of course, my role is rather *wider* in scope than might be assumed."

"Mm," Alastair returned, biting the side of his tongue. "Though I'm certain the British security services wouldn't dream of covertly installing one of their agents in the role of personal assistant to the Metropolitan police commissioner. Such a thing would be unthinkable."

"Quite so. Though I'm sure a Metropolitan police commissioner of any merit would be bright enough to spot any such additional steps to safeguard his security."

"Indeed he would. Then, given that my security is being perfectly provided for by the police service, the entire issue becomes moot."

Juliet hummed. "Every little helps," she said. "Congratulations on Jay Fieldhouse, sir."

Alastair's stomach hardened into rock. "What congratulations do you think are due?"

"He's really quite a catch, you know. Shall I authorise his background check?"

A catch I have not caught. Alastair forced the words back down his throat, turning his face without a sound towards the window.

"You've had misleading reports," he said. "There's no need for the security check."

He could almost hear her raising an eyebrow. She held her silence, waiting, until he couldn't bear the lack of sound within the car.

"I won't belittle your intelligence by claiming he wasn't there," he said. "But I don't believe he's... this isn't a case of intimacy. It's a very casual friendship, Juliet. Nothing more."

Juliet paused, the whir of her thoughts fully audible as she chose her words. "What I've heard about this weekend would place a question mark over that, sir."

Alastair took a moment to quell the small frisson of anger it caused, trying with all his might to hold it back from his face. It was hardly her fault that he was a fool and he had no right to snap at her. She was the only person on this planet who ever spoke to him with anything even approaching affection, ever seemed to find his company comfortable, and that fact had never hurt until this moment. Everything suddenly hurt.

"I'm sure you've heard all manner of things," he said, swallowing, and regarded her with a look he hoped would terminate the conversation. "Unless your sources were present in my suite, I suggest you take *my* view on this situation as conclusive."

Her forehead creased. "Frederic Hargreaves—"

The paper-thin shell of Alastair's restraint cracked. In this moment, the anger felt as safe and as comforting as a blanket, as safe as Jay's arms had been, and all he could do was release it in a torrent towards her.

"Frederic bloody Hargreaves," he barked, drowning her instantly into silence, "is not a reliable indicator of *anything*. As well you know. He took predatory interest in my guest, which I circumvented. I'm unsurprised that my intervention is being painted as some heroic statement of ownership. What *does* surprise me is that the opinion of every muckraker and gossipmonger at Cliveden suddenly means more to you than mine."

Juliet's gaze flickered between his eyes, her expression flat.

"Guest services were under the impression that you're married," she said.

Alastair's heart convulsed. "Clearly they're underworked, if they've got the time for romantic fantasies regarding their guests."

As bewilderment tightened the lines around her eyes, he decided he couldn't bear the sight of her face any longer. He retrieved his phone from inside his jacket with a scowl, his jaw set, saying nothing.

Juliet seemed to take a breath.

"Sir," she said, speaking with the greatest of care as he opened up his emails. "I appreciate that you value your privacy. The background check would be extremely straightforward and non-invasive. It just ensures that the people who become close to you have your best interests at heart."

Close to me.

It hurt more than anything so simple ever should. No wounds had actually been inflicted; no argument had taken place. Jay had simply stepped in and then stepped out of Alastair's life, as they'd agreed so many weeks ago he would. Whenever he reappeared, it would be for sexual relief, not for closeness.

He'd changed nothing at all in Alastair's world, just gently re-angled the light. Now shadows lay across it all, long and dark and lonely. Late evenings spent at work. His silent, simple flat. Small meals at the counter on his own, cooked for purposes of hunger, not for pleasure or comfort. What family Alastair had had were now gone, and even when they'd been here, they'd had so little to say to him.

Nothing was different, and yet suddenly it lay in ruins.

Alastair kept his eyes on his phone screen, his throat thick. Three decades of pride in his career kept him breathing. He spoke the words, concentrating on what a competent commissioner would sound like in this moment, what sort of things he would say.

"Jay Fieldhouse and I are not close," he said. He swept through screens, not seeing them. "We have an arrangement, not a relationship. There's no need for a background check."

"This weekend seems to have been a more... *involved* affair than your usual meetings with him," she said, proceeding with ever greater caution. "I assumed there'd been some manner of development."

Alastair's heart seemed to retch.

"There wasn't," he said, ignoring it. As he forced himself, it became easier to speak. "Fieldhouse is not my partner. He isn't anything of the sort. I've now told you everything you could possibly need to know, Juliet, and I'm tiring of this circular discussion. Shut down any gossip that you hear and don't mention his name to me again."

The silence echoed.

Juliet let out a breath, sweeping something quietly off her skirt. "Sorry, sir," she murmured.

Alastair said nothing, incapable of speech.

The car carried on towards the office, full of unspoken thoughts and regrets.

---

sorry I had to shoot off this morning... you ok? xx

Jay gazed in silence at the unsent message, sitting in his office by himself. He'd spent the last two hours in a finance meeting, trying to keep his head in the game. He'd never felt so out of place in this room before. He'd never realised it was so bloody quiet.

Though he'd slept well last night, he now found himself a different sort of tired.

Taking a breath, he deleted what he'd written and tried again.

hey... thinking about you xx

As soon as he'd finished, he winced and wiped it away. *Too much,* he thought. *Way too much. Might as well go stand on his doorstep with roses and a bloody lute.* He wanted something light, some breezy thank you for a weekend of sex. He didn't want to hand Alastair his beating heart on a platter.

Jesus, he thought, glancing nervously towards the window. *How have I done this to myself? What's wrong with me?* It was just starting to rain, a thin and half-hearted grey drizzle. The same rain would be falling on the windows of Scotland Yard.

Jay sighed, pulling his eyes back to his phone. He drank a mouthful of cold tea from the mug beside his keyboard as he typed.

just me :) thanks for this weekend, was great to spend
some proper

Jay backspaced his way to the beginning, his heart now lodged in his throat.

He should have woken Alastair earlier this morning. He should have made time for a cup of coffee together, or even just five minutes lying in bed. He wished he could have held Alastair close a little longer, told him some of this without words. Kissed his forehead, kissed his fingertips. Made him laugh just one more time.

He almost wondered what would happen if he typed it, sent it: *can we talk? I'm catching feelings for you. Kind of want to be your boyfriend.*

If he weren't so numb, he might have laughed.

He could imagine it like it was happening right now: an awkward conversation where Alastair painfully explained the importance of his work, how he hadn't really time for emotional commitments. Jay could already see the slight frown that Alastair would wear, asking why Jay had agreed to casual if he actually wanted roses and candle-light—and more than likely, that would be the last conversation that they had. Everything would end.

Jay couldn't bear the thought.

Even if Alastair had the time or the inclination, this whole thing would be over in the second he found out the truth.

Jay was building a fairytale castle on quicksand. He shouldn't have let things get this far. He was sitting here aching and in pain like what they'd had at Cliveden was any possibility at all, and he didn't have anyone to blame but himself. He just didn't belong in that world. He shouldn't have so eagerly pushed it aside. He was so far underneath a man like Alastair Harding that anyone in this world would make a more suitable boyfriend, and if Jay had been honest from the start, he wouldn't even have been allowed to wash the dishes or mow the lawns at a place like Cliveden, let alone swan around like an honoured guest. He was already punching above his weight as a police commissioner's Friday night fuck.

But a police commissioner's lover? *Partner?*

He deserved it if the world came crashing down. It'd teach him to stop gazing at the stars, kidding himself he could have them if he only tried.

Swallowing, Jay swiped the message window shut. He tossed his phone into his desk drawer, somewhere towards the back, pushed it shut and put his head into his hands.

His chest tight, his heart in his throat, he forced his eyes to close.

You need to cool it, dickhead. You need to get a grip.

This whole thing had to go at Alastair's pace, or not at all. That way, there'd still be closeness of some kind. Jay would still get to see

Alastair, touch him, sleep near him. It was more than he deserved, and he couldn't bear to gamble it on a fractional chance at an impossible more.

So just take a step back, let him drive, and be grateful for the fun while it lasts.

And if it hurts, then it hurts.

At least you'll learn something.

Six o'clock had been and gone, with no sign at all of him finishing for the night. Alone in his office with the door shut since this morning, he'd been almost ferociously productive, chasing reports and demanding updates from nearly everybody in the building, communicating only through tersely-worded emails. Replies were being returned to him at speed. They all knew what was at stake when the commissioner signed his emails with *regards.* None of them had been stupid enough to venture up here in person. Even if they had, Juliet couldn't in good conscience have let them through the door.

After three years by his side, she knew far better than that.

Whatever had occurred with Jay Fieldhouse, Sir Alastair had reached for work to soothe it—and that was the end of it. The only possible course of action was the careful application of time and space, and to hope that he found his own way to some place of peace. It was so unlike him to try to forge a personal connection. She hadn't really imagined it would end this way, locked up in silence in his office, sheltering behind his duties.

It was a shame.

She'd been delighted, hearing tales of conversation and cocktails over dinner, long walks together in the woods. Sir Alastair had been in a far better mood since Fieldhouse arrived on the scene. Sneaking the man to Cliveden for the weekend was almost breathlessly romantic, and though Juliet now desperately regretted their discussion in the car, she'd had no idea that the subject would be poorly received.

There must be some factor at play she hadn't accounted for. Alastair Harding, as private and solitary as some deep sea creature, didn't like to share the details of his heart. She'd been foolish to try fishing for them. Whatever had happened, the matter was now well beyond her reach. Her own speculation wouldn't change things, and so she was choosing not to speculate. She kept herself occupied all day, focused on responding to his emails promptly, and at seven o'clock tapped on the door of his office with professional detachment.

"Sir," she said.

There came a pause.

"Come in," he said.

As Juliet opened the door, she found him quietly rubbing his fingertips into the corners of his eyes. His sleeves were rolled up towards his elbows, his tie half-undone. A lock of red-brown hair had worked its way loose from the rest, fallen forward onto his forehead without a care. He had the distinct look of a man who'd just lifted his head from his hands.

"Is there anything you need before I leave?" Juliet asked, keeping her tone as clean as she could.

He looked at her for a moment, pale, apparently approaching a difficult decision. "Can I delay you for just a few minutes?"

Juliet masked her flicker of surprise. "Of course," she said. "Shall I come in?"

He nodded, wordless.

Calmly she stepped into his office, shut the door behind her and took a seat before his desk, catching as she did a telltale whisper of cigarette smoke. Judging by the very faint chill in here, he'd been smoking out of the window.

A few moments of uncomfortable silence ensued.

"I was abrupt with you earlier," he said. Juliet stayed still, listening in surprise. "I was rude. I snapped at you for attempting to safeguard my security, which is very literally your job. And I... I am very sorry, Juliet. I am extremely sorry."

Juliet's heart gave a tug. This had never happened before, not once in three years. It was touching—and unsettling.

"It's alright," she managed. "I wish I'd been more mindful of your privacy."

Alastair said nothing for a moment, visibly wrestling the words up into his mouth.

"Juliet, I'm... lacking in knowledge. Specialist knowledge. I wonder if it's knowledge you might have."

She spoke with care. "What sort of knowledge?"

Distinct spots of colour flared within his cheeks.

"It's personal," he said. "I'm sorry to ask. There isn't anyone else that I trust enough to speak to, and... well, you're a worldly young woman. I hoped I could take you into my confidence."

Juliet brought her hands together in her lap, folding her fingers. "As your personal assistant, I'm happy to help with personal matters. Go ahead."

As he looked into her eyes, he seemed for the first time ever a little old to her—a little weary, a little grey. She'd never seen him on the brink of defeat.

"I'm aware you've had the odd boyfriend while working for me," he said. "You... seem to have good sense in these regards."

It was true there'd been a modest collection over the years, none of them quite interesting enough to hang onto. Juliet's girlfriends generally proved more enduring than the boyfriends, but sourcing them was more difficult. She'd taken care to tidy any heartbreak away from her duties. With regret, she'd been the instigator of heartbreak far more often than the recipient.

But from what she heard of her friends' love lives, things could be going far worse.

"I'm hardly an expert," she said, her expression gentle, "but I'll share what I can."

Alastair was silent for a while, greying further.

At last, barely able to look her in the eye, he asked, "What differentiates a casual arrangement from an actual relationship? Can one ever turn into the other?"

Oh. Juliet inhaled without a sound, fighting to keep the rush of pity out of her gaze. *Oh, sir.* It took her a second to reassemble her thoughts.

"The answer will be different from person to person," she said. "I suppose that what two people decide to call their connection is their business. But there *can* be development. It's very possible for the nature of things to shift."

The lines around his mouth tightened a little. "How can you tell if that's happening? What might suggest that things have mutually changed?"

Juliet considered the matter, desperate to say nothing which would hurt him.

"A casual arrangement usually has sex as its only real focus," she said. "A relationship has other forms of intimacy."

His expression shifted. She watched him struggle with some thought, trying to decide, getting nowhere. *Most of your time with him is spent in bed,* she concluded. *Sex is a safe focus for now.*

"Are there... other signs?" he asked.

Juliet fished through her thoughts, inhaling.

"A casual partner won't usually take interest in your wider life," she said. "They won't expect to hear updates from you on work, or family, or other things. The connection is physical, rather than emotional, so there's no sense of longevity. But someone interested in a relationship will care more about what you're dealing with day to day."

He processed this in silence, nervously adjusting one of his cufflinks.

"Casual arrangements are also very private," Juliet offered. "It won't usually reach the ears of other people, while a relationship might involve that. In time, at least. There's... more of a willingness to be seen together, I suppose."

His shoulders dropped. He said nothing, glancing down.

Juliet realised he would never give it voice unless she said it first. "Has it previously been private?" she said. "What you have with him, I mean."

He nodded, his eyes still low.

She took this in, her heart drumming against her ribs. "Is there exclusivity?"

He searched her face, uncertain.

Juliet opted for the simplest explanation. "Are either of you sleeping with anyone else?"

He paled slightly, unsettled by the question. "I can tell you beyond all doubt that I'm not."

But he might be.

"Do you *think* there's exclusivity?" Juliet asked.

He took a while to answer, silently turning his cufflink. "We haven't discussed it," he said. "He... I suppose he might have other..."

Juliet nodded, sparing him from finishing the sentence. "Do you contact each other outside of your meetings?" she asked. "Casual texts? Phone calls?"

Alastair's eyes clouded. He didn't answer, apparently unable to bear it.

Juliet's spirits sunk. "Who initiates most of your meetings?"

"It's... equal, I think. He suggested the arrangement at first. Since then, we've... well, we've sought each other out fairly evenly."

"Did you ask him to go with you to Cliveden?"

In his distress, even hearing the name seemed to hurt. "He asked me on Friday evening if I was free over the weekend," he said. "I told him I was away from home, but that he was welcome to join me, if he wanted. After the first night, he offered to stay the second, and I accepted. Then yesterday, I... I then broached the subject of a third night, and he accepted..."

Juliet nodded, processing. She gave herself a moment to phrase something properly. "Three nights in a row would be unusual in a casual arrangement."

Something hopeful opened behind his eyes. "Would it?"

"I won't pry for details, but... well, I've heard that the two of you spent time together outside of your suite. That's a hopeful sign, too."

He flushed. "We took a walk," he explained. "We had dinner together before leaving. He... seemed happy."

"Has he given you any idea of when you'll see him again?"

"He said he'd contact me."

Juliet almost wanted to take his hands. She wanted to reach across the desk, gather them up in hers and hold them tightly, as she would for any female friend.

"It'll be normal if a few days now pass without contact," she said, holding his gaze instead. "I know it might be difficult, but a settling period isn't anything to worry about. He might be figuring out how he feels, too. Don't be tempted to bombard him with texts."

He listened to her, silent, following her every word.

"Later in the week," she said, "you could try texting him. Something small, something casual. *How are you,* sort of thing. His reply will give you an idea of what he's thinking."

Alastair scanned her eyes. "In what way?"

"Well, if he's open to chatting, it suggests he might be happy with more than just a physical connection. It means he'd like to know you as a person, not just... well, not just between the sheets."

He nodded slowly. "I'll... have some idea of what he wants from me."

"That's right. And starting with just a casual text will be low risk. He'll either chat and it's good news, or he won't seem keen and at least you'll have some clarity."

Alastair shifted. He glanced down at his hands again, breathing in. "I'm sorry to trouble you with..."

"It's fine," she said. "It's my job to look after your welfare. If this is distressing you and damaging your focus, then... well, I want to help." Hoping it wasn't too far, she added, "I imagine there'll be future developments in this project. Please keep me updated."

Fresh colour rose in his complexion. "Thank you," he said. He watched her get to her feet. "When should I contact him?"

"Thursday, I'd suggest. Around lunchtime."

"Lunchtime?"

"If he's busy with work in the morning, your message might get put aside or forgotten. If you text him in the afternoon or evening, it could be taken as a request to meet up."

He nodded a little, understanding. "Thank you," he said again, looking embarrassed. "These things were baffling enough when I was young. The rules of engagement have only gotten more inexplicable."

Juliet smiled, unable to help it.

"I'm happy to consult," she said. "For what it's worth, what little I've seen of him seems very positive. And he's certainly improved your mood over the last few weeks. I think you can take comfort in positive memories of your weekend, sir. You should feel safe to do that."

Cautious relief eased his gaze. "Perhaps I'll finish for the evening now," he said, glancing towards his open laptop. "I might go home and rest."

Thank goodness. "Shall I call the car?"

"That would be helpful, yes. Thank you, Juliet."

"Not at all." Juliet took his coat from the back of the door. "Will you need any food?"

"No, I... I'm sure I have something in. Oh—before I forget—"

"Yes?"

"I wondered if you'd be able to track down some information on a closed case for me," he said, sliding his laptop away into its case. "It's not an urgent matter, but... well, whenever you have the time."

"Of course." Juliet took out her phone to make a note. "Which case?"

To her surprise, he said, "A gang leader named Ian Straker. He was operating in the Greater Manchester area around ten years ago."

"Certainly. Is there... anything *particular* you're wanting to know?"

"I've been told there was an unexpected result at his trial. Misplaced evidence. I'd like to know what charges had to be dropped and what he was finally convicted for. A general summary of the case would also be helpful."

It was a curious request, Juliet thought. Then, personal assistants often dealt with far worse.

"I'll look into that for you," she said, holding open his coat for him. "I'm glad to help, sir. However I can."

Chapter 12

Alastair's salad sat untouched beside his keyboard. He'd found the thing unappetising even as he made it this morning, and his nervousness since had only lessened its appeal. As he scrolled through his previous messages, his stomach in knots at the prospect of adding a new one, the salad might as well have vanished from existence.

Thursday lunchtime had pulled itself here by its fingernails.

> **[JF - 21:16]** *go shmooze posh thing*
> **[JF - 21:16]** *think about me xxx*

All this week, Alastair's thoughts had drifted to Jay with the slightest provocation. Things he'd never considered to bear any connection suddenly reminded him of Jay: laughter through open coffee shop doorways, music played by a passing car, the sensation of stepping from his flat into the morning sun. They seemed to evoke memories he hadn't made yet. They made him feel like a part of some great and rightful whole.

It was unsettlingly wonderful.

When he dressed in the morning, he thought of Jay in their suite, gently buttoning his waistcoat for him. Whenever he ate, he thought of Jay feeding him gnocchi across a restaurant table. When he settled into bed at night, he thought of Jay there with him, kissing him, stroking his skin beneath his clothes, little pet names given like gifts.

It hadn't been an easy three days. Alastair had checked his phone far more frequently than was dignified, hoping he'd be spared the turmoil and anxiety of this moment, but there'd been no contact yet. He'd done his best to remind himself of Juliet's reassurances that silence was an expected part of the proceedings—three days for them to orientate themselves into the working week and the rhythms of their daily lives.

Now the next stage could begin.

Contacting Jay to ask for sex had been difficult enough. Contacting him *without* asking for sex transpired to be twice as hard.

As Alastair scrolled through their previous texts, rehearsing and then obliterating possible new ones in his head, he wondered how a single marriage had ever come to be. He didn't understand how such a minefield of misunderstandings could be navigated safely. It was now nearly quarter to one; any further procrastination would tip them into the afternoon, at which point Jay would likely return to his work. If casual contact was to happen, it needed to happen extremely soon.

The cheerful rattle of knuckles against the door lifted his eyes. He slipped his phone into his pocket as Juliet appeared, leaning in.

"I've got the—oh," she said, spotting his lunch, "shall I come back?"

Alastair shook his head. "Distract me," he said, beckoning her inside. "Are those the figures from Henry at last?"

"Afraid not," she sighed, closing the door with a click and strolling over to take a seat at his desk. "I'm going to shake him upside down by the ankles this afternoon, though. I'm sure something of value will fall out. These are the files you wanted on Ian Straker."

"Oh. Yes, thank you..." Alastair had almost forgotten. He reached out a hand, taking the thick folder from her with interest. He wasn't surprised to discover it had some heft to it. "Mr Straker was an industrious gentleman," he said, flipping it open.

"I went through it all in the bath last night," she said. "Reads rather like a true crime documentary. I'm amazed there hasn't been one about him."

"Oh?"

"Mm. *Not* the sort of man one takes home to mother." Juliet brushed back her hair, today's deep plum nail varnish catching in the light. "Aggravated assault," she said. "Drug offences, firearms, money laundering. An especially well-developed talent for witness intimidation, which probably explains why he was at large for so long."

Alastair raised his eyebrows. "I imagine it does."

"That's only the start, I'm afraid. If it's illegal, he's tried his hand at it. His extended family seem just as unbound by the law as he is. And he's clearly very good at persuading others to join him in his endeavours."

Alastair turned through the file, trying to keep his expression detached from its contents. There were an awful lot of victims here. Reaching the fourth set of photographs of blackened and empty buildings, he said, "Something of a predilection for arson..."

"Mm. There's a report from a forensic psychologist towards the back. She floats that the fire-setting might be pathological, but she doesn't really reach a conclusion. There's every possibility he just finds it effective."

"And all of this was his gang?"

Juliet bit down into her lip. "These are the offences linked *directly* to Ian Straker," she said. Alastair's eyebrows lifted onto his forehead. "All of this was *him.* I can bring you the files on his associates if you like, but there'll be no room left on your desk."

Alastair drew a breath, tidying up his thoughts. "For what was he finally convicted?"

"Surprisingly minor odds and ends. Far more interesting is the question of what went *un*convicted, the answer to which is attempted murder. You're right that there was a cock-up at the trial."

"Tell me."

"From what I understand, Straker torched the flat of a social worker named James Wheeler. He suspected the man of giving information to the police about him."

A gentle prickle crossed the back of Alastair's mind. "You said *attempted* murder?"

Juliet nodded. "There was a tip off," she said. "The police got Wheeler out to safety earlier in the day, then kept a close watch. Straker and two of his associates were caught quite literally holding the lighter fluid."

"What happened at the trial?"

"There's no clear picture, but we can surmise. The prosecution service blame Greater Manchester Police, and Greater Manchester Police blame the prosecution service. Either way, a box of vital evidence went missing two days before the trial. None of it was ever recovered. Ian Straker's defence lawyer did his homework, argued that Straker only intended to cause minor property damage, and the jury just couldn't convict him. Not for attempted murder, at least."

Alastair pressed his tongue into his cheek, thinking. "But they could convict for arson?"

"Mm. A few other things as well, bits and bobs from a long criminal career. Greater Manchester Police meant the attempted murder charge to be the jewel in his crown, I think, but without it the whole thing rather fell apart."

"I wonder how his defence lawyer sleeps at night."

"Knowing defence lawyers, sir, like a baby."

Alastair huffed. "And what happened to the intended victim? James Wheeler?"

Juliet gave a faint shrug, flattening one corner of her mouth. "The file doesn't say."

Mm.

"In a shocking turn of events," she added, "Ian Straker transpires not to respect the great and noble tradition of parole. He recently failed to report."

"He's missing?"

"He is. It was awarded to him on the grounds that he was a terribly nice man who'd kept his cell very tidy and always said good morning to the guards."

Alastair attempted not to sigh. "Yes, I'm sure he did."

"They're attempting to trace him, currently without success. There's an extensive manhunt underway, but apparently none of his old associates have seen him. The team in Manchester don't seem to be getting anywhere fast."

Of course no one has seen him. Alastair moved a thought around his mouth, looking down at the open file.

"If I wanted to extend that hunt to London," he said, glancing up. Juliet smoothed away her flash of surprise. "I'd need to give good reasons, wouldn't I?"

She lifted one eyebrow. *"Are* there reasons?"

"None that I'd care to present to my superiors." Alastair rested his chin upon one hand, thinking. "In all honesty, it's nothing but a vague concern."

"What manner of concern?" she asked.

Alastair supposed he'd spilled enough of his soul to her now. A little more wouldn't hurt.

"Jay has some unspecified connection to the case," he said. "While we were at Cliveden, he told me about Straker's release. He also told me that his offices were vandalised last week."

Juliet visibly added two and two together.

"Oh," she murmured. "I see. Interesting."

"There's no evidence as to who caused the damage," Alastair said. "The incident has made Jay nervous, though. And he's not usually inclined towards anxiety."

She nodded dimly, then gave him an apologetic glance. "I'm not sure it's enough to justify a full search of London."

"Hmm. I fear you're right."

"Although... if the team in Manchester had some suspicion that Straker *could* be in London, and they were willing to voice that suspicion to us, we would naturally be obliged to look into it." Juliet paused, tugging at the corner of her lip. "Shall I see whose ears I can reach?"

Alastair would never feel completely comfortable authorising her to do these sorts of covert tasks for him—but then, she was certainly willing.

And he supposed it would only take her a few phone calls.

"Don't let it eat too much of your time," he said.

"I shan't. We'll call it a side project."

"Mm. Let's do that."

"Speaking of side projects," Juliet said, "it's now lunchtime on Thursday. Will you need any help with that?"

Alastair's stomach tightened up behind his ribs. "I was just about to get round to it. I, ah... I should be fine."

"Sure?"

"Mm." He reached for his abandoned fork. "Something casual, you said?"

"Something short," she advised, getting up from her chair. "Something easy to reply to. Take a breath, type it and send it. If nothing else, it'll bring you peace."

Alastair watched her stroll towards the door, wondering how it was that such a simple task could scare him so much. Over the span of his career, he'd faced decisions that altered the course of human lives forever. He'd signed documents at this very desk which dictated the country's approach to counter-terrorism. He'd done it without a blink. When it came to his career, he knew what he was doing. He made choices he could justify and learned from his mistakes.

With Jay, he was an absolute beginner. One mistake could be the last.

Alastair drew a breath, putting on a smile.

"Fortune favours the bold," he said, as Juliet eyed him fondly from the door. "Can I trouble you for a coffee in ten minutes?"

"Of course you can," she said. "Do try to eat that salad before it rots." She let herself out, closing the door as she went.

Alastair looked down into his tupperware box of green leaves, telling himself he would be fine. This didn't need to be an enormous undertaking. It was casual contact over lunch, not the entire fate of his love life. If he treated this like a horrifying ordeal, it would be one.

He reached into his pocket, retrieving his phone.

Checking on his welfare, he thought. *Provides a reason for contact.*

Gripping his fork rather hard, typing with the other hand, Alastair composed a short message.

[AH - 12:43] *No further trouble from Ian Straker?*

He agonised over the ending for a further few minutes. En route to Cliveden, Jay had coaxed him into two anticipatory kisses per message. It seemed excessive for a casual enquiry.

Alastair added a single one, wincing. He hit send before he could rethink.

And now distraction, he thought, putting the phone aside. *Lunch. Coffee. Work. If I receive no reply, it doesn't matter.*

He ate his salad without tasting a mouthful of it, rereading emails he'd answered hours ago.

"And... well, that's the shape of things," Helena finished, a little lamely, and turned her eyes across the table to Jay. The rest of the management team followed suit. "That's where we're at."

The point had taken over twenty minutes to relay, along with a great many tables, graphs, and charts. Jay was far from fluent in the language of accountancy. What he knew, he'd picked up piece by piece over the past six years, wrapping his limited mathematics around one small problem and then the next.

But he knew how to read people's faces, and it wasn't very hard to read Helena's.

"We need more money for the doors," he translated, looking back at her. "You can't squeeze it from anywhere else. We've got to cut."

She nodded, wincing a little.

"I'm sorry," she said. "I've been over the numbers twenty times."

Jay took a second to try and think, tapping his fingers quietly against the table edge. He'd suspected this might be coming. If he hadn't been so off the ball this week, he would have started working on the solution ahead of time. Getting home after work each night, it had been far too easy to drop his coat, get a beer from the fridge and switch the television on. Abandoning his thoughts entirely had worked better than trying to fill them up.

"What about if we shift the website back a few months?" he said. "I know we're desperate for it, but we've limped along this far with the current one." He cast his eyes across the table to Connor. "Right?"

Connor gave a nod, shrugging. "We'll have to rejig some of the upcoming content," he said, "but it's not unthinkable. If push comes to shove, we can shove."

Helena cut in gingerly.

"It *would* help in the short term," she said. "It wouldn't make the problem go away, though. We'll just run into this deficit down the line, instead of now. We... well, we wondered about slimming down our active projects. Retiring a couple of them. Or even just calling a temporary break."

"No," Jay said, before so much as a breath could be drawn in agreement. "No, we're not making vulnerable kids in Tower Hamlets pay for our doors. We'll fit cardboard ones before we do that. That's not an option."

Helena hesitated, twisting her fingers together.

"Do, erm... do we *have* another option?" she said.

The silence stretched, deafening. Jay looked up at the figures projected on the wall. He sat back in his chair and raised a hand to rub the side of his neck, wishing that he'd slept better, wishing he could produce the magical solution they were all expecting. His gaze settled on the lengthy figure under *'staffing costs'*, and one possible solution occurred.

"Can you take what we need off my salary?" he asked.

Immediate protests broke out around the table. Connor led the dissent, leaning forwards in his chair.

"Jay," he said, his serious tone wildly at odds with his pineapple-printed shirt. "You're already under the London average. That's for *any* worker. Most chief execs earn three times what you do. If you drop down much more, you won't just be under the average wage.

You'll be under the *living* wage. And that isn't going to look good for us."

Jay raised an eyebrow at him, unmoved. "Are you telling me that people won't take us seriously, just because I'm not driving around in a Porsche?"

Connor didn't back down.

"Yes," he said, to Jay's surprise. "Yes, that's exactly what I'm telling you. You're not an unpaid trustee. You're not obviously from a wealthy background, doing this for a warm and fuzzy glow inside. If we drop our chief exec below the living wage, people will wonder why we can't afford to pay you properly. And you'll be managing a team who out-earn you. That's not going to be comfortable for anyone."

Jay shifted with discomfort, his eyes flashing back towards the figures.

"Well, where else is the cash going to come from?" he asked. "You've all heard the numbers. We need the doors fixed. We need our projects to keep running. I don't need a hot tub full of champagne. Helena, get your team to recover what we need out of my salary. Then we won't even have to push the website back. Job done."

Helena nodded, flushing, too surprised to argue. Her eyes dropped back to her notes and she shuffled them awkwardly. Most of the room seemed inclined to keep their silence with her.

Connor made one more attempt, prefacing his words with a breath.

"You don't need a hot tub," he agreed, "or a Porsche. But you need to eat and pay your rent, mate. And it's going to look odd if we don't supply our staff with the means to do that, especially our chief exec. I can't sit here and not point that out."

Jay didn't mean to raise his voice. He didn't mean to snap. Three miserable nights of very little sleep turned the words sharp inside his mouth, and before he could stop himself, he was speaking.

"Well, somebody's taking the hit," he said. "It's me or it's the kids in Tower Hamlets. And if anybody asks you why we're not paying our chief exec a gold pig every month, you can show them the child poverty rate in Tower Hamlets. Do you remember what it is?"

The silence rang.

"Fifty-five per cent," Jay said, shaking. "That's one in two. Pick two kids. Only one of them gets a decent meal today. There's *seventy thousand kids* in that borough. What's the poverty rate among chief execs?"

Connor withdrew his contribution at once, holding up his hands without a word.

"Right," Jay said. Nobody was looking at him, their eyes averted. The air in the room seemed to churn. "Okay. We've got our solution, then. Good." He gathered up his papers and his phone, annoyed to see the shaking in his hands. "Can somebody make the arrangements for the doors, please? Let's try and get it sorted as soon as possible."

There came a general murmur that it would be handled. No other business was brought up, nobody quite daring to speak. The meeting came to an end.

Back in his office, Jay stayed only long enough to pull on his jacket and collect his cigarettes. He didn't like putting his foot down in meetings; he never had. It wasn't often that the need for it arose, but it always left him shaken and uncomfortable, feeling like he'd overstepped his mark. A short walk to the shop for a sandwich would clear his head—and give him time to start planning an apology to Connor. He left the building before he could bump into anyone, and lit up as he stepped onto the street.

There were two routes to his usual place for lunch. His preferred route, a cut-through, took all of three minutes to walk; the other was longer and always busy with tourists, even midweek. Jay sometimes took it if he had other shops to visit, or on the very nicest days in summer.

Hoping the extra ten minutes would do him good, he picked the longer route and smoked as he walked, drafting and redrafting the email in his head.

"Sorry I took a bite from you earlier. Truth is I've not been sleeping well. I shouldn't have taken it out on you, especially not in front of everyone. I didn't mean to."

But if Connor asked, as he almost certainly would—what then? What the hell was there to say?

"Oh. Well, there's kind of a guy. He's all I ever wanted. And he doesn't even know my real name."

At the sandwich shop, Jay scrolled through the news while waiting in line. Last night he'd removed his messaging app from his easy access bar, too tired of watching himself open and close the same window. His thumb still moved instinctively towards the weather app which had replaced it, wanting to try one last time. He'd come up with and dismissed a hundred different excuses this week, each more transparent than the last. The next hundred excuses wouldn't be any better.

As he realised he was straying towards news articles which mentioned the police, dimly hoping for one he could use as an opening joke, Jay locked and put his phone away. *For God's sake,* he thought, his spirits sinking further. *Bloody one-track record.* He suddenly wished that he hadn't come out. At least holed up in his office, he could have kept himself occupied with work.

He ordered a ham and cheese sandwich and nearly asked for a macchiato to go with it, then quickly changed his mind. There was coffee at the office, and coffee back at home. Several thousand pounds' worth of fancy glass doors would be his treat for the next few months; he needed to start saving some money.

As he let himself out of the shop, holding his wrapped-up sandwich, his phone buzzed gently in his pocket.

Jesus. Probably Connor. Jay reached inside his jacket, hoping that Connor hadn't beaten him to the apology. He already felt like enough of a twat. He checked the screen with a reluctant glance, bracing himself for the worst.

[AH - 12:43] *No further trouble from Ian Straker? x*

Jay almost dropped his sandwich. He stepped quickly out of the way of a large group of Japanese tourists, then checked his phone again to make sure. It was definitely Alastair—and that was definitely a kiss at the end. As he stared down at the message, hardly daring to believe it, a businessman blundered into him and let fly some disgruntled comment about loitering on the pavement in London. He'd taken Jay for a visitor, googling the directions to Madame Tussaud's.

Pulling himself together, Jay hurried into his usual cut-through to the office. The narrow alley comprised the back doors of restaurants and shops, nothing of interest to the crowds. He'd be able to stand here for a minute and text. He stashed his sandwich underneath his arm as he eagerly opened up the message. On the surface, it seemed pretty functional. Without that tiny little x, he might have worried.

As it was, it set his heart bouncing like a rubber ball.

nah, he typed, grinning. *no trouble. I was just being paranoid :) hows y*

A door opened along the alley. Two men stepped out; Jay shifted to one side to let them pass, flashing them an awkward half-smile.

What happened next took place in seconds.

The nearest to him lunged. He locked his heavy arm around Jay's face, hauling him off balance. Blinded and muffled, Jay threw up his hands in instinct to wrench the arm away from his mouth.

A fist dug beneath his ribs.

Jay curled, spasming in pain. His knees gave way. They dragged him, his feet and his lower legs scuffing uselessly against the ground. A sudden drop in light told Jay he'd been pulled into a building.

No—

Oh, shit—

He knew what happened inside buildings, out of sight. He knew how this played out. He'd seen it all before. He struggled, kicking. They were on him in a second, raining down blows to make him stop. He couldn't shield one part of his body without them pummeling another. When he lifted his arms to protect his face, a knee slammed into his groin, agony ripping through his abdomen. Nausea rolled in its wake. With all his senses now screaming in panic, Jay deployed the only trick he had left. He forced himself to stop fighting. He slackened his muscles, shut his eyes and slumped.

They battered him for a few seconds more, then stopped as they realised he'd gone limp.

Keeping still and quiet, Jay let the two of them catch their breath. From a single foggy glance beneath his eyelashes, it looked like he was in the backroom of an unoccupied shop. There were broken down boxes, empty metal shelves. The door was pushed to, but a thin seam of light marked its edge in the darkness.

One of his attackers kept hold of him, panting. The other began to search inside his jacket for pockets. Jay waited, playing dead until the man who had hold of him let go with one hand, wiping the blood and spit off his face.

Jay took his chance.

He surged upwards from the ground, lashing out with his feet, and felt the side of his boot connect with a head. An agonised yell went up in the dark. Jay twisted, following the momentum of his kick. The hold around him broke. Scrabbling up from the dusty concrete floor, Jay ran, erupted through the door into the alley and did not stop. He didn't look back to see if he was being pursued. His feet took him straight towards the office and he let them, keeping his eyes straight ahead, sprinting without a single thought of the pain or the damage to his body. He wanted to live. On the estate where he'd grown up, the only way to have that was to run.

All the pain seemed to have gone on ahead of him. It was waiting, right there at the office. As Jay staggered through the glass front doors, now an ugly web of safety tape and cracks, every punch from his attackers finally seemed to land. He didn't manage another step. He collapsed to the floor in a heap, bleeding and broken as the tide of pain and shock swept his thoughts away. The receptionist screamed, but he heard it as if through water. It didn't matter.

As he panted against the ground, holding on to consciousness, Jay let the world shrink tight around him. Nothing mattered outside the bubble just beyond his skin. Everything was fine. He was alive. He'd gotten here, and now he could just lie down. It was over.

The noise and the chaos of help being summoned didn't reach him.

It was enough just to lie here and bleed.

At three o'clock, though Alastair hadn't asked for any, Juliet brought coffee. She put the saucer down beside his elbow, made sure the biscuit was in his eyeline, then rotated the handle towards him.

"Anything?" she asked.

Alastair continued to read without a sound.

"A busy afternoon, I imagine," she tried.

Alastair said nothing. He turned the page in his report, as silently as if he hadn't moved at all.

Juliet let herself out.

If there existed a more miserable place in the world than a central London emergency department, Jay hoped he never went there.

He'd been drifting in and out of reality for what felt like several days now, propped upright on an uncomfortable plastic seat. The sickly and the injured were crammed in all around him, phones ringing, kids howling, time no longer passing as it should.

The rest of the room were trying their very hardest not to look at Jay. After arriving and registering his place in the queue, he'd shuffled awkwardly to the bathroom to wash his hands and face, wanting to get rid of some of the blood. One glimpse of himself in the mirror, and he understood why his co-workers had wanted to call an ambulance. He looked like an extra from a very low budget Tarantino. Everything still ached and stung; every tiny movement twinged. He couldn't find any position he could hold on this horrible seat that didn't press against his pulverised balls. After hours of waiting and staring, he missed the floor of reception with all his heart. It had been quiet and comfortable there, at least.

Somewhere in the haze, there came an audible breath from beside Jay. Connor shifted, recrossing his long legs at the ankle.

"You alright?" he murmured.

Jay glanced towards the clock above the desk. "Still want to leave, if I'm honest." His split lip gave a sharp sting as he spoke. He swept it carefully with his tongue, wincing. "Nothing I can't sort out at home. First aid kit. Couple of plasters."

Connor gave him a look of apology, his eyebrows folding in the middle. "I'm sorry, Jay. If I let you waltz out of here without you being checked first, everyone at work will kill me. I promised them I'd bring you."

"Hmh."

"Won't be much longer now."

Jay snorted. "I bet you twenty quid we'll be here another hour."

Connor didn't take him up on it. He drew another breath, folding his arms. "I know it's frustrating," he said, keeping his voice down. "And I know it doesn't seem like a problem to you. But you were mugged, okay? For most people, that warrants a trip to A&E."

Jay shifted uneasily. He'd been trying to forget, pretending he was here because of some accident—tripped over a kerb and beaten himself up on the way down. He didn't want to think about the truth.

"I still can't believe they'd take a risk like that in daylight," Connor said. "Just dragging you right off the street."

Jay curled himself back into his chair. "Keep wondering if it really happened," he mumbled, crossing his arms over his chest. "All so bloody fast."

Connor hummed. He turned his gaze across the waiting room, then gave Jay's elbow a small nudge.

"Hey," he said, nodding towards the doors. "I think they might be here for you."

Jay looked around quickly. Two police constables were approaching the desk, looking like they came here often. The receptionist on duty spoke to them briefly, then stood up, gesturing with his clipboard towards where Jay and Connor sat.

"Think you're right," Jay said, bracing himself. He sat up in his seat, trying to quell his instinctive discomfort around uniformed police. Nothing unsettled him like the sight of a hi-vis jacket. "I don't know why they're bothering, to be honest. I've got nothing I can tell them."

"Just tell them what you can," Connor said. "At least it'll pass the time."

Jay grunted, tired, as the constables came this way.

At eight o'clock, Juliet finally dared to make another check.

As soon as she opened the door, her fears were confirmed. He was midway through a stack of reports, one hand supporting his head, the other annotating in utter silence with a red biro. His sleeves were rolled. His phone sat at the very furthest edge of his desk.

To stop yourself checking, she thought. *To put it out of your mind.*

She knew exactly how he felt. God knew there were enough of them out there: men who were deliciously attentive in bed, then vanished into thin air at the first hint of real connection. She didn't know what casual conversation the poor man had attempted. Whatever it was, it hadn't been inviting enough to elicit a reply in seven hours.

It wasn't a failure, precisely.

But it was a badly missed opportunity.

She'd hoped Jay Fieldhouse would jump at the chance. With a few casual texts, he could have shown Alastair that an invite to dinner would be welcome. Juliet would have aided Jay in that from the sides, encouraged Alastair, reassured him that Jay would be receptive.

But perhaps for Jay, it really was just physical. It was a shame. She'd heard such glowing reports from Cliveden. Men were enigmatic creatures, so often dysfunctionally distant from their own feelings. They lived a vague approximation of what seemed normal in a relationship, rather than what felt authentic. They took the presence of sex to mean everything was going handsomely. It meant that when finally asked to supply some authenticity, they could only offer bafflement and a swift exit.

Better you find out now, sir. Little though it feels that way.

Standing in Alastair's doorway, Juliet kept her tone gentle and clean. "Is there anything you need before I go?"

He didn't raise his eyes from his report. "No, Juliet." His voice came subdued in the silence. "Thank you."

"Would you like me to arrange a car for you?"

"No." He crossed something out in the report with a stroke of red. "I'll arrange it myself when I've finished."

Juliet hesitated, unsure if she dared.

"Sir... if he *is* James Wheeler," she said tentatively, "and he's under witness protection, he might be nervous about forging emotional ties. I've been told it can be hard for people to feel secure in their new lives, even after many years."

Alastair did not speak for a very long time, writing.

"Perhaps," he said at last, and nothing more.

Juliet nodded. He wasn't one of her friends; she couldn't tell him that she knew it hurt. She couldn't now invite him to a wine bar to put the entirety of his sex to rights. Tomorrow, she'd do her best to distract him and occupy him. The work would help. It always did.

For tonight, he'd just have to grieve.

"Good night, sir," she murmured. "I'll see you in the morning."

Alastair said nothing, reading.

She closed the door behind her as she left.

Waiting to be seen led to waiting for scans, then waiting for results. The police called back towards the end of the afternoon. They'd found Jay's mobile phone at the scene, along with his still wrapped sandwich, and handed both over in a sealed plastic bag.

"We'll get an appeal out for witnesses," one of them told him. "But... well, given that nothing was taken..."

Jay could only shake his head.

"Don't worry about it," he muttered. "It's... these things happen. London. Seriously, guys, don't waste your time."

They gave him the number of a victim support helpline to ring, thanked him for reporting it, then left.

Darkness had fallen by the time a doctor appeared with Jay's results: no bones broken, and surprisingly, no internal damage. He'd be sore for a few days, and ice packs would help with his black eye and the swelling in his groin. Otherwise, it was a case of over-the-counter painkillers and rest.

Connor held open the door of his car for Jay, one arm offered out and ready to help.

"Take your time," he advised.

Supposing he'd already lost enough pride today, Jay gripped his wrist. He lowered himself painfully into Connor's passenger seat, unable to suppress a wince. The pain was bad enough; the lingering nausea made it worse. He was glad Connor hadn't tried making any jokes. Groin injuries stopped being hilarious in the second you were given one.

"There you go," Connor said, calm and easy. "Okay. Let's get you home."

He closed the door for Jay, circled round the car, then let himself into the driver's seat.

"Connor?" Jay said, as Connor fastened his seatbelt in the dark.

"Mm?"

"Thanks. For..."

"Don't mention it," Connor said. "You'd have taken any of us."

Jay's heart gripped. It was true, though he didn't understand why it hurt. As Connor started up the engine, finally heading for home, the fear Jay had suppressed all day came welling up through the cracks.

He shut his eyes, swallowing.

Oh, shit. I don't want to lose it all.

If this was Ian, the UKPPS would move him. If he was moved, he'd never see them again, any of them, never even be able to reach out and ask how things were. His whole life would once more be a pointless and purposeless waste, back to square one. Back to the bottom line. He'd only just started to do some good. He hadn't made amends yet, not even near.

As Connor pulled out of the hospital car park, sickly orange lights giving way to quiet darkness, Jay realised he'd rather die in this life than escape into another one.

It hurt.

He wanted to live. All his stupid life, all he'd wanted to do was live. When they moved him down to London, he'd finally been given that chance. Something in his bones had realised immediately that this was it, his *one* chance, and all he wanted to do was keep living it—keep living *this* life, the one he'd built up from the dust brick by brick. He didn't have the strength to start again. He'd rather go down with his ship.

A helpless panic skittered through his chest as he understood in full that this was happening. If Ian had now tracked him down, he'd soon be paying for what he'd done. He'd cost Ian ten years of life. The only payment for that would be his own life.

Shit, shit.

Jay focused on staying completely silent, completely still, even as the world burned around him.

Shit. I don't want to die.

It seemed only minutes before Connor pulled up outside his flat.

"Do you need a hand getting upstairs?" Connor asked, watching Jay painfully push open the passenger door. He reached for his seat-belt. "Jay—"

"I'm fine," Jay managed, trying to force the pain out of his expression. "Seriously. I'm fine. I'll take it easy on the way up. I promise. No worries."

"Have you got ice and painkillers?"

"Yeah. Yeah, I've got plenty."

"Are you *sure,* Jay?"

"Yeah, I'm sure. I'm fine." Jay couldn't tell if his sudden resurgence of nausea was due to his groin injury, or to the fact he'd had no proper food since this morning. Standing here hurt. Talking hurt. Moving his arm to close the car door hurt. "I'll see you in the morning, alright?"

"You should stay home tomorrow," Connor called through the open door. "Rest your—"

Jay pushed the door shut, cutting him off, and headed across the road towards his door. He made sure to walk steadily and calmly while in sight of the car, hoping to convey the look of a man not ready to drop to all fours and vomit.

Just got to get inside, he told himself doggedly, opening up the front door. *Lie down for a bit. Be alright.*

Climbing the stairs felt like climbing Everest. Jay had never known until now that he used his groin muscles to climb stairs. By the time he reached the second floor, every step felt like being kneed all over again, his forehead hot with sweat, his stomach knotted up. He unlocked the door of his flat, fumbling with the sticky key and begging it under his breath just to let him in.

At the sight of his unmade bed, as comforting as open arms, Jay gave up at once on this day.

He pushed off his shoes without untying the laces, leaving them discarded beside the door. All the joints in his fingers strained as he fumbled with the buttons on his coat. One of the bastards had stamped on his hand. It was a miracle he could still move it at all.

Dropping his coat beside the bed, there came a loud and muffled clunk.

It took Jay a second to realise.

Shit, my phone...

The memory returned with a flash.

Oh, shit—

Al—

Crouching down caused a sharp flash of pain through his groin. He twitched and then tried to ignore it, searching, panting a little as the pain grew worse. Finally he got hold of his phone and dragged it out.

He sat down on the bed to re-read the message, his breathing tight.

[AH - 12:43] *No further trouble from Ian Straker? x*

Jay's throat thickened. He glanced at the time on his phone. Nearly nine hours ago now. Alastair would have given up on him replying.

He'd be wondering why Jay thought he had the right to play cold, when it was nice of Alastair even to ask.

Alastair was managing to be friends here, not just fuck friends.

It was Jay's fault he'd fallen too far.

Tentative, lonely in the dark, Jay typed out a reply.

[JF - 21:13] *nah nothing*
[JF - 21:14] *sorry not to text back sooner, been a long day*
[JF - 21:14] *been in A&E for most of it*
[JF - 21:14] *only just home*
[JF - 21:14] *hope your ok xx*

As soon as he hit send, Jay regretted the kisses. He shut his eyes, breathing in hard. He wasn't thinking straight. He needed painkillers, food and sleep, not awkward texting.

Too late now, he thought miserably, staring at the screen. He covered his eyes with his hands, rubbing them hard. *Put the phone down and get in the shower, idiot. You can ruin your life in the morning.*

His phone buzzed against his knee.

[AH - 21:14] *A&E? Are you alright? xx*

Jay didn't breathe as he replied.

[JF - 21:14] *nothing serious xx*

Alastair saw the text right away. He was watching the window. Somewhere out there across the city, Alastair was sitting and holding his phone, all of his focus in this moment on Jay.

The thought wrenched Jay to the brink of tears, too tired now and in too much pain to keep them in. It didn't count, crying alone. If nobody knew, it wasn't pathetic.

[AH - 21:15] *What happened? xx*

[JF - 21:15] *its not a big deal*
[JF - 21:15] *two guys wanted my wallet, thats all*
[JF - 21:15] *I got away xx*

[AH - 21:16] *I'm sorry, are you telling me you were mugged?*

[JF - 21:16] *ok not MUGGED mugged*
[JF - 21:16] *doctor says I'm fine, nothing broken*
[JF - 21:16] *just been one of those weeks*
[JF - 21:17] *one thing after another haha xx*

No response came. Jay watched the message window nervously, lying on his bed in the darkness as his groin throbbed in discomfort. *Have I said something wrong?* He read back through the short conversation, trying to see where he'd messed up. *Whining on,* he thought. *Haven't even asked about him. I've got no idea what he goes through.*

His phone began to ring.

"Oh—Jesus—"

Jay stared at the screen. *Incoming call from Alastair Harding.* He swallowed, took a second to settle himself, then answered the call with an attempt at casual friendliness.

"H-hi," he squeaked.

Great. Well done, dickhead.

"Forgive a suspicious mind," Alastair said.

At the sound of Alastair's voice, the walls of Jay's chest seemed to cave. He closed his eyes, ignoring the fresh surge of heat which rose behind them. *Jesus, I miss you. I want to go back. Back to Cliveden, back to us.*

"I wasn't certain I could take your reassurances at face value," Alastair continued, gently suspicious. "Did you say you've been in A&E for most of the day?"

Jay gripped his phone, shaking a little as it hurt. "Kind of," he admitted. "I'm alright, though."

"Exactly how injured are you?"

"I'm..." Jay's voice cracked. *I shouldn't be leaning on you. Shouldn't be needing you.* "I'm just tired, that's all. It's fine, Al. Promise."

"Jay," Alastair murmured, and Jay's own name in that voice slid between his ribs like a switchblade. It slit the throats of his defences and dropped them where they stood. In the space of one syllable, he was lost. "You're not convincing me at all that you're alright. Please tell me what on earth happened."

Jay's breath left him in a rush, ejected from his mouth without his permission. He clamped down on it, shaking. *Jesus, don't let me cry. Don't let me cry all over you.*

"S-sorry," he gasped out. "*Wow.* Shit week. I should've had more painkillers by now. I'm going to make food and go take them —sorry to—"

"Are you at home?" Alastair said.

Jay screwed his eyes shut. Sharper heat welled up behind his eyelids.

"Y-yeah. Listen," he said, inhaling, "ignore me. I just had a weird day and I'm a soft bastard. That's all. I'm pulling myself together now."

"Would it help if I brought food?" Alastair asked.

Jay's heart twisted itself in two. *Fuck. Come look after me. Please.*

"Shit," he whispered, shaking. He pressed hard at the bridge of his nose. "Shit. Shit, shit."

"Jay?"

It hurt to speak; it would hurt more not to say. Jay swallowed, hard.

"Can you, erm... can you come here, please?" he said. "If it's not a problem. Jesus, I'm sorry."

"I'll be with you shortly," Alastair said. Jay shuddered in silence, trying to keep his breathing slow. "Text me your address, please. I'll bring food with me. Are you somewhere comfortable for the moment?"

"Yeah. I'm just in bed, lying down."

"Stay there until I reach you." The slam of a door came over the line, followed by the rattle of keys. "Read something quietly on your phone and rest. I'll be with you as soon as I can."

Chapter 13

By the time Alastair reached Jay's address, three more texts had arrived.

> **[JF - 21:20]** *Im sorry to put you out xx*
> **[JF - 21:32]** *I dont mean to be a nightmare xx*
> **[JF - 21:41]** *just a crap mess today xxx*

He responded while standing in the Indian restaurant on the ground floor of Jay's building, waiting near the door to collect their food. He was still in his work clothes. He'd removed his tie and his name badge, then covered the rest of his insignia with his coat, hoping it would help him to blend in. He had nothing whatsoever with him for the night.

All the same, for the first time in days, he felt that he was in the right place.

> **[AH - 21:48]** *I'll be with you in just a few minutes. No apologies necessary.*
> **[AH - 21:48]** *Will you kindly unlock your door for me? xx*

Jay's reply came as Alastair stepped out onto the street, the bell above the door jingling behind him.

> **[JF - 21:54]** *its open*
> **[JF - 21:54]** *front door code is 1111*
> **[JF - 21:54]** *still sorry :(xxx*

Reading the texts, Alastair's heart gave a quiet thump. Jay's nervousness at asking for help was affecting him in ways he didn't usually get to feel. A lot of people answered to Alastair, but none of them ever reached out for him. He hadn't really known it could feel this compelling.

He buzzed his way into the building with the code, making a mental note as he did to encourage Jay to have it changed. Nothing kept behind a guessable 1111 would stay safe for very long. He made his way up the cold and gloomy staircase, his footsteps echoing in the dusty concrete passage, then finally reached the door of flat six.

Knocking, he admitted himself with a cautious creak of the hinges.

It wasn't a large flat by any means, with a homely lack of tidiness that could perhaps be expected of any forty-something-year-old man living on his own. It seemed perfectly comfortable, though. This was a nest, not a residence, and it was a long time since Alastair had been invited into one of those. As he stepped through the door, a familiar scent caught his senses, one he couldn't even begin to break down into its components. It was simply human, male and warm. He hadn't realised until this moment that Jay had a particular scent. The painful days without it had brought it to his notice.

He'd missed it desperately.

As Alastair glanced around, briefly overwhelmed just to be here, movement across the room called his gaze. He looked over and found Jay watching him sadly from the bed, lying on his side atop the covers. One of his eyes was ringed with heavy bruising; he had a visible cut in his lip.

Oh, God.

"Jay," Alastair breathed, abandoning his carrier bag of food upon the couch. He moved over to the bed at once. "Jay, what on earth did they do to you? Let me see..."

Attempting to sit up, Jay gave a pained and nervous shift. It seemed that he had other injuries too, currently hidden beneath his clothing.

"It's not that bad," he tried.

Alastair knelt by the side of the bed. He cupped Jay's face in his gloved hands, studying the black eye with distress.

"Should've just had my painkillers," Jay said weakly. "I'm sorry. I'm making a fuss over nothing."

"Hush," Alastair whispered, and without a thought, he pressed a kiss between Jay's eyes. In the moment, it felt like the most natural gesture in the world. Jay's eyes fell shut in response, overwhelmed by some thought or emotion. "I reject your apology," Alastair said. "It's completely unnecessary. Where else are you injured?"

Jay's expression shifted, embarrassment lowering his eyes.

"Few places," he said. "I took a knee to the groin and there's bruising. A&E told me I'll be fine. Ice and rest. It's just..." His voice skipped as he exhaled. "K-kinda sore to move."

"Of course it is," Alastair said. He laid another small kiss between Jay's eyes, resting his lips there. "Where exactly did this happen?"

"Near work. Nipped out for a sandwich, then... on the way back, two guys just..." Jay shuddered quietly. "Came out of a back door, grabbed me and dragged me into an empty shop. Roughed me up. I kicked one of them in the head and ran."

"Did you say they took your wallet?"

"They were searching for it. Didn't get it, though."

Unusual, Alastair noted silently. *Two men, lying in wait for one wallet in the middle of the day.* Recognising the thought for what it was, he stopped himself at once. Jay would already have spoken to someone about this, slogged his way through the process of descriptions and details and what could be done. Alastair hadn't attended a crime scene in years; the days of high-visibility jackets and tiny notepads were long past him. Even if they hadn't been, he hadn't been asked here to investigate. Jay didn't need a police officer in this moment. He needed someone else.

Brushing his professional instincts aside, Alastair stroked his fingertips through Jay's dishevelled hair.

"Don't move any more than you must," he said. "Rest as you are for a little longer, mm? I'll plate up our food."

"Haven't you eaten?" Jay asked, searching his face.

Alastair stood up from the bed.

"I was working late this evening," he said, ignoring the slight pull in his stomach. *Trying to forget you,* he thought. *Trying to convince myself I didn't care.* "I'd planned to make something at home, but this will do nicely."

He moved over to the kitchen in the corner, checked through the cupboards until he found plates, then set two out on the cramped counter. It was strange to be here so suddenly, so casually. This was Jay's home. These were Jay's things. Even an hour ago, he hadn't dreamed that he'd be spending his evening here.

"Will you be more comfortable out of those clothes?" he asked as he searched for cutlery, glancing across the room.

"Erm... maybe, yeah."

"I'll help you to change once you've eaten."

Jay's voice broke again. "A-Al, I... I really appreciate it. You're kind to be here."

Alastair doubted whether he could really give kindness as his reason for coming. *Desperation to see you* seemed more accurate.

"It's not a problem, Jay," he said. "Not in the least." He cracked open their container of pilau rice and divided it into two portions, glad to have something to occupy his hands. "I'm not willing to be the sort of man who hears that a friend is in pain and does nothing. Did you tell your colleagues that you were attacked?"

"Yeah. Y-yeah, I ran back there. Head of comms took me to A&E and sat with me all day, then brought me back. He offered to come in, but I... I don't really want them to... it's work, you know? I'm meant to be an example."

You don't want them to see you weak. Alastair transferred a few samosas from the foil dish to Jay's plate, his heart thumping. *But you'll let me.*

"I think you're perhaps being a little over-stoic," he said. "A mugging isn't a trifle. I'm sure no one would have thought less of you for accepting their help."

As he carried a plate of food towards the bed, Jay watched him approach with round, exhausted eyes. The poor man looked weary to the bone, all the colour and brightness gone from his face. Alastair put the plate down within his reach, then sat on the edge of the mattress.

"What about yours?" Jay asked.

"I'd like to see you eat something first," Alastair said. Jay shuffled a little closer. "I'll bring my food with your painkillers."

After a moment's visible guilt, Jay acquiesced. He reached out for a samosa, picked it up with caution and crunched quietly through its pastry casing, his eyes closing in relief. A shudder passed through his shoulders as he chewed.

You poor fool, Alastair thought, overwhelmed. *You're half-starved.* He reached out a hand to touch Jay's hair, allowing the repetitive touch calm his own nerves as well. Part of him still couldn't quite believe he was here. His heart had come tearing across London at the first possible hint that he was needed. Only now was his brain catching up, staggering up the stairs and asking in a wheeze what they'd missed.

Odd, how naturally this has come to me. Caring. I have so little experience with it.

But then, caring for Jay was rather different to caring for just anybody. Though it raised a faint flush across the back of Alastair's neck, he didn't feel inclined to stop. Being here in Jay's hour of need was a privilege; there was no shame in being proud of that.

He waited until he'd seen several spoonfuls of chicken makhani pass Jay's lips, then leant down and kissed Jay's forehead.

"I won't be a moment," he murmured. "Keep eating."

Hunting through the kitchen cupboards for a glass, he couldn't help but notice how little Jay owned. He seemed to only have two sets of everything, along with a few spare mugs sourced from corporate networking events. No two of them matched in the slightest. Damage had been repaired wherever it could be, broken handles glued back into place, chipped edges worn smooth with continued use.

Why on earth does that move me? Alastair thought, filling a mug with cold water from the tap. He found himself marveling over Jay's belongings as if they were wondrous treasures. *Why is this affecting me so much?*

He supposed this was a side of Jay that he'd feared he might never see.

"Painkillers?" he checked.

"Oh, erm—next to the sink," Jay said. "Sorry. That drawer's a state."

The packet was easy enough to find among the scattered batteries, lightbulbs and pens. Alastair tucked it into his pocket, picked up his own plate of food and Jay's mug, then carried them carefully back to bed.

Jay shifted as he approached, edging over to make room for two. "Here," he said, his face tightening. "You should—"

Alastair handed him the mug.

"Stay as you are," he said. "I'm perfectly happy to perch." He opened up the packet of painkillers, popped two pills from the blister pack and passed them over to Jay. "Here. Down the hatch."

Jay took his painkillers without protest, washing them down with a long drink of water. His muscles seemed to unwind more and more with every gulp.

When he'd finished, Alastair returned the empty mug to the bedside.

"There," he said. "A little more food now, please. I understand you want to appear invincible and unyielding in the eyes of your colleagues, but I'll be far more impressed by some self-care."

Embarrassment softened Jay's expression. "I'm sorry," he said quietly. "I mean it."

Alastair passed his fingertips over Jay's forehead. "Don't be," he said. He would have journeyed any distance to be here. If it made him a hopeless and lovestruck fool, then that was simply the truth of things. He didn't have the strength to pretend otherwise to himself, not any longer—not after the day he'd just endured. "Once you've cleared your plate, I'll help you change."

"Thanks. That'll be nice."

"Would a shower be welcome?"

"Jesus," Jay whispered, longing washing through his features. "Y-yeah, that'd be..."

"I'll run you a shower, then." Alastair watched Jay eat another spoonful of food, barely conscious of his own plate. Only its heat upon his lap really registered in his thoughts. "A good night's sleep should fix the rest. Alarms on your phone tomorrow, please, to remind you to take painkillers. Carry a sandwich with you to eat as needed."

Jay swallowed his mouthful, shivering. "Al," he whispered. "I..."

"You're either going to apologise again or thank me again. And I promise you that neither's necessary." Alastair tried a smile, hoping he'd made it seem cheerful and easy. Jay didn't need to know it was Alastair's fondest dream just to sit here, just to see him—to know they still shared some connection. "More water?"

Jay flushed. "Eat *your* food."

Alastair put his plate aside, reaching for the empty mug by the bed.

"If it puts you more at ease," he said, hearing Jay start to protest, "shall we consider you under a debt of reciprocation?"

"What do you mean?"

"It means that at some point of my choosing in the future, I'm allowed to summon you gallantly to my aid."

The smile which appeared on Jay's mouth, though small, was genuine.

Alastair smiled in return, unable to help it.

"And you'll arrive with food and painkillers," he said. "Or whatever else it is I happen to require. I can expect lavish amounts of fuss and attention to soothe whatever vexes me."

Jay's smile grew, his eyes bright at last. "Deal," he said.

"Excellent." Alastair leant close, touching his lips between Jay's eyes again. *Why do I have such a need to kiss you here today? Why does it feel so right?* Cupping Jay's cheek, he spoke softly against his forehead.

"Now relax, please. Today is just your turn for fuss. You can have as much of it as you want."

A touch of nervous hope flickered through Jay's gaze. Alastair ran a thumb across his lips, waiting for it to be voiced, and the quiet lingered on. Jay reached up, resting cautious fingertips against Alastair's jaw, and realisation dawned.

He wanted to kiss.

Oh. Alastair glanced down at Jay's mouth. He'd spent the entire afternoon in misery at his desk, feeling more wretched and more bereft with every passing hour. A few texts, a single phone call, and it had all blurred away.

Jay leaned in.

He laid his lips on Alastair's as softly as if they'd never done this—as if they were two shy teenagers outside a cinema, blushing through a first nervous kiss.

Fondness fluttered through Alastair's soul.

Don't be afraid, he wanted to whisper. He leant into the kiss, sweeping his thumb against Jay's cheek. Their lips came together deeply. *You can't imagine what I'd give to you. What I'd be for you, if you asked. You'd never hesitate to kiss me if you knew.*

He kissed Jay until his neck began to beg for a reprieve from the uncomfortable angle. As they parted, Jay seemed to shiver and dropped his gaze.

"Was that okay?" he asked.

Every part of Alastair ached. "Of course it was." He kissed Jay's mouth once last time and felt him tremble. "Let me be what you need, Jay. You've had an awful day."

He hesitated, holding onto the words a moment more.

"We're friends," he said. *No matter the pain. Regardless of whether you'll ever be...* "I'm here."

Jay's fingers threaded through his hair. "Thank you. I mean it."

Alastair leant into their gentle pull, letting Jay hold him close. "I'm glad you texted," he said, proud of the steadiness of his voice. "Have a little more food, please. It'll help."

They stood beside the bath to get Jay undressed, the two of them casting a single silhouette upon the bathroom blinds. As the shower warmed up, water raining down against the curtain, Alastair held Jay close and worked slowly through his clothes, easing them away one by one. There was no need to rush this; he had nowhere to be. Kneeling on the floor, he helped Jay step very gingerly from his jeans and his boxer shorts, Jay's right hand braced on his shoulder for balance. His grip tightened as his bruising was exposed. The purple-grey bloom extended beyond the cover of his pubic hair and up towards his thigh, already yellowing at the edges. His attackers had hurt him with full commitment as to what they were doing.

Alastair's stomach knotted even looking at it.

"I'm so sorry," he said. He kissed the skin nearby, brushing his lips beneath Jay's navel. "A few days to rest and you'll feel fine, I'm sure."

Jay huffed. "Hope so," he said. He touched Alastair's hair, moving a few strands back from his forehead. "I'm not good at being like this. Never have been."

Alastair lifted his eyes. He pressed his cheek against Jay's palm, kissing his wrist. "You're doing wonderfully," he said. "I promise you."

As he rose to his feet, Jay leant close to him again. Alastair wrapped his arms very gently around Jay's middle and held him, hands flat to his back above the waist, taking care not to press on any part of his skin. They kissed softly and unhurriedly, every motion shy.

By the time Alastair noticed, three of his buttons had been opened.

"I'm joining you, am I?" he murmured as Jay slipped apart the fourth.

Jay's lips brushed his mouth. "You said you'd be what I need."

"Indeed I did..." Alastair looked down, watching Jay unfastening the rest of his shirt. "I suppose I can steady you better if I'm there with you. Help you over the side."

Jay made a reluctant sound of agreement. "It's going to hurt getting in. Not looking forward to it."

"Are your painkillers making a difference yet?"

"Sort of. Hard to tell." Slipping apart the last button, Jay stroked the fabric open across Alastair's chest. His hands brushed Alastair's skin with deliberation, slowly taking him—as if years had passed since they'd done this and he needed to remember. "I'm glad you're here," he said, leaning into Alastair's body. His forehead tipped forwards to rest on Alastair's shoulder. "I'm really glad."

Alastair kissed the top of his head, closing his eyes. "You seem a little calmer."

Jay hummed, pushing Alastair's shirt down his arms. "I feel it." He freed Alastair's wrists from each cuff, then put the shirt aside on the radiator. The bathroom was so small he barely needed to turn. "Am I still allowed fuss if I'm feeling better?"

Alastair smiled. "Like antibiotics, I think. Finish the course."

"Mm." Jay's arms went back around his waist, returning to Alastair's hug. He laid his cheek against Alastair's shoulder, and Alastair realised with a breath how easily he fit—how perfectly their heights matched, how effortless it was for them to stand like this.

The wave of warmth and protectiveness it caused took his breath.

"You smell amazing," Jay mumbled against his neck. "You always smell so good."

Alastair's pulse stuttered. "Do I?" he said. All his life, he'd been fastidious with his grooming. Too many of his fellow police officers believed that roll-on deodorant and a breath mint could stand in place of any shower. "I'm... I'm glad you think it's..."

Jay paused, breathing in. "Kinda missed you," he said. "Being close to you."

A riot broke out at once in Alastair's head. *What exactly does that mean?* The obvious answer was that Jay meant the sex, the closeness of their skin—but some desperate and undaunted corner of Alastair's mind wanted to believe Jay meant more than that. The hope was so bright and so ferocious that it made it hard to see what was real and what was merely dreamed. It was getting harder and harder to hold onto sense.

Before he could figure out some way to ask, Jay kissed his cheek and reached towards his belt.

"Let's get clean," he said, curling his fingers around the buckle.

Alastair stepped first into the shower. He took Jay's weight on his forearms, made sure he had a solid grip, and guided him over the side of the bath with great care, feeling every twitch of pain as if they were his own.

"Come here," he said softly, drawing Jay into his arms. "Lean against me... is it very sore?"

Jay panted slightly, resting against his shoulder as Alastair adjusted the spray above them. "Only when I move. It's fine when I stay still or lie down."

"You'll be back in bed soon," Alastair promised. As the water rained from above, he held Jay close to his chest, shielding his face from the spray with a kiss to the forehead. "We'll wash this day away, then send you off to sleep. Your body can repair itself while you rest."

Jay seemed to pause. "When I'm asleep, what'll you do?"

Alastair tried to respond as if the outcome didn't affect him either way.

"Depending on your wishes," he said, "I'll either leave you to sleep—or, if you'd prefer to have someone here, I'll sleep beside you."

Jay's fingers pressed hesitantly into his back. "Would that be a problem?"

Dear God. Never.

"No," Alastair said, reaching for a nearby bottle of shampoo. "No, I'm happy to stay. Whatever you need."

As he washed Jay's hair, they settled back into kissing. Jay was gracious enough to ignore the irrepressible consequences for Alastair of their bodies being close like this, their wet skin in contact, Jay's lips searching gently for more of his kisses. The last thing Jay would want or need in his state of injury was sex, though Alastair's cock seemed disinclined to understand that. They showered slowly, washing each other clean and only breaking their cuddle when necessary. By the time they switched off the water, a sort of hazy calm seemed to blanket Jay's expression, his movements still weary but no longer stiff with pain.

Stepping out of the bath was much easier than getting into it.

"Your painkillers seem to be working," Alastair said, reaching for a towel from the radiator.

Jay nodded, drawing a long and steady breath. "Feeling better," he said. "Safe."

Safe.

"Good." Alastair kissed the top of his head, enjoying his clean hair and the scent of shampoo. "It turns out I'm useful for something."

"You're useful for a lot of things."

"Mm? You think so?"

Jay kissed the curve of Alastair's bare shoulder, his eyes down. "You are to me."

Alastair gathered the towel around Jay's body, distracting himself from the lump in his throat. He couldn't really dry Jay while cuddling him, except to rub his back. It was inefficient, but Jay seemed to want skin contact more than he wanted to be dry.

Only when he started to shiver did Alastair put an end to their embrace. He ran the towel over Jay properly, then took him back to bed.

They got beneath the covers together, turned out the lights and nestled close in the darkness. The shower had left Jay's skin as soft and tactile as anything Alastair had ever felt; it was almost impossible not to stroke him. Jay still seemed to want to kiss, wanted their bodies in contact, and the warm hug of the covers all around them began to raise guilty thoughts in the back of Alastair's mind. He kept them firmly at bay, reminding himself he was here to give comfort, not to ask for it.

Then Jay's hands wandered low on Alastair's stomach, brushing the soft and intimate skin beneath his navel. Alastair's cock gave a twitch.

"You have a groin injury," he said, cursing the slight snap of his breath.

Jay hummed against the curve of his jaw. His touch slid lower, reaching the edge of Alastair's pubic hair.

"You don't," he said, petting.

"Jay—"

"I'll be okay. So long as nothing presses on the bruising." Jay's hand wrapped slowly around Alastair's cock, squeezing its growing firmness. Alastair's pulse leapt. "If we... just like this, maybe?" Jay whispered. "Just touch."

God almighty.

"I couldn't bear to hurt you," Alastair breathed, trying to resist the light and easy stroking. His whole body ached with it, his cock begging him please to be allowed just a few moments more. "I wouldn't forgive myself, Jay."

"You won't hurt me, sunshine." Shifting, Jay eased his way down the bed, brushing kisses over Alastair's chest and stomach as he went. He tipped Alastair over onto his back. "Nothing the matter with my tongue."

Alastair swallowed. He knew he should insist—should protest even attempting something which might cause Jay discomfort.

But as Jay reached his cock, hummed and brush his tongue along its length, Alastair's ability to resist evaporated. He shuddered, watching down the bed as Jay became reacquainted with him: affectionate strokes of his tongue, open-mouthed kisses and lazy nuzzles, soft green eyes looking upwards, keeping hold of Alastair's gaze in reassurance. Even bruised and vulnerable, Jay was beautiful. He wasn't simply gorgeous, as Alastair had seen since the moment they met. He was *beautiful.*

Jay's mouth enrobed his cock, crumbling the last of Alastair's resolve into dust. He released a faint moan into the quiet and closed his eyes. The sensation of slickness and heat drove out all the rest of his thoughts, overwhelmed by the curl of Jay's experienced tongue. Jay had always been extraordinarily good at this. As he'd learned Alastair's body, he'd only gotten better at it. He tended to Alastair with as much patience and care as if they lay here every night, taking his time, winding the pressure in Alastair's abdomen slowly and steadily tighter. He varied the movements of his tongue, never letting his rhythm grow too reliable; he calmed the tremors in Alastair's thighs with his fingertips. Contentment softened his features as he worked.

He seemed happy and at peace, his breathing easy and slow. This was comforting him.

Alastair couldn't take his eyes away.

Jay was wonderful in ways that no one else had ever been. He'd never pressed Alastair for a favour, never once mentioned work or connections. He wasn't here for advancement or gain. He just wanted to be close, even while injured and exhausted. He seemed to want Alastair's deep breaths and gasps like they were painkillers.

As Alastair surrendered at last to the urge to rock, searching for the relief he could feel close at hand, Jay released a shivering sigh around his cock. His hands slid beneath Alastair's open thighs and took hold of his hips, encouraging the movement, wanting him to chase. Alastair's choked groan petered out into a whimper. He came panting only moments later, thrusting as gently as he could into Jay's mouth, one hand buried deep within the soft, damp mess of his hair. Jay swallowed him down, licking him until he'd grown soft.

When he crawled back up the bed, Jay was trembling. Alastair drew him close at once. He turned Jay over onto his back and leant down to kiss his perfect mouth, cutting off the first beginning of a restless whimper.

Jay's fingers shyly captured his hand beneath the sheets, pulling it hopefully downwards.

"You will stop me the *instant* I hurt you," Alastair breathed.

Gathering Alastair's hand around his cock, Jay's face contracted with longing.

"Promise," he gasped. He tipped his head back into the pillows as Alastair began to stroke him, the light and lazy pulls he always enjoyed. "F-fuck. Please. Please like that."

Alastair brushed back Jay's hair with the other hand, gazing into his face as the pleasure slowly came. *Like that, darling. Relax. Let me bring it to you.*

Panting, Jay looked back at him, his pupils swollen wide.

"Fuck," he breathed again, biting down into his lip. His cheeks were already rosy. "Can you..."

"Mm? Tell me, sweet."

"Lube..." Jay's eyes flashed towards the bedside. "I-in the—"

Alastair reached across.

The tube was the one Jay had brought to Cliveden, a cooling gel with mint in its formula. As Alastair pooled some in his hand, its peppermint scent filled the air, transporting him in an instant back to their suite and the noises Jay had made for him there.

Jay remembered, too. Alastair could see it in his eyes, a lost and almost nervous sort of look. As he began to stroke Jay with the gel, spreading it slowly from root to tip, squeezing just a little, Jay pushed up through his grasp. He shuddered, panting. Enjoyment wracked his face.

"Oh, God—" His voice cut and he moaned, his head arching back. "Y-you're so good at this."

Alastair leant down to the beautiful line of his throat, gliding his tongue from his collarbones to chin.

Jay's pitched cry set his heart thrashing.

"Fuck, *fuck,*" Jay gasped, spreading his thighs beneath the sheets. "Please—please can—"

Alastair knew by instinct. As he worked Jay's cock with the same tight strokes, he shifted and reached down to gather Jay's balls in his other hand, massaging them, rolling them in his palm, then finally easing Jay with the gentle tugs he loved.

Jay's back pushed up from the mattress.

"Oh, *fuck...!*" He screwed his head into the pillow, panting. Colour blazed across his face. "Oh, fuck—"

His cock began to flood between Alastair's fingers. Alastair watched in rapture as his face scrunched tight, his mouth opening with the silent cry now shattering its way through his body. He kept his hand moving, coating Jay slowly with his own spill until his features suddenly slackened in relief, his silence breaking open into panted moans. Alastair eased his hand away. He leant down, meeting Jay's desperate post-coital kiss before it could even be requested.

Jay's fingers feathered through his hair, shaking, and their breathing wound down into peace.

When he'd regained the strength to move, Alastair went briefly to the bathroom for a washcloth. He gathered Jay close to his chest, cleaning off his cock and his stomach for him, wanting him to feel comfortable as he slept. Jay barely stirred. He was drifting close to sleep already, knocked out by the rush of hormones and relief. Orgasm had done more to guarantee his good night's rest than any sleeping pill could.

Alastair cradled Jay as he cleaned him, kissing his forehead, then tossed the cloth away into the bathroom. It could be dealt with tomorrow. He didn't intend to move again until the morning.

"You okay?" Jay mumbled as Alastair drew the covers up around him.

Alastair kissed between his eyes.

"Perfectly," he said, his voice low in his throat. "Now promise me on your life I didn't hurt you."

Jay grinned, cuddling closer. "Promise. Always gentle with me."

Alastair hummed. "I'm justifying to myself that it was medicinal," he said, "and you'll sleep better."

Jay's eyes glittered. "Can I have another dose in the morning?"

"Beast." Alastair brushed back his hair, resting a kiss upon his forehead. "Of painkillers, yes. You certainly can."

"What about another dose of you?"

"If you're good and take your painkillers without complaint, yes."

"Mhm. Seems fair." Jay stirred, wrapping one arm around Alastair's waist. "Thank you for coming to look after me. I mean it."

"I'm glad you're feeling better," Alastair said. He paused, retaining the thought for a moment. He didn't know if it was a sentiment too far. "I like your company, Jay. It's no hardship being with you."

"Yeah?" Jay hesitated, pressing his cheek to Alastair's shoulder. "I'm not overstepping our—?"

Please. Please overstep it. "No. No, I'm... very happy."

"With how things are?"

"Yes. I hope you're happy, too. I hope you want to continue our association."

Jay's eyelashes brushed Alastair's neck.

"Yeah," he whispered. Alastair's heart pulled tight, suddenly incapable of beating. "Yeah, sunshine. I like what we've got. It... works for you, does it? Just like this?"

I want you to be mine. I don't even know what that would involve. I don't know how it would be different, how it would feel, but... just knowing... knowing you care for me, belong to me, wish to stay with me...

Alastair forced himself to speak, feeling as if he were teetering on the edge of a precipice.

"I'm glad you reached for me tonight," he said. "I'm glad you contacted me. If you need someone in this way again, I... hope you know I'd be here for you. I like having the chance to look after you."

Jay began to stroke between his shoulders.

"Can I text you?" he asked. "During the week, I mean? Just to check in on each other. Touch base."

Oh, God. "Of course you can."

"Won't bombard you, I promise. I know you're busy."

I'd discard it all for you. I'd find the time. I would magic time into being, just to give it to you. If you wanted me to come home at six o'clock every night, I'd find a way.

"I'd like to hear from you," Alastair said, touching his lips to Jay's temple. "That would be nice."

For a while, they lay in silence and stroked each other's skin, drifting a little closer towards sleep. A question began attempting to wrestle its way out of Alastair's throat. Once he'd noticed it, he feared he wouldn't rest unless he asked. He thought of Juliet—of what he would say to her tomorrow, regarding this evening—and found the courage.

"Jay?"

"Mm, love?"

Alastair ignored the tight contraction in his chest. "Can I ask you something?"

"S-sure."

Why did your voice skip? What are you worried I'm going to ask?

"Go on," Jay said. "I'm listening."

There was no retreat now. Alastair told himself there were a galaxy of reasons he might want to ask this—health, security, reasonable curiosity—and asked.

"Are you sleeping with other people?"

There came a long and nervous silence.

"No," Jay said, at last. He placed a small kiss against the side of Alastair's neck. "Not right now. I'm... busy with work. Barely even have time to do my laundry."

'Not right now.'

Alastair found himself unable to respond. He kept stroking the back of Jay's hair, trying to act as if the answer had only vaguely interested him.

"Is that alright?" Jay asked after a moment. "It's not... don't feel pressured by that. It's just circumstances. I'm not pushing for any kind of... you know, commitment. You and me."

Oh.

"I just wondered," Alastair said. It seemed like the right thing to say. "I like seeing you this way. This suits me."

"I like seeing you, too." Jay's arms tightened. "I don't want things to change."

Alastair said nothing, brushing through Jay's hair. He could barely feel the soft brown strands against his fingertips.

"Have I freaked you out?" Jay asked.

Alastair surfaced from his thoughts. His body felt as if it were empty, hollow space where some sense of self should be. "Not at all. Why would you have freaked me out?"

"Promise?"

"Yes, I... I promise. But why would—"

"Sorry. I'm clumsy with this stuff. Just... I like you. You like me. That's all we need, right?" Jay pressed his cheek to Alastair's. "Things're better simple."

The words felt like a rejection; Jay's arms around him felt like a plea.

Alastair closed his eyes. His throat strained with words unsaid and he didn't understand—though he would, with help. For tonight, Jay still seemed to want to hold him. That was enough.

He held Jay tighter, relieved and distressed in equal measure as Jay pulled him close to kiss.

Do you want to kiss me? Alastair wondered, his heart pounding. *Or do you want me to stop talking?*

Oh, God. You old fool. It doesn't matter. He's here and he's kissing you. That can only be a good thing.

Juliet will understand.

When their lips parted, Jay's fingers seemed to be shaking. Their noses rubbed in the darkness.

"No worries, sunshine," he said. "Let's keep it easy."

God help me. This counts as easy.

Alastair guided Jay's head to his shoulder, as if he simply wished to settle down to sleep. He didn't want Jay to notice the gloss to his eyes in the darkness, nor catch any hint of distress in his face. He didn't know if there even *was* a reason to be distressed. He felt it, all the same.

For fear that words would show more of his soul than he wanted to be seen, he said what seemed safest.

"You should rest, Jay." *Please stay with me.*

Jay hesitated. "Sleep tight, yeah?"

Alastair wasn't sure how much longer he stayed awake. It could have been another hour or more, his thoughts drifting from one thing Jay had said to the next. He finally forced himself to focus not on his panicked analysis, but on committing them to memory for someone more qualified in these matters to deal with.

He tried to sleep, unmoving in the darkness, his breathing slow and his thoughts still in chaos.

He was kept awake even longer by the strange conviction that Jay, too, lay unsleeping. He didn't know what made him think it. Jay seemed to be dreaming soundlessly, quiet and still against his chest, and he didn't dare to ask. He didn't want to wake Jay if he *was* asleep, thereby revealing that he himself had lain awake here in turmoil into the night.

It was some time before sleep finally came.

When it did, it was not restful.

Chapter 14

[AH - 06:04] *Good morning. I'm sending you a map reference for pick-up. No earlier than 8am please.*
[AH - 06:04] *<google.com/maps/@51.532...>*

[JN - 06:07] *Is that link correct? Appears to be an Indian restaurant*

[AH - 06:13] *I'll be waiting outside the Indian restaurant.*

[JN - 06:14] *The Eastern Paradise doesn't seem to be listed as one of your registered secure residences*

[AH - 06:18] *There were extenuating circumstances. I'm perfectly safe.*
[AH - 06:18] *Pick-up at 8am please.*

[JN - 06:19] *Are these extenuating circumstances also known as Jay Fieldhouse?*

[AH - 06:19] *Yes.*

[JN - 06:20] *Hope all is well*

[AH - 06:20] *Pick-up at 8am.*

COLD GREY RAIN LASHED THE LONDON ROADS. JULIET WATCHED THE pavement as they drove, drumming her rose gold-painted nails against two large take-out coffees. She hadn't slept particularly well, unable to stop picturing the poor man so quietly broken at his desk. Whether it was wise of her or not, she was now invested in this, and heaven knew that Alastair Harding was overdue some personal happiness. It would be nice to see him get it.

At last, she spotted his familiar silhouette in the distance, standing awkwardly at the roadside in the downpour with his shoulders held high and stiff.

"There, Larry," she murmured. "On the corner."

Larry gave an absent-minded nod, already switching lanes. "I see him."

"You don't mind the privacy screen again today, do you?"

"No, miss. Not at all." Larry pulled up to the traffic lights. He adjusted the windscreen wipers as they waited, trying to clear some of the deluge from the front window. "Is the commissioner alright lately, miss?"

For a moment, Juliet wondered what possible tone she might use to convey this. *He has a very serious case of feelings, Larry. It's difficult. He should never have been trusted to manage them on his own.*

"He'll be perfectly fine," she said as the lights released them. "He's experiencing a few personal troubles, but I anticipate they'll clear up soon enough."

Larry risked a glance at her in the rearview mirror. "Hope it's not strife with his fella," he said. "Never seen him like that with somebody before. It'd be a shame if it didn't work out."

Privately touched by the concern, Juliet returned him a look of very gentle warning. "Until you receive a wedding invitation, Larry, I'd advise not knowing anything about it."

He hummed, easing the car towards the kerb. "Very good, miss."

The doors unlocked by themselves with a clunk. Half a second later, the backseat blew open and admitted a dripping Alastair, who took his seat with some small blasphemy muttered under his breath. He slammed the door behind him, cutting off the roar of the rain, and gratefully accepted a towel from Juliet.

"Bloody dreadful out there," he said, scrubbing his head and his face. It left his hair in chaos, but marginally drier. "Quite certain I spotted an ark full of animals floating past..."

As he ran the towel over his coat, blotting off the worst of it, Juliet discreetly closed the privacy screen. She let him dry off and attend to his seatbelt, then took back the towel from him, swapping it for a cup of coffee.

"I'm afraid we haven't long," she said, as the car pulled back into traffic. "Richard Garston has moved your meeting with him forward to nine, and we'll—"

"Again?"

"Yes."

"Oh, for the love of—"

"Yes, I know."

"—such a despotic little tosser, just to prove he—"

"Yes, sir. I *know* he is. And you have your usual Friday with the home secretary at eleven, and I'll also need to brief you on the protection command developments before then. Now, *what happened last night?"*

Alastair looked down at the white plastic lid of his cup, steeling himself. It took him a moment to speak. "I haven't the faintest idea."

Juliet held in a sigh.

"You'd better start from the top," she said, cracking the lid from her own coffee to speed its cooling. "I'm assuming he eventually replied to your text?"

"Yes. Late. It turned out he'd spent most of the day in the emergency department."

"He'd—*what?* Why?"

"He was mugged. God help me, I forgot to even press him about it this morning. He seems determined to believe it was a completely random attack. But from what he's said to me, they were lying in wait on a route he habitually takes to buy his lunch."

Juliet bit the corner of her lip. "Sir, that's..."

"I know," Alastair said, fixing her with his stare. "I'm fully aware. And he insisted on going into work today. Short of hiding his keys or sitting on his chest, there was nothing I could do to stop him."

Juliet put the thought to one side, breathing it out. *One problem at a time.*

"Alright," she said. "So he'd been in the emergency department."

"Yes. With various injuries, chief among them a lot of painful bruising to his groin. He'd since gotten home, neglected to take any painkillers, and ended up in distress."

"And he asked you for help?"

Flushing, Alastair's eyes sought the refuge of the rainy window. "I had to call him before he'd admit it, but yes. I offered to bring him food and he asked me to come over."

Juliet thought quickly, squeezing the sides of her coffee cup. "Okay. Okay, I see."

Fieldhouse would probably have had other social contacts—friends, work mates, other people he might have relied on for assistance. She thought briefly of some of the men with whom she'd shared a purely casual arrangement, and imagined asking them to bring her food after a miserable afternoon in the hospital.

She looked Alastair in the eye. "I think it's a good sign he contacted you," she said. "A *very* good sign. That sort of comfort in relying on you indicates..."

No joy lightened his expression.

Juliet's heart fell. "Oh," she said.

He winced a little. "I'm not certain where to begin."

That wasn't promising, either. "Let's try chronologically," Juliet said, willing herself—and him—to remain level-headed. "You arrived at his flat."

"He was in pain and uncomfortable," Alastair said. "He hadn't eaten."

Again, Juliet imagined herself in pain after a hospital visit, in need of food and comfort, and ran through her mind the very small number of people she would wish ever to see her in that condition. Sex friends were not among them.

"He felt guilty for asking me to come," Alastair added. Juliet processed this, nodding, as the rain battered down against the window. "I reassured him and encouraged him to eat. I brought painkillers to him. He was... somewhat fragile and very nervous, so I suggested he could just reciprocate at some point in the future."

"How did he respond to that?"

"Favourably. He agreed. And he settled, certainly." A little colour rose in Alastair's face. "He... wanted to kiss. Asked if it was alright."

God. Oh, God. Juliet sat up in her seat, asking this with care. "Sir, my next question might be indelicate."

He braced himself, shivering. "Such is this entire situation."

"Was this kissing as a preface to sex?"

"No," Alastair replied, and took an embarrassed drink of coffee. "Not at that point. It seemed just to be in hope of comfort. Afterwards we kept on eating."

Juliet couldn't suppress the small leap of excitement within her chest.

"That sounds hopeful," she said. "What happened next?"

He visibly searched through his memories, gathering them all into order. "We showered together. It was..."

Juliet raised an eyebrow. "Intimate?"

"If you're meaning that as a euphemism for a specific form of contact, no. But we were close. He wanted touch. Affection. He was still very fragile and I comforted him."

Christ, my heart. I shan't survive this.

"And then?" Juliet said.

Slight guilt flickered across his face, his gaze back on the window. "There, erm... there was then intimacy."

Juliet managed not to sigh. "Forgive me for asking this, but... with a *groin injury?*"

"With bruising," Alastair said with a pained frown, shifting in his seat. "And it was extremely careful intimacy, *not* initiated by me."

Juliet exhaled, wishing he hadn't said it. The possibility that Jay had merely wanted sex as comfort, and taken the additional fuss as a nice bonus, couldn't be discounted. The nature of his injuries made it less likely, but it would take nothing short of full castration to dampen some men's interest in sex. Jay Fieldhouse could be one of them.

"What then?" she asked, and watched Alastair's expression tighten, nervousness holding something back.

"We... talked," he said.

Oh no. "About?"

He took a lengthy sip of coffee. "In complete honesty, I'm not sure."

"Right," Juliet said, wondering if she should just plant a recording device on him for next time—perhaps even a wire to his ear, feed him instructions line by line. It would certainly be simpler. "Tell me what you can."

Alastair inhaled. "He thanked me for coming to look after him," he said. "I told him it wasn't a problem, and I liked his company."

Good, Juliet thought. *Subtle. Hopeful.*

"He asked if I was happy," Alastair went on, "with our... with how things are. I said I was. He said, *'I like what we've got'.*"

Juliet bit her lip. "Did he mean—?"

Alastair looked into her face, struggling to find his reply.

"I don't know," he said. "I suppose I didn't want to press things, in case he... and so I said I was glad that he'd reached out to me, and it was nice having the chance to care for him. That I'd do so in future if needed."

It had been brave, Juliet thought, noting quietly that he had far more of a talent for this sort of negotiation than he credited himself.

From what he'd said, he'd been presenting Jay with shining opportunities to express a wish for greater connection. It was a wise tactic, flawed only in that it required the recipient to pick up on the chances they were being given.

"How did he respond?" she asked, preparing herself.

Alastair hesitated, swallowing. "He asked if could text me during the week. Touch base, he said. I told him I'd like that."

Juliet nearly screamed. "That's *wonderful!*"

"But then—"

"Oh, God."

"—I suppose I... well, I felt braver than I should have. I remembered what you and I had talked about. I thought that if I confirmed we're not sleeping with other people, then it might pave the way to... or at least remove an obstacle."

Juliet's blood ran briefly cold. *Please,* she thought. *Please tell me he's not...*

"And so I asked," Alastair continued, pale.

Juliet breathed in. "Tell me."

The response surprised her. "He told me that he isn't."

Juliet's forehead crumpled; she opened up her mouth.

"—'right now'," he finished, and her heart sank into her stomach. She closed her mouth.

"Ah," she said.

"He then told me he isn't pushing for any kind of commitment. Between the two of us."

Oh, no. "How did you respond?" Juliet asked, her coffee ignored in her lap.

Alastair read her face, his spirits visibly fading along with hers. "I told him I like seeing him. That it suits me. And he said he didn't want things to change."

Juliet made no reply, wishing she could see some way to revive this. She'd never really believed in the school of thought which held that men played complex psychological games. In her experience, men were by nature very likely to give direct and honest answers, even brutishly honest, at least on the first few occasions they were asked. Very few of them possessed the emotional agility for games. If they wanted something, they were usually just inclined to admit it.

"But then..."

Juliet blinked out of her thoughts. She watched Alastair's expression crease as he shook his head, something tight and unsettled gathering in the lines around his eyes.

"He suddenly seemed to worry," he said.

"Worry?" Juliet wondered if she should be allowing herself to hope. She wanted to, desperately, but it might be premature. "Worry about what?"

"I... don't fully know, to be frank. He said he hoped he hadn't 'freaked me out'. He said he was 'clumsy with this stuff', and that things are better simple, but he... well, he held me very tightly as he said it. And he kissed me. He seemed distressed, rather than..."

The silence stretched. "Conciliatory?" Juliet suggested.

Alastair met her eyes. "There wasn't pity in it," he said. "He was nervous again. Quiet. He still wanted to sleep in my arms. I... I'd have thought if he wanted to distance himself from me, and put some limits on our association, then he..."

Juliet could barely breathe. "How was he this morning?"

She watched him struggling to understand. "Bright," he said at last. "Friendly."

"Friendly?"

"Yes. I woke up to find he was already out of bed. He insisted on making me breakfast. Seemed eager for conversation. The television was on, and we..."

Alastair shook his head, bewildered, his coffee steaming by itself in his lap.

"We discussed the news," he said, shrugging. She'd never seen him shrug before, not once in three years. "He teased me about the recent set of national crime statistics. He made me coffee."

Something wasn't adding up here. Juliet could sense a space beginning to form within the unsaid; she could see its hazy outline starting to emerge. She hoped to God it was what she thought it might be.

"Would you say he was... *determinedly* bright?" she said.

Alastair inhaled, watching a streak of rain track its way down the window. "Perhaps."

"Was he affectionate towards you?"

His gaze slid into recent memories. Though he frowned, it was in confusion rather than disagreement.

"Not at first," he said. "He was busy in the kitchen, then busy in the bathroom. I... got a little anxious that he was occupying himself on purpose. I reached for him as he was dressing. Buttoned his shirt for him."

Juliet hardly dared to break the silence. "How did he react?"

Alastair looked down into his coffee.

"Stepped into my arms," he muttered. His throat muscles shifted and he took a drink, shutting his eyes for a second. "He let me hold him for... for quite some time. I touched his hair. He didn't say a word."

Juliet's heart continued to pound, watching the pieces of a much larger puzzle clicking into place one by one. "How did he say goodbye to you?"

"Showed me to the door," he said weakly, lost. "I reminded him of his painkillers, and that he should take care of his health. Told him I hoped he felt better soon. We made some small joke about him sending me a photograph of his lunch as proof of self-care. He thanked me again for coming. He seemed tense, but I... I didn't get the impression he wanted me to hurry up and leave."

Juliet gripped her coffee cup for strength. "He kissed you goodbye," she said. "Didn't he?"

Alastair looked up into her eyes.

"He was shaking." Distress caused the muscles around his jaw to clench. The rest escaped him in a rush of breath, his gaze dropping down into his lap. "I don't understand it, Juliet. I don't see what on earth went wrong."

"When he told you he wasn't pushing for commitment," Juliet said, "were those his *exact* words? That he *wasn't pushing,* as opposed to he *didn't want?"*

"If memory serves, yes."

"And when he said he didn't want things to change—sir, this is important—had you given him some indication that *you* wanted things to change?"

Alastair paled at once, shaking his head. "No," he said. "No, I wouldn't have dared."

"Did you express to him you're happy with your current arrangement?"

"I did, but... I didn't mean to the exclusion of..."

Juliet sat forwards in her seat. She reached out, placing a hand upon his arm.

"I'm about to suggest something to you," she said. His gaze flickered, worried, but it didn't leave her face. "It would be helpful to our project for you to consider this possibility very carefully."

Alastair waited, regarding her with no small amount of concern.

Juliet held his eyes.

"In trying to hold back your feelings for him," she said, "is there a chance you've given him the impression that you wouldn't want a relationship? That you're not available for an emotional commitment?"

Alastair searched her face.

"I can't see how I'd have done that," he said. "Sometimes I think he sees my every thought. He... he must realise that I'm..."

Juliet pressed her teeth very gently into the side of her tongue. "Think about it during the day," she said. "Humour me. Trial the possibility."

"If you insist," he said, still looking thoroughly unconvinced.

Relieved, Juliet sat back in her seat. She finally took a drink of her coffee, reassured there might just be hope for the poor fools yet. "One other thing I'd recommend," she said as she replaced the lid. "At one o'clock, I want you to text him, asking him where your photograph of his lunch is."

Alastair regarded her over his coffee cup, baffled. "Will that help?"

"Yes," she said. "In fact, I'll stake my remaining annual leave that he responds within five minutes. And I'll stake next year's leave that his response includes at least one question."

"A question?" He looked at her as if she were suddenly speaking Hungarian. "Why a question?"

"In the hope it'll prompt you to text him back," Juliet said. "Can we please spend these final few minutes on the question of Ian Straker?"

Alastair lifted his fingers wearily to the bridge of his nose. "Yes," he said, rubbing. "Yes, of course we can. What do you recommend I do?"

"I know you're reluctant to authorise the security check. I appreciate it's usually done when there's an agreed relationship underway. But if you're seeing him this frequently, especially overnight at his residence, he's functionally your partner. And I know," she added quickly, seeing him start to protest, "that you worry you're tempting fate by naming him as such. Normally I'd back down and leave you just to brood over there in your lily pond of nameless fears."

His mouth twisted, fighting the humour.

"But these are special circumstances," she said, raising an eyebrow. "He's quite clearly under threat. And once the security check has gone through, he becomes eligible for security measures. I can arrange covert protection for him. He won't realise that anything's in place, but he'll be safe."

Letting out a breath, Alastair surrendered. "Fine," he said. "I'll authorise it. Run the bloody checks. Do *not* bring anything to his notice."

"I'll handle it myself," Juliet promised. "It might take me a few days, especially if he's classed as a protected person. I'll run any security measures by you before I implement them."

"Good." Alastair put his head back, closing his eyes. A drying tuft of copper hair flopped forwards onto his forehead. "Excellent. Thank you. Even as a friend, he... well, I want him to be safe."

He paused, gatheringup the courage to give something voice.

"And we *are* close," he admitted, as the rain rumbled on against the window. "Just not yet as close as I'd like."

Juliet's chest tightened, moved by the sight of him like this. They'd always been very comfortable with each other, conspiratorial from day one, but he'd never shown her this much of his heart. She'd never seen him so uncertain of the world around him and his place in it.

She hoped that he would end up somewhere happy.

"Give it time, sir," she murmured. "I'm told love is a long game."

"I like seeing you this way. This suits me."

It was hard to focus on work this morning. It was hard to focus on anything. Jay had so far spent an hour scrolling dully through his emails, clicking from one to the next in the hope they might start answering themselves. He couldn't stop himself from replaying the worst parts of last night, over and over on a loop in his mind—like if he only imagined hard enough, he could somehow reshoot them and make things okay.

"I'm happy with how things are."

He wished Alastair hadn't asked about other people. He wished he'd downplayed his own reply, and better yet shut the fuck up straight after—just let the honesty be what it was. Trying to act chill and breezy hadn't fixed a thing. He'd unsettled Alastair and he knew it, then made it all so much worse by putting on a front. Alastair wasn't an idiot. He'd clearly seen through the handwaving and the backtracking.

The truth was that his silence had hurt like hell. It hurt even more each time that Jay remembered. Everything had been so perfect, then so thoroughly crap. It didn't help that he couldn't now drink coffee without stinging the cut in his lip, nor shift in his chair without a sharp wince of pain through his groin.

While his brain understood that this whole thing had been ready to collapse at any second, his heart wasn't ready to hear it—even now.

Story of my life, Jay thought, abandoning his emails to push both his hands into his hair. He rubbed hard with his fingertips as he thought. *Nothing's ever mine. Only borrowing it all for a while.* He'd never known when to quit and just be grateful for what he had. It hadn't been enough to get out of Manchester; he'd begged them to let him go to London. Once he arrived, it hadn't been enough to keep some ordinary job in a bar or in a coffee house. He'd had to start dreaming of something bigger. He hadn't even let it just stay as a small charity. He'd expanded it, pushed it, started winning bloody awards, and sooner or later it would all come crashing down in flames. He'd beckoned an entire organisation's worth of people to come join him on a plane that he knew was leaking fuel. He should have known his place, but he hadn't.

Just like he should have known his place with Alastair—kept things simple, had some fun. Instead he had to go and fall in love.

Jesus, when will I learn to just...

The knock against his door barely registered in his ears. As Jay lifted his weary head from his hands, the door opened with a click and Connor slipped inside. Today's shirt was black with an abundance of printed flamingos, his expression uncharacteristically subdued. He calmly closed the door behind him, then without invitation came over to Jay's desk, scraped a chair very carefully into place, and sat down.

Jay waited, watching him and trying not to frown.

Leaning back in his chair, Connor gave him a look of apology.

"They've picked me as the ambassador," he explained. "I'm here to persuade you to take your grisly facial injuries, and your limp, and go home to rest. But I know that's not going to happen. There's no way on this planet you'll go home. So if you could tell them all I tried very hard, but you stuck to your guns and then turned me out of your office, I'd appreciate it."

Jay stayed silent, suspecting there was more to come.

"Now that's done with," Connor said, taking a breath. He gated his hands together in his lap. "Are you okay?"

Jay's heart strained. He wasn't, and the truth sat so close to the surface that keeping it down took serious effort.

"I'm fine," he said instinctively. "Just... you know. Grisly facial injuries. And I've got a lot of..." He gestured at his screen. "Stuff to sort. Annual report for the trustees to draft. I'm fine."

Connor's mouth pulled outwards at the edges, the gentlest look of doubt.

"That doesn't usually stress you out," he said. "I've seen you write one every year, and it's never made you... well, you seem troubled lately. That's all. And I know you're very private, and you like to keep us all at a distance. But if you want to take ten minutes just to vent some stuff..."

He gave an easy shrug.

"Might help," he said. "I'm stuck here for ten minutes anyway, so they'll all think I gave it my best shot. I'll delete anything I hear from my head as I go."

Something strangely nauseous welled up in the back of Jay's throat. "What do you mean, 'keep us all at a distance'?"

Connor tried a wary smile. "Come on, Jay."

"Seriously," Jay said. "What're you... do you all think I'm aloof or something?"

"It's not a *bad* thing," Connor said. "Most places, the boss apes on as if you're best friends forever, making sure you can't ever say no to anything. Then when it's time to kick you in the face, suddenly *we are a professional organisation and we suggest you take this matter seriously.* The whiplash is unreal. But you're above all that, and it's..."

He shrugged again.

"Refreshing," he supposed. "And I get why it's a good idea. I do. But something's eating you, and I'm here if you want to get it out. Or if you want to get on with your work, that's fine too. Whatever helps the most."

Jesus.

For a few moments, Jay didn't know what to say. It was true he'd never shared much of his personal life at work. He'd thought it was only sensible, given that even the most casual discussions ran two simple questions away from disaster. *So, where did you grow up? What brought you to London?* Any conversation about his upbringing was essentially a piece of theatre, and Jay didn't like lying. He didn't like people forming an opinion of him based on things that just weren't true.

He hadn't realised his reticence was obvious, though. He'd assumed that the closed door would just blend into the wall, and nobody would care what was behind it.

It looked like he'd accidentally created a mystery.

Looking into Connor's face, Jay drew a slow and careful breath. Some things he just couldn't share. It wasn't an option, and he hated the distance that it put between him and other people. He hated that it turned out other people could see him doing it.

He supposed he could share some things, though.

He hadn't opened up in so long that it took him a moment to remember how. He swallowed a little, trying to locate the way in.

"I, erm... started seeing someone," he said. Connor nodded, listening without a word. "Someone I... well, I say 'seeing'... hooking up. Someone I maybe shouldn't have. I wasn't looking for it."

Heat broke out across Jay's face.

"You won't even believe me if I tell you," he muttered. "Seriously, I don't know how I stumbled into this."

Connor's expression didn't change. "Married?" he checked gently.

Jay huffed.

"I'm not that much of a wanker," he said. It helped somehow, the lack of judgement in Connor's face—as if he'd still be listening, even if Jay had said yes. "No, he's... y-yikes. Okay, I'm just going to tell you. Otherwise we'll be here all day. You remember the awards evening?"

Connor's forehead tightened, recalling. As he added two and two together, his expression flashed with surprise, his eyebrows popping upwards.

"Really?" he said. "The commissioner?"

Oh, shit. "I don't know how it happened," Jay said, his face turning redder than ever. "We just... well, we had a few drinks, then... somehow I was back at his flat. Stayed the night. We've been meeting up since then."

Connor let out a low whistle. "Damn," he said. "That's quite a feat, Jay. Shoot for the stars, huh?"

Jay tried to laugh. Talking about Alastair made it all feel real again. It wasn't just something in his head, a daydream he'd cooked up one day when bored—and now he'd started talking, he couldn't bring himself to stop. He felt like an old mug with a tiny little crack in just the wrong place. One jolt, and everything was spilling out.

"Have you heard of Cliveden?" he asked.

Connor shook his head.

Jay looked down at his desk, trying to find some way to describe it without choking up. "Fancy hotel out in the... we were there last weekend. Him and me. Never seen anywhere like it in my life."

"Wow," Connor mumbled. "So this is *more* than... you made it sound like you were just knocking boots. But this is a whole thing?"

Jay covered his face for a moment, then pushed his hands back into his hair. "No," he said. "No, it's... I screwed it up last night. I fucked it all up."

"Yeah? What happened?"

"He came over to keep an eye on me. Fetched food. Everything was great, then he asked me if we're still seeing other people. I told him there's just him. He went all quiet, and I... Jesus, Connor, don't let me grizzle at you about this crap. I need to do some work."

"You need to get this out," Connor said, tapping the edge of Jay's desk with his fingertips. "It's clearly killing you. So he wants to keep seeing other people?"

Jay attempted to shrug.

"I guess so," he said, ignoring the hot stab of pain it sent through his chest. "He said he likes things as they are. I don't know, I just... I guess I'd started fooling myself that he wanted more, same as me."

Connor took this on board, thinking. "He wants to keep on with you, though?"

Jay nodded numbly, rubbing the back of his neck. If he had any sense, then for the sake of his dignity, he knew that he should pull away. He should take his hurt feelings and his fluttering heart away from Alastair, keep them where they couldn't do any more damage—maybe try proper dating, meet some people. Find someone to be with who wasn't the keystone of British policing.

But that meant opening up to strangers. There'd be first dates, nervous dinners and reasonable questions. He'd just be building another house above an unexploded bomb, tricking somebody into liking him when he knew damn well he was a fraud.

Besides, he was fooling himself if he thought he wanted *someone.* He didn't want some new person to be with.

He wanted Alastair.

Connor's voice came from a hundred miles away, hazy and half-formed on the edge of Jay's awareness.

"Maybe he just needs a bit more time," Connor said. "He asked you about it, right? So it's clearly on his mind. Maybe he's just figuring out how you'd fit in with everything he's got going on."

Jay forced himself to concentrate, his heart thumping.

"I mean, if you're doing weekend breaks," Connor went on, offering a smile, "and he's bringing you food when you've been in the emergency department all day... there's clearly *something* there, right?"

Jay swallowed, staring across his desk. "You think?"

"Sure. When did he head off?"

"This morning. Stayed the night."

"Yeah? And did things seem alright?"

Jay's stomach tightened, reluctant to recall this morning. He'd been chirping away like a canary, trying to keep things bright and easy—trying not to cry whenever Alastair hugged him or kissed him.

"I think so," he said. "I kept a lid on it, at least. He didn't seem in a rush to get away."

Connor reached across the desk, giving Jay's arm a small and bracing nudge.

"Time," he advised. "Everyone starts out claiming they're looking for casual. Pretty standard, in my experience. And it's almost never true. Some people just keep it all locked up until they're sure, that's all."

"Yeah?" Jay supposed he'd never actually tried dating in London. He'd never done much dating at all, even before he'd moved. Relationships tended to simply happen to him, sprouting up out of nowhere like dandelions through cracks in the pavement. "So it's... it's maybe a case of patience?"

"If he wants to keep seeing you," Connor said, "and he was alright with you this morning, I'd say you're still in the game."

Jay's pulse skittered. "He's massively out of my league, though. He's the head of London policing."

"So?" Connor said. "You're a catch, too. Hold your head up, Jay."

It was a kind thing to say. Jay hadn't expected to hear a lot of kindness this morning, and even if the hope seemed small, it was far more than he'd had ten minutes ago.

He smiled a little, releasing some of the tension in his shoulders.

"I'm sorry to dump this on you," he said awkwardly.

"I offered," Connor said, amused. "Besides, this week's been a shocker. You were literally mugged less than twenty four hours ago. Out of interest, was there any chance at all you'd have considered going home?"

Jay huffed. "No. Not one."

Connor's smile seemed to twinkle. "See?" he said. "I knew I knew you." He leant forwards in his chair, peeked inside Jay's coffee mug and found it empty. "And *there's* why you're getting nowhere fast. Shall I fix this?"

As Connor picked up the mug and got to his feet, Jay found his heart lodged in the back of his mouth.

"Connor?" he said, as Connor strolled towards the door.

Connor looked back with a smile. "Yep?"

"Thanks for listening," Jay said. "I mean it." He hesitated, hoping this wasn't too much. "I don't mean to keep you all at a distance. It's... there's good reasons I... just please don't think it's anything to do with you, will you? You all mean the world to me."

"No worries, boss," Connor said. "If you ever fancy a pint after work, let me know."

He let himself out of Jay's office and tapped away down the corridor.

Jay turned his eyes back to his emails, numb. Whatever was going to happen with Alastair, he couldn't do anything about it now. Sitting here sulking certainly wouldn't help. There were things he should be doing, people waiting on him. Long after Alastair and his human comforts were gone, there would still be kids in this city circling the drain. Jay had brought himself to London to make amends, not to bag a posh husband and swan around Cliveden playing pretend.

Sitting up straight in his chair, he returned to the top of his emails and opened up the first in line.

Borrowed time, he told himself. *Use it wisely.*

He worked solidly until twelve, determined not to waste any more of the day. He ate his sandwich and took his painkillers, ignoring the uncomfortable clouds of memory it kicked up. He limped downstairs for a smoke, limped back up, made himself another coffee and got on with his report for the trustees. *At least there's plenty to do,* he reflected, taking comfort in small mercies. He'd achieved more today than he expected.

When his phone gave a bleep not long before one, Jay checked it without thinking, expecting something to do with work.

The name on the screen stopped the world spinning.

Jay opened up the message at once, barely breathing.

> **[AH - 12:59]** *I think you promised me something this morning.*
>
> **[AH - 12:59]** *Slipped your mind? xx*

"Jesus," Jay whispered. *Checking on me. Friendly with me.*

He glanced at the remnants of his lunch, now crowded by paperwork beneath his monitor: crumpled cling film, the crust from a ham sandwich, an empty crisp packet and a yoghurt pot with an apple core tucked inside it.

Nervously, Jay pulled them forwards and arranged them into a suitable picture. As an embellishing touch, he retrieved the empty blister pack of painkillers from his waste paper bin, placed it in shot and took a photo.

He attached the picture to a message, praying as he typed.

As the typing bubble appeared, Alastair resisted the urge to dig his fingers into his desk. He breathed in and out with purpose, waiting as calmly as he was able.

The photograph appeared with a soft chime: the debris of lunch, a finished painkiller packet, heavy stacks of paperwork in shot. Alastair's heart heaved against his ribs. *Your desk,* he thought. *Your working day.* Jay had a chipped mug featuring his charity's logo, a pot full of highlighters with the caps mismatched, and photographs of innumerable grinning teenagers, all framed as if they were family. He used blue ink to write, and he ate salt and vinegar flavour crisps.

The messages which unfolded beneath the photo tightened Alastair's grip on his phone.

> **[JF - 13:01]** *100% responsible adult*
> **[JF - 13:01]** *dont judge my milky bar yogurt*
> **[JF - 13:01]** *hows your day? xx*

"You owe me two years' worth of additional annual leave," said the voice at his shoulder.

I owe you a good deal more than that.

"Bring me the form," Alastair said, "and I'll sign it."

Juliet hummed. "I'll trade it for you to reply to him with a question."

"Now?"

She nodded. "Yes, now. Trust me."

Obediently, Alastair typed.

> **[AH - 13:02]** *Fairly well. Midway through my usual green salad. Now sadly disappointing compared to Milkybar yoghurt.*
> **[AH - 13:02]** *How are you? xx*

"Jesus," Jay whispered again.

[JF - 13:03] *bit sore but in one piece*
[JF - 13:03] *nearly got my unread emails under 100*
[JF - 13:03] *and dont take the piss, they were on offer at the supermarket xx*

[AH - 13:04] *You've confused envy for piss-taking. Distraught I wasn't offered one last night. xx*

[JF - 13:04] *save you one for next time*
[JF - 13:04] *busy day? xx*

[AH - 13:04] *I've been in meetings all morning. Only just escaped. xx*

[JF - 13:05] *good meetings? xx*

[AH - 13:05] *I would love to tell you Jay.*
[AH - 13:05] *But then of course I'd have to kill you. xx*

[JF - 13:05] *sounds good to me... no more emails...*
[JF - 13:05] *hows your salad? you allowed to talk about that? xx*

[AH - 13:06] *I can. It is uninspiring. xx*

[JF - 13:07] *dont remember ever having an inspiring salad xx*

[AH - 13:07] *Now I think about it, no. Nor can I. xx*

[JF - 13:08] *need to get yourself some milkybar yogurts, mate*
[JF - 13:08] *theyre magic xx*

[AH - 13:09] *'Mate'!*
[AH - 13:09] *I see they go very nicely with painkillers. xx*

[JF - 13:10] *classic foodie combo*
[JF - 13:10] *like cheese and tomato*
[JF - 13:10] *coffee brb xxx*

Alastair squinted at the message. He got up from his desk, crossed to his office door and opened it. "Juliet?"

Juliet looked around from her laptop, swiftly closing the Manolo Blahnik website. "Yes, sir?"

"What does *coffee burb* mean?"

Her cheek twitched with humour. "Is it the letters *b-r-b,* by any chance?"

"Yes, it is."

"It means *be right back.* It's contemporary digital parlance." Juliet leant back in her chair, turning a rose gold fountain pen between her fingers. It matched her nails and the accents on her heels. "He's indicating that he'll be occupied for all of the three minutes it takes to boil a kettle, for fear that you'll think he's abandoned your conversation and stop replying. Clearly a distressing thought to him." She raised an eyebrow, smiling. "In other words, *coffee burb* means he's in love with you."

Alastair's expression shuttered. "He is not in love with me."

"Is he not?"

"No. No, of course he isn't."

Juliet's smile widened. "Ask him to dinner," she said.

The thought took the breath from Alastair's lungs. "God almighty."

"Ask him. And with his next reply, the two of you will officially be dating. Take him somewhere romantic. Tell him through the candlelight that he's the most enchanting man you've ever met, that he occupies your thoughts day and night, and that Cliveden offers a comprehensive range of wedding packages to suit all couples."

Alastair felt himself flush to his hairline. "I approached you for *sensible* advice."

"This is my sensible advice," Juliet said, smiling still, and tossed one stockinged leg over the other. "Ask the idiot to dinner."

"He... he could well say no. I couldn't bear it."

"He shan't. He'll say yes, probably very loudly."

"If he was willing to go to dinner with me, why on earth would he have suggested an arrangement between us and not dinner in the first place?"

"Probably because he thought you'd agree to one but not the other. Now tell the poor man you want him to be yours, and prove him wrong."

Alastair's message alert sounded from his office. He flushed ever darker, his heart racing.

"Excuse me," he muttered.

"Ask him," Juliet called as the door began to close, "or I'll ask him on your behalf."

Alastair opened it again. "You'll do no such thing!"

[JF - 13:14] *hey listen*
[JF - 13:14] *you were amazing yesterday*
[JF - 13:14] *got me back on my feet*
[JF - 13:14] *can I do something to thank you? xx*

[AH - 13:15] *Sincerely, Jay. Thanks aren't needed. xx*

[JF - 13:16] *I want to*
[JF - 13:16] *you didnt need to look after me xx*

[AH - 13:16] *What sort of thanks are you proposing? xx*

Alastair attempted to eat a little of his salad as he watched Jay reply. The typing bubble appeared for a while, then vanished entirely

—reappeared, quickly vanished—and on its third attempt remained for some time.

The eventual ladder of messages made his heart buck like a hare.

[JF - 13:20] *come round this weekend*
[JF - 13:20] *let me cook for you*
[JF - 13:20] *watch a film maybe*
[JF - 13:20] *you can have your milkybar yogurt xxx*

Across London, Jay attempted not to stare at his phone screen. Now he'd sent it, he knew for sure it was too much.

Or is it? That could still be casual, couldn't it?

It was just food and a film. Friends did that with each other. He hadn't necessarily shown his hand here. His text didn't necessarily read like his internal organs were all trying to squeeze their way out of his throat, which they very much were.

Alastair began to type.

Oh, Jesus. Here it comes.

He could almost hear Alastair's voice. *"Jay, I fear you've misjudged the nature of our arrangement."* Closing his eyes, Jay told himself this would either be a success or a lesson.

As his phone vibrated gently, he forced open one eye.

[AH - 13:21] *That's very kind of you.*
[AH - 13:21] *I'd love to. xx*

"Oh—oh, thank fuck..."

[JF - 13:21] *saturday evening?*
[JF - 13:21] *give me time to clean :P xxx*

[AH - 13:22] *Saturday. I'll bring wine. xx*

"Oh, shit. Oh, Jesus. What do I cook?"

As Jay googled the phrase *recipes to impress someone out of my league,* his phone gave another sly buzz.

[AH - 13:23] *And there's no need for you to clean. Your flat is perfectly acceptable as it is. xx*

The typing bubble appeared. Alastair watched it, oblivious to his own growing grin. He fanned his fingers as he waited, rolling them with happy anticipation against the edge of his desk.

[JF - 13:23] *we talking about the same flat? xxx*

[AH - 13:24] *The perfectly acceptable one in which I woke up this morning? xx*

[JF - 13:24] *wow*
[JF - 13:24] *thought youd have higher standards than that :P xxx*

[AH - 13:25] *It seems that you've misjudged me, 'mate'. xx*

[JF - 13:26] *:P*
[JF - 13:26] *am I distracting you from work? xxx*

[AH - 13:27] *Only from my uninspiring salad.*
[AH - 13:27] *Should I let you return to Mount Email? xx*

[JF - 13:27] *doing them in between texts*
[JF - 13:27] *don't go if you don't have to*
[JF - 13:27] *nice to chat :) xxx*

[AH - 13:28] *Very well. Coffee brb. xxx*

Chapter 15

The knock came five minutes ahead of the time they'd agreed. Jay tossed his tea towel over one shoulder and hurried for the door, taking a second to fix his hair in the mirror as he passed. He'd bought a brand new shirt, olive green with subtle stripes, and unbuttoned it just low enough to offer the edges of his ink. The place was spotless, the candles were lit, and he'd spent nearly two hours creating the playlist. For this critical moment, the fates had picked Adele's *One and Only,* and Jay wasn't going to argue with their choice. He'd done everything he could to make tonight perfect. From now on, he simply had to see.

Pulling open the door, he found Alastair waiting in the hallway in his long black coat and leather gloves, holding out a bottle of red wine. His grey eyes glittered at the sight of Jay, the hint of a smile playing at corners of his mouth.

Jay squeezed the edge of the door, grinning. "Hi," he said.

Alastair's smile grew. He stepped over the threshold, put the bottle on a nearby surface without a glance, and took Jay's face in both his hands.

"Hello," he murmured, gathering Jay close.

As their lips came together, Jay's soul seemed to exit his body. It rocketed immediately into the stratosphere, there to stay for good, floating somewhere thirty thousand feet above the earth. *Oh, God,* he thought, and leaned in closer, sliding his arms around Alastair's waist. *Fuck, you're really here. This is happening.*

They kissed slowly beside the open door, warm fingers wrapped in leather supporting Jay's face. Already this was everything he'd dreamed. When the kiss finally ended, their foreheads stayed together and the floor beneath Jay's feet seemed to sway.

Alastair stroked his thumb over the cut on Jay's lip.

"This is healing well," he said. "And this..." He kissed just beneath Jay's black eye, as carefully as if it were fresh. "I'm glad you're alright."

The gentleness of his voice would never fail to ruin Jay. He shivered a little, unable to help it.

"Scrappy, me," he whispered. "I bounce back fast."

Alastair hummed, pleased, and softly recaptured Jay's lips. Settled back into kissing, it took Jay several seconds to pick up on the bleeping from the kitchen.

"Sorry," he mumbled into the kiss, stroking his hands up Alastair's sides. "I think that's our garlic bread."

Alastair smiled against his mouth. "I hope you haven't gone to trouble."

"Not too much," Jay lied, wishing he could sound just a little less breathy. Alastair's pupils seemed huge at this close distance, deep and soft and warm. "Nice to spend time with you, that's all. I wanted to make it special."

"You're too kind," Alastair said, nuzzling the side of Jay's nose. The oven timer continued to beep. "Shall I let you tend to that garlic bread?"

"Y-yeah," Jay admitted. "Probably best. Don't want it to burn."

Alastair released him, fingertips brushing along his jaw. "I'd hate to waste your efforts," he said, stepping back. "Don't let me get in the way."

Lightheaded, Jay attended to the oven timer. His lips tingled from Alastair's kisses, his hopes for this evening even higher than they were before. He couldn't help but steal glances across the room, watching as Alastair closed the front door and removed his coat. Beneath it, he was wearing a silver-grey jumper over a simple white shirt, the fine-knit wool almost silky in texture. It was a far softer look than anything Jay had seen him in before. He'd dressed comfortably, not formally, and it did things to Jay that he couldn't quite explain. Alastair looked as if he'd feel magnificent to hug—not just for a quick squeeze, but a cuddle that went on for hours, arms wrapped around each other on the couch.

Pulling off his leather gloves, Alastair looked around.

"Dear Lord, Jay," he remarked, teasing. "Is this the same flat?"

Jay grinned, scraping his tray of garlic bread from the oven. "Looks bigger tidy, doesn't it? I was overdue for a proper clear out."

Alastair brought his bottle of wine over to the kitchen. "Can I help you with anything?" he asked, setting it down on the counter top.

"There's a corkscrew in the drawer to your right," Jay said, turning the garlic bread slices carefully with his fingers. They only needed another few minutes. "You could open the wine, if you want. Get us started."

"This drawer?"

"Yep. That's the one. How's your weekend been so far? Have you done much?"

"A few work tasks," Alastair said absently, retrieving the corkscrew. "I ended up on the couch with a book. Nothing too exciting."

"Good to rest at the weekend, though. Have a bit of down time. It sets you up for the week."

"Mm, very true. How was your day?"

In truth, Jay had spent every moment of it in anticipation of this one. Knowing that Alastair would be here all evening made him so happy it was hard to keep his head fixed on anything else.

"Pretty good," he replied, smiling, and returned the garlic bread to the oven. "Did some laundry at last. Went for a run. Tidied up."

He set the timer with a few quick presses of the button.

"There," he said. "Couple more minutes, just to crisp up the cheese."

"Excellent. And in honour of the occasion..." Alastair handed Jay a glass of very dark red wine, the liquid gleaming in the candlelight. "Roagna La Pira, 2010."

Jay took a gentle sniff, catching notes of berries and roses. He didn't know all that much about wine, but he had a feeling this might be romantic wine. He certainly hoped it was.

"Before I drink this," he said, relaxing back against the counter edge, "how long was the number printed on the price tag?"

Alastair chuckled, pouring himself a glass. "A number of sensible length," he promised. "Indulgent but not obnoxious."

"Two digits?"

"Two digits. Jay. I'm not a maniac."

Reassured, Jay took a sip. The flavour flooded through his mouth, warm and rich and full of fruit. This was *definitely* romantic wine.

"Damn, Al," he murmured, helpless. "You've got amazing taste in booze."

Alastair tested it for himself; the verdict was a small hum. "I've been saving it," he said, as he licked his lower lip. "It's nice to have an excuse to finally open the bottle."

I'm worth saved wine. Jay's heart resumed its eager skipping. "I don't know if my dinner will live up to this, you know," he said. "Glad I made dessert as well."

"Mm? What is it we're having?"

Jay checked the over timer. "Chicken," he said, "baked with roasted sweet balsamic tomatoes, garlic butter and provolone. Rice and side salad to accompany."

Alastair's eyebrows lifted, apparently impressed.

"You've got rather a knack for cooking, haven't you?" he said. Jay attempted to hide his flush of pleasure in his wine glass, drinking. "Is this a hidden passion of yours?"

"I don't know if I'd go *that* far," Jay said. He didn't want to admit he'd been happily preparing things all day. That was a lot of pressure to put upon Alastair. In truth, Jay had been waiting a decade for an excuse to cook like this, and he'd enjoyed every minute of it. "I like throwing ingredients together, that's all. You don't mind that we're eating on the couch?"

"Not at all."

"I swear this place looked bigger when I viewed it."

"It's delightfully compact. And I'll be very happy eating on the couch with you." Alastair moved closer, put his arm around Jay's waist and placed a small kiss upon his forehead. "For what it's worth," he added, "we could have dinner together in a cardboard box and I'd still be happy."

Jay attempted not to glow.

"You're sweet," he said, leaning into Alastair's body. He let his cheek get comfortable on Alastair's shoulder. "I know you're used to finer surroundings."

Alastair huffed. "Dull company makes even the finest surroundings seem dull," he said. "I'd much rather be here with you. Are you wearing a new fragrance?"

Argh. Jay had hoped he would notice.

"Not really new," he said. "Team got me it last Christmas. Do you like it?"

"I do," Alastair said. He followed Jay's cologne to its source at his throat, nuzzling beneath the curve of his jaw. "Mmhm. Very much."

As Alastair's mouth stroked his neck, Jay's eyes fluttered shut. He'd missed being like this, close and happy; it felt like Cliveden all over again. Everything was right where they'd left it, just waiting to be picked up and continued. He bit down into his lip, lifting his chin in hope of more, then realised he was still holding his wine glass. He moved it to safety on the counter, not wanting to spill it down Alastair's back.

Alastair hummed, followed suit, then backed Jay up against the fridge.

Oh, God. Jay sucked in a breath. Alastair pressed himself close, raising a shiver across Jay's chest, then nudged playfully beneath Jay's chin to gain access to his neck. As his warm, searching mouth began a feast of Jay's throat, Jay scrunched a hand into his hair and let himself relax, trembling a little. His tattoos suddenly burned to be touched.

"Fuck, I missed you," he thought—then realised he'd said it aloud. He couldn't take it back, even if he wanted to.

Alastair teased aside the collar of Jay's shirt, murmuring his name against his skin.

As the oven timer began to beep again, Jay contemplated tossing all the food out of the window. He tightened his grip on Alastair's shoulders and sighed in protest, not wanting to stop.

Alastair's amused rumble felt more like a purr than a laugh. "I believe that's your garlic bread," he said, flashing his tongue behind Jay's ear.

Jay bit back a gasp. "Tastes better burned."

"Mm?" Alastair said, stealing a nip of Jay's earlobe. "Convenient."

Jay's eyes rolled back into his head. Before he could draw breath to moan, a second timer exploded across the kitchen. The novelty Father Christmas's shrill ringing was much harder to ignore.

"The chicken?" Alastair said, audibly smirking.

"Yeah," Jay groaned. "Probably not as good burned."

Alastair hid one last kiss against Jay's neck and eased back, releasing Jay from his embrace. "Can I help you serve up?"

"Think I can manage," Jay said, breathless. As he gathered up the shards of his thoughts from the floor, he glanced around for something for Alastair to do. "You could take the wine over to the couch, maybe? Get comfy?"

Alastair nodded. He retrieved the bottle and both glasses, and with a last dark-eyed smile, he strolled away towards the sofa.

Jay watched him go, every inch of his body still echoing. *Jesus, I'm not going to survive this.* He was glad he'd suggested the cosy privacy of a home-cooked meal, not the very public setting of a restaurant. If they ended up eating their dessert in bed, then so be it.

Jay took his time to arrange everything properly on both plates, making sure it all looked nice. Everything had turned out well in the oven, the cheese just starting to brown, the tomatoes juicy but not soggy. It seemed as if the universe was looking out for him, giving this date every sprinkle of luck it could spare. As he portioned out the rice, Jay wondered if Alastair knew this *was* a date. He'd brought fancy wine as a gift, which seemed like a hopeful sign, and he'd worn nice clothes. Something about a cashmere jumper said 'new boyfriend' to Jay, not 'casual hook-up', and he hoped he wasn't the only one who thought so. Alastair had picked up on Jay's fragrance; he'd noticed how tidy the place was. Surely he realised Jay was pushing the boat out, too.

Surely. Surely you know.

As Jay brought both plates towards the couch, Alastair waited with a pleased look of anticipation. He looked as comfortable and at home on Jay's couch as if he spent most evenings sitting there. For a few giddy moments, Jay let himself imagine what it might be like to do this several nights a week—cooking for Alastair, relaxing together on the sofa after work. Back rubs, candles, conversation.

Please, God. Let me have this.

Jay put the plates down on the coffee table with care, biting his lip.

"I hope it's alright," he said. "If it's crap, there's almond peach galette for afters. If that's crap too, we'll just binge on Milkybar yoghurts. I bought two packs, just in case."

Alastair smiled without comment, patting the vacant cushion beside him. *Come here.*

Trying to ignore his building nerves, Jay settled down at his side. Alastair's arm went around him, coaxing him closer, and even *this* felt like they'd done it a thousand times. They fit together to eat like a happily married couple in a film.

Jay gathered his plate from the table into his lap, hoping against hope he'd not overdone the garlic.

"Where did you learn the recipe?" Alastair asked, reaching for a piece of bread.

Jay held his breath.

"My head of marketing gave it to me years ago," he said, watching Alastair scoop up a little of the sauce. "I wrecked it the first time I made it. Massively over-cheesed it. Think I've cracked it now, though."

Alastair lifted the garlic bread to his mouth. He bit down, and time itself seemed to execute an emergency stop. Jay's heart stopped with it. He watched, motionless, as Alastair began to chew.

Alastair's eyes closed. He lifted his fingertips to his mouth.

"Oh, Jesus," Jay said, his stomach plunging through the floor. "I'm sorry. I'm so sorry. Don't eat any more. I'll fetch the Chinese menu. Pretend this never happened."

Alastair stifled a laugh around his mouthful, chewing determinedly, then swallowed.

"You'll do no such thing," he said. "It's wonderful. It's *delicious,* Jay. Now please relax. I've never felt someone go so tense in all my life."

Jay let out all his breath at once. "Are you *sure* it's alright? You can tell me if it's awful. I won't mind."

"It's magnificent," Alastair said. He leaned close and kissed Jay firmly between the eyes, his face filled with affection. "It's perfect. You can relax, darling. I promise you."

Darling. Jay's toes curled tight inside his socks. *Oh, fuck. Darling.*

"I'm glad I brought a decent vintage," Alastair said. "This more than deserves it." He took another bite of garlic bread, reaching for the bottle. "Shall I top you up?"

Jay smiled, happy little bubbles streaming through his veins. "Sure. Thanks, sunshine."

Jay had planned to put a film on with dessert—something classic and soft, maybe funny. In the end, the whole idea slipped his mind. Sitting and talking was too good to interrupt. Long after the dishes were soaking in the sink, he and Alastair remained together on the couch, laughing and kissing as they chatted. On Alastair's request, they had a second portion of dessert. He scraped the bottom of his bowl clean, chasing down every last little speck of peach galette.

The candles soon began to flutter, their flames idling low in deep pools of hot wax.

I don't want you to go, Jay thought, watching Alastair lean over and fill their glasses with the last of the wine. Being together like this felt as natural as anything in the world.

Alastair looked up into Jay's eyes, his pupils dark and soft.

"Thank you for dinner," he said. He put the empty bottle aside on the coffee table, then gathered Jay's socked feet into his lap. "You're an incredible cook, Jay."

Jay grinned, shining with the compliment. "Thanks for coming to look after me," he said, resting his cheek against the back of the sofa. As Alastair's thumbs began to rub slow circles into his arches, his toes flexed on their own. "It meant a lot. I was a mess, and you just..."

"You realise it was an honour, don't you? There's no reason to thank me."

"An honour? Seeing me all sad and pathetic?"

"Seeing you vulnerable." Alastair's smile grew soft, his expression tender as he rubbed Jay's feet. "Besides, I'm still holding you to your debt of reciprocation."

Even the dream of it raised warmth in Jay's chest—being the person Alastair reached for, the one he wanted in a moment of weakness. *I'd literally cross oceans to look after you,* Jay thought, briefly lost for words as he looked back into Alastair's eyes. *I'd fetch you the moon if you needed it. You know I would.*

"Just say when," he said. "I'll come running. No matter where you are, I'll be there."

"I look forward to it," Alastair said, as his thumbs found somewhere special near Jay's left heel. A helpless shiver travelled up Jay's back, stretching him out and cutting his breath.

"Ahh—"

"There?"

"Mhm. There."

Alastair peeled off Jay's sock, wrapped both hands around his foot and concentrated on the knot he'd found, watching with pleasure as Jay squirmed.

"Should I be rescuing that wine glass from you?" he asked.

Jay tipped the glass's contents back in one swig, clicked it down on the coffee table and pushed it away.

"Problem solved," he said, fanning his toes.

Chuckling, Alastair continued his work, rubbing his way upwards from Jay's heel. Jay slumped into the cushions and swallowed most of a groan. He let the rest escape him as a sigh, so happy in this moment that he feared he might just melt. Little curls of enjoyment were swirling through his blood, his cheeks flushed with the warmth of candlelight and wine.

"Al," he whispered, closing his eyes. Alastair stripped off his other sock for him, humming. "God, you're..."

"Mm?" Alastair set about giving his other foot the same care and attention, working idle patterns with his thumbs. "More than deserved, for that dessert of yours."

Jay gazed up through his eyelashes, settling his arms behind his head. "I can make other desserts, too."

"Can you now?" Alastair murmured, his eyes flashing.

"Mm hmm."

"My waistline should run screaming, should it?"

Give your waistline here. I'll sort it out. "Everybody needs a vice," Jay said. "It's the people without one you need to worry about. They're the dangerous ones."

"Given that I already smoke and drink wine," Alastair said, "it seems I'm already well-supplied with vice."

"You drink *good* wine," Jay pointed out. As Alastair began to massage his instep, his back arched up off the couch. "Mnnhh—doesn't count if it's good wine—and I only ever see you smoke when *I* start one up, so..."

"How interesting," Alastair said, his voice soft and teasing. "In fact, I drink wine, smoke, *and* eat to excess when I'm with you. If memory serves, we also have an ambitious amount of sex. Apparently you're good at tempting me into things."

Jay grinned, stretching enough to tug the hem of his shirt free from his jeans.

"You never complain," he said. "I inspire you to live life to the fullest. I'm your *joie de vivre,* keeping you young."

Alastair's smile became a smirk, delight dancing in his eyes. "I think you're overestimating the magnitude of an eight year age gap. You're hardly performing services to the elderly."

Biting the corner of his lip, Jay decided that he dared. "I think you were probably born elderly, weren't you?" he said. It earned him a huff, but no denial. "You're having a lot more fun since me."

Alastair smiled, gliding his fingertips up around Jay's ankle. "I am," he said. "Vices and all. I'm... happy when I'm with you, Jay. A little more myself somehow."

Jay's heart gave a tug. He looked up into Alastair's eyes, wondering if this was the right moment to start the conversation.

"Happy to help," he murmured. He watched Alastair lean down to kiss the narrow strip of bare stomach exposed by the bottom of Jay's shirt. "Must wear you down sometimes, putting on a front at work. Being what everybody needs you to be."

Alastair nodded, nosing beneath the fabric. "Very much," he said. "It's... comforting, being able to put that aside."

Jay smiled a little. "You haven't had many boyfriends over the years, have you?"

Even the word, *boyfriend,* seemed to cause a tentative shift in the air. Jay couldn't be certain it had happened outside of his imagination, but it lifted Alastair's eyes to his own.

"Hardly any," Alastair said. It looked like it brought him relief to admit it. "I never consciously turned away from relationships. They just... well, dwindled as I rose up the ranks."

Listening, Jay down to stroke Alastair's cheek.

Alastair kissed his palm. "These things take time to establish," he went on. "Time I didn't have. I can't regret the choices that I made. When I made them, I barely even saw them for choices. But you're right. It's... been a lonely journey to success."

Jay nodded quietly, unsurprised to hear it. "Tough at the top?"

"Mm." The edge of Alastair's mouth lifted. "Still," he said. "Only two years of it left."

"Two years of...?"

"Commissioners usually serve no more than five. I'm approaching the end of three. No plans to challenge tradition."

Jay hadn't realised. He blinked, brushing his fingers through Alastair's hair. "Do they really just demote you after five years? Seems harsh."

"No," Alastair said, half-amused. "We normally retire."

"Really?"

"Dropping down after leading the force would be very strange. And the new commissioner won't want a predecessor haunting the hallways, questioning all their changes. It's an expected part of the role."

Jay smiled, wondering why the thought made him happy. He supposed he'd be glad for anyone lucky enough to retire young, good years of life left ahead of them. In Alastair's case, it seemed like it was deserved.

"That'll be great for you," he said. "Taking down the front you've built, I mean. Getting your personal life back."

"I'm planning to keep myself busy, but... well, you're right. A new stage of life." Alastair's eyes brightened, his expression fond as he nuzzled his nose against Jay's stomach. "Thank you for helping me to practice."

Jay grinned. "I'm a glimpse of freedom, am I?"

"You're a glimpse of many things," Alastair said, running his hands up Jay's side. "Would you say that you put on a front?"

"You mean at work?"

"At work. In general."

Jay thought about it, curling his fingers gently at the back of Alastair's neck. There was an obvious answer, one he quietly swept aside. This conversation wasn't about that. "Honestly?" he said at last. "I sort of think we all do."

"Mm?"

"Yeah, I mean... the world's a stage, right? We want everyone else to think the best of us. Want them to know that we're trying, and we're handling things as well as we can."

Alastair seemed almost proud to hear Jay say it, still dotting little kisses on his stomach.

Jay smiled, wondering what about it had pleased him.

"It's life," he went on with a shrug. "Just have to hope you meet someone who fancies what's actually there. Wants what you've got, even when you think you've got nothing."

Alastair took a moment to weigh some risk in silence. "And do you?" he said.

Uncertain, Jay tilted his head.

Alastair clarified, looking up into his eye. "Fancy what's actually there."

If you knew, Jay thought. *If you had even the tiniest idea.* He paused as the words settled over him, and in their wake a realisation unfolded.

You won't know though, will you? Unless I tell you.

The room seemed to fall still. Even the music seemed to soften, whispering away into quiet, and Jay gazed down into Alastair's face, his throat suddenly dry. He'd felt this way beneath the boughs of the beech tree at Cliveden. In that moment, he'd kept it all in, convinced he'd blow everything apart if he dared to let it out. But this moment didn't feel half as fragile.

Fuck me up. Jay realised this was it, the time to speak. He held his breath. *Here goes.*

"You make me feel brand new sometimes," he said. "Like I'm a kid again. Like I just want to run around with you and play."

Alastair's eyes sparkled with humour and more than a little understanding. It was enough for Jay to push onwards, overjoyed and terrified at once, so in love he suddenly couldn't cope.

"The first time I ever made you laugh," he said, "sitting there at that dinner in your uniform, I just... I don't know. It lit me up inside. I watched you laugh, and I wanted to see you laugh until you cried."

Alastair listened, now looking at Jay as if the secrets of the universe were written on his face.

Jay went on, begging those perfect eyes to understand.

"First time I saw you naked," he said, "I wanted to make you come so hard you never forgot me as long as you lived. Now I've cooked you something, I want to cook you everything. I want to see you lick the bowl. I just... Jesus, please don't take this wrong. I love that you've poured your life into working for something. It's part of you, and it's your heart, and I can't tell you how much I admire that."

Alastair's eyes began to shine.

"Just don't think that work's all you've got," Jay whispered. Swallowing, he cupped Alastair's face. "Okay? Don't ever think that. Don't worry about retiring. I'll still fancy you like mad."

Alastair's gaze didn't move.

"That will be two years from now," he said.

Jay's entire body braced. This was it. He couldn't stop this coming out. He'd just stepped free from the cliff, and there was nothing he could do but fall, hoping that he landed somewhere soft. All the air shook its way from his lungs.

"Al," he said. His gaze flickered. "Come on."

Alastair said nothing, still searching his face.

"Don't act like you don't know," Jay begged, his cheeks burning in an instant. "Don't tell me it's not obvious I'm..."

Alastair didn't seem to be breathing, watching Jay as if afraid he might explode. "Are you planning to be with me two years from now?"

Fuck. Jay loosened his hands from around Alastair's face, suddenly on the verge of throwing up. *I've fucked up. I've—fuck—*

"Al," he said. His brain scrabbled wildly for more words. Nothing came. "Al," he whispered, his voice breaking.

Alastair didn't move for a moment, his eyes still fixed on Jay's face. He shifted suddenly, leaning forwards, and Jay had time to drag in half a breath before Alastair's fingers drove through his hair, hauling him up into a kiss.

As Alastair kissed him fiercely, Jay clung to his shoulders and tried to hold on. *Fuck. Oh, fuck.* Within seconds, he was lying flat against the cushions with Alastair's weight on top of him, pinning him, kissing like they needed each other to live.

Desperate, somewhere close to panic, Jay managed to gasp the words between their mouths.

"It's not just sex," he said. He hadn't planned for it to sound like a plea, but it was too late now. "It's... i-it's more for me. I want us to be something."

Alastair's hands surrounded his jaw. "You are perfect to me," he gasped, holding Jay hard enough to bruise. "Why in God's name didn't you say something?"

"Are you *serious?* You're the fucking Met commissioner. You're amazing. You're important. I didn't say anything because I was afraid you would end this."

"Why would I want to *end* it?" Alastair demanded, searching Jay's eyes from an inch away. "Isn't it obvious I'm in love with you?"

Holy shit.

Holy fuck, I...

"Al," Jay managed. He felt his heart begin to break. "Jesus, Al—"

Alastair's kiss cut off his whimper. They kissed until the need for oxygen had Jay panting, raking his hands through Alastair's hair. He'd never needed to hold onto someone so much in all his life. It didn't feel like their bodies could get close enough, too many fragments of space in between.

You're mine, Jay thought, reeling as he wrapped his legs around Alastair's. *You're in love with me. It's real, you're mine, you're actually—*

A short stretch of vibration came muffled from somewhere in between them. Jay's breath stalled, distracted. He tried to ignore the steady buzzing as it continued, concentrating on Alastair's tongue inside his mouth and Alastair's fingers buried in his hair, Alastair's hands holding tight to his body. The call kept on, thrumming insistently.

After almost a minute, Alastair released Jay's mouth with a shudder. "I'm sorry," he said, flushed. "It's... I probably need to—"

Work.

"It's alright," Jay whispered, trembling a little. "No worries. I-I understand." He slipped his hand down, retrieving Alastair's mobile for him from the pocket where it was still buzzing. Handing it over, he caught a glimpse of the name on the screen. "Juliet?"

"My assistant," Alastair said. "She only bothers me out of hours if it's urgent." He looked into Jay's eyes, flushed and pale at once, his lips swollen red where they'd been kissing. "I really am sorry for this timing."

Jay's throat tightened at the sincerity.

"Don't be," he said. He reached up to brush Alastair's hair back from his forehead, marvelling that he was allowed. *And you love me,* he thought, dizzy. *It's real.* "Answer her, sunshine. We can kiss in a minute."

Alastair huffed, glancing at his lips. "I just hope it's not an emergency."

"Won't know unless you answer," Jay murmured. He nudged the phone. "Go on."

Alastair swallowed, swiped his thumb across the screen, and lifted it to his ear.

He spoke before she could, hoping to make the situation quite clear.

"This is spectacularly poor timing," Alastair began, gazing down. Jay smiled up at him, his cheeks pink and his green eyes bright, soft with patience and affection. The thumping of Alastair's heart was likely audible on the line. "What is it?"

"I wouldn't contact you if it weren't important," Juliet said at once, no trace of humour in her voice. "Are you with him at the moment?"

"Yes, I am. As well you know. What is it?"

"Can you take this call in another room?"

"No, I can't. For the third and final time, what is it?"

"It's about him. It's his background check."

Alastair's pulse seemed to skip. He kept his concern from his face, still looking down into Jay's eyes. "Unless it's *extremely* serious—"

"Please listen," Juliet cut across him fiercely. "I'm not calling to tell you about a fine for speeding. If this could wait until Monday, I would have waited. I know he implied to you he's a police informant that Ian Straker tried to kill. But he's not."

Alastair steadied himself, wishing he couldn't see his own rising apprehension now reflected in Jay's eyes—gaze dimming, smile fading.

"I see," he said, shifting to sit up. Jay moved to sit beside him, looking nervous. "Go on."

"He *is* in the Protected Persons Service," Juliet said. "He entered into it because of the Straker case, but he's not James Wheeler." Her breath broke. "Oh, Alastair. I'm so sorry. I've found his criminal record. I've found all of it. Some of it was excused when he—but I couldn't keep this from you, couldn't let you spend the weekend there without knowing."

Oh, God.

"Juliet," Alastair said, as the blood drained from his face. "Please say what you have to say."

Juliet's voice shook.

"His real name is Jason Straker," she said. "He's Ian's younger brother."

Chapter 16

THE WORDS RANG IN ALASTAIR'S EARS. FOR SEVERAL SECONDS, nothing at all seemed to exist as he tried and failed to affix that name to the face still gazing at him, those gentle green eyes full of concern.

Looking back, Alastair swallowed without a sound.

"Thank you for informing me," he said. His voice sounded hollow to his own ears. "The... the record that you mentioned. What manner of—"

"It's bad," Juliet murmured, and no more.

The silence gathered in again.

"I see," Alastair said, forcing himself to speak. The walls appeared to be shrinking, the ceiling closing in. A wave of cold spread out across his back. "If you don't mind, I'll hang up and look into this myself."

She understood. He could hear it in her silence, somehow. He could almost feel her pain for him, transmitted along the line.

"I'm here if you need me," she said. With the tiniest of clicks she vanished, gone from his side.

Alastair quietly locked his phone, surprised to see no shaking in his fingers. There would be soon. The shock would reach them. He could feel it passing down his shoulders and into his arms, creeping through him like a slowly spreading poison.

"Everything alright?" Jason Straker asked, in a voice as soft as his kiss had been. He stroked his fingertips along Alastair's arm. "If... if you've got to go, sunshine, it's okay. I'll understand."

Will you? Alastair looked into his eyes. He found himself overwhelmed by the urge to lean in for one last kiss—one more gentle press of their lips, here in the final seconds of a world about to end. There would be no going back after this. Their first loving kiss might well have been their only one.

He couldn't bear it.

My Jay.

My...

As Alastair's throat tightened, a lifetime's worth of faith in duty and honour rose to the fore. Instincts he had trained for thirty years, instincts which refused to let him suffer this indignity, hardened his veins into steel, forcing out all space for blood to flow. Whatever he had felt, it did not matter. He was a fool for having felt it at all.

The name left his mouth. It spoke itself, and in an instant, there was nothing left to say.

"Jason Straker."

Jay's face opened. For a moment or two he didn't move, soundless and pale as he read Alastair's eyes. His lips came apart and then closed as he swallowed.

"You had me checked," he said.

It was not a question.

So I could use my resources to protect you. Alastair's heart twisted, burning with the humiliation of it: all his softness, all his concern. He'd been so eager to do anything and everything he could. *For my Jay,* he thought, and the misery stung in his throat, so sharp and so fierce it took his breath. He clamped down on the feeling, shaking, and spoke as a police officer.

"Did it occur to you," he asked, "that I might want to be told this information?"

Jay hesitated, turning even paler.

"You... you get that we *can't* tell people, don't you?" he said. Something in Alastair's chest caved, something he feared couldn't be fixed. It must have shown in his face. Jay sped up, leaning back from him, his eyes growing wide with anxiety. "We're literally forbidden from telling people, Al. From telling *anyone.* That's the first thing they—"

The words exploded out of Alastair's mouth.

"I'm the *bloody police commissioner!"* he shouted, shocked at his own force. "I do not class as *anyone!"*

Jay's mouth opened. "Wait—are you *angry* with me?"

"Angry?" Alastair demanded. "Why on earth would I be angry to discover that for weeks now, I, the Commissioner of the Police of the Metropolis, have been fucking the younger brother of a notorious Manchester ganglord? What about that could *possibly* upset me?"

"Why *would* you be upset?" Jay asked, pulling away along the sofa. "What's the problem?"

Alastair scoffed, dearly wishing he had the strength to laugh. "Must I really explain to you?"

"Maybe you should."

"My position is founded on a certain degree of respectability. A certain distance from criminality. Caesar's wife must be above suspicion. And *you* are—"

"What?" Jay snapped. "A criminal?"

Heat flooded across the back of Alastair's neck. "According to your record," he cut back, "that's *precisely* what you are! I don't know what other word there is!"

Jay's hands dug into the sofa cushions underneath him, his knuckles blanching white. It seemed to take him a second to find the strength to speak.

"And you got the whole story just there, did you?" he asked, shaking. "Half a minute on the phone, and you know everything about it?"

"I heard what I needed to! Which is far more than *you* ever supplied to me!"

"Jesus, what was there to *supply?* I've told you the truth, Al! I've never told you a single lie about this! What exactly did—"

"How *dare* you."

"What?"

"The *truth?*"

"The truth! The truth that I pissed someone off, I got out of Manchester—"

"And you simply *forgot* to mention that the person you pissed off is your own bloody brother, did you? Or did you decide to skip that particular detail for a reason?"

"What difference does it make if he's my brother?"

Alastair got up from the sofa in a fury, no longer willing to discuss this at close quarters. "For God's sake, it makes all the difference! How can you ever think that it wouldn't?"

Jay struggled to his feet as well.

"Because it tells you something, does it?" he demanded, shaking. He jabbed his fingers into his own chest. "Something about me? Fruit never falls far from the tree, right? When you thought I'd just crossed paths with him, that was fine and you were offering to protect me—but you're saying if you'd known that we were family, you'd never have come anywhere near me, is that it?"

Alastair's fists balled. He didn't want it to be true. He wished for his own honour that he could let fly some condemnation of Jay's view of him, retort that he would of course have seen past this if Jay had just had the decency to disclose it at the outset. He tried to imagine his way back to their table at the awards evening, when the only thing he'd wanted in the world was to talk and grow close with this man whose playful flirting set his heart awhirl like snowflakes in a storm. He tried to ask himself what he would have done, learning this information then.

But the truth was, he would have thought twice.

He'd have kept Jay Fieldhouse at the same polite distance he kept the rest of the world—admired him, perhaps, for attempting to steer his life onto a better path, but never contemplated taking him home. They'd have shared pleasant but meaningless small talk over a plate of beef wellington, parted with a handshake, then likely never met again. There'd have been no arrangement, no Cliveden, no home-cooked meal by candlelight. He'd let Jay close, closer than anyone in his entire wretched life had ever come, while never knowing anything about him.

Alastair filled his chest with air.

"It is not unreasonable that I would have wanted to know this!" he shouted. "You withheld information in order to influence my decisions! And I don't appreciate you suggesting that puts me in the wrong!"

It struck a heavy blow. Pain scattered through Jay's expression, tightening up the muscles in his jaw.

"Jesus," he breathed. "You're... th-this is why I've never told anyone. This bullshit right here."

"It's bullshit of me to expect honesty, is it?"

"Al—"

"When I've never given you anything less?"

"Al, just—s-seriously—you've had more honesty from me than I've given anyone else in ten damn years. I've never even come *close* to telling anyone else. You know why?"

"Because they would use it to make informed decisions?" Alastair snapped. "Outrageous of them."

Red anger flooded through Jay's face. "Because when I do, people make decisions about me!" he shouted, his voice ringing through the flat. "Decisions based on things that *aren't fucking true!"*

Alastair turned away, inhaling hard in an attempt to control himself. He dragged both hands backwards through his hair.

"Because the last decade of my life suddenly disappears," Jay went on. "Everything I've done. Everything I've changed. Written off in an instant, like it never even happened. Thirty seconds and I'm not even me anymore. I'm just Ian Straker's little brother and it's all I'll ever be."

He jabbed two fingers in the air towards Alastair, shaking.

"So fuck you," he spat. "Fuck you for being like this. Fuck you for proving I was *right* to hide it."

Alastair paced from the couch towards the mantelpiece, his thoughts reeling and raging from one extreme to another. "How else did you expect me to be?" he demanded. "My position—for God's sake, my *entire career*—if it's found out I've been—"

"What?" Jay said. "Consorting with the criminal underclass?"

Alastair wasn't nearly stupid enough to agree with the sentiment—but nor was he prepared to back down.

"That is how this would be perceived by my professional connections," he said, bracing both his hands upon the mantelpiece. He dropped his head forwards and shut his eyes. "Don't you dare reproach me for being protective of what I've worked for."

"God forbid that you correct people," Jay breathed back at him. Alastair looked up, finding Jay white in the face. "God forbid that you challenge their assumptions and stand up for me. Point them towards the full story."

Alastair's jaw clenched. "Jay—"

"Five minutes ago, you were in love with me. Now I'm a stain on your good name."

Alastair turned from the mantelpiece, shouting. "At *no point* did I say that—"

"Did she even tell you I'm the reason that Ian's in prison?" Jay raged back. His eyes were ablaze. They began to shine as he shouted, welling over with anger and frustration. "Your assistant? In the single half a minute that you spoke?"

Alastair's objection died in his throat, too shocked by the sight of tears to carry on with it. He'd only ever seen tears in Jay's eyes once before. At the time, Jay had been helpless with pain and too exhausted to move, embarrassed to have reached out for comfort. The memory was overpowering, and in an instant, some part of Alastair was prepared to withdraw all his anger without another thought. He wanted to replace it immediately with reassurance, with groundless promises that this did not matter. The need to reach out and brush his hand up Jay's arm nearly choked him.

He forced his fingers to remain where they were at his side, but made an effort to level his tone.

"She didn't tell me," he said, looking into Jay's eyes, "because I'd rather hear the rest from you."

Jay's expression creased. He huffed, trying his hardest to make it all into a joke.

"Sure," he said. He reached up to wipe his hands across his eyes, forcing the distress aside. "Because I'm desperate to tell you now. I can't wait to hand you more things you can screw right up and throw back at me. That's just what I want."

Taking a breath, Alastair gathered himself back into a state where he could speak his mind and not merely shout from his heart. He took a moment to ensure that his voice was calm, that his hands were released from their fists, and that the words he said were measured and meant.

"Without my career," he said, "my life would contain next to nothing. It is *all* I have. I've allowed you to understand that to a much greater extent than most people, and I'm not going to apologise for reacting angrily in its defence. If you want me to understand something about you, then this is your chance to explain it to me how you wish it to be explained. Otherwise the official records will tell me. And from what I'm hearing, they're not going to speak of you kindly."

For a few awful seconds, there was silence. Jay's throat muscles worked without a sound, his face pale and empty, his eyes dark with tears.

"I'm not answerable to you," he said. His voice broke, though his head stayed high. "I won't explain myself to you. I'll set you straight, but it's because I've come too far to stand here and let someone like you shit on me. This is for me. Not for you."

"Very well," Alastair said. Nothing would be solved through further arguing. This would continue as a discussion between adults, or not at all. In aid of more productive exchange, he moved over to the couch and seated himself on the edge. "Go ahead," he said. "Set me straight."

Jay paused, taking this in. He kept his distance, staying where he was beside the mantelpiece, but loosened his hands from their fists. His fingers rubbed as he gathered the words.

"You don't get born a Straker and become a teacher," he said. "Or a doctor. Or a police officer. Your job is to be useful to your family, because you're nothing and they're all that you've got. You do the shit that makes your parents pat you on the back and feed you. You *don't* do the shit that makes them pull a face and tell you you're being a little wanker. Shit like fetching story books home from school."

Alastair opened his mouth, already on the brink of apology.

"Don't," Jay barked over him, shaking. "Fucking *don't.* Do *not* talk to me. Just sit there and listen. Whatever they've told you that I did, I did ten times worse. I've done things that would stop you from sleeping next to me ever again. I did those things until *I* couldn't bear to sleep next to me. But there wasn't any way I could live *without* doing those things, and if you'd grown up on the same street as me, you'd have done them too."

Something in his face changed. The pain quietened, dulling.

"Then I met someone," he mumbled. "Usually when you're in prison, they... they put you in front of these people who couldn't give less of a shit. You're just a criminal. They know you won't change. They skim over some options for when you leave, talking like they're about to fall asleep. They tick your name off on the list and tell the system you got given all the support and guidance you could dream of. Usually it's like that. But... but then someone wasn't."

Alastair took a cautious guess. "James Wheeler."

Jay's forehead creased. "How the hell do you know about Wheeler?"

"I read your brother's case file," Alastair said, earning himself a wince.

"Stop calling him that, will you? I know what Ian is to me. You're just being a shit, making me hear it."

"I didn't intend that."

"And I don't care what you intended." Memory had roughened Jay's accent, his northern vowels now blunt and heavy, as unwelcoming as a palisade wall. "My sessions with Wheeler were meant to last twenty minutes. He'd be in my cell over an hour each time, showing me leaflets for stuff he thought I could do. GCSEs, NVQs. Telling me that I was bright, that I could make something of myself. You know how many times I got told that as a kid?"

Alastair said nothing, numb.

"Never," Jay said, staring into his eyes. "Not once. Not even a possibility. How often did you hear it?"

Something twisted its way through Alastair's insides. "Too often."

"There's no such thing."

"I assure you there is. The pressures I—"

"Fuck your comfortable childhood," Jay cut in, cold. He took a second to unclench his jaw, then went on without contrition. "When I got out, Wheeler kept on ringing me. Checking up on me. I couldn't do any of the stuff he'd found for me, not with Ian looking over my shoulder all the time. But Wheeler didn't... he wasn't disappointed. Didn't act like I'd wasted his time."

His chest expanded with his breath.

"We met up when I could," he muttered. "Cheap hotels. Usually talked for a while, then went to bed."

Alastair attempted to give no reaction, unsettled by the hot and strangling rush of jealousy towards a man who'd now been gone into the ether for ten years.

"Don't," Jay huffed across the room at him. "Don't even make that face at me, Al. Either I'm a criminal and you're ashamed, or you're jealous. Pick."

Alastair loosened out his jaw, breathing in. "I never said ashamed. Please go on."

"Fine. Just don't bother hating him. He got the ugliest version of me I've ever been. I'd usually start crying halfway through. Telling him I was unhappy and I hated myself. Hated all the things I'd done. Wanted just to be a normal person, live a normal life. And he'd tell me he could get me out."

Jay pushed his hands into his pockets, gathering himself in the direction of an end.

"He used to mention the UKPPS to me," he said. "I used to tell him he was off his head, thinking I'd ever do that. Eventually he passed some stuff that I'd told him to the police. Small stuff about Ian, scraps of things. I didn't care too much. None of it would've amounted to anything. But somehow Ian found out about it, got hold of Wheeler's name."

Realisation dawned. "You were the anonymous tip off," Alastair said, his chest tight. "You warned the police that Ian was going to kill him."

Jay nodded, numb. "I knew Ian would figure out it was me. So I thought... Jesus, if I'm doing this... if I'm stabbing him in the back, I might as well stab until he's dead."

He looked away across the flat.

"I told them everything," he murmured. "Told them about things they'd never even realised were going on. They were interviewing me for days, all anonymous. One night, some woman called Kim strolled into my hotel room, told me she was from the Protected Persons Service, and said I needed to consider her offer."

He returned his eyes to Alastair, broken, and gave the slightest shake of his head.

"She said it'd be a completely new start. I'd never see my parents again. The place I grew up. Any of my mates. Couldn't ever see Wheeler again. He was going into witness protection as well, and if someone found their way to one of us, they could follow any connection to the other. All my life—everything I knew, everything I was—I signed it away on a gamble that Wheeler had been right. He said I could do something good with my life if I tried. So I tried."

"You were brave," Alastair said.

Jay's expression contorted. "Yeah?" he shot back. "I was stupid."

"What on earth makes you stupid?"

"Stupid to trust I'd be alright. They screwed up the trial, then they gave him parole. He's going to find me someday. And he'll probably try and burn me alive."

I will not let that happen. Alastair almost said it, the words fighting to get out of his mouth. *I will die before I let that happen.*

Before he could find his courage, Jay went on.

"Now I've built up a company I can't run away from," he said, exhaustion filling up his eyes again. "If I vanish now, all my people'll lose their jobs. And no matter how much good I do, no matter how many years go by, it won't make up for all the bad I did. There's no way I can ever undo it. That kills me. Cripples me."

He reached up, wiping his eyes with the back of his hand.

"I don't dare to make friends," he said. "Can't kid myself that I deserve them. Nobody'd want to anything to do with me, if they knew. Wouldn't want to work with me. Wouldn't want to be seen with me."

His throat seemed to grip, its closure catching in his breath. It was the closest sound to a sob he seemed prepared to make.

"Fuck this shit," he whispered, pressing his sleeve against his eyes. "I should've known."

Oh, God. What have I done?

"I'm sorry," Alastair said. Sickly, guilt-stricken heat rolled through his body in waves, lifting the hair on his neck onto end. "Jay, I... I didn't mean to suggest there's anything about you that... I-I'm truly sorry."

Jay huffed, the sound strained. He rolled words around his mouth with the tip of his tongue, then gave another shake of his head.

"You made it so easy to forget," he said, his eyes red. He reached a hand into his back pocket, retrieving a packet of cigarettes and a lighter. "Holy shit, you had me fooling myself. Police commissioner's boyfriend. Cliveden."

"Jay..."

"When I was a kid, I didn't know places like that even existed."

"Jay, I never meant to—"

"Like castles made of rainbows. Then we're there in your suite, and you're just good to me. Kind to me. Telling me you want to help me and keep me safe."

Jay lit his cigarette, his wrist shaking.

"Like there's something about me that just deserves to be happy and safe," he muttered around it. "No questions asked. What a rush."

"You do," Alastair said at once. "I'm sorry I suggested otherwise."

"Get fucked, Al," Jay murmured, as soft as *I love you.* He dragged on his cigarette, eyeing Alastair darkly across the several feet of space in between them. "If you want honesty from me now, at least be honest back. I'm a liability. I'm an embarrassment. Who'll ever respect you,

Commissioner of the Police of the Metropolis, when they find out you've had your dick in some criminal?"

Alastair's bones ached with guilt. "I spoke in anger," he said. "I shouldn't have. I'm sorry. I was hurt that you'd deceived me."

Jay's eyebrows lifted. *"Deceived* you?"

It wouldn't help to withdraw the remark, or try to shape it into something better. The only sustainable way out of this would be honesty. Without that, anything they managed to preserve would be unreal.

"I was hurt you hadn't confided in me," Alastair said. "Jay, I haven't been this close to someone in a long time. An *extremely* long time. It hurt to think that I'd grown close to an illusion."

"Jesus. I'm not a fucking illusion. I'm standing right here. I'm everything I was an hour ago."

"I realise that. And I'm sorry for how I reacted. I'm sorry if I brought to life some fears for you. I wish that I'd discovered this differently."

Jay's shoulders stayed stiff.

"Me too," he muttered. He blew smoke towards the carpet, not looking at Alastair. "I'm not going to say I wish I'd told you. If I'd been able to tell you, I would have. You rolled up in my life and everything was amazing, and there's no way I would have risked setting fire to it. I loved you too much to tell you. If you don't understand that, I don't care. It's still true."

Distressed by the use of past tense, Alastair swallowed.

"Love is founded upon trust," he said. "Trust is founded upon honesty. I wish that I'd heard this from you instead of someone else. If you don't understand that, it's still true."

Jay took this in without a sound. His eyes flickered towards Alastair's lips, hurt, then away across the room. He returned his cigarette to his mouth.

"Shame I only got a grand total of two minutes as something more than your fuck buddy," he said. "Maybe if I'd had five minutes, I'd have told you."

Oh—oh God, I...

"Are you saying you're finished with me?" Alastair asked. He held Jay's stare, suspecting he was about to receive a wound from which he would never recover. "Is this over between us?"

Jay didn't miss a beat. "Caesar's wife must be above suspicion."

Alastair took the blow. He'd thrown it first; he deserved it back.

"Or perhaps," he said, "Caesar could grow himself a spine." He steadied himself, his heart thudding with panic and hope. His honesty had caused this damage. Honesty might still stand some chance of repairing it. "You mean everything to me, Jay."

Jay hesitated, nervous colour flushing through his face. He expelled another stream of smoke towards the floor.

"Don't read my criminal record," he said awkwardly. "Please. I'm not the guy who did those things. I don't want you picturing him when you look at me."

"I won't," Alastair said. He didn't need to think. The promise came as easily as standing here, as solid as the ground beneath his feet. "I won't reopen your past. It's your business. Share only what you want with me."

Jay looked up into his eyes. "Why did you have me checked?"

There was nothing to be gained in hiding this. It hurt, thinking this had all arisen from an act of protective love.

"I thought I could keep you safe," Alastair said. "From... well, from anything that would pose a threat to you. Scotland Yard takes steps to secure the safety of a police commissioner's partner. I asked my assistant to register you, but the process requires a regulation background check. I didn't realise there'd be anything for her to find."

Jay's gaze dimmed.

"They won't let you have me now," he murmured, and his voice seemed impossibly small. "Will they? A shit like me."

Alastair paused. It was true that this would have to be handled with great care. Certain things would have to be forefronted; certain assumptions would have to be faced down and challenged, perhaps repeatedly. Rehabilitation had always been a part of his platform, always a focus, and even if Jay made a sensational example, he was a *strong* example. It wouldn't necessarily lead to ruin.

"I might face an uncomfortable discussion with my superiors," he said, looking into Jay's eyes. "And I'd lose credibility in the eyes of certain subordinates, if it ever came to light. But... ultimately, no one can forbid anything. I forced the world to respect me as a gay police officer. I can force them to respect my choice of partner."

Something moved across Jay's face, a flash of longing quickly suppressed beneath his drained and injured calm. Alastair had a feeling he knew which word had caused the hope.

He gave himself a moment to hope as well, then voiced something he couldn't leave unsaid.

"I don't mean to pry," he said. "But it'll help if there's been no addition to your criminal record since you left Manchester."

Jay answered without pause or doubt, looking straight into Alastair's eyes. "Nothing," he said. "Not one thing in ten years. I left all that behind me. I swear down to you."

A knot in Alastair's chest quietly loosened, slipping free. *Thank Christ,* he thought, letting the very worst of his fears fall away. His choice of partner would be controversial, but not completely out of the question. There might just be hope.

As the silence ached around them, bruised and sore, Alastair's heart seemed to nervously unwind. He realised that Jay was waiting for him to speak.

"You've made remarkable changes," he said. "In your circumstances, I mean. In your life. It's incredible what you've done, Jay."

Uncomfortable with it, Jay shrugged. "Doesn't mean a thing unless I help other people do the same," he muttered. "Too many kids in this country don't see a careers advisor 'til they're in prison. Witness protection shouldn't be the best thing that ever happened to someone."

He looked away.

"Okay," he mumbled, took one last drag of his cigarette, then tossed it with a hiss into his glass of wine. "This isn't how I wanted tonight to go, but... well, you know now. It's all out. It's your decision what you do with it."

Alastair's stomach tightened. "Would you rather I leave?"

"No," Jay said. "No, you... you don't have to. Can if you want. But don't think that I want you to."

He hesitated, glancing towards the kitchen.

"I, erm... I might go down the road to the shop," he said. "Get some air. I'm nearly out of cigs. But you could hang on here, if you want. Then when I get back, we'll..."

Alastair drew a careful breath. "Talk," he said.

Jay gave a fraction of a nod. "Figure something out."

"I'd like that." Alastair wished his voice hadn't broken. He steadied it with a squeeze of his own hands. "We'd... just reached somewhere rather special."

Jay did not react.

"Tell your assistant to work on her timing," he said, lifting his leather jacket from a hook on the back of the door. He checked through the pockets for his wallet. "For what it's worth, I meant everything I said. Still do."

"So did I." Alastair hesitated, struggling with the childish urge to cling. Part of him didn't want Jay to leave, not until everything was settled. He'd not felt this fragile since he was a little boy. "Shall I come with you?"

"Honestly, I... I kind of want a few minutes to chill. If we're going to talk, I need to breathe first." Jay pulled on his jacket, casting Alastair an uneasy glance. "Do you want me to make you a coffee or something before I go?"

Alastair flushed. "It's alright. I know how to use a kettle."

Jay remembered. The memory echoed in his eyes, a little soft, a little sad—but it was there.

"Shop's about ten minutes away," he said. He held Alastair's gaze. "I won't be long. Just sit tight, and we'll..."

Alastair gave a nod, trying to smile. It felt weak upon his mouth. "Alright."

"Do you want me to fetch you anything back?"

Though the honesty hurt, Alastair owed it. They'd come too far to only come this far. "Just you."

Jay huffed, barely audible. He glanced at Alastair's lips.

"See you in a bit, then," he said. "Make yourself at home. If you're hungry, there's... eat whatever you want, I don't mind."

He pulled his eyes away. He slipped out through the door, closing it quietly behind him, and his key rattled in the lock. He was gone.

In the silence, Alastair lifted both hands to his face. He pushed them back into his hair, his fingers splayed, his eyes closed, and kept them there. *Twenty minutes,* he told himself. Twenty minutes to find some sort of calm, bring his rioting heart under control, and prepare a more lasting apology. The damage that he'd done could be repaired. This night wasn't over.

Switching on the kettle, he scrolled through the log of his recent calls. She would be waiting somewhere, worrying, and he couldn't keep her on edge until the morning.

"I'm alone," he said, as soon as she answered. "He's gone out for air."

Juliet's voice, though quiet, was full of concern. "Are you alright?"

Alastair exhaled, unsure how to answer. He wasn't even certain where to begin. He closed his eyes for a moment, listening to the rumbling hush of the kettle, and told himself that he'd never kept the fullness of a situation from her before. She'd seen him through much more complex problems than this.

And if she was going to give up on him, she'd surely have done it weeks ago.

"There's a chance I'm about to appall you," he said, "but I want to be upfront. I owe you nothing less."

Juliet murmured her response, unafraid. "Go on."

"I'm... resolved, Juliet. To stand by him. He made the tip-off which saved James Wheeler's life. He turned traitor and provided enough information to bring down his brother's organisation. If the Crown Prosecution Service had done their job, Ian Straker wouldn't have seen daylight again. I don't see any reason to distance myself."

Juliet spoke with extreme care. "He has an ambitious criminal record, brother or no brother."

"I'm sure," Alastair said, his pulse quickening uncomfortably. "I imagine Jason Straker's credentials are toe-curling. But I'm not involved with him. I'm involved with Jay Fieldhouse, who tells me he's never received so much as a parking ticket. Is that true?"

"Not since his move to London," Juliet admitted. She seemed to pause, audibly gathering her courage. "You'll raise eyebrows, if it ever becomes known. You'll raise them very high."

"And I'll point them towards the prestigious award we just handed him. He's dedicated his life to rescuing young people from a path he knows too well. There couldn't be a better example of reform."

"All the same..."

"No," Alastair murmured, quiet and firm. "No, not 'all the same'."

He reached for the kettle as it started to boil, switching it off.

"If someone challenges me over this," he said, his heart beating hard, "and they're stupid enough to express on record that a criminal is always a criminal, I'll annihilate them for it."

He tipped hot water over the coffee granules at the bottom of his mug, letting the gentle hiss and tumble soothe his nerves.

"Direct people to me if you're asked about this," he said. "Don't say a word."

"Only agents of the British security services would have the authority to access UKPPS records. As you know, I'm an ordinary personal assistant. There's no way I could know any details of this."

Alastair stirred his coffee, exhaling. "Quite."

"I worry you'll face questions," she admitted. "But... well, I can see you're prepared to answer them. And I certainly won't stand in your way." A smile warmed her voice. "Something's changed, hasn't it?"

Alastair's chest swelled.

"We talked," he said. "He wants more, Juliet. For us. I want to give him that."

Juliet made a soft, contented noise. "Who said something first?"

"He did." Alastair opened up the fridge, glad she couldn't see the nervous smile threatening to form on his mouth. He must look like an idiot, smiling to himself in the dark. "He thought I knew already. That it must be obvious he..."

"Loves you?" Juliet said.

Oh, God.

And it might still be alright. We'll talk, and...

"He didn't realise I have feelings for him." Alastair concentrated on adding milk to his coffee, trying to say this like a man in his fifties and not a fluttering teenager. "He said he wants us to be something. And I'm... I'm not sure that I've ever in my life... he really does matter to me, Juliet. I'm sorry for the problems this might cause you."

"In the grand scheme of things, I'm happy with my lot." She was smiling; he could hear it in her voice. "Where is he at the moment?"

"He's gone out to buy cigarettes. Wisely, I think. It wasn't an easy discussion for either of us. But he'll be back soon, and we'll talk. I'm hoping I can reassure him that I'm—"

A small, unexpected noise stalled Alastair's thoughts. He paused to listen, falling still. It seemed to be a cautious sort of scraping, as if a thin metallic implement was being rattled very gently around a cylinder.

It was coming from somewhere close at hand.

"Is that him?" Juliet asked.

The lock, Alastair realised. His stomach gripped oddly. Unless twenty minutes had passed at lightning speed, it couldn't possibly be Jay. The smallness of the sound raised the hair on his arms; it didn't sound at all like an ordinary key.

Some nameless instinct stalled his breath.

Chapter 17

"Please stay quiet and listen," Alastair said, scanning his immediate surroundings. The one-room flat offered very little cover. In lieu of anything better, he opened up the tallest of Jay's kitchen cupboards and positioned himself behind the door, shielded from obvious sight. Juliet had fallen silent in his ear; she never needed direct commands from him twice. He switched his phone to speaker mode, locked it and dropped it into his pocket, freeing both his hands. He wanted to believe they wouldn't be needed, but in the event that they were, he wouldn't have time to fumble with his phone.

The rattling continued.

As the seconds stretched on, Alastair began to doubt himself, scrambling for an innocent explanation. Perhaps Jay had simply forgotten to mention his room mate who picked locks as a hobby.

A low, hollow clunk sounded through the flat, followed by the lazy whine of hinges.

Footsteps came into the lounge, too slow and too cautious to be Jay.

Alastair listened, unbreathing. He thought he could discern a second set accompanying the first, quieter and lighter on the floor.

He shut his eyes for a moment, forcing back the instinctive rush of panic, then pushed aside his second even more unhelpful instinct—the one which seemed to speak in his mother's voice, chiding him for being so embarrassing and dramatic, telling him to step out, say hello, and clear up this strange misunderstanding. That instinct was usually the one which turned ordinary people into victims. He'd attended too many crime scenes in his life to fall prey to it, seen too many corpses wearing pyjamas and shocked expressions.

"Where is he?" a male voice grunted, low with suspicion. "Not back from work?"

A derisive snort answered.

"Then who lit the fuckin' candles?" asked a younger, more sarcastic voice. "He's in here. Check the bathroom."

Alastair glanced quickly at the contents of Jay's cupboard: a mop with a cheap metal handle, too flimsy to withstand any force; an apron, too thick to twist into an effective garotte; heavy tins of soup and baked beans.

Taking up two tins in utter silence, Alastair braced himself. Physical altercations had been rare, even twenty years ago. He'd not expected to be involved in one this evening. His mother's voice gasped in horror in the back of his mind, outraged at his mortifying rudeness towards these unexpected guests. *"Alastair, what in heaven's name are you doing? Put those down at once."* Alastair ignored her, his pulse quick and fast.

The bathroom door squeaked open across the flat.

"Nothing," the deeper voice muttered. "Maybe he's gone out?"

"That coffee's fresh," replied the younger voice. "Who makes a fuckin' coffee then goes out?"

Alastair stayed still, sensing their eyes move as one to the slightly ajar cupboard door.

The silence boomed.

"Go on," the young man said.

Not making a sound, Alastair waited. He couldn't throw with any accuracy or force, not at an unknown target. His best chance here lay in speed and surprise. He held his ground, allowing the heavy footsteps to bring themselves closer to the door, his every muscle as taut as a bowstring. Once the footsteps stopped, there came a long and painful pause.

As a hand threw open the door, Alastair launched himself from inside. He brought the heavy tin down onto the intruder's skull with force, then aimed a second swing towards his nose. It connected with a sickening crunch. The man howled, staggering backwards into the fridge, and Alastair registered with a glance his tattooed and shaven head, his enormous bulk—and the switchblade he carried in one hand.

Alastair didn't wait to see anything else. He released the tins and bolted for the door, dodging the foot that lashed out to stop him. He vaulted the two canisters of petrol they'd brought and threw himself against the door, grappling for the handle.

Before he could get it open, the second intruder slammed with force into his back.

The blow shocked the breath from Alastair's lungs. He arched, trying to fight, then shouted out with pain as his arm was wrenched up behind his back. The intruder pinned it into place, then dug the flat of a blade against the side of his throat.

"Don't move," the boy barked, panting—and a boy he was. From his voice, Alastair doubted he could be more than twenty. He spoke with a northern accent, so painfully familiar now that Alastair couldn't help but shut his eyes. "Don't fuckin' move. You draw one more breath and I'll take an ear off you, right here and now."

Alastair said nothing, forcing himself to count through the pain and the panic. He'd not needed this technique in twenty years. *Juliet,* he reminded himself with a breath, and shifted just enough to make sure his pocket could hear. Whatever was about to happen, he needed her to know about it.

"You know who sent us to fetch you?" the boy grunted. "You know why we're here?"

Alastair didn't move. He didn't speak, didn't breathe, didn't think.

The intruder he'd incapacitated was hauling himself up from the kitchen floor, blood pouring down his face.

"Is that him?" the man asked, dazed. He reached up to try and wipe away the mess with his hands. "That's Ian's brother?"

The boy sneered at him, tutting. "I dunno, dick-for-brains. D'you think?"

"Thought he was supposed to look like Ian."

"Can you even fuckin' see anything right now?" the boy snapped. "Of course it's him. This is his flat and he tried to run. Case closed. Now pass me the ties before he kicks the shit out of you again, and let's go."

Alastair's pulse slugged inside his chest. Ties meant a move to a secondary location, a possibility to be avoided at almost any cost, but the knife at his throat made resistance unwise.

And there was something far more serious to consider.

If he spoke up in this moment, pointing out their mistake, they'd quite likely cut his throat, stuff his carcass back into the cupboard, and then lie in wait for Jay. But if they moved him on to another location, they would be gone by the time Jay returned. They wouldn't realise their error for some time. Juliet could use that time to track Alastair, trace him.

All he needed to do was keep his mouth shut, and Jay would be safe.

"They won't let you have me now, will they?" he'd said. *"A shit like me."*

Alastair swallowed, making his choice. He clenched his fists and forearms to create as much bulk in them as possible, shaking in silence as the boy secured his wrists behind his back. It was done before he could even consider second thoughts.

"Right," the boy panted. The stronger man seized hold of Alastair by the shoulders. "Take him down to the car. I'll finish in here."

Alastair kept his head high and his eyes straight ahead as he was forced down the stairs in the darkness, stumbling on the bare stone steps. The thick fingers wrapped around his wrist ties held him upright. He could feel the switchblade pressed flat in the middle of his back, a quiet warning not to draw attention to himself or cry out. With a minimum of effort, it could sink into his back, drive its way between his ribs, pierce his heart. It was an unnecessary precaution. He had two better reasons to stay silent than they could ever have provided him. One of those reasons would still be listening on the line even now, summoning help, waking the war machine of Scotland Yard. The other was a few minutes' walk from here, quietly clearing his head, trying to air the wounds that Alastair had just left in him.

A brief flutter of fear skimmed between Alastair's ribs.

Please don't let those be the final things I ever...

A battered blue Nissan waited by the pavement, its engine running. As the shaven-headed man forced Alastair into the backseat, the driver of the car glanced around. Alastair lowered his face from sight as much as he could, his heart beating hard.

"That him?" the driver asked.

"It's him," the bulky man replied. Alastair suppressed his flood of relief, keeping his eyes to himself. "Milo's just sorting out the flat. Won't take long. Place is tiny."

"What happened to your face, man?"

"He brayed me with somethin'. Bust my nose."

The driver laughed, turning his eyes back to the wheel. "Sounds about right," he said. "It's an improvement, mate. You should be thanking him."

The bulky man gave a grunt. He reached across to the open door and slammed it shut.

"Ian can thank him for me," he said.

Alastair closed his eyes.

Even the bell above the door sounded weary. It announced Jay's arrival into the shop as if he'd interrupted it doing something important, a dull and reluctant tinkle that he absolutely understood.

Squinting in the glare of the halogen lights, he made his way directly to the aisle where they kept the booze, too tired to pretend that he'd come for other things. Alastair's fancy wine was meant for savouring over a meal; what they needed now was several litres of vinegary paint-stripper. They had a lot of ugly things to drown in it. He chose a bottle by price, barely glancing at the label, then moved on towards the wall of magazines and chocolate.

As a child, corner shops like this had been his training grounds. He'd started young, too young for shopkeepers to think he should be watched. When he got good at pocketing sweets, and could do it without turning bright red and shaky in the knees, he'd started lifting bigger and bigger things. Soon he'd trained out the embarrassment and the nervousness. It was only a question of practice. By the age of nine or so, all he ever felt as he slipped undetected from a shop was a quiet, sure-footed sense of victory. There had come a point in his life when he almost never paid for anything. Popping to the shop was as casual for him as for anyone else, the only difference being that what he needed went up his sleeves rather than into a basket.

Even now, the sight of a wall of chocolate and sweets triggered an automatic analysis in the back of his mind: how clear the shopkeeper's line of sight was, how vigilant they seemed, how much interest they'd taken in him already. The calculation happened separately from conscious thought. He didn't have to intend anything for those razor-sharp skills to kick into motion, supplying him with the odds and the risks and the gains within the span of a second.

Sometimes, a flash of his old instincts brought him guilt, along with strangling distress that those deeper parts of him would never truly change.

Sometimes, there was a weird and savage comfort about it: *I won't. But if I had to, then I could.*

As a boy, knowing how to steal what he needed had meant his needs were always met. He'd always had food in his pockets, toothpaste and soap, anything a shop could sell. The only person he relied on for those things was himself. He'd been proud of it, and pride hadn't been easy to come by.

Numb, gazing at the wall of shiny wrappers and logos, Jay let the sense of comfort come. *I'll always be alright,* he thought. *Even on my own.* His chest ached a little as he thought it, understanding all too well why he felt this way tonight.

He wondered if Alastair Harding had ever gone into a shop on his way home from school and lifted a multipack of Mars bars, just in case his parents were too drunk to make food.

It was difficult to let go of the anger.

Numb, Jay gathered up a Crunchie, two Toffee Crisps and a large bar of Galaxy, then took the small pile to the counter. The girl gave him a smile, scooping his haul across her desk to tap them one by one through her till.

"Rough day?" she asked. She had a lip ring and the tips of her hair were bright blue, the rest a fading fairy pink.

Jay huffed, disarmed. Something about a friendly stranger would always get to him. He didn't ask how she knew, supposing it wasn't a surprise to hear that he looked like shit. His eyes might even still be red.

"Wasn't so bad at first," he said.

"Yeah?" She rang through his bottle of wine, then handed it over. "What went wrong?"

Jay wondered for a moment how to put it into words. The weird humour of it almost made him smile. *I'm in love with my fuck friend, the Met chief. But he's just found out my whole family are crooks.*

His smile faded, realising what sat at the heart of it.

"Think I've disappointed my partner," he said. "That's all. Didn't mean to disappoint him, but..." His throat clamped shut, stopping the rest.

She took this in with sympathy. "Will he forgive you, d'you think?"

"Hope so." Jay watched her search his Galaxy bar for a price sticker, her snowy pink nails sparkling as she turned it. "He's... y'know. Won't see another him. Not in this life."

Jesus, why am I telling you all this? The pain sat too close to the surface to keep it out of sight.

"Just want him to think the best of me," he muttered, flushing. He tried a shrug, hoping it made this seem a little less weird. "I don't know if he can anymore."

She reached somewhere beneath the counter, pulling out a crumpled plastic bag. "If he'd done what you did, would you get over it?"

Jay didn't have to think. "Probably only love him more, to be honest."

She dropped him a gentle wink, sliding his chocolate into the bag.

"Don't tell him you're sorry," she advised, folding it over. "Tell him what he means to you, and why you did it, and how you'll make it right."

For a second or two, Jay couldn't speak. He almost wanted to ask if she would maybe come with him, help him fix this without a risk of making it worse. He took the bag from her and swallowed, loosening his tongue. "Feel like I should be tipping you," he managed.

"Won't stop you," she said. "Did you need anything else?"

"Y-yeah. Twenty Benson and Hedges, please. Ta."

Walking home, Jay rehearsed what he would say.

Hey... that got a bit mad. I shouldn't have been so defensive. It's just that you're perfect and I don't want to lose you. Can we start again?

Hey, I didn't mean to blow up at you. I think I've still got some shit to work through. I came from nothing, and you're... you're everything, and I honestly don't know how to...

Hey, listen. I was out of line. It's fair you'd want to know what kind of man you're sleeping next to. It just kills me, thinking you'd be scared of me. You don't have to be.

Just please don't go.

It ripped him apart, realising how much he wanted this—how close they'd come. If they could just sort this out, the whole thing would stop being a game of pretend. What they'd shared back at Cliveden would stop being a fairy story and start being Jay's actual life, and in the morning he'd wake up in his boyfriend's arms, cook Alastair breakfast and say *I love you,* not just think it.

As he started to get anxious, worrying too much over the words, Jay swept the whole lot from his head. He would know what he needed to say when he was looking at Al. He couldn't do this on his own, guessing the responses.

All he could do was open up, give it his best, and hope Al understood.

Tangled in his thoughts, Jay was only vaguely conscious of the crowd of people gathered outside his building from some distance away. Only as he got close enough to see coats pulled over pyjamas, scared faces turned up towards the roof, did he truly start to notice them. Concerned, he quickened his pace. Maybe someone had triggered the fire alarms for a prank. It wouldn't be the first time, if they had.

Closer to the building, he realised he could hear two alarms, fighting each other to be heard.

Jay broke into a run.

At the edge of the crowd, a familiar face turned towards his approach. Ghufran owned the restaurant on the ground floor. He had four daughters and an Arsenal season ticket, and his wife made qatayef worth dying for.

"Ghufran," Jay panted, stumbling over to him. "Ghufran, what the hell's going on?"

"We've got a fire," Ghufran replied, tipping a weary nod towards the upper floors of the building. Black smoke was pouring through a bathroom window on Jay's floor. "We've had to evacuate the whole building. Fire brigade's on its way."

Jay looked across the crowd of worried people, his heart pounding.

"Where's—" *Oh, Jesus.* "Did everyone get out okay? Is this everybody?"

"Why? Who's missing?"

No. Oh, no—he's—

"Al," Jay said, searching every face again in panic. None of them were right. "Alastair, he's—h-he was in my—which flat is the fire in?"

"We don't know yet," Ghufran said. "Nobody's seen it. We heard the alarm, then someone came downstairs to say there was smoke, and that was only two minutes ago."

Oh, shit.

"It's mine." Jay dropped his bag. The bottle smashed against the pavement. "It's my flat!"

He sprinted towards the door.

"Jay!" Ghufran roared after him. "Jay, you can't go in there!"

Jay didn't hear the rest.

"Alastair's still inside!" he shouted, barging through the door with his shoulder and racing towards the stairs.

A storm cloud of smoke awaited him on his floor, a black and brooding presence as malevolent as a poltergeist, swirling thickly as it gathered beneath the ceiling. This wasn't an ordinary fire. They didn't grow this fast, get this dark, without help. Hauling his jacket up around his nose and mouth, Jay struggled along the hall towards his door.

Smoke was seething from all four edges, churning and curling and rising fast.

Shit—

Jay grappled for the metal handle, yelping as it burned his fingers. He wrapped a fistful of his jacket around it, twisted and wrenched, throwing himself to safety behind the door as heat and smoke belched forth with the force of a river. The reek of petrol waved in its wake. Coughing, stooping as low as he could, Jay staggered into the flat and screamed over the shrieks of the alarm.

"Al!"

Everything was lost in black smoke. Jay could only see the couch and the bed by the light of the flames licking across them, striping up the walls towards the ceiling.

Filling his lungs, Jay howled.

"ALASTAIR!"

The roar of the fire drowned out any hope of a response. He didn't know if he could hear a voice calling back to him in panic, or if it was just the piercing screams of the alarm, ringing in his ears. He dropped to the ground beneath the smoke line, clamping his jacket over his nose, and crawled on one arm towards the kitchen.

"Al—"

Someone's blood was spattered across the floor, smeared up the front of the fridge. It gleamed scarlet and black, flashing in the light of the fire.

"Oh, *shit—*" Jay choked, his eyes stinging with the petrol fumes. *"Al!"*

He stumbled on his hands and knees across the flat, checking under everything he could, shouting Alastair's name. There was no sign of him. The bed had become a solid column of flame, pouring more and more black smoke towards the ceiling by the second.

Fuck—shit—if you were—

Jay hauled himself to the bathroom door, checking inside.

"Al—" He coughed, hacking. "Al, are you—"

Above the bed, a vast triangle of wallpaper swung free, burning as it fell, sweeping flames across everything it touched. Something within the wall of smoke let out a loud, echoing crack. Part of the ceiling gave way.

Choking, Jay crawled back towards the door.

You're not here. You're not in here, you're—there's nowhere you could—

Even as he dragged himself out to the landing, Jay's instincts screamed at him to go back, to search, to check everywhere once more, reach properly behind the couch this time. Alastair could be lying there, overcome by smoke, burning. He would die because Jay didn't go back. These were Jay's last seconds to save him, and Jay was spending them trying to escape.

Shit—

Oh, shit—I can't leave you to die—

As Jay clawed by his fingertips back towards his door, footsteps came pounding up the stairs. Heavy arms dragged around his chest, hauling him up. Someone else seized hold of him around the legs. He tried to shout at them, beg them to go into his flat and check, but sucking in a breath filled his lungs with smoke. He choked and hacked, unable to fight as his rescuers staggered down the stairs with him.

As they reached the floor below, another deafening crack sounded from above. More of the building's structure had given way, eaten up by fire.

Oh, fuck. Jay clung to the arms fastened around him, coughing and retching as his lungs struggled to expel the smoke. *I left you. I love you and I left you to burn.*

Blinded by tears, coughing fit to die, Jay only realised they'd reached the outside air when his rescuers rolled him onto the cold hard surface of the road. He lolled onto his back, barely conscious, still gripping the arms that had carried him.

"He's alive!" Ghufran shouted to the crowd. Jay could hear people crying, sobbing in panic. "He's alive! Get an ambulance!"

It's too late, Jay thought. He tried to speak, his lungs straining. *It's over. I left him. He's gone.*

Someone pressed a hand to his forehead.

"Jay? Jay—"

The building was ablaze. Tongues of flame lapped the sky from an upper floor window, drinking the darkness as smoke billowed in torrents from the street-level entrance. A small crowd had gathered to treat someone lying in the road. The rest of the building's occupants hung back in fear, frightened children sobbing as they clung to their parents.

As Juliet looked twice at the man in the road, her heart lurched into her throat.

"Larry, stop the car!" she gasped, grappling for the door handle. The vehicle jolted to a stop. She staggered out, threw shut the door and hurried towards the knot of people, her heels snapping against the asphalt. "Excuse me! Excuse me, I know this man—I need to—"

Jay Fieldhouse was panting on the ground, his face and his hair black with soot. His watering eyes had tracked clean paths down his cheeks. Juliet knelt at his side, assessing him quickly as he hacked and strained, struggling for breath. He didn't seem to have suffered any burns other than the palm of his right hand, the skin there branded with an inch-wide strip of shining scarlet-red. He was coughing like he'd breathed in half of hell.

Larry appeared at Juliet's side, hovering just within her sight. "Is he alright, miss?"

Juliet swallowed back her fear.

"We need urgent medical assistance for this man," she said quickly. "Get an ambulance here as fast as you can. Then call the deputy commissioner, tell him I've reached Jay Fieldhouse's flat and there's a major fire underway. I'm taking him to London Bridge Hospital. I'll need people to meet us there. There's no sign of the commissioner."

Larry nodded quickly, fumbling his phone from inside his jacket. "Ma'am."

As he made the call, Juliet looked down into Jay's face, feeling faintly sick as he continued to cough. She reached out, pressing her cold hands against his cheeks.

"Jay?" she said. He didn't seem to hear her, wheezing, every breath laboured. Juliet's jaw locked. "Jay—"

His eyes flickered, green irises appearing amongst the soot. He stared up at her and searched her face, a dazed spark of recognition firing in the depths. The awards evening seemed to have happened centuries ago. The two of them had exchanged no more than a few words—Alastair's business card offered, turned down—and though Jay clearly recalled her, he couldn't quite place her.

"My name is Juliet," she said. "I'm Sir Alastair Harding's assistant."

He lunged at once for her wrists.

"Al—" He choked, writhing as he gripped her. "H-he's inside —please—"

Juliet's stomach gripped. *You went into the building,* she thought. *You searched for him.* The reaction certainly seemed authentic. Those wild eyes were difficult, if not impossible, to fake.

It stood as a mark in his favour, but questions still needed to be asked.

Juliet reapplied her hands, one across his forehead and one secured firmly at his shoulder, forcing him to lie flat.

"He's not inside," she said. "I know it for a fact."

Jay Fieldhouse wheezed up at her, uncomprehending.

"Now I suggest that you concentrate on breathing," she said. "In through the nose, then out through the mouth. The sooner you can talk, the better."

Chapter 18

THEY'D GIVEN JAY BABY BLUE PYJAMAS TO WEAR, EMBROIDERED WITH the hospital's logo. The nurse had turned the lights down low, encouraging him to put his head back and sleep, with a promise that his oxygen mask would stay in place overnight. This private room was bigger and far cleaner than his flat; no sound filtered in from the corridor outside.

Jay would not be sleeping, though.

The last thing he had any right to do was rest.

He bitterly regretted leaving his flat. Of all the mistakes he'd made tonight, though he didn't yet understand why, that had clearly been the biggest. Something had happened in the few short minutes he was gone. Whatever it was, he wished it had happened to them both. Juliet had seemed certain that Alastair wasn't in the building, but Jay couldn't let himself believe it—not until Alastair walked into this room, took a seat beside Jay's bed, and swore to Jay he was alright.

Until then, there was nothing to do but face the featureless white ceiling and wait, trying and failing to make some sense of it all.

The empty hours sat as heavy on Jay's chest as a boulder. What time it was now, what stage of the night, he couldn't even guess. His perception of its passage was mangled out of shape by the feeling that he was urgently needed. Part of him was still crawling along the corridor to his burning flat, trying to go back and check. Once or twice, he'd wondered if he should just discharge himself, get a taxi to Scotland Yard and sit in the lobby until someone finally agreed to take him to Al. But the nurses had taken away his clothes, along with his wallet and his phone.

Shutting his eyes, Jay filled his lungs with the oxygen coming through his mask. He'd never had one of these before. When they first put it on him, he'd expected the air to seem cleaner or colder, just *better* somehow, good air with all the badness removed. But it was just the same as normal air.

A quiet click from the door broke through his thoughts. He opened his eyes to find a nurse leaning into his room, her expression gentle.

"Two men and a lady are here to talk to you," she said. "Do you feel strong enough? Or would you like them to wait until morning?"

Al. Jay shifted to sit up, alert at once.

"I'm okay," he said, his voice muffled beneath the mask. "I want to see them."

The nurse nodded. "If you get tired, just press your call button and I'll come."

Jay wondered what the touch of protectiveness in her voice was about. "Alright," he mumbled. "I'll... th-thanks."

She stood back, holding open the door, and gestured his visitors inside.

Neither of the men were Alastair. Though Jay had never met them before, he recognised them both in an instant as police. It was something about the unapologetic eye contact, backed up by the way they nearly prowled into the room, hands in the pockets of their coats. Jay looked between them as they flanked his bed. Little differentiated their hard-lined faces. One was slightly older, slightly taller and slightly wearier, which led Jay to assume he was the senior. Both were forty-something and white, dressed in nondescript shirts and ties, and sporting the standard father-of-two haircut. They seemed annoyed to be out of bed at this hour, frowning before a single word had been said. Neither spoke as they took their places.

Behind them, apparently removed from the proceedings, Juliet had taken a chair in the corner without a sound, one leg crossed over the other. Jay hadn't noticed her enter the room.

Wary, he glanced between his visitors' faces.

"Jason Straker?" the older of the two asked.

Jay's muscles tightened. That was *not* a good start. He gave no sign of acknowledgement, his pulse drumming out a nervous warning to him as the officer took ID from inside his coat.

"Detective Chief Superintendent Curlew," the man said, flashing his credentials. The other one produced a small notebook and a biro. "This is Detective Superintendent Young. We're here to ask you a few questions about your relationship with Sir Alastair Harding."

What the—?

Jay glanced instinctively towards Juliet, who looked back at him without speaking.

"It's Fieldhouse," Jay said, pulling in a breath through his mask. "My name's Jay Fieldhouse. Where's Alastair?"

Curlew's expression didn't change. "We were hoping you'd like to tell us."

Jay faltered, concerned. His eyes flashed back towards Juliet and found her watching him still, analysing his reaction with her shrewd brown eyes. His heartbeat sped.

"Why don't you know?" he asked. "You told me he wasn't in the flat. You said that you knew it for a fact. Are you now telling me there's a chance he was—"

"Your building," Juliet interrupted, her expression unreadable, "is the only place on this planet we can be certain that he isn't."

"Then where is he?"

"If you care for his welfare, you'll respond to DCS Curlew's questions honestly and in full. Alastair would want you to do so."

Jay didn't respond. He knew what a police interrogation sounded like. He'd had his first at the age of fourteen, lied his way through it, spat and sworn and kicked the chairs until the duty solicitor told the officers they were distressing a minor unduly. She'd fired the magic bullets, *charge him or let him go,* and that was that. Jay had used them in every subsequent interview.

He'd hoped never to find himself in one again.

"Am I suspected of something?" he asked. "What's going on?"

His questions bounced off Curlew's face like sunlight off a mirror. "How long have you known the commissioner?"

Jay forced himself to swallow, coughing as the motion irritated his throat. "F-few weeks," he said.

"In what circumstances did you meet?"

"Small charity of the year. My charity won. I'm their chief exec. We were sat together for dinner."

"And you spent that night at his residence, did you?"

"Yeah."

"Doing what?"

Jay widened his eyes, staring directly into Curlew's. "How much detail do you want?"

"You're saying that you commenced a sexual relationship with him," Curlew said.

Jesus Christ. "We slept together," Jay muttered, heat breaking out across his face. "What's going on?"

"And you've met him for sex on several occasions since then?"

"Whoa—okay. Okay, listen. I get that you're leading this somewhere sordid. I get that you're setting out some horrible little path, hoping that I'll prance my way along it. Why don't we jump right to the end, and you tell me exactly what's happening?"

"I'll take that response as a yes," Curlew said, as calm as stone. "At what point in the proceedings did you make Sir Alastair aware that you're a convicted criminal and a close family member of the ganglord Ian Straker? Or did you conceal that from him with a particular purpose in mind?"

Jay's jaw clenched. He looked past Curlew's shoulder into Juliet's face, his shoulders starting to shake. "Are you kidding me?" he bit out.

"Please answer the question," she said.

"Why don't *you* answer the question?"

"I have." Her eyes were dark and glossy, fixed upon his face, and she was pale. "Now I'd like to hear you answer it."

"Yeah?" Jay shot back, annoyed. He coughed into his mask as his lungs strained. "I'd like to hear where Alastair is. I'd like to hear why none of you are telling me, and I'd like to hear what exactly I'm being accused of. I'd like to hear it right now."

Curlew slipped back into the fray. "Why did you hide your true identity from the commissioner, Jason?"

"Jesus," Jay breathed, staring at him. "Could you three maybe have googled the UKPPS before you came in here? I'm *not allowed* to tell people. It was a *new* relationship. Why am I getting the third degree?"

Curlew changed track without a blink. "What were the events of this evening as you see them?"

Jay lifted a hand and adjusted his mask, buying himself a second to level his tone.

"Al came round about seven," he said, trying his best to stay calm. He'd not done anything wrong. All he needed to do was tell the truth. "I'd cooked dinner. He brought w—"

"This was at your flat?" Curlew cut in.

Jay took a breath. "Yes."

"Did you specifically invite him to your flat?"

"Where else would I be able to cook him dinner?"

"Your flat isn't listed as one of Sir Alastair's authorised residences," Curlew said, one eyebrow flicking upwards. "Why would he put his security aside like that? Did you persuade him it was a good idea?"

"I wanted to cook for him," Jay said, approaching the brink of despair. "Where is he?"

"What did you discuss over dinner?"

"All sorts. We just... Jesus, we were just chatting. I don't remember every single thing we said." As the silence stretched, Jay dragged in a rasping breath. "What do you *want* me to say?"

Juliet spoke from across the room. "What did you discuss *after* dinner, Jay?"

Jay looked at her, trying to read the strangely haunted expression on her face. He didn't want to share this information with two arsehole detectives, talking to him like a truculent teenager they'd found skulking somewhere he shouldn't.

He told her instead, begging her with his eyes to explain.

"Al and I set this thing up as casual," he said. "For a while now, I've wanted it to be more. See each other properly. Last night, he told me that he feels the same. He wants more too."

"Though he still had no idea who you actually are?" Curlew checked.

Jay bit down into the side of his tongue. He lifted his stare in silence to Curlew, holding still for a second, simply breathing.

As he spoke, his voice shook.

"My name," he said, "is Jay Fieldhouse. I'm the founder of the Fieldhouse Foundation. Last year, my charity got 164 kids back into education or apprenticeships. We got another 209 into full-time employment. We oversaw 14 separate youth-led projects for the benefit of local communities in London, and we arranged networking, consultation and training for over a thousand youth professionals."

Curlew waited, entirely unaffected. The dullness in his eyes twisted Jay's upper lip back into a snarl.

"That's who I am," he said fiercely. "And a few weeks ago, I met a guy a million miles out of my league. He liked me back somehow. And I'll grant you I had a whole lot of shit to tell him—shit that keeps me awake, shit that I regret *every single day* of my life—but we were just getting somewhere, somewhere *good,* somewhere I'd never been before. I didn't know if I meant something to him or if he was just in this for fun. I didn't know how he'd take it. That's why I kept it."

Curlew gave a dry huff. "And how *did* he take it?"

Jay's stomach pulled.

"Not great at first," he said. If he tried to claim anything else, they'd see that he was lying. They would wonder why. "A lot of shock." He took a breath, glancing towards Juliet. "I told him everything you hadn't," he said. "Filled in all the gaps you left. You know I'm the reason that Ian got sent down, don't you? You know I'm the one who put him behind bars?"

"This is Ian Straker, your older brother," Curlew noted with interest, "who absconded from parole several weeks ago. How often do you speak to him these days?"

"Funnily enough, I don't. I've not said a word to Ian since the day I—..."

As the pieces suddenly slotted into place, Jay stopped dead. He snapped his head towards Curlew.

"Wait," he said. "Where is Al?"

Curlew made no reply, waiting.

Jay's heart slid up into his throat. "What are you telling me?" he demanded. "Why am I being grilled like I—h-holy shit—"

"What happened after the two of you argued, Jay?" Juliet asked.

"We didn't argue," Jay bit out. "We talked for a while, and it got intense, but he... he seemed to understand why I'd... and I thought maybe if I stepped out for some air, went to the shop, bought some cigs, we'd be able to talk better when I got back. Sort things out. Why are you—"

Juliet pressed on. "What time did you leave the flat?"

"I don't know. I didn't check."

"Why did you choose a shop so far away?"

"Are you for real? It's ten minutes."

"There are shops closer to your flat."

"Are there?" Jay said, staring into Juliet's eyes. "I always go to that one. It's just habit. *Where the actual fuck is Al?"*

Juliet paused, preparing something unwelcome behind the blankness of her expression.

"He's wherever your brother's associates have taken him," she said. The bottom dropped from Jay's stomach. The walls around him seemed to fall. "We're now working very quickly to find him."

For several seconds, Jay couldn't breathe. Words wouldn't arrange themselves into the proper strings in his head. His oxygen machine gave a questioning beep, noting the sudden pause in flow.

"He's—y-you're saying Ian's—and you think *I'm* in on it?" he said.

Juliet's gaze flickered. "We think it's odd that the Metropolitan commissioner has been kidnapped by a Manchester ganglord within weeks of starting a relationship with that ganglord's younger brother."

Fuck.

"Okay—*or,*" Jay said, "the fact that Al's involved with me is exactly why Ian would've targeted—"

"We think it's odd that it happened in the very hour your history came to light."

"Look, this isn't—"

"We think it's odd that you conveniently stepped out for air," Juliet went on, as cold as ice, "and returned when Alastair was gone."

Jesus.

"Can you all just turn it in," Jay said, starting to shout, "and listen to me for *one minute* without barking at me? Can we give that a try, maybe? Please?"

None of them moved.

Jay proceeded slowly, trying to ignore the lightning storm now taking place inside his chest.

"Ian starts fires," he said, shaking. "This is what he does to people that cross him. He tried to kill a guy called James Wheeler back in Manchester, and I warned the police, and they stopped it. Ian knows it was me who ratted on him."

They all waited, their eyes on him like cats studying a rat inside a cage.

"And if Ian's now got hold of Alastair," Jay said, "you should *not* be in here wasting time talking to me. You should be out there looking for him, *now,* because Ian's waited ten fucking years to punish me for what I did."

Curlew scoffed, a dull and empty sound.

"You're suggesting the Metropolitan police commissioner's been kidnapped to teach you a lesson?" he said. "Didn't you just admit to us it's only been a few weeks since—"

To Jay's surprise, Juliet interrupted. "Detectives," she said, sitting up in her chair. "I think you've seen what you came to see. Please leave. I'll finish up here."

Displeasure flashed across Curlew's features, too quick for him to hide. His mouth flattened and his eyes grew small and tight, puckering at their edges with annoyance. With effort, he formed the expression into a smile, then turned to Juliet.

"Miss Naughton," he said, with the air of one asking a cat please not to sit upon the kitchen counter. "I know your role turns out to be a bit more *involved* than we were previously told. And I realise your people are providing us a lot of support on this. But this is a Scotland Yard investigation, and that means it falls under my autho—"

"I spoke clearly," she said, watching him with absolute calm.

Curlew shuttered to another halt. His jaw rolled in a circle, irritated. He released the rest of his breath in a snort, determined to have the last sound, even if not the last word. He glanced at the other detective, nodded stiffly, and the notebook was folded away.

The two of them left without speaking—though Curlew took pains to pull the door ahead of its assisted swing. The buffer in the frame muffled his slam into a feather-soft click.

In the silence that followed, Jay kept his eyes on Juliet. She unfolded herself from her chair with grace, brought it with her, and placed it soundlessly beside his bed.

"You're the last person to have any contact with Alastair," she said, sitting back down. "Whether you mind me saying it or not, your criminal record is the stuff of nightmares. DCS Curlew would be failing us all if he didn't question you harshly."

It was the first time Jay had properly taken her in. On the night of the awards evening, she'd registered in his mind as a glossy but anonymously professional woman in a little black dress, probably about to ask if he could join them all for photographs. The second time, he'd been too blinded by smoke and his own leaking eyes to make her out. Now that he saw her clearly, she struck him as far too young to wield the kind of composure that she did. She moved with the same measured grace as Alastair, and she gave the same thought to her words. Although she was pretty, her eyes big and brown in a heart-shaped face, the overall effect was strangely disconcerting—as if whoever sat behind those eyes, working the controls, had selected them with purpose somehow, put them on like a battlesuit specifically designed to distract and disarm. Her beauty was the clean and misleading beauty of a show home, everything deliberate, nothing out of place.

Are you worried? Jay thought, trying to read her face. There was nothing to be seen, no clue he could find. *Have you just decided not to be worried? Do you even understand what you're dealing with?*

There was no easy way to put this.

"My brother's a killer," he said. His throat closed over, hating the words, wanting them to stay unvoiced and locked in his chest where they might not be real. He didn't want any of this to be real. "He's killed several times that I know about, and probably a few times that I don't. If you want to judge me by the record of the man I used to be, alright. Judge me. But you won't see murder on that record. I had lines and I didn't cross them."

He held Juliet's eyes over the blue rubber edge of his oxygen mask.

"But there's murder on Ian's," he said. "You can question me for days, there'll still be nothing I can tell you, and Alastair will die. Do you get that?"

Juliet took a moment to process this, laying her hands together in her lap.

"We're following several lines of inquiry," she said. "Scotland Yard and the security services are working together to find him, and we're doing so at speed. Nobody is sitting idle."

"Right. Good. What can I do?"

A small frown line appeared between Juliet's eyebrows. "You, personally? Very little."

"There must be something," Jay said. "You can't expect me just to sit here and wait."

"Well... if Curlew wishes to question you again, please be calmer. I appreciate that it's frustrating to be dogged by your history. I can imagine how irritating it gets. But the best way to keep Curlew from wasting time is to show him coolly and collectedly that that's what he's doing."

Jay pushed his tongue behind his teeth, wondering how many charities he would have to establish before his present began to outweigh his past. At least one more, it seemed. "Right," he said again. "Fine. I'll..."

"If you're defensive," she said, one eyebrow lifting, "he'll assume that there's a reason."

"There *is* a reason," Jay snapped. "It's that I'm—"

"I know," she cut in. "And for what it's worth, I'm *also* terrified. But Curlew doesn't know the commissioner in the way that you and I do."

Jay closed his mouth, listening for a moment.

"Nobody had any real idea of your relationship until tonight," she went on, weighing his reaction with her eyes. "Alastair Harding is known as an unmitigated man of duty. It came as a shock to almost all of his people to hear that he was taken from a boyfriend's flat. Without him here to speak for you, some of them are dealing with that shock by doubting your sincerity. It's not a surprise," she added, seeing him start to protest. "And I'll point out to you that for most of these people, it is very literally their job to doubt the things they're told. Their entire skillset involves poking holes in unlikely stories and seeing where the leaks appear."

Her eyes gentled, taking in his pained expression.

"But I need you to hold water," she said. "I need you to be calm, dignified and helpful. Alastair needs that from you."

Jay looked away across the room, his heart thudding. It was hard not to shake his head in disbelief. He'd been interrupted, sneered at and forced to beg for answers to the simplest questions, even while lying here in an oxygen mask. No one had treated him calmly or with dignity, and his attempts to be helpful had so far been batted aside. His home and all his possessions were probably still smouldering right now, and the man that he loved was in the hands of a killer—but what mattered was being polite to the nice policeman.

Jesus.

"Would any of your people be willing to speak for your character?" Juliet asked, somewhere on the edge of his thoughts.

Jay focused himself with a breath. If he had to deal with these people in order to help, then so be it. Alastair had put up with these bastards all his life. Now Jay would put up with them, too.

"All of them," he said. "Ask any of them. Anybody on the payroll. My head of comms—Connor—he'll tell you."

Juliet produced her phone from inside her sleeve, unlocking it.

"And I can get you my UKPPS contact's details," Jay went on, watching her type. "She'll tell you I'm a different person now. She'll... J-Jesus, she'll send me to the arse end of nowhere when she finds out what's happened. But she saw who I was ten years ago. She can tell you that I've changed."

Juliet hummed. "It crossed my mind to contact guest services at Cliveden," she said, distracted as she typed. "I don't think you'd find better advocates anywhere in the world. They were all very taken with the pair of you."

The memory of Cliveden, all its privacy and comfort, brought a rush of almost physical pain through Jay's chest. He put his hand up over his oxygen mask and held it in place as he breathed, trying to push back the rising flood of panic and guilt. He could have told Alastair then. He *should* have done. If he had, Alastair could have taken steps to protect not only Jay but himself, and none of this would be happening.

This is all because of me. All of this. All because I didn't want it to be true.

It's my fault, and Al will pay for it.

"Find him, will you?" he said, shaking. He tightened his grip around his mask. "Please. Don't let Ian hurt him. I won't be able to fucking live if Ian hurts him. Please, just..."

Juliet locked her phone.

"Save this," she said, slipping it away inside her jacket. She gestured at his face. "This. You're wasting it on me."

Smoothing her skirt, she stood up from her chair. Jay's pulse gave a kick.

"Where are we going?" he asked. "What happens now?"

"I'm returning to Scotland Yard," she said. "My team is involved in the operation to find Alastair, and they need me to lead them. You'll stay here and be treated for smoke inhalation."

"Are you—erm—do PAs usually do that?"

She reached inside her jacket, withdrew a slim black leather ID and opened it towards him.

"Standard policy for Met commissioners to be assigned additional security," she said.

Jay scanned the complicated ID card, clueless.

Juliet raised an eyebrow. Apparently, this usually prompted a better reaction. "I'm a member of the British security services," she clarified, folding her ID shut. "I'm not just his assistant."

Jay's mouth opened.

"Oh," he said, startled. It certainly explained a few things, not least her ability to interrogate someone through eye contact alone. He wondered if Alastair had ever realised. "Oh, you mean like—"

"If you say James Bond, I'll shoot you."

"Yep. Sure. Shutting up now."

"I've been in charge of Sir Alastair's private security for the past three years," she said. "Working publicly as his assistant provided excellent cover. He's never given me so much as a moment's trouble." Eyeing Jay, she added, "Until you."

Jay suspected that might haunt him.

"Do we know for sure that Ian's behind this?" he asked, filling his lungs with clean air from the mask. "He's *definitely* got Al?"

She gave a somewhat reluctant nod. "Alastair was speaking to me on the phone when intruders entered your flat," she said. "I could hear some of the call, but not all of it. They moved him into a vehicle, your brother's name was clearly mentioned, and the call cut off not long after. I assume they entered a tunnel."

"He, erm... he rang you after I'd gone, did he?"

"He did. We spoke for three or four minutes."

Jay didn't know if he dared to ask. He'd said so many things he now wished he could take back. For all he knew, Alastair had called her in despair, telling her he'd made a horrendous mistake and would distance himself from Jay as soon as he could.

"What did Al say?" he heard his own mouth ask, and braced himself to hear the worst.

Juliet took a moment to give her answer. She seemed to be

deciding if it was her place to tell him, or if this was a violation of trust.

"That he loves you," she said at last. Jay's heart gave way. "He told me that if your relationship with him raises eyebrows, or raises questions about his judgement, he doesn't care. He's chosen you and he's committed to being with you."

Incapable of speech, Jay tightened his hands in the hospital bed sheet. It somehow hurt more than if Alastair had told her he was an arsehole and a thug.

Juliet searched his face. "Do you understand why I'm willing to tell you that?" she said. "Do you understand why it is I'm willing to trust you?"

Jay swallowed in silence, waiting.

"It's because I trust Alastair," she said. "He's not a sentimental man, nor a gullible one. Plenty have tried their luck at fooling him over the years. And yet within a minute of meeting you, he seemed to decide that you were safe."

Her eyes grew dark, her tone forcefully steady.

"I need to believe he was right to do so," she said. "Otherwise I face the dawning realisation that my mentor could now lose his life and all his dignity over a giddy flutter of the heart. I'm not willing to face that possibility, not until there's no other option available."

Jay looked into her eyes, his chest pounding. He could feel its echo in every part of his body.

"I want to help," he said. "I want to get Al back. Bring me with you to Scotland Yard and I'll help."

Juliet's gaze shuttered. "Out of the question."

"You've already got someone with first hand experience of Ian's operations, have you?"

"No. But if I take on Curlew's prime suspect as a third party consultant—"

"Either you *trust* me," Jay said fiercely, his throat ripping itself open, "or you *don't,* princess. Choose which one and choose quickly. Because every minute you stand there sneering at me is a minute that Al will pay for."

Her eyes flashed. "Please do not shout at me."

"Then please don't ignore me. If I was in on this, my part would be over. All I'd have to do now is keep it zipped and let things happen. But I'm not doing that. *I'm trying to help."*

Juliet considered this, her expression guarded. "If I take you to Scotland Yard, you'll have to answer to Curlew first. You'll need to satisfy him that you're to be trusted. Then you can possibly advise me."

"Fine," Jay snapped. "What else am I going to be doing? Sat here like piffy on a rock." He reached behind his head, trying to find the clasp of the oxygen mask. "Get the nurse, will you? I'm leaving."

"I'm not sure you've completed your treatment yet."

"Fuck that for a game of spades. Al wouldn't lie here and wait if it was me."

They drove north-west through London, past Regent's Park and Finchley Road. As they reached Brent Cross and joined the M1, Alastair gave up trying to track the route. He knew where they were going.

With nothing to fill his thoughts but his own panic and the silence, the journey passed in wild and shapeless lumps of time. Passing cities stood for distance markers. Near Leicester, they pulled into the furthest corner of a motorway service station and relieved themselves against a nearby wall, then unclipped Alastair's ties just long enough for him to do the same. He thought of running, but with three much younger men to pursue him across entirely unfamiliar ground, he didn't rate his chances. A minute later, they rejoined the motorway with his wrists re-secured.

Alastair watched the service station shrink into the distance, trying to ignore his nervous flickers of regret.

The rest of the journey seemed to take much longer. The night was passing and they'd driven nearly two hundred miles. Alastair couldn't be certain if he was hazing in and out of restless sleep, or simply staring forwards in silence. The two men crammed on either side of him were sleeping, the younger one curled around his phone and listening to music through earbuds.

As they passed signs for Manchester Airport, Alastair experienced a surge of new and much sharper panic. He found himself staring at the nape of the driver's neck, trying to work out if there was a way he could take control of the car with his hands still secured behind his back. Even causing the vehicle to crash might improve his chances. Depending on what these men had planned, he might shortly be wishing with every scrap of his soul that he'd chosen injury and possible death in a car wreck.

His heart beating hard, he forced himself to think of Juliet—of the rescue operation she'd probably put in motion already.

I'm not alone, he told himself, gripping his wrist ties. *It only seems that way.*

The entirety of the UK police force would be looking for him. He had to trust the invisible presence of his people over his own compromised emotions, or he stood no chance at all.

Approaching the city, their route seemed to take a number of irrational and unnecessary turns. *Muddying any CCTV,* Alastair thought, making the deductions as if this were happening to somebody else. *Avoiding plate recognition technology.* The two men either side of him were reluctantly waking up, stretching their arms and legs as best they could within the confined space. They reached a set of traffic lights two spaces behind a dormant IRV for Greater Manchester Police, and Alastair again experienced the crazed instinct to crash the car, draw attention to the vehicle in some way. Before he could bring himself to do it, the lights changed. The police car vanished, its siren silent.

This time, the regret did not ease. Alastair began to sweat. He locked his focus tightly around his breathing, trying to count each slow contraction of his lungs. Calm would serve him better in this situation than panic.

The car turned at last down a sidestreet past a condemned block of flats. They emerged into a large expanse of what seemed to be former industrial land, thick with weeds and fly-tipped broken furniture, overlooked on all sides by Victorian red brick cotton mills and warehouses long fallen into disrepair. The buildings stood like hollow shells, eerie in the glow of the sparse yellow security lights. Their windows were smashed, their once-proud faces now spattered with graffiti. Misery seeped from the structures like radiation.

At the far end of the wasteland, a derelict power station awaited them.

Recognising a final destination, Alastair's panic sharpened into something he couldn't self-tend. His heart began to slam against his ribs, his muscles suddenly tight enough to tremble. *This is the sort of place where people are taken to be killed,* he thought—and once he'd thought it, he couldn't think of anything else.

The car pulled to a weary stop outside a worker's entrance. The driver unlocked the doors. Beside Alastair, the young man with acne drew his switchblade from inside his sleeve, flicked it open and gestured.

"Out," he said to Alastair. "Now."

I'm going to die. There were three of them, three fit and healthy young men for whom physical violence was an everyday part of life. Alastair was restrained, alone, and unarmed. *But I can't go with them. I can't go into that building.*

The moment's indecision cost him dearly.

As a hand closed in Alastair's hair, wrenching him sideways out of the car, agony blistered across his scalp. He twisted with a cry, struggling against the vicious grip. A second hand clamped over his mouth to muffle him, cruel digging fingers and rough, sour-smelling skin, and his captor began to drag him towards the door. Alastair's socked feet stumbled without purchase over the rough ground, jagged by sharp rocks and shards of old glass.

Resist. Try.

This could be the only chance to try.

Alastair utilised the firm grip on him to provide the balance his own arms couldn't. He moved suddenly, quickly, twisting at the point of contact and slamming his knee up into something soft. The man groaned, buckled and started to drop. The arms around Alastair loosened. He staggered free and turned to run. If he was to be a statistic, better a statistic on his feet.

He managed all of four metres before the driver lunged into his path, seized him by the shoulder and buried a fist into his abdomen. The blow forced all the breath from his lungs. Pain burst throughout his body, swift and sharp and unbearable. It grew and grew until he contained nothing else but the pain, every sense rendered white and useless with the ferocity of it. He couldn't breathe. He could only coil around it and try to retrieve himself from the agony, blinded, ringing in every cell.

"You should've guessed he'd try that," came a grunt, somewhere on the edges of his consciousness. "Hold onto him properly, will you? The boss didn't want him injured."

Alastair retched as heavy hands forcibly uncurled him. He could barely move. *I got old,* he thought as two of them hefted him up. They half-carried and half-dragged him into the building. *This isn't my world anymore.*

The slam of metal doors echoed in the concrete space behind them. Alastair stumbled between them through the gloom, still nauseous with pain, the stench of natural decay overwhelming his nose and mouth. His feet burned upon the cold stone floor.

They've had hours. Hours to find me. And yet—

Corridors and doorways blurred. Halfway down a long stretch of hallway, the young man finally shouldered open a door and held it wide.

The room beyond was a small concrete chamber, little bigger than a cell. Banks of decommissioned switches covered one wall.

They shoved Alastair inside, dragged him across to one corner and forced his back against the concrete wall. Heavy hands on his shoulders ordered him to sink down. They wrenched his wrists back against a thick metal pipe protruding through the floor, then produced more zip ties.

As they bound him into place, cold spread through Alastair's chest. Struggling wouldn't do a thing to loosen zip ties. He was more likely to lethally lacerate his wrists in the attempt than to free them.

They've done this before, he thought, now on the verge of vomiting. *This is the usual procedure.*

"Shall we get—?" the young man said. Alastair kept his eyes shut, still trying to cope with the pain in his abdomen.

"Yep," came the short reply. "You stay here."

Alastair tensed his wrists against the ties. The teeth of the thick black bands dug into his skin; the pricks of controllable pain brought him enough clarity to breathe, deep and measured, forcing himself towards calm. Traces of Jay's roasted garlic still lingered on his shirt collar. He hadn't been able to sense it in the airless car, overpowered by the odour of marijuana and body spray, but he could smell it now.

At least...

He couldn't bear it—the thought of what might otherwise be happening in this moment. Jay, beaten and bound to this pipe, screaming out in silence for help.

Alastair swallowed, leaving his eyes closed. As two men left the room with an echoing bang of the door, he gathered his own panic close to him and showed it something better. Jay would be in the care of a police liaison officer at this moment. He'd be sitting somewhere safe and warm, comforted, surrounded by support and by people. He wasn't here, experiencing this.

Numb, Alastair laid his head back against the wall.

I'll take this for you. There was a strange and crippling comfort in it. Everything Alastair was about to suffer, Jay would be spared. *"I want us to be something,"* Jay had whispered, kissing him—their first and only loving kiss. *"You're amazing."*

Shaking, Alastair filled his chest with air. He sat up taller, prouder, his heart pounding in his throat. Jay was safe, and it meant the very worst would not happen. There was peace in that.

He had made the right choice, no matter what.

Chapter 19

THE SQUEAKY CRUNCH OF THE DOOR HANDLE ECHOED ALONG THE empty corridor. Jay's eyes snapped up from the steel floor tiles, broken out of his thoughts at once. He'd been sitting here motionless for at least an hour, worrying, trying not to imagine the things being said inside that room.

Connor appeared in the doorway, looking tired and underdressed with shadows beneath his eyes. It was unnerving to see him in an ordinary sweatshirt and jeans. Without his usual flashy outfit, he had the look of someone who should really have stayed home with their cold. Behind Connor came DCS Curlew, frowning and self-important as ever, gesturing Connor out into the corridor.

Shaking, Jay got to his feet.

Curlew locked the interview room, taking his sweet time about it, then turned around to Jay. With a breath, and with only the most reluctant eye contact, he said, "Don't leave London. If anything new comes to light, we'll need to speak with you again."

A muscle in Jay's jaw twitched. *Guilty until proven innocent,* he thought—and by Curlew's definition of proof. He worked to relax his expression, trying to come up with some polite thing to say in acknowledgement. In the end, he couldn't manage it.

"Good," he said. "Now go find Al."

Curlew glowered. He pocketed his keys, turned his back, and headed away up the metal staircase, his every footstep marked with a clang.

Inhaling, Jay turned at last to Connor.

"Hey," he began, all the fear flooding right back. "I don't know what exactly they told you, but—"

Connor stepped forwards. Before Jay could move, he put his arms around Jay and held on, waiting as Jay petered into silence.

Fuck.

Swallowing, Jay laid a nervous arm around Connor's back. It didn't feel the same as hugging Alastair. Connor was too tall, too slim, and his fragrance was too strong and too citrusy. It still brought a lump to Jay's throat.

"They told me all sorts," Connor murmured. "I told them you're the most decent guy I've ever worked with, and this world would be a different place if the police cared half as much as you. Do you want to stick with Jay, or go for Jason?"

Shit. Shit. Speechless, Jay gripped Connor harder.

Connor didn't let him go.

"I signed all the stuff about not telling anyone," he said in Jay's ear, his voice quiet. "I wanted to promise you in person too. It's safe with me. You can forget I know."

Jay clamped down on his gathering tears, forcing himself to keep breathing. He wasn't going to start sobbing in a Scotland Yard corridor. He couldn't break down, not yet, not now, or he'd never get back up again.

"And I'll tell you that I wondered sometimes," Connor went on. "Not wanting photos of you, I mean. I figured there was *something* in your past. So it's not a shock. It's not a problem. If we all turned out like our parents, I'd be a long-haul truck driver with anger management issues."

Jay released his breath in a rush.

Connor patted him steadily between the shoulders. "Is this why you struggle to let us in?"

All these years. Jay had tried so hard. His life had been built upon a false floor, and his brother had always had control of the lever. He'd hoped that if he kept everything at a distance, never truly claiming it as his own, then losing it all wouldn't hurt as much.

The one thing that Jay had pulled in close, and held onto, was the one thing that Ian had now taken.

Shaking, he managed an exhausted nod.

Connor gave him a careful squeeze. "You know they'd all just admire you more?" he said. "Pulling yourself free from that? I do."

Jay forced himself at last to speak. He didn't know if he deserved to be admired for what he did, especially if it was Alastair who now paid the price. But the words were kind, and he was grateful for them.

"Thank you," he said. "Thanks, Connor. Thanks for... I-I'm sorry that you got dragged out of bed."

"Don't worry about it," Connor said, easing back from the hug. He kept his hands on the tops of Jay's arms. "I'm glad I could clear things up."

"He's got some idea that I... Curlew, the—" Jay gestured vaguely, too tired now to think straight. The word clicked into his head. "The detective," he said, sighing. "He's decided I'm in on some plot to kidnap Al and hold him to ransom. Al's not here to speak for me, so..."

"Well, I'm here at least. I hope it'll make some difference." Connor surveyed Jay gently, still holding onto him. "The fire's all over the news. I'll tell everyone at work it's your building and you won't be in. Will you keep me updated on your guy?"

"S-sure. Yeah, I will."

"I hope they get him back. Looks like they're doing everything they can."

"Yeah. Yeah, they're..."

"If you need somewhere to stay, you're welcome at mine."

"Connor—"

"Do you want to head there now? Few hours' sleep?"

Oh, Jesus. "That's kind," Jay said, struggling not to stutter. "Really kind. I just feel like I need to stay here, in case they... you know. In case there's updates."

"Alright." Connor offered Jay a smile. "Shall I stick around?"

The quiet clang of high-heeled footsteps caught Jay's ear. He glanced towards the stairs and found Juliet descending towards them, looking calm and composed. She'd found clean clothes from somewhere and put her hair back into a ponytail.

As Jay met her eyes, she stopped where she was, waiting her turn to speak to him.

Jay drew a breath.

"It's okay," he said to Connor. From somewhere deep down, he summoned up the strength to smile. It felt like laying wallpaper over a pile of loose bricks. "You head home. Get some sleep. I'll ring you, if there's..."

Connor nodded. "Call for anything. I'll keep my phone on."

Jay's heart gripped. "Thanks, mate."

Connor pulled him in again—quick, tight, two short thumps between Jay's shoulders, then let go. As he turned away, Jay swallowed and tried not to watch him leave, too close to tears to risk it. He didn't want Juliet to see him choked up.

She flashed Connor a polite and close-lipped smile as he passed her on the stairs, her eyes averted, then made her way down towards Jay.

"I take it you've been cleared of suspicion," she said.

Jay's jaw clenched, thinking of Curlew.

"Not sure I'm cleared," he muttered. "It's been reluctantly put on pause." He pushed his hands into the pockets of the borrowed tracksuit bottoms they'd given him, dug up from some ancient Scotland Yard lost-and-found box. The pockets still had debris from the previous owner: biscuit crumbs, a penny, a bus ticket from 2015. He half-wished he'd stuck with the hospital pyjamas. "Curlew told me I'm not to leave London. Like I'm going to waltz off while Al's still..."

Juliet restrained a sigh, keeping what looked like some choice comments to herself. "I'm afraid it's his job to ask the obvious questions first."

"Yeah, well... he's asked them now. Got his obvious answers." Jay shivered, suddenly aching for coffee. "He had me for at least another hour before he even spoke to Connor. Kept coming back to the same things, just phrased a little different each time."

"It's a standard technique. It's... well, it's an attempt to catch you out."

"Could've done without him assuming Al pays me for sex."

"I'm sorry. I imagine he's trying to suggest something about the nature of your connection."

"Not surprised some of your boys are hanging tight to their homophobia. How the hell did Al ever make commissioner?"

Juliet smiled weakly. "If he were here," she said, taking a breath, "and this were several months ago, he'd make his usual joke... which is that he's not exactly a *practicing* homosexual."

Jay huffed. He could imagine Alastair saying it. He could hear his deadpan tone, see the quiet glint in his eyes and the slight lift at one corner of his mouth, curling upwards and ready to smile.

"I'm sorry this happened before your relationship was made official," Juliet said. She looked at him gently, her eyes full of sympathy. "When I called the deputy commissioner to tell him Alastair had been kidnapped, and where from, he didn't believe me at first."

Jay's stomach pulled. "Am I really such a mad choice?"

"To me, no. Not especially. To the men who serve as his direct subordinates... yes." Juliet hesitated, trying to soften it. "I'm sorry if that upsets you. Most of them had only the vaguest awareness that he's even gay."

Jay lowered his gaze, supposing it shouldn't come as a surprise. He couldn't really imagine what Alastair had battled through, trying not only to thrive here but to convince the rest to follow him. Even for Jay, the head of his own company in a liberal field, being out was not a case of flicking a switch—gay or not gay, proud or not proud. There were ever-shifting layers of outness to be navigated: people who were fine but still visibly skipped hearing *'boyfriend';* people who could cope with mentions of a same sex partner, but not more than once a month or so; people who knew the phrase 'inappropriate work environment' and wielded it like an axe, chopping down any conversation they didn't think should be happening. Living honestly was a game of constant analysis, always monitoring how open was *too* open, how gay was *too* gay.

From Monday to Friday every week, Alastair played that game with the highest possible stakes. It seemed like his preferred strategy was to keep his barriers close and cautious. The more time Jay spent around his colleagues, the more he understood.

As Juliet gestured towards the stairs, Jay quietly followed her lead.

"I sort of switched off at one point," he murmured as they walked together. "In the room with Curlew, I mean. Started daydreaming. Imagining what Al's gonna do when he hears what was being implied."

"I'm doing something similar," Juliet admitted. Her heels rattled quietly on the metal grids. "Telling myself that he'll return at any minute, and ask why all the things that I've already suggested weren't implemented faster."

"Suppose if it gets us through..."

"Mm. It's important to stay calm."

"What's happening, anyway? Are you getting close to—?"

"Things *are* happening," she said, "though I wouldn't say we're getting close. We have a full media blackout in place and officers searching nearly every inch of London. Patching together CCTV will take time, especially now the footage from your building is irretrievable, but we've got street teams out collecting as much of it as we can. We're also trying to locate a signal from Alastair's mobile phone."

"That's... pretty easy for you guys these days, isn't it?"

"If we were trying to track *your* phone, and we could justify it later in court, yes. Sadly, Alastair's is fitted with as many security measures as our budget could afford. We were diligent in making sure that third parties couldn't hack it or track his movements."

"Oh, so—now that *you* need to find him..."

"We can't. Not easily and not quickly." As they stepped off the stairs, Juliet took her phone from inside her jacket. "We've never had a commissioner kidnapped before," she said, checking it. A string of messages awaited her. "All our precautions were focused on preventing this from happening. Now it's happened, we're in an unprecedented situation. Coffee?"

"Oh, erm—sure. Alright."

She showed him along the corridor to a coffee dispenser, stationed beside a floor-to-ceiling glass window with a view looking east across the Thames.

"You're... handling things kind of on the fly, then?" Jay said. He'd hoped to hear that they'd rehearsed for this day a hundred times, that everyone knew their job and what to do.

"There *are* procedures," Juliet said, taking a paper cup from the stack. "We've put them into place. But because it happened from an unauthorised location, which has since burned down..."

Shrugging, she slotted the cup into place.

"On the fly is all we have," she said.

Jay watched, numb and empty, as she tapped a few buttons on the machine. *This shouldn't be happening,* he thought, lost in the hiss and the sad trickle of hot liquid against paper. *I should have stayed with him. Should've let him come with me.*

Jesus, all the things I should've done.

"How are they getting on up in Manchester?" he asked, trying to push his thoughts towards something productive. Regret and wishes wouldn't get Alastair back. "Do you want me to call some of the people I used to know? See if they've heard anything?"

Juliet seemed to pause.

"Greater Manchester have told us they don't believe your brother's in the area," she said. "They've had no sign of him for weeks."

Something cold whispered across the back of Jay's neck. "They're still looking though, right? They're going house to house in Moss Side?"

Juliet said nothing.

Jesus. Jay took a second just to breathe, forcing his surge of anger to quell. He leant closer to Juliet, lowering his voice.

"Listen," he said. "That's... that's not good."

She made no reply, her eyes on the machine.

"If they've not seen Ian," Jay said, "it's because he's been lying low, planning something. Planning *this.* When you're lying low, you do it somewhere familiar. You tell as few people as possible, and you make sure the ones you *do* tell are ready to lie through their teeth when the coppers come asking if they've seen you. When you're holding someone against their will, you hold them on your territory. That's not London. This has *never* been about London."

Juliet turned her head to look at him. "I'm sharing authority over this operation with a number of people," she said. "Some decisions are mine. This one isn't."

"Then you need to convince whoever it is to change their decision," Jay said. "You need to make them understand. If you don't, then—"

Juliet's jaw locked tight.

"Forgive me," she cut in, and spoke until he stopped. "I now realise that I've failed to explain something to you. Silly of me, really. I don't know why it slipped my mind. It's all I've been able to think about all night. Let me bring you up to speed."

Jay waited without a sound, hot prickles still tracking across his skin.

"I'm supposedly responsible for Alastair's personal security," she said, staring into his eyes. "I've now failed in that. Utterly. He is gone. It happened on *my* watch. I knowingly allowed him to spend nights at an unauthorised residence with a man whose background I neglected to check. It makes it hard for me to argue that I know what I'm doing."

"Then tell them *I* know what I'm doing," Jay said furiously. "Tell them I know Ian. Tell them I know how he—"

"I've just spent several hours attempting to *downplay* your connection to your brother. I'm not going to stride into the next briefing and present you as a consummate expert."

"Jesus. Look," Jay said, shaking, "I don't *care* how you usually do things here. I don't care about all this political crap. I'm just telling you that when they haul Alastair's body out of the Irwell, not the Thames, I'm going to come find you and look right into your face. I won't say a word, princess. I'll just look at you and wait. And you can explain to me how I'm supposed to go on with my life, constantly picturing how scared he'll have been as he died, how he'll have felt in the moment that he realised we weren't coming for him. You can tell me how I'm supposed to cope seeing the light go out in his eyes every single time I close mine. Alright?"

Juliet's mouth flattened. She took the coffee from the machine and snapped a plastic lid onto it, her motions stiff.

"This isn't gangland Manchester," she said as she passed it to him, her voice lethally soft. "Power doesn't rest in the hands of the man who gets angriest and makes the most compelling threats."

Jay's throat clenched. "This *is* gangland Manchester. It became that way the second Ian showed up."

"Mm. Well, unfortunately—"

"And Ian's the only person holding any power here. Not you. Not me. Not DCS Shit-for-Brains. Not anybody else. You realise that, don't you? And I'm the only person who knows a single thing about Ian."

"Noted," Juliet said, toneless, programming in a second coffee. "How does this change the fact that my hands are tied?"

"Untie them," Jay snapped, "or Al's going to die."

Juliet's expression hardened. She said nothing, watching the coffee trickle down with an almost ferocious steadiness, her eyes fixed into place.

Jay pushed on. He couldn't stop, not until she understood.

"If Ian had taken one of us," he said, "and we were in danger, Al would be breaking every single rule in existence to get us back. And you know it," he added angrily, drowning her out before she could start to tell him otherwise. "He wouldn't be standing here, shrugging, telling himself he's powerless. He'd be better than that."

Juliet reached out for a plastic lid. "What exactly do you expect me to do?"

"You need to get Manchester onboard," Jay said. "You need to call every copper who's ever dealt with Ian and ask them where they think he'd take a hostage, and you need to get armed officers out to those places *now*. You need to get people watching the roads, stopping every car with more than a couple of passengers in it. You should've suggested all this hours ago."

Juliet fitted the lid on her coffee with a snap. She spun prettily to face him, smiling hard.

"Bless you for thinking I didn't," she said, sugar sweet and suddenly dead behind the eyes. "It's so reassuring to hear we're on the same page, Jay. Really. I'm thrilled you can now suffer this with me, making perfectly sensible suggestions that sink like fucking stones into the endless swamp of men who believe they know better."

Jay's pulse stuttered. Unsettled, he opened his mouth—what to say, he didn't know.

"Let me show you somewhere you can sit," Juliet chirped, striding past him. She didn't look to see if he followed. "They never show all the waiting around in the police dramas, do they? I hope you like staring helplessly into space."

The cold had found its way into Alastair's bones, seeping upwards through the concrete floor. He'd been here for at least an hour now, if not longer, though the passing minutes were impossible to track. Pain kept his senses sharp; every shift to ease his cramping muscles sent a stab of agony of his abdomen. He wished he could wrap his arms around it and curl.

His thoughts ran like water sputtering from a half-clogged pipe—sometimes in a rush, sometimes only by the drop. With little else to occupy his mind, he lapsed often into memories of Jay. This evening had, at one point, been idyllic. He found himself trying to imagine how it might have continued, had it not all gone so desperately wrong. The two of them would likely be asleep by now. He would be warm and comfortable in bed with the man who loved him, safely wrapped in Jay's arms. If he closed his eyes, he could almost feel Jay's quiet, steady breaths against his neck, almost catch the familiar scent of his skin.

It was a trauma response, and Alastair knew it. He was powerless to change the situation in which he found himself, weaving in and out of shock, and his brain's only recourse was to distract him with comforting nonsense—a puppet show to keep him calm. It was working, though. With no other way to keep time passing by, he allowed himself to dream.

The thuds of approaching footsteps came as a shock. Alastair jolted from his thoughts with a start, wrenched painfully back into the present by the sound. The door hinges echoed as they squeaked, admitting heavy boots into the room, followed by a lighter and more nervous set of feet. Alastair waited, tensing his wrists against his bonds.

For some time, there was no noise. Alastair kept his eyes low, barely breathing as the boots crossed the room towards him. They came to a stop within his eye line, a little too close for comfort.

The silence strained.

"Has he spoken much?" asked a low and lethal voice.

"Not a lot," replied the voice of the young man with the acne. "Don't think we've had a word out of him this whole time."

The owner of the boots knelt down, lowering himself into Alastair's field of view.

As their eyes met, every muscle in Alastair's body turned to rock. The resemblance was desperately unsettling. Jay was a cub, bright-eyed and always willing to play; his older brother was a wolf. Ian's neck seemed broader, his eyes somewhat darker, his features aged by a thick and well-maintained beard—but the shapes were all there, brothers in their bones. Genetics had given both the sort of symmetrical features and strong jaws often associated with honesty, with working-class respectability. In Jay, they'd earned Alastair's trust within seconds. In Ian, it was easy to see why he'd been granted parole. He looked like the type to describe himself to a judge as a family man, a loving father, and be believed. No stereotypes of the northern criminal applied. His clothes were clean and new, his appearance well kept, his stare perfectly steady.

Alastair inhaled, looking back into his face.

You tried to burn a man alive, he thought.

Ian read Alastair's expression in silence, his eyes crinkling at the edges—a touch of amusement, a flicker of disbelief. He seemed to be working something out, making connections.

After what felt like an eternity, he slowly straightened up to full height.

"Come here," he said, looking over his shoulder.

Warily, the young man edged closer. When he was near enough, Ian scooped an arm around him and pulled him in the rest of the way, then gestured for the boy to look at Alastair.

"I'm going to ask you a question," Ian said, his voice soft and conspiratorial. His grip had closed around the boy's upper arm, his fingers held solid, his eyes still fixed on Alastair's. "Take your time on it, okay? Have a really good think, then give me an answer."

The boy nodded, pale, staring at Alastair with mounting concern.

Ian gave him a moment to prepare. "Who," he asked, "the fuck is this?"

The boy hesitated.

"It's Jason," he said. "It's your brother." Swallowing, he risked a glance at Ian. "Isn't it?"

Ian's mouth curved, his smile slow and ugly.

The punch came from nowhere, hard enough to send the boy reeling into the wall. Blood showered from his mouth in a spray. The sheer speed of it made Alastair flinch, panic lurching up from his stomach into his throat. He watched, his heart banging out an alarm call as the young man slumped in a whimpering heap to the foot of the wall, cradling his jaw.

Ian inhaled. He straightened up, easing back under his own control, and wiped his sovereign rings upon his sleeve.

The smile was gone.

"You've now caused me a problem," he told the boy, checking his rings for damage. "I've had this thing planned out for weeks. I asked you to do a simple job for me, and suddenly everything's gone to hell."

Sobs emanated from the shaking young man on the floor.

Ian, accustomed to the accent, understood more of it than Alastair.

"Yeah?" he said. "I didn't want you to bring *the right flat.* I wanted you to bring *the right person.* Did you take care of the place when you were done?"

Whimpering ascent was given.

"Anybody see you?"

"N-no," came the sob.

Ian loosened his jaw, sighing. "Get up," he grunted. "And don't ever kid yourself into thinking you're smart again. Do you hear me, Milo? You're not. You're a moron. You're a worthless piece of shit, and crawling out of your mum was the peak of your achievements. I don't know why I bothered even giving you a chance."

As the young man struggled to his feet, Ian turned the full force of his stare onto Alastair.

"And who the hell are you?" he asked.

Alastair steadied himself, keeping his fear a safe distance away from his face. Cringing and cowering wouldn't help him. A man capable of casual brutality clearly wouldn't be moved by tears or pleas. Instead, Alastair used the tone of calm and simple honesty he would usually use for his superiors, hoping that it carried enough respect.

"My name is Alastair Harding," he said. His accent prompted a huff of dry humour, Ian's mouth twisting upwards. "There's been some mistake. I'm not the person you seem to think I am."

"Noted," Ian said. "But you and him *are* fucking, aren't you?"

Alastair hesitated, disarmed.

Before he could even try, Ian crushed his words from the air. "Don't," he barked, anger flashing through his face. "Don't try. Don't think. Don't dare. I don't have time to deal with lies, and I don't have any respect for people who think they can manipulate me."

His heart leaping in fear, Alastair stayed quiet.

"Here's the facts," Ian went on, his voice hard and his eyes sharp, burning into Alastair with all the force of a brand. "For this to happen, you were in his flat and you were on your own. He never shared his space easy. You didn't say a word the whole way here, didn't ask what was going on, which means it made sense to you for *someone* to get taken from that flat. You've not asked who I am. You already know. That means he's violated his witness protection and told you. You let my boys drive you four hours down the motorway at knife point, saying nothing, making them believe that you're him, and it's because you're protecting him. That means you're close. For Jason, that means you're fucking. Never lie to me. Don't ever even think about lying to me."

Alastair gripped the pipe to which he was bound. He spoke calmly, steadily, resisting the urge to avert his eyes.

"In a spirit of clarity, Mr Straker, you'll want to put my name into a search engine. I'm afraid this is more serious than you realise."

Ian's eyes tightened up at the corners, suspicious. "Why will I want to do that?"

Alastair braced himself. He hoped that a full disclosure would prevent any decisions being made in haste—that this would buy him time, not cost him it.

"Because you'll discover I'm the Metropolitan police commissioner," he said. He shifted painfully, trying to quieten the cramping in his lower back. "I'm Alastair Harding, head of the London police force. There are photographs of me online and on the Scotland Yard website."

Nothing changed in Ian's face. Only the quick sweep of his eyes registered that anything had been said at all.

Alastair continued with care.

"The authorities will pay you for my safe return," he said. His own pulse hammered in his ears, fast with hope. "They'll pay generously. This entire mistake will reverse itself and go away."

Ian said nothing for almost a minute, thinking, weighing and analysing.

His stare then seemed to close. He seized Milo by the scruff of the neck, throwing him roughly towards the door.

"Stand outside," he said. "Let no one in. Tell nobody what you've heard. Not a soul. Do you hear me?"

Milo promised him through broken stutters.

Alastair gathered his grip around his restraints and held onto them, resting the back of his skull against the concrete wall. *God help me,* he thought, and his heart carried it on through his body: *God help me, God help me, God help me.*

The door slammed, raising a twitch in his muscles. Silence fell. Whether he'd now saved or condemned himself, he didn't know. He wasn't sure if Ian Straker knew yet either. The quiet rang, bright and cold, as Alastair stretched his aching legs against the floor.

Please get here, he thought, closing his eyes. *Please. Get here quickly.*

Chapter 20

THE BURNS MADE IT PAINFUL FOR JAY TO WRITE. IT HURT EVEN FORMING his hand into a shape that could hold a pen, creasing the sore strip of skin across the middle. They'd given him the crappiest blue biro in the world, so old and dried up that Jay couldn't form the letters with any speed, and the process felt far more like carving than writing.

Now and then as he scrawled, it flashed through his mind that the things on this table—this pen, these sheets of paper, this cooling cup of tea—were his only possessions in the world. They weren't even really his, borrowed from a reluctant receptionist. Everything he'd ever owned was gone.

But dwelling on it wouldn't change it. He was making the most of what he had.

"I'm told you've now requested four separate rounds of paper," Juliet said from the open doorway. "Dare I ask?"

Bracing himself, Jay cast her a glance.

"Nearly done," he muttered. He carried on scribbling the last part of an address, digging it into the paper with his worn-out biro. "Nothing else I can remember. Kicked what I could out of my head ten years ago... told myself I wouldn't need it..."

He flipped over the sheet of paper, added it to his finished stack and shuffled the pages together.

"There," he said, holding them out.

Juliet made no comment as she approached, her expression wary. She took the pages from him and briefly riffled through.

"I did the same for the police back then," Jay said. "People he associates with, names and addresses. The addresses I can remember, at least. If they're on that list, they'd willingly hide him. Plus all the places he used to go. Narrows it down for you. Manchester's big."

He reached for his cold cup of tea, not really wanting to look at her.

"Use it if you want," he said, shrugging, and took a drink. He didn't know when he'd started to shake. Perhaps he'd never really stopped. "Just wanted to feel like I'm helping."

Juliet was quiet for a moment, looking down at the reams of his scruffy blue scrawl.

"Thank you," she murmured. "I'll... pass this onto the right people."

Jay's throat thickened. He couldn't tell if she meant it or not, but he supposed it was out of his hands. *At least I did it,* he told himself, drinking so he didn't have to speak. *At least when they find him, I'll know I did something. Didn't just sit here and wait for him to die.*

"I'm sorry if I've been short with you," Juliet said.

Jay kept his eyes to himself, offering an awkward shrug. "You're not allowed to be short with them. Better if you take it out on me."

"I realise you want to help. And it's frustrating, not to be able to."

It took Jay a second to find the words, then another second more to say them.

"Ian's hurting him. Right now." He took a silent drink, trying to act like it was nothing. "It's my fault this happened. It's your fault it's not being stopped. I'm not frustrated. I don't even know what I am, but it's not that."

Juliet paused, taking this in. When she spoke, her tone was gentle. "Ensuring that blame is handed out in accurate proportions won't mean we find him faster."

Jay said nothing, staring across the room at the wall of victim support posters. He'd been seeing them all night now, though he hadn't yet registered a single detail of their contents. Colours and reassuring faces and words all muddled together, shouting about helplines and not being alone.

Breathing in, he pushed his thoughts elsewhere.

"Where did you grow up?" he said.

Juliet took a careful seat beside him, lowering herself onto the scratchy navy sofa.

"Surrey," she said, resting her hands together in her lap. Her fingers were slim and she kept her nails short and round, painted a shade of mushroom-grey. "Walton-on-Thames."

"You go to some old boarding school?" Jay said.

She gave a small nod. "Wycombe Abbey."

Jay paused. "Al went to Harrow," he mumbled, "not Eton." He looked down into his lap, too exhausted now to cry. "I remember every word he's ever said to me. Since we met, it's... my brain just grabs onto it all, holds it. His life's been so different to mine. Everything he says is amazing."

Jay's throat threatened to close. He kept on talking, needing to let this out.

"My school was just the nearest to our house," he said. "I got mates by messing around. That's all school was for me. Turn up every day and try to keep my friends laughing, pass the time 'til we could all slope off to the shop and buy cigs. Teachers knew we wouldn't be doing anything with our lives, so they didn't bother. Can't blame them. And I was Ian Straker's little brother, so..."

He shook his head.

"Ian was a celebrity at that school. The teachers were all scared of him. Scared of my dad, scared of my mum. Scared of all my uncles. Everyone knew it. Just by being Ian's brother, I was famous too. Then I started to act a bit like Ian, and everyone loved me for it."

Juliet nodded. "I don't imagine you had much chance after that?"

Jay huffed.

"Kids want love," he said. He put his hands over the back of his neck, lacing his fingers together. "Want to feel safe, see people smiling at them. They'll follow love where they find it. A teacher would sit me down and bollock me once a week or so, telling me I was lazy and irresponsible and had no future, and I'd sit there thinking of my mates. Thinking of the people who liked me how I was."

"So... you had no incentive to change," she murmured.

Jay shook his head. That had come later, with Wheeler and his skills assessments. Making Wheeler smile had been addictive.

"Not until I was grown," he said. He looked up into her eyes, holding them for a second. "You know the biggest problem with this world?"

"Tell me," she said quietly.

"Lucky people, thinking they earned it. Telling the unlucky that they should've just tried harder."

Juliet said nothing, lowering her eyes.

Misery suddenly struck Jay in a wave.

"I wish Al was here," he breathed. His eyes shut themselves just to cope; he dropped his face into his hands. "I wish he was here to tell you all to listen to me. I walked in, and you all just... I mean, look at the way you've dressed me."

Juliet glanced at his borrowed clothes, uncomprehending.

"You could've given me anything from the lost and found," Jay said. "Why not a shirt and a tie? Why a tracksuit? Then I had to sit in an interview, trying to sound professional and calm while I'm dressed like I just robbed an off-licence. It's no wonder none of you will listen to me."

"Jay," Juliet said, her features tightening. "I'm sorry if you—"

"Twelve hours ago, I was chief executive of an award-winning London charity, making dinner for my partner. Now I'm Jason Straker all over again, sat here just... and my whole life is gone. Everything. *All* of it. You know the worst part?"

Juliet made no sound, searching his eyes.

"I *listened* to you people," he said, his voice shaking. "You told me

I'm not unlucky and I should've just tried harder. *So I tried harder.* I put the effort in. I started out from nothing when I got to London. Took my GCSEs at an adult learning place while working nights in a bar. Then I built something good enough for you lot to start inviting me to fancy dinners, giving me awards."

"Jay—"

"But it doesn't actually work that way, does it? Now you've found out I'm really *one of them,* you've taken it all off me. Like I shouldn't rightly have all this success. Like I must've stolen it all from its proper owner, must've tricked Alastair into some disgusting sordid affair with me. Do you know how many times I've had to deny that I'm a rent boy?"

"Jay, I'm sorry—"

"Jesus, I hate those words. They mean so little. Two words and I'm obliged to say, *oh no, it's fine, don't worry about it,* and you'll click off in your heels and forget every word that I've said."

"I won't. I assure you."

"Al's suffering somewhere."

"We're doing everything we can to—"

"You're not," Jay said. He let the silence drop between them, heavy and awkward. "For one thing, you've got an expert on your prime suspect sitting by himself in some room, staring into space." He shrugged. "But I'm wearing a tracksuit. So why would you listen to me?"

Juliet was silent for some time, looking down at the notes that she'd given him.

"I'll look into these," she said. She brushed the edges of the sheets with her thumb, neatening them together. "I might have to keep it from anyone's notice, but..."

One last try, Jay thought. *One last damn try.*

"Juliet," he said, letting his despair into his voice. She looked up at the sound of her name, unsettled. "We *can't* wait. I know Ian, and I know how he operates. You know what Al would be doing right now if he was here, if Ian had taken one of us. He wouldn't be restricting this to London."

Juliet paled. Her eyes shut for a moment, surrendering to something. "I realise that," she said. "And I'm extremely concerned."

Shit. "Yeah?"

"The deputy commissioner is approaching this as a hostage situation, waiting for a demand to arrive. He's convinced that we'll get one within twenty-four hours. He believes there isn't an idiot on this planet would harm the Metropolitan commissioner."

A tide of horror washed through Jay.

"Jesus," he whispered, his stomach clenching. "They're waiting for —okay, listen. Ian didn't *do* hostage situations. If you need some proof, check his file. He didn't mess around like that. If he got hold of someone and took them somewhere, he wasn't doing it for money. And believe me, he'll harm anyone and everyone he wants to."

"Then we're waiting for nothing. We're wasting time we don't—"

"Yes. *Yes, you are.* And I know it feels crazy for you and me to say we know better than the rest of them combined, but we just *do,* princess. That's the truth, whether they like it or not."

A long breath shook itself from Juliet's mouth. "I'll push some things covertly," she said. "It might cause friction between the security services and Scotland Yard when it's discovered, but—"

"If the commissioner of Scotland Yard gets killed," Jay cut in, "how much friction is *that* going to cause?"

Juliet took the point. She stood up, holding his papers to her chest.

"Do you want another drink?" she asked. "Something to eat? I'll... get someone to bring you better clothes."

Hesitating, Jay turned his eyes towards the posters. "Is there anywhere else I can sit?" he said. "I don't want to be in here. This is the victim support room. I'm not a victim."

"Jay, your flat was burned to the ground. You're very much entitled to be in here."

Jesus. Jay shut his eyes. "Look, you know what I mean."

"Okay. Alright, I... I'll take you to the conference suite where my team is set up. It might have to be a chair out in the corridor, but... well, at least you'll be on hand."

Stretches of numb lucidity divided the panic into stages. Alastair noted the recurring pattern and began to use it as well as he could, thinking things through when he was calm, comforting himself with recent memories when the fear closed its claws around his chest.

He started to approach the situation as if it were a training exercise, compiling ideas and possibilities, weighing their chances of success. Soon, he'd isolated a number of opportunities that should be taken immediately if they arose. The first day and night of a kidnapping were critical. With each passing hour, and with no signs of rescue on the way, the need to forge some escape plan of his own became more pressing—and the consequences of simply sitting here in silence grew more daunting.

Alastair waited, cycling over and over between methodical planning, irrepressible fear, and concern over the increasing pain behind his ribs.

The chance which finally came to pass was one that he'd considered at some length.

As the door to his makeshift cell creaked open, all his planning over the last few hours kicked into life. Slouching footsteps shuffled inside. He lifted his chin, waiting for the glance to come around the corner.

In the moment that it did, he spoke.

"Wait."

The boy blinked in alarm, startled to find Alastair looking up at him. Blood had dried in a crust around his mouth and nose; he hadn't dared to leave his post even to wash.

"I want to talk to you," Alastair said, speaking as calmly as he could.

A scowl snapped into place at once. "Shut the fuck up," the boy grunted. "We've got nothin' to speak about. And you're not s'posed to talk."

"I imagine Ian's used to people doing what they're supposed to,"

Alastair said. "It probably doesn't cross his mind they could look after themselves instead."

The boy's eyes narrowed. He said nothing, guarded, visibly trying to work out what was happening here.

"What's your name?" Alastair asked him steadily.

The boy's expression shifted. "Milo."

"Milo, you work for a stupid man. I can see why you do. He's useful to you from time to time, and work is hard to come by. But sometimes he misses what's right in front of him. I think you understand me."

Milo scowled ever harder, unmoved. "What the fuck do you want?"

Alastair held his glare.

"I want to leave here," he said, his heart pounding. "I want to walk quietly through a back exit before the trouble starts. You know what's coming, of course. Ian hasn't realised, but I think that you have."

"Have I?"

"The longer I stay here, Milo, the more likely it becomes that Scotland Yard will arrive."

Milo snorted. "And?"

"And it will either end in violence or in arrests. Ian will be quick to tell the police that *you* were the one who took me. He'll let you sit out his sentence for him."

Milo said nothing in response, visibly taken aback. This thought had clearly not occurred to him; he didn't like it.

Alastair kept his voice level, easing more weight onto the pressure point he'd found. "Or this could work out well for you. I could be a useful opportunity. More useful than anything Ian has ever given you."

Milo's concern retreated behind an ugly smirk, hurriedly pulled into place. "You think?" he jeered. "What's useful about you, tied to a pipe? Fuck off."

"I have money," Alastair said. "Plenty of it. Within a few hours, you could have plenty of it too."

The smirk dropped from Milo's mouth.

Alastair gripped the pipe and went on. "Here's what would happen," he said, "if you agree. You'll cut me loose—"

"Fuck off! Ian'll batter me."

"He won't get the chance, Milo! You and I will be out of a side door before anybody sees us. We'll walk a short distance from here and I'll call my people. When they arrive, I'll explain who you are and that you helped me to escape. Ian will be in police custody within an hour, where he can no longer reach you—and for assisting me, you can name a figure."

Milo glanced towards the door. Alastair's heart clenched.

"Any figure, Milo," he hissed. "I'll empty my bank account to leave here alive."

The boy flushed, unsettled. "Any figure?"

"Name it," Alastair said. "Name it now. It'll be in your hands by the end of the day."

"Yeah?" The corner of Milo's mouth twitched, his eyes darting quickly over Alastair's face. "What if I tell you I ain't doin' it for less than ten grand?"

Uncomfortable guilt crept through Alastair's chest. For this young man, the unfathomable upper limits of wealth capped at the price he'd seen colleagues spend on one holiday.

"Then I'll give you thirty thousand," he said. He watched the boy struggle to process it, glancing wildly again towards the door. "Milo, you'll earn more money in five minutes than most people in this city earn in a year. This chance won't come again in your life."

"Fuck off," the boy let out in a rush, shivering. "I can't trust you. You'll tell the police it was me what took you from the flat, won't you? I know you will. They'll fuckin' throw me into prison along with Ian."

"Then wait until the police get here," Alastair said, "and you'll take Ian's place in prison for him. Do you think he'll do the decent thing? No. You'll take the blame for arson and kidnapping—for kidnapping the highest-ranking police official in England—or you'll untie me, *quickly,* help me to the exit and make enough money to buy everything you've ever wanted."

Milo had turned grey, almost nauseous with indecision.

Alastair stared into his eyes.

"This is your chance to become the winner," he said. "Ian is going to use you as armour. He thinks you'll take a bullet for him. And I think you're too intelligent for that."

Milo's face twisted with distress. It was too much.

"Piss off," he spat. "You... y-you prob'ly don't even have the money. You're just fuckin' with me."

Before Alastair could stop him, he turned on his heel. He slapped the switch and the light snapped out. With an angry bang of the door, he was gone.

Alastair closed his eyes against the sudden darkness. He shifted, wincing as a fresh spike of pain twisted through his abdomen. He'd hoped to find comfort in at least having tried, but there was none.

Prickles of panic began the next stage of the cycle. He gripped his wrist ties, swallowing, and tried to imagine Jay here with him—pressing gentle kisses to his temples, a voice whispering against his cheek. *"Don't worry, sunshine. Help's coming. We're on our way right now."*

Alastair clenched down around the fear and shook, heat breaking out between his shoulders and across his back. In his mind, Jay's arms wrapped around him, whispering to him as his heart sped out of control.

"Easy, sweetheart. Just breathe for me."

Alastair put his head back, resting his skull against the solid concrete wall, and breathed. Help would be here soon. He'd given his life to the force. It wouldn't now leave him here to die. They all knew where he was and had some plan in motion to retrieve him, and in his panic, the delay seemed longer than it was. His legacy was not about to shift. He was the country's first ever gay commissioner; he was not about to become their first murdered commissioner.

That wasn't happening.

Oh, Christ. This can't be happening.

Time was out of order. Some mechanism of the universe had broken, the machinery left dormant and unmoving. Jay turned the wheels by hand with coffee and cigarettes, one after another, willing something to change. Now bundled in a faded black sweater two sizes too big, he sat by himself in the corridor and listened to his memories of Alastair, trying to keep him present in the world. Thinking about Al felt like holding onto him. If he was here in Jay's thoughts, talking and laughing and breathing, nothing could wipe him out. He'd make it through somehow.

The call would come at any second, and all of this would end.

And Jay would go to... somewhere. Some other room. Some other corridor. Wait there until somebody took him to Alastair. He'd sit beside Al in the quiet, hold onto him and nestle into him, and finally face the fact that this was all his fault. He'd finally feel something other than this numbness. He kept trying to picture his home again, burning, all the daft little comforts he'd collected over ten lonely years twisting and blackening and swallowed up by fire—but all he could register in his soul was this paralysing absence. He wouldn't feel the rest until Al.

And if there wasn't Al, there wasn't anything.

There just wouldn't be.

It would all stay like this without end, stopped. Like a smashed clock. Nothing would move. No matter where Jay went, no matter what happened around him, he would stay sitting here in this corridor forever, waiting for news that couldn't come. He couldn't walk away from this building without Al. He'd still be here a thousand years from now, still watching the distant double doors as if they'd open at any second and the other half of his soul would stroll in.

No me without you.

It wasn't a choice. It was a statement of being, and the pain it caused was crippling. Since the moment they'd sat down at that table together, started talking, some space inside Jay's soul had been filled up. That moment wasn't a meeting. It was a recognition.

He should have told Al weeks ago.

Think I might've been made for you. Think you might've been made for me.

I don't want to be alive if you're not.

Shaking, Jay reached into his pocket for cigarettes. Juliet had bought them from the vending machine for him; nicotine was the only thing keeping him functioning. As he stood from his chair, fumbling a cigarette from the packet, Jay wondered what he would do when he'd smoked the last of these—how he would keep time from crashing.

Maybe I won't, he thought, his fingers shaking. *Maybe I'll just...*

The double doors squeaked open at the end of the corridor. Jay looked up, hating himself for hoping, and discovered Juliet striding towards him. She had her mobile clasped to her ear, listening to someone intently.

Jay watched, numb, as she approached.

Reaching him, she took his arm without a word and dragged him along towards the conference suite.

"What's—?" Jay mumbled.

Juliet ignored him, still focused on her phone.

"Yes," she said, agitated, "immediately. Put it through to Ravi's laptop, will you?"

As she shoved open the door, she hung up the call.

"The mobile phone," she said, leading Jay quickly between tables of hardware, stepping without a glance over tangled wires and extension cables. "I decided to cut out Scotland Yard and outsourced it to a third party hacker. We have a signal."

Sleep-deprived and dazed, it took Jay several seconds to understand.

"Wait—*Al's* phone?"

"Yes—"

"Jesus, where?"

"The area's very broad. I'm having a map reference sent through. I need you to identify anywhere nearby that—"

"Where, Juliet?"

Juliet took a breath. "Manchester," she said, hauling him by the arm towards the corner of the room. A young man sat there alone with a laptop, frowning through his glasses at his screen. "Ravi?"

Ravi looked up quickly at the sound of her voice.

"Ma'am," he said, "I'm getting a request to—"

"Load it." Juliet pulled Jay over, stationing him at Ravi's side. "Show us the map."

Ravi's fingers rattled across the keyboard. A map of the north west popped into place, its focus sweeping downwards as it zoomed, closing in on Greater Manchester. Jay watched, one hand over his mouth in case he threw up.

"So—so this is where Al's phone is putting out a signal?" he asked, glancing sideways at Juliet. "This is where he is?"

"This is the general geographic area where his phone was last able to connect to the system," she said. "There's a chance he might have been separated from the phone, or that he's been moved in the time since this signal, but given the facts..."

The map locked into place.

"Here's the base stations used to triangulate the location," Ravi said, pointing out three white glowing dots upon the screen. "The signal came from somewhere within them. I'm sorry, it's fairly huge."

Jay leant closer, scanning the screen at speed. "Can you make it any bigger for me, mate?"

With a few quick taps, the map expanded.

"Is this somewhere familiar?" Juliet asked, watching Jay.

Jay's stomach lurched. "This bit," he said, pointing. "Old industrial area. Warehouses, buildings waiting to be scrapped. Most of them are uninhabitable."

"Most?"

"Ian had his hand in a drugs outfit here. Years ago." He gestured to a building on the screen. "See that? Abandoned electricity station. We, erm—hydroponics. Two hundred grand worth of cannabis grown in there. The place was creepy as hell, but it meant no one ever came sniffing round."

Juliet's eyes widened. "In other words, it's isolated and easy to secure."

"It is." Jay bit into the side of his cheek, holding her stare. "This is guesswork," he warned. "It's all instinct."

"I'm willing to trust your instincts."

"This is it, then. There's my instincts."

"Do I understand you have knowledge of the building's layout?"

"Donkey's since I was there, but..."

"Would you be able to find your way around?"

"Think so. Why?"

"Because I don't want to risk a raid on this," Juliet said. "If that building can be fortified and we screech up outside with all sirens blazing, it'll turn into a stand-off. Alastair might be harmed."

Jay drove the possibility out of his mind with force, steadying himself before he spoke.

"Okay," he said. "Whatever you're suggesting, I'll do it. You know Manchester's four hours away, don't you?"

"Not by helicopter." Juliet unlocked her phone, flashing through her contacts at speed. "Not for us."

The sound of the door dragged Alastair back to consciousness. As his eyes snapped open, nothing changed. He found himself facing the same pitch darkness which had lulled him to sleep. There came a click from near the door, then a blaze of light so perishing that the back of his eyes seemed to scream, blinded in an instant by the glare. He shut his eyes and curled into himself, coughing. The teeth of the plastic ties bit into his wrists.

Footsteps came into the room. Alastair forced himself to raise his head and squint, hoping and praying it was Milo, a miraculous second chance to convince the boy.

The sight of Ian Straker stopped his heart. He braced in silence, trying to breathe more quietly as Ian collected a rusting metal chair from one corner. He moved it across the room, placed it within a metre of Alastair, then took a seat.

His heart banging, Alastair warily met his gaze.

Ian made no comment. He stayed motionless for some time, his expression blank and searching. He seemed to be grappling with some question, looking for the answer in Alastair's face.

Alastair gripped his ties. "You seem conflicted," he tried.

Ian's expression barely registered that he'd spoken. A moment passed.

"This was going to be so simple," he murmured. "Easy. Clean."

"For what it's worth, it still can be."

"Nah. Not like I wanted." Ian sat back in his chair, folding his arms across his chest. "I didn't believe you at first."

"I don't blame you."

"Little dickhead always liked his posh toffs. Staring at them on the telly... films and that. Didn't think he had ambitions as high as you, though."

Alastair made no reply, wishing his pulse would slow down.

"He kicked me in the face for one," Ian added dimly. "Ten years ago. So much for family. My whole life spent looking after him, then one day just..."

Alastair chose his words. "I imagine you've spent some time planning your revenge."

Ian reached absently into his pocket.

"Keep it simple," he said. He slipped a lighter free and turned it between his fingers, apparently out of habit. "Draw a line under it all, you know? Now I've got a fucking hostage."

"You've an opportunity to make a great deal of money," Alastair pointed out.

Ian grunted. "Don't shit me around, will you? Nobody ever gets to keep the money."

"You'll be surprised."

"Nah. I don't think so. The only surprise I'll get is the handcuffs slapped around my wrists the second I turn my head. Like I'm going to hand you over in an Asda car park? Swap you for a briefcase of fifty pound notes, give everyone a cheerful wave, and off I go to catch my bus? That's not how this'll go."

Alastair watched, saying nothing, as Ian rolled the lighter between his fingers, snapping its lid in a brief flash of flame.

"Question is," he murmured as if to himself, "how *will* it go?"

Alastair shifted, trying to ease the discomfort in his lower back. As the pain in his stomach had dulled, the pain around his kidneys had only sharpened. He likely needed medical attention, but getting out of here alive would come first.

"You could release me in a remote location," he said. "It'll take time for me to be found, time you can use to make your escape. This needn't end in arrest for you."

Ian sucked his teeth. "Thought about it," he admitted. "Cut my losses, as it were. Cancel the whole thing. You'll send people after me, but I could just go off abroad."

"A neutral outcome. Not to be dismissed."

"Problem is," Ian said, still toying with the lighter between his fingers, "and sadly for you, I think this might be a dealbreaker... that outcome won't fix Jason."

Alastair hesitated. "Fix him?"

"Mhm. He'll carry right on with his cushy new life. Running his dinky charity. He'll have the Met chief there to suck him off at night, and all the Met chief's money in the bank. He'll go on thinking he's some kind of golden-hearted hero who turned his little life around, instead of a back-stabbing shit-tongued cunt who threw his family into the fire when it suited him. And that's..." Ian threw his hands up, shaking his head. "Nah. We can't leave that broken and ugly. That won't help me sleep."

Alastair's pulse echoed in his ears. "Do you really want to risk arrest and a return to prison, just to prove a point of honour?"

Ian's low chuckle raised the hairs upon his arms.

"See," he said, tipping the lighter towards Alastair, "you've made a hell of a mistake, there. You were doing well, too. Shame I'm pretty big on points of honour. Ever since literally everything else in the entire fucking world got taken away from me, you could say points of honour are all I've got. So you'd do well not to toss those aside."

"Surely it's a point of honour to survive," Alastair said, willing himself to stay calm. "To endure. To live to fight another day."

"Maybe," Ian conceded. "But if I let you stroll out of here, I'll never get another shot at Jason. That's for sure. Either you'll keep him locked up nice and tight, or witness protection will spirit him off somewhere smart this time. They won't put up with his star-gazing, wanting to make a big deal of himself in London. They'll just drop him in some backwater shithole and tell him to keep his head down. And that'll be that."

Alastair curled his fingers around his ties. Drawing out the conversation seemed as productive a plan as any. Every second the man was talking was a second he wasn't doing anything worse.

"How was it that you located him?" he asked.

Ian took the bait. "Had a feeling he'd only stab me in the back if he won big from it," he said. "He was always dreaming about London as a kid. Don't know why it fascinated him so much."

He sighed, spinning the lighter with another flash of fire.

"I've got contacts down there," he said. "Got chatting to one of them, not long after I got out. He told me his business had been struggling lately. Some new charity, working its way through the kids who normally supplied for him. Telling them they all deserved better. And I got this tingle over the back of my neck when I heard it. I thought to myself... would he *really be* that much of a wanker? Would he *honestly* set himself up like he's some kind of saint?"

Ian shook his head, snapping the lighter shut.

"Calling himself Fieldhouse," he grunted. "Like I wouldn't remember."

Alastair spoke with care. "Remember?"

For the first time, Ian smiled. "Soft little tosser," he said. "Found a fieldmouse out in Alexandra Park one day. Fetched it home in his pocket and decided it was called Fieldhouse. Said he was gonna keep it."

Alastair paused. "Why would he name himself after a mouse?"

"Because I killed it," Ian said. He flicked the lighter with his thumb.

"Probably thought I forgot. I'm surprised *he* remembers, actually. He was only about four."

As icy cold poured down Alastair's back, he kept his face as empty as he could.

"Why?" he asked.

Ian shrugged. "Our dad would've taken it off him anyway."

Incapable of speaking, Alastair stayed quiet and unmoving. He found himself suddenly aware of how far from any other human beings they were, how completely and desperately alone.

Ian clicked his lighter shut, slipping it away into his pocket.

"So I can't just pull the plug on this," he said, briskly and business-like, putting the conversation back on track. "I've got to make the most of it. Won't get another chance."

Alastair forced himself to speak. "Chance?"

"To make Jason understand," Ian said. "Make him realise exactly what he did. How much he hurt me."

Alastair swallowed hard, gripping onto his ties to keep his shoulders from shaking. "Hurt *you?*"

"We're family. That's meant to mean something."

"You tried to burn a man alive. Someone he cared about."

"Which part of 'family' aren't you getting?" Ian asked, his forehead creasing. "Besides, you think he didn't burn *me* alive? Jason ripped my heart from my chest. My own brother. He cost me ten years of my life, and judging from how he's been carrying on since, he doesn't seem to think he did a single thing wrong."

God almighty.

"Mr Straker," Alastair said, unable to keep an edge of desperation from his voice. "This whole thing could cost you a lot more than—"

"Listen," Ian interrupted, fanning out his hands. "I'm talking about fairness here. Okay? Maybe wankers like you don't care about things like that. But right here, in *my* world, we do things properly. Jason brought my life to an end. He's got no place to complain when I do the same to him."

"He didn't *end* your life," Alastair said, shaking. "A prison sentence is not an execution. You're here, your life is continuing, and you can still walk away from this entire situation with honour."

"He took a decade from me. I want it back."

"And how exactly do you propose to retrieve a decade from someone? This is madness."

"Depends." Ian shrugged. "How long will he take to get over you?"

Alastair didn't move. He took a moment just to breathe, trying to form words out of the screaming chaos blotting out his every thought.

"In this moment," he said, staring into Ian Straker's eyes, "everything can still end well. All decisions can be reversed. Most of the British police force will be searching for me, even as we speak. It's in your interests that they find me alive."

"Unless," Ian said, his tone bland, "they're thinking that you died in the fire. That's all over the news, by the way. Nothing whatsoever about you."

Alastair's mouth opened. "That's—y-you'd be risking a—"

"Jason'll realise what happened, of course. Even if nobody else does. Too much of a coincidence for him not to, really. That's the important bit covered. And does it matter if you burned there in his flat, or if you actually burned a few hours later?"

Oh, God. I...

"Same outcome," Ian went on. "My brother finally understands that what I want is what happens. Even makes the delay a bit poetic, really. Ten years of thinking he got away with it, then at last things get settled... plus, it sorts out the question of what to do with you."

Alastair struggled to speak. "They won't give up on me so easily. None of them. If you think they'll shrug—think they'll assume this was an accident—y-you are wrong. And it will cost you."

Ian pulled at his lower lip. "They've had a while to start looking for you, though. Haven't they? And I've not heard any sirens."

Alastair said nothing.

Ian's smile spread across his face. "Huh," he said, getting up from his chair. "This was helpful. I can see why he likes you—you're good to talk to. Thanks."

As he moved towards the door, Alastair's heart leapt into his throat.

"You're making a mistake!" he cried, twisting against his ties. "You have another choice!"

Ian huffed.

"Do I?" he said, reaching for the light. He switched it off. "Sorry you got caught up in this, mate. Should've picked yourself better friends."

He left, closing the door behind him.

Chapter 21

"And does it matter if you burned there in his flat? Or if you actually burned a few hours later?"

Two hundred miles away, Jay would be grieving. He'd have specialists with him, trying to help him cope with the thought of those final few minutes—Alastair trapped by fire, trying to escape. These were the first few hours of Jay's new world. He'd lost his home. He'd be mourning everything he had.

Alastair was mourning, too.

It might even be daylight by now. The world would be continuing without him—the city, the commuters, the morning papers. Reports of a fire somewhere in a block of London flats; among the fatalities the head of the Metropolitan Police.

Does it matter? Panic and distress shrieked at each other across the wreckage of Alastair's mind, arguing, fighting. *Did any of it matter?*

Whether Jay was grieving him or not, Alastair would never know. He wished he'd fought harder in the flat. He wished his ashes were already mixed with the ashes of the rest of Jay's life, all cooling together, nothing worse left to come. He wouldn't have to feel this fear any longer.

He kept thinking of Jay grieving; of Juliet grieving. They could still find him if they looked.

But why would they? Alastair thought. *I'm dead.*

These were almost certainly the last minutes of his life.

His throat clenched. He soothed himself to breathe, letting the heat break at last in his eyes. This might be the last chance he ever had to cry, and there was a painful, frightened comfort in it: his own tears, his own emotions. He hadn't cried since he was a child. He'd learned from a young age that it was unseemly and pointless to cry.

But if these last few minutes would be pointless, then so be it.

It was distressing to be unable to dry the tears. The bands around his wrists dug into his skin more sharply than ever, even tiny movements now tightening them. Shaking, Alastair tried to draw his focus away from the pain, up to his chest and to the feeling of each breath as he took them in, air in his mouth, air in his throat.

I don't want to die alone. I wish you were here.

I wish you—

He would never see those soft green eyes again. *One glance,* he thought, sobbing. *One last glance. What I'd give.* One moment in the window at Cliveden together, sharing a cigarette as they watched the day's fading light spill across the river. One breath beneath the branches of a beech tree, kissing as if the whole world could wait.

'It's more for me,' he had said. *'I want us to be something.'*

Misery burned in Alastair's eyes. He'd never even said the words. He wished he had, just once. *I love you, darling,* breathed against Jay's forehead. *I love you very much. You were my brightest joy.* No one else in the world had ever made him feel cherished. Though they'd only had weeks, they'd been the happiest weeks.

'Sunshine.'

Alastair twisted his arms as he shook, digging the edges of the ties into his skin. He needed the pain to breathe. He needed it to try and calm down.

Your sunshine. Not for long. But I was.

It made it so much harder to die. They could have spent happy years together. Instead Jay would walk through those years by himself, followed only by Alastair's shadow. Those fragile threads they'd gathered around each other were about to be snapped, severed for good. Jay thought they were already cut.

Shaking in silence, Alastair tried to gather his thoughts.

If happy years were out of reach, he would allow himself a few happy minutes instead. He'd spend this time imagining how he and Jay would have spent their lives. These precious last minutes were his own. He had a lifetime of joy to experience before the chance was gone forever, and if he only got to live it in his mind, then so be it.

Dinner out once a week. Those fond green eyes by candlelight, crinkling at their edges as Jay smiled. Their fingers tangled on a tablecloth. Weekends together—long weekends, large breakfasts eaten in bed. Two more years of work. In time, a weekend at Cliveden and a walk through sunlit woods to a beech tree where time held its breath, sheltering them safely within its bounds.

A ring.

And then a perfect day—guests, photographs, a slow dance leaning together beneath the lights. Juliet would have cried. She would have been so happy for them.

A hand to hold always. A husband. A family. Dogs, perhaps—cats if Jay preferred. Sundays, walking through woods hand in hand. Filling Jay's life with comforts he never had, growing human and warm in the light of his love. Growing old wrapped in arms that had been worth a lifetime's wait.

Jay would have wanted for nothing. Not one thing.

Instead—

And I can't even be there to comfort you. You'll need me and I won't be there.

Alastair wrenched against his ties. *Oh, God. I don't want to leave you.* Tears blurred the darkness into ghosts of light and shade. The pain in his wrists wasn't sharp enough to dull the rage any longer. It wasn't easing. He wanted to howl.

I don't deserve to die.

Wild with grief, he thought the bang of the door was in his imagination. The sudden blaze of light made it real. He winced, dropping his head as voices filled the room.

"But—for real, though? Now?"

"Now."

Alastair shut his eyes. He didn't want to see. He let every other thought burn to nothing in his head, except for one: Jay. Jay's eyes, Jay's face. His hands.

Someone came close, heaving Alastair forwards to access his wrists.

"In here?" Milo's voice asked as the ties were cut, sounding nervous. "You're—you're just gonna—"

"Not in here," Ian said. "There's not enough air. It'd eat it all up, then just go out. The others are setting up in one of the warehouses."

Alastair kept his eyes closed, his heart pounding itself apart. *Jay,* he thought. Jay's smile. The way he laughed, the way he kissed. The way he sounded waking up.

Ian's hands closed around Alastair's shoulders. He flinched, bracing, but Ian only dragged him to his feet. He forced Alastair's wrists behind his back and held them, then slung another arm across his chest from behind.

"No sudden moves," he said in Alastair's ear. "Mm?"

A cold metal edge pressed flat to the front of Alastair's throat.

"We're taking a walk," Ian said. "You're coming nice and quiet."

As Ian forced him forwards, Alastair walked. It didn't matter where his feet were going. He would keep his eyes closed and die in his own mind, in Jay's arms in the suite at Cliveden where they'd fallen in love. He could feel the warm weight of the covers. He could see Jay's eyes, looking into his own, watching him from the pillow with that quiet, loving smile.

Corridors passed; Alastair didn't see. He let his feet move him forwards without thought. In his mind he was stroking Jay's cheek, brushing back his tufts of hair. Juliet would be good to him. She'd take care of him. Jay would take care of her.

"Listen—just—" Milo's voice scattered through Alastair's thoughts.

"He's got money," Milo said. "He told me. Why're you—instead we could—"

"Milo, how about you just fucking turn it in? The only reason this is happening is because of you."

Alastair shut his eyes tighter, desperate for them to stop speaking. Jay was fading from his mind; he wanted to hold on. In his thoughts, he pushed close to Jay, kissed him more desperately, stroked through his hair and felt its texture between his fingers. *Mine, my Jay—*

"Look, he's loaded," Milo tried, hurrying along beside them. "He's seriously loaded. He offered me thirty grand, okay? He wasn't kidding, Ian. You don't have to kill him. We could—"

They turned a corner.

As they staggered to a sudden halt, a voice spoke from several metres up ahead.

"Stay where you are."

Alastair's eyes snapped open.

The corridor ahead was blocked. Five figures in coal-black body armour stood in a V-formation, four with firearms pointing this way.

At their head, deathly calm, stood Jay.

The noise which Alastair let out cracked Jay's heart in two. He kept the feeling off his face as he scanned the situation, taking in what it was that they were facing. Ian had Alastair by the throat, a switchblade open and ready to go. Behind them stood a horrified-looking teenager with acne, staring open-mouthed at the guns now trained in their direction.

The sight of the knife spilled ice through Jay's blood. *Holy shit. Just in time.*

At last, he moved his eyes to the one place they didn't want to be.

Ian looked right back at him, his features set in stone.

"Okay," Jay said, inhaling. He hadn't seen that face in ten years. He hadn't missed how small the sight of it made him feel, nor how helpless. "Let's just... let's everybody chill, alright? No sudden movements."

His brother gave a huff. "Drop the guns or watch him die."

Jesus.

"If you do that," Jay warned, "they'll shoot you. There's four of them and one of you. Do the maths."

Ian moistened his lips.

"Shame your boyfriend's only got one throat," he said. As Ian tensed, Alastair flinched, his eyes snapping shut. The blade threatened to dig in. "Drop the guns," Ian barked.

Jay threw up a hand.

"Easy," he said, fighting to keep the panic out of his voice. One quick flick and this would be over. Ian would open Alastair's throat like it was nothing, and nobody in the world would ever be able to put that right. "Let's take a minute first, okay? This can end just fine for everyone."

The teenager in the back unleashed a choking sound, twitching with the urge to turn and run.

"Let him go." The boy's voice broke as he pleaded. "F-fuck's sake, Ian. Just fuckin' let him go, will you? He's not shitting around."

Ian didn't move. He kept the knife as it was, flat against Alastair's throat, his stare piercing into Jay's.

Jay risked a quick glance into Alastair's eyes. *It's alright,* he tried to convey in silence, keeping his breathing steady. *Not leaving without you.*

Alastair seemed to swallow, gazing back.

"Got more than you bargained for, Ian?" Jay asked, as calmly as if they'd bumped into each other at the pub. He looked back into his brother's face. "Guess you didn't know that he's the Met chief."

Ian's jaw worked. "You're gonna stand there and chat to me, are you? After everything you did?"

Jay measured his response, giving it with care. "You know I didn't make the rope."

"Nah," Ian said, huffing. "Just slipped it round my neck."

"What choice did you give me? You knew I was sweet on Wheeler. I saw it in your face, the day you told me what you were planning to do. You only did it to find out if I'd stop you. You just wondered if I had those kind of balls."

Ian said nothing, visibly sweeping his tongue around his cheek.

Swallowing, Jay forced himself to carry on.

"All I've ever done is stand between you and what's mine," he said. "And you make me do it, Ian. You put me into that position over and over again, just to let me know that you could. But you can get it right this time. You can put the knife down, let Al go, and everybody walks out of here. Nobody has to lose this time."

Alastair spoke, his voice quiet and simple. "Milo," he murmured. The nervous teenager at the back reacted to the name, twitching. "I warned you."

The boy flashed a panic-stricken look towards Jay.

"I don't know what's goin' on," he tried. "I'm just—I—I ain't involved in this. I ain't caused none of this." His hands bunched into fists at his sides. "You're Jason? You're the brother?"

Ian shouted without looking. "How about you shut the ever-lasting fuck up now, Milo?"

Jay kept his eyes on Alastair's face, trying to read what he was being told. Alastair seemed to be breathing again, shallow and slow, watching Jay closely in return.

"They'll let you leave," Alastair said, his eyes forward. "You'll be allowed to walk out of here. If you do the right thing, you won't be harmed."

Ian's upper lip curled back. "How about you shut up and all?" he snapped, snarling directly into Alastair's ear. "The right thing to me is emptying you out across the floor. So just pipe down, hey?"

A small, urgent instinct prickled through Jay's blood. Something about Milo, hovering just outside Ian's eyeline, caused his heart to speed up and beat out of rhythm. He wasn't certain who Alastair had been addressing, but he was starting to get an idea.

Wetting his lips, Jay said, "We don't want bloodshed, Ian. We don't want *anybody's* blood shed."

"So drop the guns," Ian raged, "and back the hell away! I'm not moving a muscle until you're halfway down that corridor and the guns are on the floor. Do you understand me?"

Behind Ian, out of his sight, Milo took a first silent step.

Jay kept his focus fixed upon his brother. "How'd you find me, Ian?"

"Followed the stench of hypocritical do-goodery," Ian jeered. "Led right to you. Asked an old London mate to help me out, get some of his boys to watch your office and put the frighteners on you. Make certain you knew what was coming."

"The vandalism? Mugging me?"

"Should've guessed you wouldn't take a hint. You could've kept your head down, you little shit, and we wouldn't even be standing here right now. Could've slunk off somewhere quiet with your thirty pieces of silver. But no. You just had to go ahead and prove you're so much *better* than the rest of us."

Jay waited for a moment before he spoke, trying to judge his response. He needed Ian distracted, but not enraged. That had never been an easy line to walk, even without ten years of betrayal in between them.

"Do you honestly think I did what I did just to look good?" he asked. Behind Ian, Milo edged another nervous step nearer, his staring eyes locked on the back of Ian's head. Jay took a risk, buying time. "You don't get it at all, mate, do you?"

Ian let out an ugly laugh.

"What's to get?" he said. "You're an ungrateful little tosser who decided you're too good for our family."

"You're talking like we ran a fucking bakery."

"And?"

"And it wasn't like that, was it? You were going to burn Wheeler alive in his flat. I shouldn't have to explain why it's bad that you would do that."

Ian scoffed. "That goody-two-shoes social worker cunt was poisoning you," he said. "Whispering in your ear, turning you away from your own flesh and blood. Telling you that he'd give you the world if you turned on me. The only mistake I made was letting it go on so long. Maybe if I'd stepped in and stopped it earlier, I could've saved you."

"And this time?" Jay said, raising his voice. It echoed off the concrete walls, covering Milo's last few footsteps. "What are you trying to teach me this time?"

Ian's face set.

"I'm done giving you lessons," he said. He screwed his fist in Alastair's hair, dragging back his head to expose his throat. "Now I just want to give you nightmares."

As Jay cried out, Milo lunged. He lashed his arms around Ian's neck from behind and wrenched him backwards, grabbing wildly for the knife. All three of them lurched. They staggered as one; the knife flashed. Shots rang out as they fell.

Jay moved before they hit the ground. He ran forwards without a thought, ignoring the shouts of the operatives behind him. He reached Alastair within a second, dropped to his knees and grabbed for his body, hauling him up from the floor.

His weight lolled against Jay's shoulder.

No—

No, you—

Jay scrabbled to find his neck, searching in desperation for a pulse. Ian and Milo were sprawled out on the ground nearby, as loose and limp as puppets with the strings cut. They weren't moving. For all Jay knew, they were dead. He clamped his fingers to the side of Alastair's neck, gasping as he realised there was blood.

"Al," he begged, shaking too hard to feel a thing. "Al, no—please—please don't—"

With a sudden gasp, Alastair stiffened. His arms locked tight around Jay's chest. His hands formed fists in the back of Jay's clothing, his grip like iron as he clung.

"Jay—"

The ground seemed to pitch and tilt beneath Jay's knees. He expelled every molecule of air in his lungs, so relieved he almost passed out. Nothing would ever scare him again as long as he lived. Nothing would ever matter. He shifted enough to hook an arm beneath Alastair's legs, no longer caring who the firearms team had hit. It was done; it was over. They were going. He lifted Alastair up without a second's delay, braced him against his chest and carried him back the way they'd come, staring straight ahead towards the exit. Two of the operatives tailed them, their guns still drawn. Two stayed behind. Jay didn't care.

Alastair curled into his chest, burying his face against Jay's shoulder. His hands shook where they'd locked around the back of Jay's neck.

"I've got you," Jay murmured as they moved, his heart slamming against his ribs. One of the operatives was speaking into a radio at speed behind him. The words were nothing, a gabble of meaningless noise. "I've got you, sunshine. I've got you and we're getting out of here."

Alastair's body convulsed. "Jay," he gasped, barely able to speak. "Oh, God—"

"Everything's alright," Jay said, hushing him, shaking. "We'll get you off to hospital. Everything's going to be fine."

"Milo—the boy, did they—"

"Let's concentrate on you, okay? We'll sort the rest out later."

As they approached the familiar back entrance, Jay steadied his arms beneath Alastair's weight. He booted the door open with his foot, caught its recoil against his free shoulder, and carried Alastair out into the air.

The security services were waiting fifty yards away, gathered behind a blockade of police vehicles. Cries went up as Jay and Alastair appeared. Jay breathed in, held Alastair close and simply walked, focusing on putting as much distance as he could between the two of them and the building.

Nearer to the line, a swarm of people came rushing forwards to try and help, gasping panicked questions, issuing orders. At the noise, Alastair shrank against Jay's chest, his fingers twitching on Jay's neck. Someone in a uniform intervened to try and take Alastair from Jay's arms—and while Jay would never be proud of the language he released in response, it worked. The space around them emptied, the situation now abundantly clear. Jay carried Alastair onwards through the clamour.

She appeared at Jay's side as if from nowhere, perfectly calm with her mobile clasped to one ear.

"Here," she said, seizing him by the elbow and pulling him through the crowd. A hired taxi was bending to a stop by the road. "That car there. It's ours. The Royal Infirmary's expecting us."

Jay followed her lead. She got the door for him and held it open, still speaking quickly into her phone.

As Jay lowered Alastair into the backseat, Alastair clung on. His breath crackled with panic in Jay's ear.

"It's okay," Jay said at once, gathering his arms as tight as he dared. Being gentle in this moment wasn't easy. He wanted to hug and to grip and to squeeze, reassure himself that Alastair was in one piece and that he was real. He couldn't bear to cause any pain, though. He didn't know yet what Ian might have done. "It's alright, love. I'm coming too. I'm getting in with you. Can you shuffle over for me?"

Alastair shifted backwards, shaking, his face a mess of half-cried tears and sweat. His eyes were huge and he was bloodless, as pale as if he might throw up at any second. Jay got in, slammed the door, and pulled Alastair close to him again. Alastair crawled into his lap without a word, latched his arms around Jay's chest and buried his face against Jay's neck, sobbing in absolute silence.

Jay wrapped both arms around him, shaking too.

"Shhh..." he hushed, carding his fingers through Alastair's hair. *Oh, Jesus. Oh, fuck.* He could hardly get the words out, struggling to piece together the sounds. "Shhh, Al... it's alright..."

Alastair twitched, still not making a sound.

"We'll get you to hospital," Jay whispered, shutting his eyes. The lack of a visible world somehow helped. Whatever was unfolding around them, it was unimportant. He had his face pressed to Alastair's hair, Alastair's hands gripping onto his back, and the rest could attend to itself. "We'll get those wrists looked at, yeah? I won't let you go, I promise. I won't let anybody take you off me."

Juliet got into the passenger seat. She pulled her door shut, thanked the driver quietly, and the car set off.

Jay kept his eyes closed for most of the journey. He brushed Alastair's hair back from his ear and murmured to him as they drove, reassuring words which came without needing to think. Alastair's face stayed hidden against his neck, silent tears tracking their way beneath Jay's collar.

Not far from the hospital, a chime sounded from the passenger seat. Jay slowed in his murmuring, lifting his eyes to the rear view mirror. He watched Juliet read the text she'd just received; her shoulders expanded in relief.

Looking up, she found Jay watching her in the mirror and paused.

"Was it Ian they hit?" Jay asked. "Is he dead?"

Juliet didn't move for a moment, weighing his expression.

She answered with a single, simple nod.

Jay lowered his head, pressing the tip of his nose to Alastair's temple. *My Al,* he thought. *My sunshine. My whole world and all my dreams.*

"Good," he said, and nothing more.

Chapter 22

THE TRILL OF THE PHONE RANG BRIGHTLY THROUGH THE LOBBY, CLEAR above the chatter of the guests. Setting aside her check-in list, Katie reached for the receiver and tucked it against her ear.

"Cliveden House," she said pleasantly. "This is Katie speaking. How can I help?"

The caller was a younger woman, polite and well-spoken, who presented herself with the graceful efficiency that usually belonged to a PA.

"Hello, Katie," she said. "I hoped I could book some accommodation for this evening. There'll be a few special requirements, if that's alright."

Katie reached for the wireless mouse. "Of course," she said, giving it a wiggle to wake the screen. "We have plenty of availability. What can I arrange for you?"

"My employer and his partner have been through something of an ordeal overnight. They'll need a lot of peace and privacy, and they'll have a security officer with them. Would a quieter area of the hotel be possible? One of the smaller suites, perhaps."

"That's not a problem. Just the one night?"

"Ah, no. I imagine a little longer than that. Could you please reserve the room for a week? I'm happy to pay in advance."

"Of course. Let me just bring up our booking system." Katie pulled at her lip, watching the screen as the software automatically refreshed itself. For their usual clientele, 'something of an ordeal' could be anything from an assassination attempt to a dinner party where the soup course was served before the shellfish. She supposed she didn't need to know the details. "Okay, there we are. Can I take the names of the guests who'll be staying, please?"

"Certainly. The names are Sir Alastair Harding and Mr Jay Fieldhouse. Sir Alastair has stayed with you previously."

Oh, my God—

Oh my God, oh my God!

"Oh—yes, I remember their last stay," Katie said, gripping the phone as twin tsunamis of excitement and concern flooded through her system. She'd hoped to see them come back soon, but hadn't dreamed it would be *this* soon. Strictly speaking, she shouldn't ask what had happened. It wasn't her place to know. But she couldn't simply brush it aside and breeze onwards. "I, erm... I hope they're both okay?"

The woman on the phone briefly paused, then seemed to decide it was best to confide.

"I'm afraid Sir Alastair was held hostage last night," she said. "He wasn't treated kindly."

Oh, shit. Katie wrapped a hand in silence around her own throat, holding the instinctive reaction in. *Oh, my God.* It felt like hearing it had happened to a friend or a family member. A thousand questions exploded at once inside her mind, none of which she dared to ask.

"His injuries are minor," the woman on the phone went on. "But he's suffering from a lot of shock. It's... been a bloody awful night, to be candid. Mr Fieldhouse's flat was destroyed in the fire you might have seen reported on national news. Both of them are in desperate need of peace."

It took Katie a second or two to speak, so horrified that it was hard to bring her thoughts together properly.

"I see," she said, breathless. The words arose through instinct alone, a product of years of practice. "I'm so sorry to hear that. I'll make sure they're undisturbed and have everything they need."

"Thank you, Katie. That would be wonderful." The speaker paused, considering something. "And... could you also reserve a single room for the same nights? Under the name of Juliet Naughton, please. Somewhere nearby, if you can."

Katie arranged for them to come in through the staff entrance. From the sound of the situation, a busy lobby filled with people was the last thing either of them needed. She kept their booking forms to be dealt with later in their stay, then put a message through to the cleaning team, asking them to prioritise the Orkney Suite.

Shortly after twelve, Juliet Naughton called again, saying that the car was approaching the estate. Katie waited just inside the door to the staff parking area, watching the light rain now falling across the courtyard and trying her best not to worry.

The crunch of approaching tires on the gravel track brought both relief and new waves of trepidation. They parked as close to the entrance as possible and Sir Alastair's assistant got out first. It could only be her that Katie had spoken to on the phone. Miss Naughton suited her voice, elegant and calm, the sort of woman whose lipstick would survive armageddon. A touch of tired shadow beneath her eyes was the only suggestion of anything amiss. She stepped from the vehicle and opened an umbrella in the same fluid motion, faultless in her high heels on the gravel. She circled around the car and opened the door to the back seat, shielding the passengers from the rain as they emerged.

At the sight of Sir Alastair, Katie's stomach turned. The poor man looked ready to drop. He was wearing borrowed clothing far too big for him, his hair dishevelled and dirty, and his complexion was grey with exhaustion. Jay helped him from the car, dressed for war in black cargo pants and combat boots, but holding his partner as gently as if every bone in Alastair's body had been broken. As they made their way towards the entrance, Alastair leant wearily into Jay's side, too drained to speak, Miss Naughton covering them from the rain with her umbrella. A security officer came behind them, bulky and anonymous in his boxy grey suit. They didn't seem to have any luggage.

"I'll be here this evening," Miss Naughton said at the door, directing the promise towards Jay. They'd clearly known each other for years, as close as family. It tore Katie's heart into ribbons. "I'll bring everything the two of you will need. Text me if anything specific comes to mind. It won't be a problem."

"Thanks, doll. I will. Just clothes and stuff for now."

"Yes, of course. I'll bring a selection." She paused, glancing nervously at Sir Alastair. "I'm a single text away. I hope you sleep well..."

Sir Alastair hesitated.

As he reached for her, Jay beckoned without a word for the umbrella.

They embraced beneath its shelter for some time. Sir Alastair's expression tightened as he held her, gathering the back of her hair very gently with his palm. Seeing him start to cry, Katie tore her eyes away and concentrated on dealing with the lump in her throat.

When the two of them parted, still visibly overcome, Miss Naughton transferred her hug at once to Jay.

"Look after him," she said against his shoulder. She held onto him, her jaw tight. "For God's sake, look after him. Please."

Jay dipped his nose into her hair, rubbing her gently on the back. "He won't leave my sight," he said. "You know he won't."

"Thank you... and I'm sorry for—"

"Forget about it," Jay murmured, squeezing her. "We got him back. That's all that matters."

She released him with a tearful nod and a glance of gratitude, pale. She dried her eyes very quickly with her fingertips, then retrieved her umbrella from his keeping.

As Juliet strode back through the rain towards the car, Katie watched her go, her heart in her mouth.

She held the door for the two men and their security guard to come inside, then gestured gently towards the staff lift, addressing herself through instinct to Jay.

"If you want to follow me, sir, I'll show you up to your room."

It was the suite they'd had before. Everything was just as Jay remembered it: the window seat, the fireplace, the heavy velvet drapes, all perfectly the same. It felt like the space had been waiting for them all this time, empty and unoccupied, their room with all their things still tucked away inside the drawers. Jay had never been so glad to see a room in all his life.

"Can I bring you anything?" the assistant asked as he guided Alastair carefully through the door. She'd been waiting for them in the courtyard, watching for the car. Jay had a feeling he could ask for a bowl of snow from the top of Mount Everest and she'd fetch it within the hour.

All they really needed was privacy, though a couple of other things would help.

"Could you do something like a malt drink?" Jay asked, glancing at Alastair. He hadn't said a word during the journey here. He'd hardly moved, barely looked at anyone. Stepping into the hotel, he'd sagged against Jay's side as if releasing his very last scrap of strength. "Horlicks, hot milk. That sort of thing. It's... Katie, isn't it?"

Her expression softened, moved to be remembered. "It is, sir. And of course I can."

"Thanks. And maybe a chair for..." Jay looked at their security officer, whose name he didn't know. The guy was built like a bomb shelter, and almost certainly armed. "You don't mind me putting you out in the corridor, mate, do you? Just need some privacy for a while."

The man dipped his head. "Not at all, sir."

"Thanks..." Jay hesitated, glancing back at Katie. "And... listen, I know this is cheeky... but you've got the spa downstairs, haven't you? Would they lend us some bubble bath? I don't mind what's in it. Just something to..."

He tightened his hold around Alastair's waist.

She nodded, understanding completely. "Of course," she said. "Is there anything else I can do?"

Jay let out a breath, unsure why her kindness was killing him. "No," he said. "No, that's... that'd be brilliant. Thanks."

Their security officer let her out. She disappeared along the corridor at once, away on her mission without a moment's pause. With a nod to Jay, the security officer left as well, closing the door behind him with a soft and simple click.

Nervous silence fell. It seemed unreal to be alone at last—hours of anguish, suddenly all over. Some part of Jay had never expected to hear silence again in his life. He'd almost thought the noise and the fear and the panic would go on forever, endless into eternity.

He turned to look at Alastair, placing a cautious hand upon his arm.

"You alright?" he asked. It was a stupid bloody question and he knew it. Anyone could see that Alastair was a mess. His eyes were sunken and lost, struggling to meet Jay's gaze. "Sorry," Jay said, swallowing. "I know you're not. I know you're nowhere near alright. But if we get you clean, get you something to drink... that'll be a start, won't it?"

Alastair said nothing, looking down between them. He reached silently for Jay's hand, touching his fingers as if unsure whether he would find them solid or not, then lifted them from his sleeve, turning Jay's palm upwards to his sight.

The skin there was still red and mottled, some patches shiny, some starting to peel.

"How did—?" Alastair said.

The fire seemed like years ago. Though Jay had been conscious of the sting across his palm all this time, he'd more or less forgotten what it meant. The injury and the memory had disconnected themselves, unimportant.

"It's nothing," he said, quietly closing his fingers. "Nothing compared to what you've been through."

The silence pulled.

Honesty, Jay thought, breathing in. He didn't want to start hiding things now.

"Burned it on my door handle," he admitted. It was enough to lift Alastair's eyes into his. "When I got back to the flat, there was smoke pouring out of all the windows. Nobody had seen you. I went in, tried to find you. But I couldn't."

He hadn't realised that Alastair's face had any colour left to lose.

"You could have been hurt," Alastair responded, horrified, staring up at Jay in alarm. "Jay, you could have been killed."

Jay couldn't believe his ears.

"*I* could have been hurt?" he said. "You've just spent the whole night as a hostage to my psycho of a—a-and you're upset because *I* could have been hurt?"

Alastair didn't move, looking at Jay as if no words could ever be enough. Tears wavered in his eyes, but didn't fall. His cheeks tensed as he swallowed something back.

"I'm sorry," broke out of him at last. "I'm sorry for the things I said to you. I'm so, so sorry. I had no right to say those things."

Jesus Christ.

"Al," Jay said, shaking. He ran his hands up Alastair's arms. "Al, you're *alive.* I thought I'd never see you again. Do you really think I'm still upset about—"

Alastair's expression folded. All at once, he started to cry. He dropped his head towards Jay's shoulder, leaning in, and Jay gathered both arms around him without a thought. Alastair held onto him as if suddenly afraid to fall. He pressed his face against Jay's shoulder and didn't move.

Jay ran his fingers through the back of Alastair's hair, combing it as gently as he could.

"I wish I hadn't left you on your own," he said, whispering the words against the side of Alastair's head. "If I'd known, I'd have stayed. We'd have talked. And I'd have torn apart anyone who came for you."

For a moment, Alastair made no sound.

"He was going to burn me," he said. His voice cracked. "H-he was going to burn me alive. He said that you'd realise it was him."

Jay couldn't bear the thought. They'd averted it all at the very last moment, and it was still going to keep him awake.

"Ian's dead," he said softly. "He's gone. You made it out of there and he didn't."

"I—I-I don't know how to—how to cope with—"

"You will. I promise."

"Jay, I..."

"I know it feels like nothing's real," Jay said, wrapping his hand around the back of Alastair's head. "I know you feel like you've been shot out of a gun and you're still going. I know that getting away from him feels like you climbed up a rope of barbed wire to do it, and you're bleeding all over, but I promise it won't always feel like that. I know because I've been there. It takes time, but it all fades away. So we'll handle this one minute after another, alright?"

Alastair seemed to shiver. He nodded, drawing the first full breath Jay had felt him take in hours.

"Please be patient with me," he said.

Jay's chest ached. He loosened his fingers in Alastair's hair. "I'm not going anywhere," he said, stroking through the matted copper strands. "I got you into all this crap. I'll get you out."

They held each other in silence for a few minutes, rocking very slowly side to side. By the time the cautious knock came, the shaking in Alastair's shoulders had subsided. Katie slipped back into the room, accompanied by another member of guest services. She laid a tray with two malt drinks on their coffee table, placed a box of chocolate truffles beside it, then turned to the young man who'd come with her, carrying a gift basket wrapped in cellophane. At her nod, he placed it with care at the end of their bed.

"With the compliments of the management," she said. "We've also added a couples' treatment in the spa to your account. If you let us know when you'd want to make use of it, we'll make sure you're the only guests there. We're on hand twenty-four hours if there's anything else you need."

Jay had never wanted to hug a stranger before. It was hard to know how else to express his gratitude, how to turn the vastness of this sensation into something as tiny as words.

"Thank you," he told her, overwhelmed. It didn't seem enough. He tried again, looking into her eyes. "Thank you for... it means the world. Seriously."

Katie dipped her head. "Always happy to help, sir," she said. "I wish you both a peaceful stay."

She and her colleague left, closing the door.

Jay picked up the tray from the coffee table. He'd never helped anyone come down from a traumatic event before. All of this was instinct, cobbled together with hope and love. He knew nothing about recovery.

He knew a little bit about Al, though.

"Shall we get you clean?" he murmured, nodding towards the bathroom. Alastair came with him as he carried the drinks through, trailing at his side like a ghost. "It'll be hard for you to settle while you smell of borrowed clothes."

If Alastair was confused by Jay resting the tray beside the bath, he didn't show it. He watched mutely as Jay stripped the cellophane from the gift basket, searched through the selection of products and picked out a bottle of bubble bath. *Cedarwood and juniper,* Jay read from the label. *Seems legit.* It would help to wash away last night, and that was all he could ask of it.

Water gushed from the tap into the tub, piping hot at once. Its rumble filled the small space with sound, as soothing as rain against a window, and the pale gold mixture turned to bubbles as soon as Jay added it to the water. He swirled it a few times to help it along, straightened up and dried his hand off on a towel, then turned with care to Alastair.

"Be honest with me," he said, looking into Alastair's eyes. Alastair quietly stiffened. "I don't mean to make this awkward. I want you to feel comfortable, and I'm fine with whatever the answer is. Do you want me to—"

"Don't go," Alastair said at once. He hesitated, embarrassed, then said more steadily, "Don't leave. There's no need for you to..."

Jay proceeded gently. "I won't leave," he said. "I'll stay in the room. And—again, I'm fine with whatever the answer is—"

Alastair flushed a little as he spoke. "I wouldn't be uncomfortable if you joined me," he said.

Jay considered that kindling hint of colour, and concluded that *I wouldn't be uncomfortable* might just mean *I want you to.*

"Alright," he said, trying to look like this was simply a piece of information and not a desperate relief. He'd lost Alastair less than one hour after admitting what this was to him. Since then, Alastair had been through hell, all because of the connection they'd shared. It was a miracle he could even stand to look at Jay, let alone share a bath. Nervous of the silence, Jay tried a careful smile and some humour. "Suppose I've had my kit off in front of you a few times now. Nothing you haven't seen before."

Alastair's flush deepened. Though he didn't exactly smile, he seemed to like that Jay was smiling. It put a moment's brightness in his eyes, a single glimpse of the man who'd once dropped everything and raced across a city to look after Jay. He took a tentative step in Jay's direction, quietly seeking something out.

Gathering him in with one arm, Jay gently bumped their foreheads.

"Shall we get these hospital clothes off you?" he said. "Juliet'll be here later with your things. But we'll manage in dressing gowns until then, won't we?"

Alastair nodded, leaning into his hug.

With care, Jay set about unfastening the unfamiliar buttons. It had been good of the hospital to lend Alastair the clothes. He couldn't have travelled all the way to Cliveden as he was when he was found, grimy and dirty with blood around his cuffs, but these clothes didn't smell like him. They didn't smell like his home, his ordinary life. They were a temporary measure, and if there was one thing Jay didn't want

Alastair to feel right now, it was temporary. As he helped Alastair undress, he stripped himself as well, matching the process garment for garment. *Can't have you standing there naked,* he thought, *while I'm kitted out like Action Man.* The combat boots looked bizarre discarded on the cream marble tiles. The cargo trousers joined them, then Jay's boxer shorts and Alastair's briefs, until finally they could hug skin to skin within the swirling, scented steam.

"There," Jay said, running his hands up Alastair's back. Alastair trembled against him, breathing slowly at the side of his neck. "Quiet bath, hot drink, then we'll get into bed. If you just want to lie down and rest, we'll do that. If you want to talk, we'll talk. If you want to go to sleep, we'll go to sleep."

Alastair nuzzled nearer to Jay, shivering.

"Thank you," he whispered, wrapping his hand around Jay's left shoulder. His fingertips grazed Jay's tattooed wing as if he could really feel the feathers there, stroking them. "I'm not sure if I could sleep. But resting would be..."

Jay smiled a little, watching his face. "Alright. Shall we get you in the bath? Here, I'll help you. Take your time."

The hot water seemed to curl around them, holding them safe as they settled beneath its surface. Jay laid back against the side, gathered Alastair to rest upon his chest, then reached for one of the mugs of malted milk.

"Here," he said, guiding it into Alastair's hands. "Should be cool enough to drink now."

Alastair shivered, sipping it with care.

"We can stay like this as long as you want," Jay said, watching him, stroking his back. *Worried I'd never hold you again,* he thought. *Never have you close again.* "The hot water'll ease your aches. We'll get you clean again, get you comfortable. If you want to stay right here all afternoon, that's fine. We can do that."

Alastair took another nervous drink. He swallowed, then gathered the mug against his chest, looking down. "I'm sorry about your flat."

"Jesus, Al. Don't worry about that. Not for a second. It's not your fault."

"I can't imagine what it feels like, to lose everything you've..."

Jay reached out, brushing back the strands of Alastair's hair. "Hey," he said softly, easing Alastair into quiet. "Don't give it another thought. Believe me when I say that all I'm feeling right now is relief."

"All your things..."

"They're just things. The shops are full of new things." Jay pressed his lips to the top of Alastair's head. "Could've lost a lot more than things."

"Jay..."

"When I realised Ian had got hold of you... holy shit, I didn't want to live."

"Jay—"

"I mean it. I wouldn't have been alright again, ever. I wouldn't have coped."

Alastair stirred in Jay's arms. He moved his mug to the side of the bath and shifted around in Jay's lap to look at him, his eyes reddened and shining. He took Jay's face into his hands.

Emotion tightened the lines around his mouth, gazing down as if holding the world.

"I love you," he said.

Jay's mouth opened. He wouldn't forget Alastair's expression as long as he lived. There was something almost overwhelmed in it, as if he couldn't quite believe it. As if half-certain he was seeing things.

Alastair searched his eyes, shaking.

"I love you very much," he whispered.

Jay wrapped his fingers around Alastair's sore wrists, holding his hands to his face. "I love you, too," he said, his heart breaking. "I'm here, sunshine. I'm not going."

Alastair was silent for a moment, grappling with some thought he couldn't bear.

"I want you to stay," he said at last, watching for reaction. Nervous tears refilled his eyes. "I want you to care for me."

"I will," Jay breathed, sliding his fingers between Alastair's. "You're everything to me. Of course I'll care for you. Of course I'll stay."

Alastair swallowed hard. "I want you to be mine. Only mine."

"I'm yours. I'm all yours, all of me. I've been yours since the second you shook my hand and said hello." Jay looked into Alastair's eyes, wishing he could let their nervous gaze straight through into his mind, let them scan and search and analyse whatever they wanted, see it all laid out for themselves. "Give me time and you'll see, sweetheart," he said. "I promise. I'm not going anywhere."

The gloss in Alastair's eyes thickened. His tears grew heavy enough to fall.

"I want you to be mine for some time," he said.

Jay gathered his hold around Alastair's fingers, taking care to be gentle as he brought them to his lips. "Unless you chase me off with a brush," he said, kissing them, "I'm not leaving you."

Alastair's eyes flashed, more tears rising. "I'm being serious."

Jay nodded, not looking away. "So am I."

A silent tremor passed through Alastair's hands. Jay squeezed them gently, rubbing them.

"I'm not leaving," he whispered, shaking his head. Alastair leant towards him. As their noses rubbed, Jay shut his eyes. "I'm not going, Al. I'm never going."

Their lips came together.

Jay had never kissed and cried in the same moment before. Alastair was crying, too. He could feel Alastair's tears easing down onto his cheeks, a warm and silent stream indistinguishable from his own.

"I love you," Alastair breathed against his lips, shaking. "Please, Jay."

Jay ran his fingers through Alastair's hair, his throat thick. "Everything you ever want," he whispered, "I'm going to bring you. Everything you ever need, I'll find for you. I love you. And whatever he put you through, whatever you worried was going to happen, it's over now. You're here with me and we're safe."

"I want to stay for a few days. Here, at Cliveden. A week perhaps. Until..."

"Until you're ready. Until you feel like yourself."

"U-until then."

"I'll be here," Jay promised in between kisses. "I'll be here afterwards, too. As long as you want me, Al, I will be here."

Chapter 23

Alastair woke the next morning to a feeling of dazed surprise. He hadn't really expected to sleep, nervous of the near certainty of nightmares. He couldn't remember drifting off. In the end, he'd had no dreams—or if he had, his mind hadn't bothered to keep them. Sleep had returned him to the world in far better condition than it found him, wrapped up warm and deeply calm.

As he shifted, stretching out his feet, the protective cocoon around his body gently tightened. There came a kiss to the back of his neck, a murmur of words he didn't catch, and the covers gathered up about his shoulders.

Alastair let out his breath.

You're here, he thought. *You're with me.* It was no wonder the nightmares had kept their distance.

Slowly, he opened his eyes. His blurry vision muffled the sunshine, softening the room around him into foggy shapes. As it cleared, he found ribbons of mid-morning light shining between the drapes. One of Jay's arms was wrapped around his torso from behind, his palm flat against Alastair's heart; his other arm lay along the top of the pillows. He had his mobile outstretched in his free hand. He was texting very carefully with his thumb, attempting not to disturb Alastair's sleep.

As he spotted the recipient's name at the top of the window, Alastair smiled.

He watched the conversation, sleepy and at peace.

[JF - 11:27] *still fast asleep*
[JF - 11:27] *must need it*

[JN - 11:27] *Very understandable. Did he eat much yesterday?*

[JF - 11:28] *didnt expect he would but in the end yeah*
[JF - 11:28] *staff brought us up fish pie for tea, he had the lot*
[JF - 11:28] *I got a few biscuits into him in the evening too*

[JN - 11:28] *Good. An appetite is very normal after shock*

[JF - 11:29] *figure his body knows what it needs*
[JF - 11:29] *best just to get him it*

[JN - 11:29] *Is there anything that I can get for you?*

[JF - 11:30] *god no, dont worry about me*
[JF - 11:30] *I'm fine*

"You need breakfast," Alastair murmured. "It's nearly noon."

Jay smiled against his temple. "You're asleep."

"Mhm."

"I'll have some food when you do. Not hungry just yet." Jay pushed his phone away across the pillow, gathering Alastair back against his chest. "How're you feeling?"

Alastair almost didn't know where to begin. *It's real,* he thought dizzily. *All of it. I'm alive.* He lifted his head into Jay's gentle nuzzle, enjoying the scratch of stubble against his cheek. "Tired," he admitted, "but content."

Jay's arms tightened around him. "That's fine for now, love. I can work with tired but content."

"Did you sleep well?"

"Like a log. Did you?"

"Mm. I don't think I've ever slept this late in all my life."

"It's alright. I won't tell anyone."

"I hope you've not been bored."

"Just drifting in and out of sleep, really. We had a rough time yesterday. It's good to get some rest."

Alastair placed his hand quietly over Jay's, holding it there against his chest. "I'm glad we're here," he said. "Cliveden, I mean. Where we were."

Jay nuzzled behind his ear. "Yeah? Think it's going to help?"

"Mm. Very much."

"Whatever you feel like doing today, just let me know. Juliet says she's handling work. You don't have to think about any of that. Your only job is resting and recovering here with me."

"Has anything been announced to the press?"

"Not yet. Juliet says they will at some point. But she'll check with you first what you want said."

Alastair exhaled. When the news did break, journalists would be camped outside his home within ten minutes. It was a relief to be here, so far away. He didn't know if he had the strength to appear calm and composed before the cameras yet.

"Some of the details will attract a lot of interest," he said, putting it mildly.

Jay hummed, stroking a small pattern on Alastair's chest. "Maybe," he said. "Think about it later, mm? All that can wait."

Alastair smiled a little. "I'm under orders to rest, am I?"

"You are. And before you think of giving me trouble, they're orders from Juliet. I'm just the enforcer. So let's have no fuss from you, ta."

"Have I ever spelled out that you're wonderful?"

"Lucky, is what I am." Jay dotted a line of kisses along Alastair's shoulder, laying them one by one along the seam of his pyjama shirt. "And I'm going to remind you every single day."

Alastair closed his eyes, overjoyed and lost for words. "Jay," he whispered. Saying it only made him happier. He said it again, glowing inside. "Jay..."

The tip of Jay's nose brushed against the side of his neck. "Will you promise me something, please?"

"Anything." Alastair didn't need to think. His soul responded for him. "Anything you ask."

"Promise that you'll always say my name like that."

"Like—?"

"Like I leave you speechless."

Alastair wrapped their fingers together, holding them over his heart. "I'll have no choice in the matter," he said, "given you're an expert at taking my breath."

"I'm sorry we... you know. It was a bad moment to get pulled apart. I didn't get to tell you even half the things I wanted to."

"I'm sorry as well. I'm sorry for how I reacted. I want you to know, Jay—"

"It's alright, love. We both over-reacted."

"No, I... I *need* to," Alastair said. "Really. It's important to me."

Jay settled into silence to listen, rubbing the back of Alastair's hand with his thumb.

Alastair took a breath.

"I'm sorry I suggested you had any cause for shame," he said. "I haven't a clue what it's like to lead the life you have. But those circumstances and your choices have combined to make you into an honest and honourable man, and I want you to know how clearly that shines from you. I only admire you more, now I understand what you've overcome. I'm distraught that I gave you any impression otherwise."

Jay's hug tightened all around him.

"Al," Jay murmured. "It's fine. You were freaking out and you had half the information. Your job's your life. You had every right to flip your lid."

"That's kind of you," Alastair said, flushing. "And you're right that I value my career very deeply, but... well, for a long time, it was the *only* thing I valued. I defended it as if that's still true. It isn't. And I want to make that clear."

Jay's soft, flattered laugh came as a puff of air against Alastair's skin.

"So long as you know you're always safe with me," he said. "There's stuff in my past I'm not proud of. Stuff that I can't wash away. I did those things, but I'm not those things. I'm lucky I got the chance to make some other choices. *Those* choices are me."

"I feel safer with you than any man in this world. I mean it, Jay."

"Yeah?"

"Yes. Totally and utterly. I just hope you can feel like you're safe with me, too."

Jay seemed to release a silent breath, letting go of something heavy. How long he'd held onto it, Alastair didn't know. He suspected it had been a long time.

"I wish I could have told you like this," Jay said, pressing his cheek to Alastair's temple. "Here at Cliveden, lying in bed. I should've told you everything from the start. Just taken a big breath and come clean."

It would have spared them considerable distress. Certain that Jay already realised it, Alastair chose not to give it voice, resting his head back against Jay's shoulder.

"I imagine it felt like a lot to share," he said. "A lot of pain to unearth. I can see why you were reluctant to trust me."

"I'm sorry. I'd been so bloody lonely for so long, and you were just... I-I was so dazzled by you. By everything in your world. It was beautiful and I didn't want to lose it."

Alastair understood. He himself had been so nervous to lose Jay that he hadn't dared to reach for him. If he had, perhaps the trust would have come before this point. Perhaps everything would have unfolded differently.

The miracle of hindsight, he thought, half-smiling. He lifted Jay's hand to his lips, kissed it, and forgave himself. *At least we got here in the end.*

"We certainly took the more dramatic route to closeness," he said fondly. "In lieu of difficult conversations, I opted for kidnap and you led an armed recon mission into an abandoned power station to save me. We're quite a pair."

Jay broke into a grin at once. "I didn't *lead* it," he said. "I knew the layout of the place, that's all. I just showed them through the side door. It wasn't a big thing."

"I'm rejecting that utterly, I'm afraid. I won't have anyone discrediting your daring heroics, not even you."

"Argh. Alright. If you insist."

"I very much do."

"So... given that I've led an armed recon mission into an abandoned power station to save you... can we go ahead and agree that I'm your boyfriend now?"

Helpless, Alastair smiled. "I think that's very certain, yes."

"Yeah?" Jay nuzzled hopefully into the side of his neck. "Kinda want it in writing."

"I'll have Juliet draft something. Would you like it framed?"

"Yep. Official Certificate of Boyfriend, presented to Jay Fieldhouse on the occasion of his daring heroics."

"Pride of place above your desk at work?"

"Oh, yeah. Blown up so big it covers half the wall. And I want a heart-shaped photo of me in your wallet."

"Ridiculous man." Grinning, Alastair lifted his chin for more kisses. "It'll be a photograph of us both."

The day which passed was short and gentle, a practice day where the sun stayed low in the sky. They rested together in their suite until nightfall, talking softly in bed, sharing cigarettes in the window while watching boats out on the river. Alastair drifted between wanting to eat, wanting to nap and wanting Jay to hold him. In a few days, maybe these instincts would seem childish or indulgent, a fragility to be put aside. But for now, his world stretched no further than the walls of this room.

By the time darkness fell, they still hadn't dressed. There was no need to get changed before bed. Alastair hadn't spent this much time in his pyjamas since he'd had his appendix out as a teenager, but he couldn't bring himself to care.

"It's just your turn for fuss, love," Jay said, scraping around the bottom of their ice cream bowl. "You can have as much of it as you want." He smiled, offering out the spoon. "I want to be what you need."

Alastair's heart squeezed. He leant forwards, taking the spoon contentedly into his mouth.

Jay's eyes warmed, watching him.

"I love you," he said.

The words washed through Alastair's senses, just as perfect as the first time he'd heard them. He held Jay's gaze, lost in the look of affection shining back at him, and realised all over again that he was alive.

In what he'd believed were the final minutes of his existence, he'd imagined the entirety of it with Jay.

He could imagine it even now, no less clear. Such a realisation should surely scare him; that scale of commitment was enormous. He'd never really expected to form a lifelong bond. He'd thought the odds were too short on finding someone he could love indefinitely and without condition. In chronological terms, he'd had access to Jay's true feelings for no more than a matter of days.

And yet the idea seemed so comfortable in his mind.

Because I lived the alternative, he thought. For a few minutes, it had been their reality. They'd lost all chance of forever. Having that chance back could never frighten him.

Overwhelmed for a moment, he could only gaze at Jay, taking in the shapes of his face.

Jay smiled, biting the corner of his lip. "It's good stuff," he said, "isn't it?"

The ice cream, Alastair realised.

"It is," he agreed. He rested his head upon Jay's shoulder. "It's perfect."

When the bowl sat empty on the bedside, Jay ran a warm bath for them to share. He all but carried Alastair to the bathroom, undressed him just as carefully as the day before, then joined Alastair in the water, cuddling him close skin to skin.

As he stroked his soapy palms across Jay's tattoos, something about Jay's hands resting either side of his waist sent a flutter of unexpected hope through Alastair's stomach. His memories of Cliveden, and the intimacies they'd shared here, were stored in his body as much as in his mind. Jay's hold was protective and gentle, and familiar in a way that warmed his blood. Though it startled him that his libido could be prepared to recover so quickly, it stood as testament to Jay's excellent care. He made it easy to forget.

For a few seconds, Alastair contemplated it: shyly catching hold of Jay's hands, relocating them underneath the water. He didn't doubt that Jay would, if he asked.

But it seemed so soon. Sex was surely too frivolous to count as a comfort. There was a difference between wanting Jay's arms for reassurance and wanting Jay's touch for pleasure. Physicality could wait.

All the same, it was odd—and not a little disappointing—to put on pyjamas before getting into bed. Jay had opted to forego any kind of top covering, which helped. Alastair nestled close to his tattoos, rested his cheek upon Jay's collarbones, and let his thoughts begin to slow.

Almost asleep, a quiet buzz from nearby caught his ear.

Jay shifted, reached across to the bedside and checked his phone.

"Just Juliet," he said. "Hopes you're getting on alright..." He began to respond, typing quietly. "Is there anything you want from home, love? Anything you need?"

Everything Alastair needed was right here.

"Please tell her that I'm well," he said.

Jay kissed the top of his head. "I will. You get comfy there on my lion, mm? Won't be a minute."

At peace, Alastair closed his eyes.

He fell asleep to the feather-soft tapping of keys.

"Al?" Jay's voice flickered through Alastair's consciousness. "Are you with me?"

Still soaking in the shallow end of sleep, Alastair lay in the quiet and simply drifted, half aware of Jay's fingertips passing through his hair.

"Still out," Jay said fondly, as if to somebody else. His smile was audible in his voice. "Come on in."

High heels crossed the carpet, a confident stride which Alastair recognised in an instant. "You don't mind?" Juliet whispered, keeping her voice down.

"It's fine," Jay said. "I bet PAs see a lot worse. Pull up a pew."

There came the sound of a chair being dragged very gently to the bedside.

"I have your..." Juliet said.

"You star," Jay breathed, carefully holding Alastair with one arm as he reached out to take something from her. "What's he paying you? It's not enough."

Juliet made a quiet sound of amusement.

"No PA in this world is paid enough," she said, as Alastair became dimly aware he could smell bacon. "Most of this could wait until later, really. Just updates."

"Nah, go on. I'll pass it all along when he wakes up."

"Are you certain?"

"Certain I'm certain," Jay said, taking a careful crunch from what sounded like a toasted sandwich. Alastair tried not to smile. "Hit me with it."

"There's only really one thing of any importance. The deputy commissioner is hoping to inform the press tomorrow morning. He thinks it's better to release an official statement before unofficial rumours get too far, which is possibly fair."

"Will Al need to be there for it?"

"God, no. It's better if he isn't."

"What's going to be said exactly?" Jay asked in a whisper. "I mean... there's a lot of stuff to explain."

"It's been recommended that we keep things simple," Juliet replied. "We'll say that Sir Alastair is recovering well after being freed from a hostage situation earlier this week. The media will want to know more, of course, but Alastair can decide whether they get it or not."

"Sounds fair to me. At least we're here where journos won't bother him."

"Quite. Scotland Yard aren't expecting him back for at least two weeks, by the way. He'll be sent straight home if he tries."

"No worries," Jay said. "Sure I can keep him occupied."

Alastair's stomach squirmed a little.

"What about the kid?" Jay asked, taking another bite of his sandwich. "Miles?"

"Milo," Juliet said. Alastair held his breath. "He's recovering excellently. Discharged from hospital now, and extremely willing to talk."

"Good."

"He's provided us with enough information to lay hands on the other members of Ian's fledgling new gang. We've spoken to them all, made sure they understand just how closely they're going to be watched by the security services from this day forward. You won't be troubled, Jay. Either of you."

"Jesus, that's a relief..."

"I'm not sure if this has already been made known to you, but in case it hasn't... we realised through speaking to the other gang members that Alastair wasn't the intended target. Most of them were astonished to find out that they'd kidnapped the head of the London police."

Jay hesitated, swallowing a mouthful of his sandwich. "What do you mean, not the target?"

"The plan, so far as they've all told us, was to retrieve you from your flat and bring you back to Ian in Manchester. Most of them were under the impression this had happened."

"But... wait, I don't know if I'm following—"

"The men that Ian sent to London hadn't met you previously. They had details of your address, but no idea what you looked like."

"So... so you're saying they thought that they'd got me, but really they... holy shit. Why didn't Al tell them?"

"We're not sure. Apparently he gave no indication whatsoever that there'd been a mistake. It's... likely that he realised what was happening, Jay. Why they were there."

A long, aching silence fell.

"He went in my place," Jay said. "He let them think..."

"Yes," Juliet replied. "From what we can tell, that's... quite probably correct."

Jay's fingers curled against the back of Alastair's head. He didn't speak.

"You were asking me about Milo," Juliet said, a little awkwardly. "I hope you don't mind. I took the liberty of contacting your people, and asked if there might be some support for him. Something to improve his situation in life."

Jay swallowed. When he spoke, his voice came perfectly steady.

"That's good," he said. "I'm glad. I'll give them a ring later. Make sure he's getting the works."

"Are you quite alright?"

"Me? I'm fine, doll. Sound as a pound. Don't ever fret about me."

Juliet made a gentle noise of dubiety. "If it's all the same," she said, "I think I will. Alastair's welfare has always been my greatest priority. A large part of his welfare is now you. That means your happiness counts among my duties."

"That's kind of you. Really, I mean it."

"Not at all." There came a comfortable pause, a silence which seemed warm with understanding. "Would you say that he's settling a little?"

"He's doing brilliantly. Taking things nice and slow, day by day. Not rushing. Couldn't be prouder of him."

"Good. I'm so pleased."

"I was thinking maybe a walk later." Jay took another bite of his sandwich. "Get some air, stretch our legs a bit. I'll see if he fancies it."

"I'm sure that would help. I'll leave you both to rest for now, if there's nothing I can do. Please tell him I have a very long list of kind wishes to relay. Everyone at Scotland Yard is thinking of you both."

"Both?"

"Mm. The general consensus about you shifted somewhat when you quite literally carried him from the building in your arms. I understand that DCS Curlew is preparing a lengthy apology."

Jay gave a snort, polishing off the last of his sandwich.

"Tosser," he remarked as he chewed, dusting his fingers on the sheets. "Hope it's a good one. Just wait til Al finds out how many times he implied that I'm a rent boy."

Alastair bit down into the side of his tongue. *Oh, indeed?*

"No doubt he'll be thrilled," Juliet said. "I look forward to seeing Curlew hide from you both at the Christmas party. Is there anything I can do before I go?"

"Nah, doll. You head off. Thanks for the..."

"My pleasure." There came a careful clunk as Juliet returned her chair to the corner. "Give him my love."

She strolled away, her heels quiet across the carpet. The door of their suite opened with a hush and then closed, leaving a silence in her wake.

"How long've you been awake?" Jay asked.

Alastair stirred, cuddling into his arms. "Not very long."

Gathering him close, Jay pressed a silent kiss against his temple. "You let Ian's boys think you were me. You let them take you away, knowing they were going to hurt you."

Alastair said nothing, enjoying the steady thump of Jay's heart against his own.

"Why?" Jay asked, barely audible.

Alastair wrapped his arm around Jay's back, reached up and laid his hand where he knew from memory there were black ink feathers.

"I love you," he murmured, and let it be his answer, whole and complete on its own.

Not quite ready for the woods, they stayed within the gardens.

"Have they recovered anything from your flat?" Alastair asked, leaning his head upon Jay's shoulder. The crunch of their footsteps on the gravel seemed the only human sound in the world. This late in the afternoon, midweek, the grounds were almost empty. Only their security officer, trailing them at a discreet distance, shared the view.

"Nothing," Jay said with a sigh. "The building's gone. Landlord's sent an email saying he won't charge us for the rest of the month."

Alastair tutted. "A compassionate soul."

"I know, right? I'm hoping he'll at least give back the deposit."

"As the fire wasn't your fault, he really should..."

A sparrow flittered across their path, a tiny burst of wings blurring between one hedge and another.

"We'll see," Jay said. He looked rather magnificent in the clothing Juliet had acquired for him. Whether she'd purposely chosen the dark grey jeans and leather jacket to cheer Alastair's spirits, Alastair couldn't be certain—but it was working. "Still feel like I'm lucky," Jay added, kissing Alastair's forehead.

Flushing, Alastair leaned into the contact. "You're extremely sweet."

"I mean it, you know. If I had the same choice a million times, you or that flat, I'd pick you every time."

"Jay..."

"It's true, sunshine. You can *Jay* me all you want."

"It was your home for ten years," Alastair said. *And you've been mine for less than a week. Surely you...* "I'm sorry it was taken from you."

Jay's arm hugged around his waist, bringing him closer. "Been thinking about it, to be honest. Wondering why I'm not more fussed."

"Mm?"

"I'm kinda realising my roots weren't that deep. I saw the place as somewhere to sleep and cook and shower. It wasn't... *home,* you know? Not with a capital H."

"Even after all those years?"

"Not really. It's... honestly it's weird, what happens when you get moved. I signed all the papers in a daze, then they gave me two hours to collect the bits I wanted from my flat. Then that was it. Driven to Piccadilly, smuggled onto the train to Euston. Done. Gone."

Jay shrugged, shaking his head.

"I suppose I've always worried it could happen again," he said. "Sometimes at night I lie there, looking up at the ceiling, and I plan out what I'd take. There's a massive suitcase stashed under my bed. Well, *was* stashed. Never been abroad in my life. It was there for... well, the day Ian found me. The day I'd have to pull my heart out, leave it there on the floor and go."

"I'm so sorry," Alastair murmured. "I can't imagine how it felt, living with that anxiety."

"I'm sort of only realising now that *is* how I felt. Now it's all over, I mean. Is that weird?"

"Not in the least."

"If you'd asked me a week ago, *how's life?* I'd have told you I had a pretty good deal. It's like... alright, this might sound tragic."

"Go on. I'm listening."

"I didn't really think I'd ever see this day. I couldn't imagine a life where *I* survived *Ian.* I thought I'd always just be scrabbling to do some good while I still had the chance. Now I'm..."

Jay's shoulders expanded.

"I'm here," he said. "I'm not on the run any longer. I'm just alive. Free, like everybody else." He looked down at Alastair, breaking into a smile. "Feels pretty amazing. Brand new start."

Alastair couldn't help but smile back, happiness bubbling through his heart. "I'm so glad for you, Jay. Really, I am."

Jay's smile became a grin. He pulled at the corner of his lip with his teeth, glancing down at Alastair's mouth. "You know the best nights I ever had in that flat?"

Alastair paused, not daring to hope.

Jay's eyes sparkled. "The two when you were in it."

"Jay," Alastair said, blushing. They stalled upon the path together, facing each other. "Jay, you're..."

Jay slipped both his arms around Alastair's waist.

"Yours," he said. "Signed and sealed, Al. I mean it."

Alastair's chest seemed to swell, dizzy with the joy of it. He couldn't pull his eyes from Jay's, afraid to miss even a moment. No sight in the world would ever compare to the easy affection in Jay's face.

Coaxing Alastair close, Jay rested their foreheads together.

"I know it's early days," he said. Their noses rubbed, his voice soft. "I know we've only just... don't let me freak you out."

"I don't believe you could," Alastair said. "Truly."

Jay seemed to hesitate, cradling the small of Alastair's back with his hands.

"You know I've got it bad for you. Don't you?" He pressed his lips to Alastair's. "Really bad. I mean I... I can't even tell you how close I want to get. I don't know how to put it into words without scaring you."

"Jay..."

"You make me feel like I'm really here. *Properly* here. Like it's all finally started at last, no more just stumbling through."

Alastair swallowed, quite certain his pulse could now be heard.

"I feel complete when I'm with you," he said. "I don't see any possible way that will change. I can't imagine a moment I won't be thrilled by the sight of you. By your voice, your warmth." His throat pulled tight. "I've never ached for someone like this before," he said, shaking. "I hope you feel the same, Jay."

Jay's lips met the words with a kiss. "I promised you I'd be there when you need me," he said. "I never put an end date on it."

Speechless, Alastair cuddled tighter into his arms.

"I wouldn't have been able to cope if I lost you," Jay murmured. "You know that? You'd better mean that you want me to stay, or you're going to have a problem on your hands."

Alastair nuzzled into the warmth of Jay's cheek, certain beyond all doubt that this would never be a problem.

"I'd like us to be something," he said. "Something special."

Jay shivered, resting their foreheads together. "I want that, too."

As his eyes closed, shining inside with the rush of love, Alastair realised there was no better time to bring this up. "I was thinking," he said softly. "About the press. I wanted your opinion before..."

"Yeah? What've you been thinking?"

"I'd like to tell them I was taken from the home of my partner. Tie it to the media coverage of the fire. If you're comfortable, we'd name you. There'd be some media interest in you, and in your charity, but I believe it would be sympathetic."

Jay took this onboard, gently studying Alastair's face. "What about Ian? Are you going to mention him?"

"No. No, I think he's dictated quite enough of your story already. I'd like to erase his name from this entire business. Leave the perpetrators anonymous, and tell the press we've no interest in glorifying kidnappers."

"Are the press going to be satisfied with that?"

"If we tell them it's to prevent any risk of copycat kidnappings, they'll have no choice but to comply." Alastair hesitated, stroking his fingers through the back of Jay's hair. "If this is too much for you too soon, please tell me. I realise our relationship is new."

Jay gave a gentle huff. "It's not," he said. "Newly honest, maybe, but not new." He brushed his lips against Alastair's cheek. "Will I need to do anything?"

"Perhaps warn your people there might be interest," Alastair said. "If we supply a photograph of the two of us, there won't be any need for paparazzi to try to acquire one. Otherwise..."

He tightened his arms around Jay's shoulders.

"Stay here with me another week," he said. "We'll have privacy and peace. The story will fizzle out, then we can both return to London. Together. If that suits you, of course."

Jay smiled against his cheek. "Of course it suits me."

Oh, God. Alastair almost didn't dare believe it. "You're... you're happy to be publicly linked with me?" he said.

Jay squeezed him around the middle, grinning. "You're fucking adorable," he said, sending Alastair's heart into orbit in an instant. "Why wouldn't I want to be linked with you? I've wanted that for weeks."

"I just don't want to rush you," Alastair said, blushing desperately. "I've waited so long to be like this that I'm... *erupting* with it, Jay. I haven't a clue how fast these things are meant to go. I haven't had a proper boyfriend this side of the millennium. Just promise me you won't let me rush you."

"Daft arse," Jay chided, chuckling. He nuzzled into Alastair's neck. "Rush me. I dare you."

They embraced for several minutes, happy together in the sunshine. Every inch of Alastair's skin seemed to be tingling, every nerve aglow with possibility. They had so much time laid out ahead of them. There was no reason any longer to hold back, nothing that he needed to hide. There was just togetherness, a wide open ocean of it.

And here they were, standing on the shore.

"Hey," Jay murmured, running both his hands up Alastair's back. The softness in his voice caused a bump in Alastair's pulse. "Let's have dinner. In the restaurant, I mean. Make an evening of it."

A date? Alastair inhaled, thrilled by the thought. *Our first date. After all this time.*

"Tonight?" he said.

"Sure. You feeling up to it?"

"Yes, I think so. If we... a quiet corner, maybe. Privacy."

"The staff'll put us somewhere cosy if we ask. Do you reckon Juliet can get hold of a nice shirt for me?"

Alastair smiled, utterly certain of it. "I imagine she's got four or five already."

Grinning, Jay kissed him on the cheek.

"Right," he said, taking hold of Alastair's hand. "Sorted. It's a date, then. Shall we walk on a little bit? This path takes us down to the river, if I'm right."

Chapter 24

"What're you having?" he asked, stroking Alastair's palm with his fingertips.

Alastair cast him a smile over the menu. Even the light brush of contact made it difficult to concentrate on the choice of desserts—then, he'd been struggling to concentrate all evening. From the moment Jay emerged from their bathroom in a fitted dark red shirt, open at the neck to show the tops of his tattoos, Alastair had been lost. Several glasses of wine since then had only sealed his fate.

He focused himself with a sigh, gently catching his lover's fingers.

"Still agonising," he said. "The pavlova looks incredible, but I don't think I can turn down chocolate parfait. Not when it comes with dulcey crémeux."

"Tough choice."

"Have you decided?"

"Mm hmm."

"What are you having?"

Jay's eyes glittered, dark and playful. "The suffle."

With a lift of one eyebrow, Alastair glanced back over the menu. His mouth twisted as he spotted it. "*Soufflé,* darling."

Jay visibly masked a smile. "I think you'll find it's pronounced suffle, sunshine."

"Oh? I'm certain it was soufflé last time I had it in Paris."

"Nah," Jay said, eyes sparkling with mischief. "Definitely suffle. We're big on the stuff up north. Suffle for all three meals sometimes."

"In that case, it seems I've been mistaken all this time. Suffle it is."

Jay winked. "You can have a spoonful," he said. "Seeing as it's you."

Am I even drunk? Alastair wondered, dazed. *Or is this just love?*

"How kind," he said, as Jay's fingertips soothed across the sensitive skin inside his wrist. The candlelight gathered around them both, warm and quiet, everything at peace. "I'm sure I'll find it in me to return the favour."

"Al?"

"Mm?"

"Got a question for you."

Lord. "I'm listening."

Jay's gaze seemed to stroke Alastair's face, adoring every fragment of him. "What the hell is dulcey crémeux?"

"Crème anglaise," Alastair said, smiling helplessly, "combined with chocolate."

Jay's face lit up with amusement. "Chocolate custard," he translated.

"Mm."

"You're having chocolate parfait served with chocolate custard."

"Or pavlova," Alastair added. "Depending on what gets startled out of my mouth when the waiter reappears."

"Will it be as good as my almond peach galette?" Jay asked.

Alastair's stomach gave a happy flip. "No," he said with certainty, "but I doubt they'll allow you into the kitchen to make it for me."

Jay chuckled, reaching for his wine glass. "Shame."

Alastair took a breath, and a risk. "When we're home, perhaps."

He watched Jay take in the words, memorising every detail of the expression they caused.

"Home?" Jay checked. He smiled a little, drinking. "Yours, you mean?"

Alastair inhaled, hoping this didn't change the character of the evening. "I don't know if you've made plans already. If you haven't, then... well, when we've left Cliveden, you'd be very welcome to stay with me. Finding yourself a new flat will take some time, I imagine."

He tried a cautious smile, brushing his thumb against Jay's wrist.

"Mine is open to you," he said. "You can share it as long as you like."

Jay's eyes seemed to shine, his pupils soft and swollen in the candlelight. He finished his wine, placed the glass to one side, then took both of Alastair's hands in his own.

"You sure you won't mind if I take you up on that?" he murmured.

"No. No, not at all." *God almighty. Say it, man.* "I'd like you to be there, Jay. I'd love your company."

Jay pulled at his lower lip. "Suppose it'll help you get back into daily life, won't it? Having someone around."

Alastair's heart thumped. "Having *you* around."

Jay squeezed his hands, bright-eyed. "I meant what I said." He slipped his fingers free and reached for their menu. "Until you chase me off, I'll be following you around forever."

The waiter reappeared beside their table. He refilled their wine glasses for them, then asked if they'd like to order dessert.

Jay handed him the menus with a smile. "Pear soufflé for me please, mate. And my partner's having—?"

"The parfait," Alastair said, his heart skipping happily. "Thank you."

Alone in the lift, Alastair took the chance to nestle into Jay's side. Jay put an arm around him, pressing a small kiss against his shoulder as they hugged.

"Holy shit," he whispered, breathing in. "You smell good..."

Alastair stirred, lifting his chin with hope. "Do I?"

Jay took the invitation, nuzzling beneath his jaw. "Like wine," he said. "Candles and posh chocolate mousse. It's nice."

Alastair corrected him with a smile, warmth now glowing across his face. "Parfait, dear heart. Not mousse."

"Looked like chocolate mousse to me," Jay said, smirking, and pulled Alastair closer into his body. As their chests pressed together, something in the depths of Alastair's stomach uncurled, shivering and sparking as it awoke. "Chocolate mousse with chocolate custard and chocolate ice cream on the side," Jay teased, kissing his throat. "That's what I just watched you eat. Because posh people are six-year-olds gone mad with power."

Alastair bit down into his own lip, taking hold of his lover's biceps. "It was *malt* ice cream, thank you, Jason."

"Why did it taste of chocolate, then?"

"Because you *mixed* it," Alastair said, dangerously close to laughter, "with the chocolate mousse—*parfait!*—like a barbarian."

"Did you know that you're gorgeous when you're drunk?"

"Excuse you. I'm hardly drunk."

"Think you are a bit, love. You're all pink and calling me Jason."

"Oh, I... is it alright that—? I'm sorry if..."

"Everything's alright when it's you," Jay said fondly, rubbing his nose against Alastair's neck. "Especially when you're giggling, full of wine and chocolate."

"You're *causing* me to giggle, beast. You're amusing me on purpose, then accusing me of drunkenness. You're a scoundrel."

"Mm." Jay swiped his tongue beneath Alastair's ear, a hot flash of sensation which took Alastair's breath. *"Your* scoundrel."

Alastair's heart heaved. He couldn't hold in his hope any longer, tightening his hands on Jay's upper arms.

"Jay," he began, breathless. "Jay, I..."

Before he could ask, the lift bumped to a stop. It informed them with a happy ping, and the metal doors slid apart.

Kissing Alastair's neck one last time, Jay took hold of his hand.

"Come on," he said, pulling. Alastair's heart thumped. "Let's get you tucked up in bed with your cocoa. Don't want you roaming the halls, pissed and singing."

Their fingers tangled as they walked along the corridor to their room. At the door, Jay leant against it to look through his pockets, searching for the key.

After a few moments he glanced up at Alastair, visibly amused.

"Penny for your thoughts," he said.

Alastair surfaced with a blink. "Mm?"

"Penny for your thoughts, love. You're miles away."

Alastair hesitated, watching him—his exquisite face, the warmth of his eyes, the triangle of chest and tattoos offered to Alastair's gaze by his shirt.

After a moment's indecision, Alastair quietly stepped closer. He cuddled into Jay, still leaning against their door. Jay's arms went around him without question. He secured Alastair cosily against his chest, gentle fingers soothing through his hair.

Alastair found his lips resting close to Jay's ear. He kissed its shell and said, "I might have been drinking with purpose. The last glass or two, at least."

"Mm?" Jay nosed at his temple. "Why, beautiful?"

'Beautiful'. So naturally. So easily.

"I want to make love again," Alastair said. Even emboldened by alcohol, it felt reckless and demanding. "I'm not sure how to tell you. How to ask you."

Warm, tender hands gathered around his jaw. As Jay tilted up his head, Alastair's heartbeat stuttered out.

They came nose to nose with a brush of their lips.

"I know we said it was about the sex." The pad of Jay's thumb brushed beneath Alastair's lips. "Maybe the first couple of times, it was. But we both know it's been more than physical for a while now. A lot more. For a long while. Having sex again won't somehow turn things back."

Alastair's stomach fluttered. He exhaled, relieved to hear his worries voiced so plainly, and tightened his arms around Jay's chest.

Jay kissed his forehead. "You can have everything from me," he said. "Just as easy as it ever was. If you want a little love, come and tell me. If you want me to tell you with my hands, just say."

Alastair shivered, unsure if a more arousing offer could possibly exist. "I want that," he whispered. "Very much."

Jay's lips curved against his forehead. "Here's the plan, then. We'll let you in, and you can get comfortable. Shower if you want. Get into bed if you want. I'll nip back down and have a quiet word with guest services. I'll be back soon, I promise."

"If you're meaning to source certain items, I... I may have done so already."

"Yeah?"

Alastair blushed. "Juliet kindly brought them. Along with your shirt."

Jay chuckled, fishing the key from his pocket. "She knew what this shirt would do to you, huh?" he said. He fitted it into the door. "Let's get settled."

Inside, as Jay attended to the lamps, Alastair drifted quietly over to the dressing table. He removed his cufflinks, watching his own reflection in the mirror as he stored them carefully in their case. The room seemed quiet all around them; he found himself curiously shy.

As he slipped his jacket back over his shoulders, Jay appeared.

"Here," he said, stepping close to help. Alastair glowed, enjoying the show of chivalry. "I love seeing you take a jacket off. Does things to me."

Nervously amused, Alastair glanced over his shoulder. "Why?"

"Not many people see you like this," Jay said, draping the jacket over the back of a nearby chair. "It's nice. Feels intimate."

He came close to Alastair again, drawing him back against his chest. In the mirror, Alastair could only see their torsos reflected—Jay's arms wrapping over his own, his thicker fingers sliding between Alastair's.

"It's like you're in your lingerie," Jay murmured in his ear. "Makes me feel like a lucky boy."

Alastair laughed, unable to help it. *"Jay...* for heaven's sake..."

"I mean it." Jay nosed against his cheek, grinning, stroking a gentle kiss near the corner of Alastair's mouth. "Sexy, seeing you unwind."

As he skimmed his hand slowly over Alastair's stomach, he slipped his fingertips between the waistcoat buttons.

"Can I undo these?" he asked, his voice soft.

Something about the tender seeking of permission sent a ripple of heat through Alastair's blood. It made him feel precious somehow, revered. After all this time, all the things they'd done together, Jay took nothing for granted. Alastair nodded, a little breathless, and watched in the mirror as Jay slipped the buttons apart one by one, taking his time.

"You know we don't have to go all the way tonight?" Jay said. "If you just want to lie down together, that's okay. Just touch for a while... whatever we do, we'll take it slow."

A shiver tumbled down Alastair's spine. He swallowed, letting his head rest back against Jay's shoulder as the last button came apart. Wine, love and a deep breath filled him with bravery. "I want you inside me."

Jay's chest rose up against his back. "Yeah?"

"I've missed you. Having you that close."

Jay stroked Alastair's waistcoat apart, easing it back from his shoulders. "We'll still take it slow," he said, slipping the fabric down Alastair's arms, and laid the garment aside. "Take our time to remember how this goes."

He loosened Alastair's tie for him, pulled it open, then started on the buttons of his shirt. As soon as he could, he teased aside Alastair's collar and leant down to kiss his neck, every movement gentle and steady, his hands tender as they wandered Alastair's chest and stomach. Alastair relaxed as best he could, focusing on his own breath as Jay's mouth stroked and soothed the back of his neck. Only his wrists and his collarbones were uncovered, but a flattering hardness nuzzled against his tailbone already.

"You're beautiful," Jay breathed in his ear, reaching up to finish off his shirt buttons. "You're just so beautiful..."

Alastair flushed, watching in the mirror as more of his own chest began to appear. Jay remained fully dressed behind him, still gorgeous in his jacket and cufflinks, his eyes as dark and deep as midnight.

"I'll look after you tonight," he said. "I promise." He eased the fabric of Alastair's shirt back, exposing the slope and curve of his shoulder. As his mouth trailed along it, warm and soft, Alastair's chest began to rise and fall a little faster, overwhelmed by the sight of them together.

Jay shivered against Alastair's back. "Jesus, Al, I've missed you. I've missed your skin."

A few more buttons came apart. Jay loosened Alastair's shirt from his trousers, unfastened the final button and brushed his hands beneath the open fabric, gliding his hands over Alastair's bare chest. Alastair's pulse hit the ceiling. He shuddered, unable to hold in a moan. Jay's hands felt like heaven; he wanted their touch even more than he'd realised. He trembled as Jay petted him, mapping his skin in long and careful sweeps. One hand strayed low onto Alastair's stomach, two fingers tracing along his waistband. It felt like a question.

Alastair nodded with a shiver, flushing.

Jay reached down, infinitely gentle. He cupped Alastair's cock through the fabric, almost protective with the curl of fingers, then slowly and steadily began to rub. The sensation cut Alastair's breath in his throat. He rocked his hips forwards for more as Jay's other hand kept up its tender sweeping, skimming over Alastair's torso as if he were water Jay wanted to ripple.

"Oh, God," Alastair gasped, his throat closing over. His skin felt like it wanted to sing. He felt alive.

Jay hummed against his neck, soft and proud.

"Nice?" he said. "You're so smooth. You feel so good to touch." His fingertips grazed over Alastair's left nipple, barely brushing the sensitive point. Alastair's cock twitched behind his zip and he whimpered. "Oh, sweetheart... you *have* missed me, haven't you?"

Alastair could only nod, shaking.

Jay undid the fastening of his trousers with care. With the zip lowered, he slipped his hand inside Alastair's underwear and gently freed his cock from the fabric, handling Alastair as if it were the first time he'd ever had the pleasure. Alastair shuddered, arching. He reached down to hold Jay's wrist, feel his hand moving as it stroked him.

Jay kept his fingers light and loose, almost maddening in their gentleness, settling Alastair to his touch.

"Don't think I've ever seen you look so good," he whispered. "Look, Al."

Alastair's eyes fluttered open. He met his own heavy-lidded gaze in the mirror, his cheeks flushed and his lips slightly apart. He took in the sight of his clothing eased open, his body bare, his cock fully hard within the wrap of his lover's fingers. He looked debauched; his eyes were glittering. Jay, still fully clothed behind him, seemed as powerful and at ease as a king. Gasping a little, Alastair thrust forwards into the circle of Jay's hand. Jay smiled against his shoulder. He tightened the sleeve of his fingers and began to stroke in rhythm, his touch still gentle as it glided up and down from root to tip. Alastair stiffened, moaning under his breath, and began to rock his hips in hope of more.

Jay nuzzled into his neck, his breath revealing a restless edge as he sighed. "Shall we get the rest of these clothes off you?"

Alastair nodded, desperate.

Jay kissed the back of his neck one last time. "Alright, love. Turn around for me."

Alastair turned. Jay gave him a gentle smile, cupped his face and kissed him for a moment, then knelt down to undo Alastair's shoes. Alastair leant back against the dressing table as he did, gripping the wooden edge in an attempt to calm his pulse. It was hard to think of anything but the aching in his cock, still exposed and yearning for the stroking to resume.

Jay helped each foot from its shoe with care, then dealt with Alastair's socks as well, casting him a smile.

"You alright?" he checked.

Oh, God. Please hurry. "Must you be so beguiling?" Alastair asked, cupping Jay's cheek.

Jay grinned, leaning into his hand. "I'm a bit overdressed though, aren't I?"

"Not necessarily a bad thing."

"No?" Jay shifted forwards on his knees, pushing Alastair's shirt apart to nuzzle into his stomach. "Do you like me all posh?"

Alastair's pulse reeled and skittered as he watched. He touched Jay's hair, tousling the messy brown strands with his fingers. "It's... evocative."

"And I like you all scruffed up. Interesting." Jay trailed the tip of his nose in a line leading south from Alastair's navel, gazing up at him with deep and loving eyes. "Maybe we just like what we do to each other."

Alastair smiled, shivering. "I can't argue with that."

Jay grinned. He brushed his hands up Alastair's thighs, then hooked his fingers around the open front of his trousers.

"Don't worry, love," he murmured, easing them down. Leaning close, he lapped his tongue against the underside of Alastair's cock, a deliciously short sweep of wetness and warmth. Alastair tightened his grip on the edge of the dressing table. "I'll always be here to put on a nice shirt and scruff you up. Just ask."

Alastair shivered again, deeper. His trousers passed his knees. "Jay..."

Jay continued to lick his cock as he freed one ankle then the other, more than capable of concentrating on both. Alastair quivered, unable to pull his eyes from the sight of Jay's soft pink tongue reacquainting itself with his cock. He exhaled a long and restless breath, let his head fall back, and swallowed in the quiet.

At last, Jay's open palms stroked up his sides. "Bed now?"

Alastair took a moment to compose himself. He could hear his own heartbeat, quick and fast and hard. "Bed now."

Jay got to his feet, scattering small kisses here and there on Alastair's body as he rose.

"I can't wait to watch you come," he whispered, pulling Alastair close. The stroke of expensive fabric against Alastair's bare skin sent an almost electric surge through his body. He arched with a gasp, pressing closer. Jay anchored one arm around his waist, then with the other hand, he slipped Alastair's open shirt down his arms, leaving him naked at last.

"You're perfect," he breathed in Alastair's ear. Alastair put both arms around his shoulders, raking his trembling fingers through Jay's hair. "You're so gorgeous I can't think sometimes. I just look at you, and... damn, it's like the world goes quiet. There's just you, Al. There's nothing but you."

Alastair had never come so close to swooning. "Jay..."

Jay knelt a little, hooking his right arm behind Alastair's knees. He lifted Alastair from his feet as if he weighed nothing, then carried him with care across the suite. He laid him in the middle of the bed, resting him atop the soft and cool expanse of the covers. Alastair kept his arms around Jay's neck, pulling gently in hope of being joined.

Jay grinned and stole a kiss from his mouth.

"One sec," he said. Shifting, he toed his way out of his shoes. They clunked to the floor beside the bed, then in his socked feet he climbed up to be with Alastair, crawled across the bed to him, eased on top of his body, and leant down to claim Alastair's mouth.

Alastair's blood burned as they kissed. Jay's weight was warm and familiar, and his mouth as soft as silk. He tasted like the wine they'd just shared. As they explored each other's mouths Jay caressed down Alastair's sides, encouraging him to arch, and the rasp of his clothing felt so good that all thoughts of dry cleaning bills blitzed themselves from Alastair's head. He pulled Jay closer still, grinding up against him with a whimper. He wrapped his bare legs around Jay's thighs.

Jay searched Alastair's mouth with his tongue, humming.

They kissed until the need to feel Jay's body became so strong it nearly hurt. Gasping, they grappled their way through his clothing together. It ended up strewn all around them on the bed, discarded piece by piece in the struggle to connect more and more of their skin. At last, shuddering with relief, Jay hauled off his open shirt and cast it away across the room, crawling back to Alastair at once.

The full body rasp of their skin resounded through Alastair's senses. He moaned against Jay's mouth, shaking, and clung onto the broadness of his back, wishing he could see his own hands holding tight to those angel wing tattoos. He wanted photographs of it one day. He would pay any price. Shifting, Jay reached down with a hand and brought their cocks into alignment, gathering them together so they could rub.

"Yeah?" he breathed, his voice soft and low, accompanied by a hot flash of his tongue. Alastair panted his eager assent between their mouths. What Jay wanted, he wanted. Nothing in the world appealed more. He gasped a little as Jay began to grind against him, setting a slow and restless pace which he knew from experience would satisfy and tease in equal measure, and leave him so desperate to fuck he couldn't think.

Helpless, Alastair arched his back from the bed and rocked in time. He whimpered into the kiss for harder. Jay caught hold of both his hands, pinned them up against the pillow, and kept his thrusts long and lazy.

In only a matter of minutes, Alastair was prepared to beg.

"Please," he gasped into the kiss, every inch of his skin now hot and prickling. The words shook themselves free. "Please, Jay—please, I want—"

Jay shuddered against him, breathing hard. "Mm, love?"

Alastair swallowed. He gripped Jay's back as tightly as he could, trying to plead with his eyes. "Please," he whispered. "I need... oh, Christ, I *need...*"

Jay's fingers brushed his cheek, cupping his jaw. "Where's the things Juliet brought?"

Flushing, Alastair glanced towards the bedside.

Jay reached across. He opened the top drawer, retrieved the white paper bag acquired from a nearby pharmacy, and shook its contents out onto the bed. To Alastair's relief, Juliet had avoided anything adventurous: a very ordinary water-based lubricant and a pack of twenty standard condoms.

Reaching for the pack, Jay set about removing the cellophane with his teeth. Alastair hesitated, but brushed the thought aside at once, content to settle in with Jay's decision.

Sensing his pause, Jay glanced down. His eyebrows quirked in question.

It was impossible to ask this without blushing. Alastair did his best, reminding himself that he and Jay had shared far more intimate experiences.

"Perhaps we can go without," he said, tentatively. "Unless there's some reason to..."

Understanding dawned in Jay's face. He removed the cellophane from his mouth without a word, brushed it from the bed, returned the condoms to the bedside cabinet and leant down to kiss Alastair deeply.

"Do you want my fingers first?" he breathed between kisses, unboxing the lube. "Help relax you?"

Alastair swallowed. Jay had always been gentle and patient enough to trust; he didn't want to wait much longer. "Not necessary."

"Sure?"

"Can I... on top of you? Just to start."

"Of course." Jay stole one final kiss, then eased up onto his elbows. "Whatever's easiest."

They switched places on the bed, Jay lying back against the pillows, Alastair sitting nervously across his thighs. As he made himself comfortable, Jay's hands stroked reassuringly up his arms.

"You okay?" Jay murmured.

Alastair reached for the bottle of lube with a slight shake of his fingers. "Yes, are you?"

"I'm fine, beautiful." Jay bit his lip, watching calmly as Alastair snapped open the cap and dispensed several pumps of clear gel. His hips shifted a little. "Go as slow as you need, alright?"

Alastair had no intention of rushing. After everything he'd been through, everything he'd survived, this was not going to be a hurried experience. This was the first fuck of the rest of his life, with the only man he wanted to feel inside him ever again—and it was love. His body had been telling Jay for weeks that it was love. Finally, he would let himself listen and hear it back.

As Alastair gathered both hands around his cock, coating him in the cool gel, Jay drew a ragged breath and swore. He gathered his hands within the covers, restless already. Alastair began to stroke, spreading the gel slowly with his palms, and it earned him another low gasp of profanity. Unable to resist the flushed look of pleasure on Jay's face, he kept going for a little while, allowing the rhythmic motion of his hands to calm his own nerves.

At last, Jay's hips shied back from the contact. His face tightened, enjoying it too much, and he mumbled out a warning. "Al?"

His mouth dry, his heart beating hard, Alastair shifted forwards. He placed one hand on Jay's chest for balance, spreading his fingers wide across a gleaming black rose. Reaching down, he guided Jay's cock carefully into place between his legs. He closed his eyes and forced himself to take a breath or two, trembling—then sank down as slowly as he could.

Halfway, the inevitable twinge of pain made him twitch. His breathing skipped and he stalled.

Jay's hands stroked up his chest at once.

"It's alright, sunshine." His voice seemed to blur and soften the discomfort, lifting Alastair free of its sharpness. It jogged his thoughts enough to remember to breathe. "Take a minute..."

Swallowing, Alastair drew his focus to the long and loving sweeps of Jay's hands, letting them soothe him and slow his breath. He flexed his fingers against Jay's tattoos. "You're bigger than I..."

Jay's hands grazed down his sides, whispering across his skin. "We've got all night," he said. "No need to rush."

After a few more deep breaths, the sensation of impossible pressure began to ease. Alastair adjusted his grip on Jay's chest, forcing himself to wait just a moment or two longer. He opened his eyes to find his lover watching him gently from the pillows, his soft green gaze full of concern.

"Any better?" Jay said.

Alastair's heart fluttered. He nodded, breathing out. "Yes, a little."

Jay smiled, perfectly easy. "Good," he said softly, caressing his hands down Alastair's thighs. "No worries."

As Jay stroked him, slow and steady, Alastair pressed on. He paused now and then to breathe, even when the discomfort was bearable; his body needed time to remember Jay. It needed to feel safe, to know that this was happening gradually. Jay's hand appeared on his cock, petting him to revive his erection and distracting him from the worst. At last, with a long breath, Alastair closed his eyes and sank down on the final few inches. It ached inside him, a deep and slick and squeezing burn—almost good. Almost there. His mouth dropped open and he moaned out the feeling, dry-throated now, bearing down around Jay's cock. *In me,* he thought, his heart pounding. *Inside me. Want you in me.*

"Okay, love?" Jay whispered, brushing a gentle thumb against his hip bone.

Alastair nodded, incapable of words. This would always feel intense. Without knowledge of the pleasure beyond it, it could easily feel too much. He leant forwards, wrapping both his hands around Jay's shoulders; Jay's touch found its way up to his waist.

With a first careful shift, Alastair barely moved. He simply stirred his pelvis a little, accustoming his body to the feeling of thickness and intrusion. The sensation reassured him enough to start breathing again. He shivered, letting himself have this careful half-movement for a minute or two, gazing down into Jay's face, Jay watching him gently in return.

Breathing together, it grew easier. As Alastair tested cautious rocking, raising and lowering himself with care, the first flush of real enjoyment warmed through his nerves. His breath left him as a moan, then again as Jay shuddered underneath him, hands flexing at Alastair's waist.

Patient with me, he thought. *Waiting.*

The pleasure began to come more easily, warmer, the motions of Alastair's hips a little bolder as he relaxed. A rhythm developed almost without his notice. All his focus had drawn tight around the feeling: the thick, gripping fullness, Jay's cock moving through tightly hugging muscle; the faint stomach swoop as Jay pushed a little deeper; the protective hands anchored at his waist. The familiarity of Jay's chest beneath his fingers set his heart racing.

As he realised he was enjoying it, Alastair released all his breath in a rush.

Jay exhaled beneath him, too. His expression warmed with relief, his eyes soft as he smiled.

Trembling, gazing down, Alastair let himself move with more vigour, grinding down upon Jay's cock like he meant it. No pain arose, only pleasure. Jay's heady moan caused his own in response, and Alastair found himself lost in the look of relief which flooded

Jay's features, committing every detail of it to memory. He wanted to keep this forever. *My lover,* he thought. *My happiness. My home.* This was no longer sex for relief; these were words of comfort spoken by their skin. *You make me happy,* his body breathed as they rocked. *You make me whole.* Jay's gaze flickered, his throat muscles shifting as Alastair's groans grew helplessly in volume. *I love you.*

He rode Jay until the motion felt so smooth and so easy he didn't understand how it ever could have hurt. Each push of Jay's cock only left him softer and more open, more eager to keep going. Jay was wonderful underneath him, patient and self-controlled, his longing expressed in gentle twitches of his fingers or deeply-drawn breaths. He wanted to chase the sensation, but he was resisting. He wanted Alastair's pleasure more.

At last, as the lighter pressure grew frustrating and his body ached for harder, Alastair shifted his grip on Jay's shoulders.

"From behind me?" he begged, surprised by the fragility of his own voice.

Jay nodded, swallowing. He lay still for Alastair to dismount him, passing a gentle hand down his side. Alastair shifted into a new position, kneeling up by the pillows with his hands upon the headboard. He was wholly unsurprised to see them shaking. Jay eased into place behind him, kneeling too, his chest warm and solid against Alastair's back.

"Tell me if it's too much," he whispered, reaching for the bottle of lube on the bedside. As Jay reslicked his cock, Alastair shivered, feeling so open and so empty it was obscene. "Don't let me hurt you."

A little shifting, some gentle testing, and Jay eased his way back inside.

Alastair arched, gripping the headboard.

"Jay—" He swallowed, panting, dropping his head back against Jay's shoulder. "Jay, please—"

Nuzzling into Alastair's neck, Jay wrapped a strong arm around his chest and buried himself deep. Alastair clenched with the force of the sensation, dug his teeth into his lip, and moaned.

"Jay!" he gasped out, shaking. "Fuck—"

Jay shifted, breathing hard, and braced his free hand against the wall. As he withdrew, Alastair quivered, rocking back with hope.

"You're my world," Jay breathed against his shoulder, thrusting deep again. "You're my everything."

Overcome, Alastair's jaw dropped. His mouth unleashed a sound he'd never heard himself make, a keening sort of whimpered plea, all the muscles in his back tightening with pleasure as Jay moved in him. His thrusts came deep, slow, and easy, angled to perfection. Jay's hand soothed down to the side of Alastair's hip, strong fingers curling there to keep Alastair arched back against him. Alastair gripped the headboard, breathed, and tried not to whimper with every single stroke. His resolve crumbled in less than a minute. Helpless, he let the sounds come pouring from his mouth, fragmented with panting and gasps of Jay's name.

Jay kept the pace gentle and slow, the rhythm unfaltering. It was almost hypnotic: the long and thick glide in, the deep pressure and pleasure at its end, then the relief of lazy withdrawal. Alastair's body began to tighten with anticipation of each thrust. It felt like being rocked somehow, safe, no effort to make except to hold onto the headboard and moan out his soul. Jay's breath was reassuring against the back of his neck, the lamplight warm upon their skin. Everything was alright.

It always would be.

Jay's gentle fucking turned time and thought into nothing, gathering Alastair safe into some altered existence where his sole and single purpose was to enjoy. He was close even before Jay reached around to stroke his cock. Whenever the need to come grew intense, when Alastair's sounds began to heighten in pitch, Jay slowed their rhythm and took him shallowly for a little while, comforting him until he'd cooled. His touches stayed gentle, kept Alastair simmering at a perfect heat of just enough, just close, just right.

How could I not have fallen in love with you?

Lost in pleasure and rhythm, Alastair realised in such a rush it took his breath. It felt like a climax of the heart. It left him reeling, his pulse staggering, his mind and his soul blown open.

This was fate. Ever since the moment that I met you.

Jay nuzzled into the side of his neck.

"Is this alright?" he whispered, still moving, still rocking Alastair forward into the soft, familiar pleasure of his hand. Alastair tipped back his head, rubbing his cheek against Jay's. "Anything I can change, sweetheart?"

Alastair's entire body seemed to inhale. Joy spilled through his veins, bright and wonderful.

"Don't change," he begged, rocking back. He bit down into his lip, so happy he could die. "Oh, God. Don't change a thing."

"Penny for your thoughts," Jay murmured, brushing his fingertips down Alastair's naked back. His tattoos gleamed in the lamplight, his pulse still deep against Alastair's ear. The scent of sex and sweat laid over them, every inch of their skin still in contact. What time it was, Alastair didn't know.

He smiled, lifting his head to kiss beneath his lover's chin. "That you make a remarkable pillow," he said.

It earned him a sleepy chuckle.

"Yeah? Good to hear." Jay's fingers skimmed against the small of his back, tracing some absent-minded pattern. "Did you mean it?"

"Mm?"

"Staying with you. When we go back to London."

Alastair cushioned his cheek on Jay's collarbones, letting his eyes drift shut. "Of course I meant it. You don't know the comfort it brings me, the thought of falling asleep like this every night."

Jay was quiet for a moment or two, his fingertips still drawing their gentle shapes.

"What if I get comfy?" he asked.

Alastair smiled, slipping his ankle around Jay's right knee.

"Lucky me," he said, and touched his lips to Jay's tattoos. Opening his eyes, he found he'd kissed the ace of hearts. It seemed fitting; he kissed it again. "I've never felt this happy. I didn't think I ever would."

Jay stretched, his fingers curling against Alastair's lower back.

"You deserve to be happy," he said, kissing Alastair's forehead. "More happiness than you can handle. So much happiness you float."

Smiling, Alastair nuzzled along the line of Jay's jaw. "Certainly floating now."

His lover's eyes glittered, their pretty green turned golden by the warmth of the lamp.

"Good," Jay said, and held Alastair's gaze as he stroked over the curve of his hip, tracing his fingertips against his rump. "Sunshine?"

"Mm?"

"Do you think we've re-awakened something?"

Yes.

"Perhaps we have," Alastair said, picturing the night now ahead of them: waking Jay in the small hours to beg sleepily for his touch; waking Jay in the morning to pull him into the shower, press him up against the tiles and make him glad that he'd been born; strolling with Jay into the breakfast room, safe and happy at his lover's side. "After everything we've been through, I think we're entitled to a little comfort."

Jay's mouth curved. He gathered his hand around half of Alastair's arse and gave it a slow squeeze, his eyes sparkling.

"Only a little?" he said.

Alastair grinned, helpless. "Perhaps more than a little."

"Do you reckon twenty condoms was a guess or a challenge?"

"Mm. It's kind of Juliet, making sure you're well-stocked with everything you need to ensure my happiness. Then, I suppose if we're not using them, there's no risk of running out."

Jay's grin seemed to light up the room.

"Come here," he husked, pulling Alastair to kiss him.

Chapter 25

Two Weeks Later

JULIET SCANNED THE HEADLINE WITH RESTRAINED AMUSEMENT, supposing it could have been worse.

Met Chief's 'tattooed hunk' sets Twitter aflutter. For the benefit of readers unfamiliar with Twitter, and so that everyone might judge the matter properly for themselves, the paper had supplied no less than three photographs of Jay on his Saturday morning jog, gloriously sweaty and grinning ear to ear. His grey marl tank top exhibited his body art to perfection. The photographer had made sure to catch him stretching at the traffic lights near Holland Park, all the muscles displayed in his shoulders and upper back. *Online meltdown over police commissioner's partner. Alastair Harding back to work 'in excellent spirits', say Scotland Yard.*

"Cheeky swines," Juliet tutted, folding the paper shut with a rustle. "'Excellent spirits' indeed."

In the driver's seat beside her, Larry chuckled. "Not that they're gossiping, of course," he said. "Just passing along that some other folks've been gossiping."

"Oh, naturally. They'd never dream of it themselves, I'm sure."

"Think the commissioner'll be upset?"

"I think they're lucky he's had a pleasant two weeks," Juliet said, returning the paper to the dashboard. "But as it stands, no. I can't imagine he'll be too dismayed." As they made the familiar turn onto Kensington Church Street, she reached inside her coat for her phone. "We half-suspected something like this might happen. Really, it's surprising that it took this long."

"Suppose he *is* an unusual choice," Larry remarked. "Mr Fieldhouse, I mean."

Juliet hummed, typing. "You're not wrong. There was bound to be a frisson of interest sooner or later..."

> **[JN - 07:57]** *Two minutes away. Possible press outside, just to warn you*

"And he *is* terribly eye-catching," she added, sending the text with a tap of her thumb. She cast Larry a smile along her shoulder. "I suppose we all need a little something to brighten our moods on a dull Monday morning, don't we? One can hardly condemn the British public."

Larry smiled, keeping his eyes on the road. "Afraid I wouldn't really know, miss," he said. "He's not much my type."

Juliet smirked.

"Just ignore them if they're kissy in the car, Larry," she said, loading up Twitter. "They've been together around the clock for a fortnight. I imagine they'll be sorry to part."

A huddle of hopeful paparazzi had gathered some distance down the street, held at bay by two sizable bodyguards. Sir Alastair was not the only resident of the street who lived and worked in the public eye. It looked as if one of his neighbours had dispatched their own security to supervise the problem before it could start.

As Juliet stepped from the car, there came a flurry of clicks and a few calls for her attention, which she contentedly ignored. If she ended up in the background of some shots, then no matter. This coat was Max Mara; it could handle it. She opened the backseat of the car and stood ready, the ends of her hair lifting in the breeze. A curious sense of happiness seemed to permeate the air this morning, raising an unprompted smile on her face. *A return to the world of Mondays,* she supposed. *A new and peaceful normal.* It was certainly worth smiling about.

The front door twitched, then started to open. Louder calls broke out from the paparazzi. Under a hail of frenzied clicking, the two of them appeared: Alastair first, resplendent in his uniform, looking so well-rested and at ease that the sunlight seemed to brighten just to keep up with him; grinning at his side, utterly unfazed by the cameras, came Jay. He'd opted for a mid-grey blazer and a simple white t-shirt—entirely himself, just smartly so, with his hands held casually in his pockets.

They moved directly from the doorstep to the car, paying no attention to the shouts of the photographers. As they reached the vehicle, Alastair took the door from Juliet with a twinkling glance, thanking her in a murmur. He held it himself for Jay to get in.

If the protective hand upon Jay's lower back was staged, it was *well* staged. The paparazzi devoured it, snapping away in a frenzy. Their shouted questions went ignored. Once Jay was safely inside the car, Alastair acknowledged them with a single wave and joined his partner in the back, dipping out of sight.

Juliet shut them in, trying not to smile too broadly.

"Full uniform?" she checked as they set off, turning in her seat to regard them both.

Alastair cleaned the smirk off his face.

"They're likely to run with some variant of *'police commissioner returns to work','*" he said, resting one arm around Jay's shoulders. His eyes sparkled as Jay leaned comfortably into his side. "They might as well have decent pictures to go with it."

Helpless, Juliet smiled. "I take it you've already seen the papers?"

"He spent nearly all of yesterday glued to Twitter," Jay told her, grinning. "Giggling to himself at all the comments. You know I've gone viral? Connor says our website crashed trying to handle all the traffic. He's joking about doing a nude calendar of me."

"Only if I'm allowed a free copy," Alastair said, planting a kiss on the top of Jay's head.

The pair of you, Juliet thought. *You'll be the end of us all.*

"I'll tell the lawyers to unload the cannons," she said. "If any photographers cause a nuisance at your office, Jay, let me know and I'll see that they're dispatched."

"Nah, they're not doing any harm. Besides, they'll get bored soon enough." Jay stretched happily, reaching up to Alastair's hand on his shoulder. "Mad how life turns out," he said, playing with Alastair's fingers. "If you'd told me five years ago that I'd one day go viral for shagging the Met commissioner..."

Alastair's expression warped with mirth. "Mm?" he said, tangling their fingers. His eyes flashed as he looked down at his lover, prompting a broad and delighted grin. "What would your reaction have been, pray tell? Unqualified delight, I hope."

Jay nudged their noses together, glowing. "Once they'd shown me a picture of you, yeah. Over the bloody moon."

"Beast. That was self-deprecating wit, not a window to flirt with me."

"Sorry, love. Don't think I'm sorry."

Their affectionate nuzzle became a quiet, gentle kiss.

In the front seat, barely able to contain her smile, Juliet cast her eyes askance at Larry. He had his gaze trained firmly above the wheel, watching the traffic ahead with the corners of his mouth distinctly high.

"You'll text me if you can't make lunch, right?" Jay murmured behind them. "If you're snowed under, I mean. Just let me know."

"I will not text you," Alastair replied, his voice soft, "because at one o'clock, I will be at Bocca di Lupo come hell or high water."

"It's your first day back, Al. Might walk in to find chaos."

"Chaos that can wait while you and I finish a plate of langoustines together, I'm sure."

"Still. If something changes..."

Alastair gave a fond huff. "Juliet," he said, amused. "Please reassure my partner that I'll be meeting him for lunch at one as planned."

Juliet glanced around from her phone. "He'll be there, Jay," she promised. "If I have to smuggle him out of the side entrance in a sack, he'll be there."

Grinning, Jay relented. "Alright," he said, flushing happily as Alastair kissed his forehead again. "Don't let anyone push him too hard, will you? I want him to come home in one piece."

"He will. He's leaving on the dot of six all this week, whether he likes it or not. He's not to work at home in the evenings either. Can you—?"

"Sure," Jay said. "You do days, I'll do evenings. Sorted."

"Do I have any say in this?" Alastair asked, amused.

"No," they answered together, prompting a laugh. Juliet gave him a smile from the front seat. "Apologies, sir. Jay has clearly done wonders for you these last two weeks. I won't be allowing anything to imperil his good work."

Alastair hummed, his eyes bright. "Then nor will I," he said, kissing Jay's temple. "If you think you'll be finishing close to six, let me know."

"For a lift, you mean?"

"Mm. A lift home."

Jay lifted his head, rubbing his nose against Alastair's cheek. "Alright," he said. "I will. Thanks, sunshine."

Even before they'd made it upstairs to the office, Alastair's return to Scotland Yard was widely celebrated. Everyone they passed was delighted to see him, then even more pleased to find him in good humour. When a fourth person stopped him in the corridor to chat, Juliet left him to it with a smile and headed up to make coffee.

At five minutes to ten, she came back down to retrieve him ahead of his meeting with the command team.

"Social butterfly today," she teased as they made their way towards the conference room. "Your coffee went cold. You hardly seem to need it, though."

"It's important to reassure everyone I'm well," he protested. "I disappeared without warning for a fortnight. I just want them all to know it's now business as usual."

Juliet wondered if he was underestimating his present chirpiness or overestimating how sunny he'd been before the kidnapping. Either way, she supposed that it was moot. A brief glance through today's papers would explain to anyone why the commissioner was now shimmering about the place like a dragonfly. If he'd been a rank or two lower, he might have been getting high fives in the corridor.

As she held the door of the conference room for him, a round of applause welcomed him inside.

"You're all far too kind," he said with a smile, a picture of grace as he shook hands and received hugs from almost every person present. "How sweet of you all. Thank you. Yes, reports of my demise were much exaggerated..."

It took almost ten minutes to settle everyone around the table with their coffee. These meetings usually ran with military precision, Alastair's time too valuable to waste with trivial or irrelevant issues. Today, there was laughter and biscuits. Sitting in her usual seat at Alastair's side, Juliet scribbled quick notes in shorthand as the deputy and the assistant commissioners all gave updates, the discussion easy and productive. Though two weeks off had brightened his spirits, it hadn't dulled Alastair's attention to detail in the least. He listened warmly and with interest to what he'd missed, asked a few pertinent questions here and there, and within ninety minutes was entirely back up to speed with the happenings of Scotland Yard.

"Thank you all for your updates," he said at last, with a glance towards Juliet to ensure she'd got it all. She nodded absently, still writing. "I have only two items to add. The first, a piece of news... during my recent emergency, I understand you were all made aware of the twin role occupied by my assistant Miss Naughton. Juliet's connections to the security services proved invaluable in my retrieval, but now make it unfeasible for her to continue in her current role. As a result, and following discussion with the Home Office, it's been decided that she'll be retained at Scotland Yard in the position of special advisor to me. We're still attending to the finer details, but I imagine it's henceforth my job to make the tea."

As laughter bubbled around the table, Juliet gave a smile and pretended to note it down.

"... *Alastair's* job..." she murmured, to further amusement. "Thank you, commissioner."

"Not at all," Alastair said neatly. "I'll update you all on Juliet's new role as soon as the details are finalised. Until then, she's indicated that she's happy to continue with the duties of my assistant, so please contact her with any of the usual inquiries."

Reaching for his cup of coffee, he took a small sip.

"Secondly," he said, putting it aside, "you might have seen that my partner's, ah... fitness regime has garnered some attention on social media over the weekend."

A rash of quickly hidden smiles broke out, smothered away behind faultless expressions.

Alastair's eyes glittered.

"Please do remind your teams that all media inquiries should be transferred to the public relations department without comment," he said. "Public relations, please do remind the press that we are the Metropolitan Police Service, not the cast of *Loose Women.* They can gossip very nicely amongst themselves without our input. With that said, if there's nothing else to add, thank you all for your time and have an excellent week."

Over the general scraping of chairs, chat and conversation broke out. As everyone filed towards the door, Juliet finished her notes with a flourish and flipped shut her pad.

"Just to remind you," she said, standing up with Alastair, "you'll need to leave for Bocca di Lupo in around an hour and fifteen minutes. I've told Larry and he'll be ready to pick you up at the front door."

"Excellent," Alastair replied, pleased. "Thank you."

"You're more than welcome." Glancing over Alastair's shoulder,

Juliet spotted a nervous-looking figure shuffling against the flow of people, coming this way. "Curlew," she said, covering the sound with a cough.

Alastair's expression smoothed.

"Thank you," he murmured. He turned around as Curlew reached him, assuming a blithe and close-lipped smile.

Curlew was already red in the face.

"Commissioner," he said, offering out a hand. "Great to have you back."

"Christopher," Alastair said in greeting, warmly clasping the offered hand. "How nice of you to say. Thank you."

As Juliet took her phone from inside her jacket, needing something to occupy her eyes, Curlew cleared his throat.

"Glad to see you're alright," he said, trying a hopeful smile. "Must have been a hell of an ordeal."

"Mm. A once-in-a-lifetime experience, I hope. Before I forget," Alastair said, his tone as light and fluffy as a fairy cake. Juliet braced herself, suspecting this might become a moment to remember. "I wanted to thank you for keeping Jay company during my absence. A victim support officer, a cup of tea and some reassurance might have been better than several hours of questioning with no solicitor, but I'm sure you had a lot on your mind."

Cringing, Curlew sucked in a breath.

"About that," he said. "I, erm... I just hope you know it wasn't anything personal, sir. Crossing the obvious off the list, that's all."

Alastair gave a short hum. "It was obvious Jay isn't to be trusted?"

"Oh—erm, I don't know if I'd put it like *that,* but..."

"No? How would you put it?"

"Well, we... we had no record of the association, and... given his previous connections... we just figured it was better to eliminate him from suspicion early," Curlew concluded, unwisely attempting a shrug. "That's all."

Alastair hummed again.

"Strange," he said, with a fractional raise of one eyebrow. "Such dogged commitment to eliminating Jay from suspicion, and yet you ignored Juliet's assurances as to his character. You ignored the assurances of all of his employees over the past six years. For what it's worth, you also ignored *my* assurances."

"Sir?"

"The fact I trusted Jay enough to spend my evening alone in his home with him might possibly have stood in his favour. Unless of course," Alastair added in a murmur, his eyes flashing, "you believe that I'm a gullible old fool who would fall like a dream for whatever convoluted honeypot scenario you'd envisioned."

Curlew's mouth opened, his cheeks now stained a bright and burning red.

"I don't think that," he managed, his voice breaking. "I-I don't think that at all. It's just... his past was... I'd have been an idiot *not* to check."

Alastair didn't miss a beat.

"You didn't *check,* Christopher," he said. "You wasted the critical first hours of a major kidnap investigation parroting the same questions over and over at an innocent man. You committed the cardinal sin of any criminal investigator. You decided on a perpetrator and then attempted to fit the evidence around him, rather than considering the evidence as it stood."

"Sir, his... his previous record—"

"A man's previous record does not override the clear evidence of his present."

Curlew exhaled in a rush. "Sir—"

"Your record, for example, has previously suggested to me a rational and responsible detective. The current evidence puts before me an oaf who decided he'd spotted a criminal and hung on like a dog to a postman's leg."

Juliet screwed her toes into her shoes without a sound, keeping her attention fixed firmly on her phone.

"I'm sorry," Curlew managed, shaking. "If I'd known the facts—"

"You're a detective, man. It's your job to ascertain the facts."

"And that's all I was trying to do."

"No," Alastair murmured, utterly calm. "You were trying to bend the facts to fit your prejudice. You mistook your key witness for a suspect, then you ignored a small mountain of evidence that you were wrong."

Curlew paled.

"Sir," he said, speechless.

Alastair drew a breath.

"Jay was retrieved from a *burning building,"* he said quietly, staring into Curlew's face. "He entered in the belief I might be trapped there. A more visceral demonstration of devotion and concern is hard to imagine. What in your mind *possibly* negated that?"

Curlew didn't speak, waiting nervously for more.

Alastair's jaw tightened. "Perhaps you suffer some belief that a same sex bond, by its nature, is less meaningful than a straight one. Less loyal. That such connections are founded on physicality rather than affection."

He leant closer, lowering his voice.

"It is *not* the case," he intoned. "I've now performed you a valuable service by bringing these misguided assumptions to your notice. I expect you to thank me by putting enormous effort into correcting them."

He tipped his head calmly towards the door.

"Out," he said.

Curlew practically crawled from the room.

As he disappeared off towards the stairs, pale and shaking, Juliet reached out. She found Alastair's wrist, gathered her fingers gently around his hand, and moved it without a word to her arm.

Finding her skin goose-pimpled, every hair lifted on end, Alastair gave her a quietly flattered look.

"I was clear enough, was I?" he murmured.

Juliet let out a breath. "Magnificently clear."

Huffing, Alastair reached for his half-empty coffee cup.

"I'll tell Jay at lunch that his honour is restored," he said. "A rent boy indeed. Ask HR to schedule Curlew's division for an equality and diversity refresher, will you? Make sure he gets the hint."

Juliet managed to sit on her thoughts for nearly an hour.

"He means the world to you," she said, laying a fresh stack of unsigned forms in Alastair's in-tray. "Doesn't he?"

Alastair smiled, his gaze still occupied with this month's frontline policing report. "You're only just seeing this now?"

She smiled, unable to help it. "No. Just... freshly marvelling at its depth, perhaps."

Quietly, Alastair turned his page.

"It was hard to believe at first. Every day I get to spend in his company, I grow more sure of something." He looked up into her eyes, his grey-blue gaze gentle and at peace. "I think I... fascinate him, Juliet."

Juliet's heart thumped. "I think you might be right."

"I've stopped asking myself why. Quite honestly, it feels amazing just to let him. Whatever we're doing, he seems happy that we're doing it together. Truly, deeply happy. As if it's all he could ever really want."

Oh, God. "You make a very affecting couple, sir."

Alastair's mouth lifted a little at one edge, uncertain. "Affecting?"

Juliet attempted to put it into words.

"His love for you is very open," she said. "Very perceivable. And yours for him. It... rather shines from you both, if I'm honest. As if you can't help yourselves but show it."

He considered this, an understanding sparkle in his eyes.

"It's wonderful to be loved," he said.

Juliet's heart ached. She found herself reaching for humour, hoping it would stop her from welling up. "Shall I ring Cliveden this afternoon?" she asked. "Get you the number for their wedding co-ordinator?"

He visibly fought back a smile, dropping his gaze to his report. "Far too soon to discuss such things."

But it doesn't shock you to hear. "Is it?"

"Mm. He's only just claimed himself the title of boyfriend. If I offered him an express upgrade to fiancé, I think he'd run a hundred miles."

Juliet spoke with care, pulling at her lower lip. "Out of sheer curiosity... if you *knew* beyond all certainty that he'd say yes..."

Alastair took a moment to reply, searching through his pen holder. "This seems academic."

Juliet held her nerve. "So did asking him to dinner."

He paused again, his expression unreadable, full of everything at once. Selecting a green biro, he uncapped it with a tug and jotted a short note in the margin of the report.

"Be that as it may," he said at last. "I'm not going to rush things. I couldn't bear to ruin what we have, not when we've gone through so much to have it."

Juliet smiled. She saw it all in a flash, laid out in front of them as clearly as a map.

"A few months from now," she said, "I'm going to be back and forth between the two of you, promising you both that if you just hand over the ring, he'll say yes. You'll be lying awake at night to watch each other sleep, wishing he could be your husband. I guarantee you that this will be happening. It's going to be unbearable."

Alastair lifted his eyes from the report, casting her an entirely dubious smile. Warning, humour and hope fought for dominance in his face. "If he ever expresses even the slightest interest in marrying me, you are to tell me at once. You will run, not walk, to inform me."

"So that you can make the arrangements?"

"So I—" Alastair inhaled. "Juliet."

"Alastair Fieldhouse-Harding," she murmured, and watched his pupils blow to twice their size. "Rather softens you, doesn't it? Such lovely harmony, all those Ls and Ds and Hs."

"Juliet."

"Still carries the necessary clout in full form. Sir Alastair Charles Fieldhouse-Harding QPM."

"Juliet—"

"Unless you're given a peerage at retirement, which we can probably bet on, and will make you the Right Honourable the Lord Fieldhouse-Harding Kt QPM... and Jay will be... oh, dear. I may have to consult Debrett's for this. Would he be styled the Honourable Jay

Fieldhouse-Harding, perhaps? To differentiate the two of you? Or will they just let *both* of you be Baron Fieldhouse-Harding? You'll be completely inseparable by that point anyway, so I suppose you're quite right. It *is* academic."

"Juliet," Alastair said, now rather breathless and turning the shade of a tomato. "I'm almost certain you're teasing me."

Juliet smiled. "Am I really?"

"I believe you are."

"Mm. When the day comes that I'm sitting at Cliveden, with a flute of the very best champagne in my hand, watching you dance with your new husband beneath a glittering chandelier to the sound of happy sobbing from everyone who knows you, you'll realise I wasn't teasing in the least. Shall I fetch your coat now? I think it's about time for your lunch."

Halfway through Juliet's salmon salad, there came an apologetic knock against the open office door. She glanced up from her copy of *Vogue,* mildly surprised to find an unknown lady in a belted raincoat smiling very gently from the threshold.

"I'm so sorry," the stranger said. "I didn't mean to disturb your lunch. I'm looking for Alastair Harding's office—is this right?"

Juliet paused, wondering what on earth was going on. They weren't expecting any visitors until much later this afternoon, and reception would surely have checked the lady's ID before allowing her up here. She looked like the most ordinary woman in the world, perfectly average and mild in every way, carrying the sort of canvas tote bag one might use to pick up a few groceries. Nothing about her suggested a wily assassin or terrorist.

"Can I ask if he's expecting you?" Juliet said, cautiously laying down her fork.

"He isn't. But I do have identification."

Sitting up a little, Juliet waited to be shown.

The stranger stepped into the office, reached inside her tote bag and produced a simple leather wallet, the sort that might contain an Oyster card. As she opened it for Juliet's inspection, the logo of the National Crime Agency lifted Juliet's eyebrows onto her forehead. She scanned a few more details, noting that the card carried a photograph but no name.

Realisation dawned.

"You're with the UKPPS," she said, looking up into the other woman's face. "Is this about Jay?"

The stranger gave a hesitant smile, quietly closing her ID.

"My name's Kim," she said. "Is Sir Alastair available? I don't imagine it'll take that long."

Juliet put a hand inside her jacket, retrieving her security services badge.

"Juliet Naughton," she murmured, offering it out, and gave Kim a moment to check her details. "I'm Sir Alastair's special advisor. They've gone out to lunch together, I'm afraid. Probably still flirting over langoustines. Can I help at all?"

Kim handed back Juliet's badge, her smile rather shy.

"Possibly," she said. "It's... really, I should contact Jay to confirm everything. But I know my sudden appearance always makes him very nervous, and given the circumstances, I thought I might as well just come here."

"Is there a reason for him to be nervous?" Juliet asked, gesturing Kim to a chair.

"Oh, no," Kim said. "Not any longer. There's nothing for anyone to be worried about." She settled down, resting her tote bag by her feet. "Do you know Jay?"

Juliet smiled. "Quite well by now," she said. "He's a sweetheart, for sure. Are you aware of the situation we had two weeks ago?"

"I am. I didn't realise at first that Jay had actually been involved, but as more details reached me... is it true they're both recovering well?"

"Like a dream. I've never actually seen either of them happier."

Kim's eyes brightened. "That's good to hear. I opened the paper this morning, saw Jay's photograph, and I thought... well, it all seems very clear. All that's left now is to confirm things."

"What is it you're hoping to confirm?" Juliet asked, resting her chin upon one hand.

Kim smiled, looking almost quietly proud.

"I don't know how much you know about the UKPPS," she said. "For most of the people that we help, they stay within the service permanently. Even if years go by without any problems, that small chance of still being tracked down means they're on our books for life, as it were."

Juliet was already following. "Unless, of course, the person who wishes them harm..."

Kim nodded. "Ian's death takes away most of the danger for Jay. It's not often this scenario rolls around, but... well, for the person who's been living under threat, it's a big relief."

"He's definitely happier for it," Juliet said. "Can I check, though —*most* of the danger?"

"No known threats exist," Kim replied, swift to reassure. "Personally, I believe very strongly that Ian was the only person who still wished Jay harm after all these years. We've seen no attempts by anyone else to trace Jay, nor to discover his whereabouts, and that's the main thing to take home. But it's nothing we can rule out conclusively. There's always a possibility."

Juliet nodded a little, thinking. "In normal circumstances, what would you now recommend?"

"I'd usually want to meet with Jay first. Ask his opinion on it all, and make sure that any decision is one which he feels comfortable with. In normal circumstances, there might be a case for moving him again. His identity has been compromised, his new location discovered, and even though Ian is dead... well, friends and family live on. There might be a case."

"But?" Juliet prompted, transferring half a cherry tomato to her mouth.

Kim smiled a little. "But it seems to me he might have entered a brand new protection scheme. One more specialised to his needs than we can ever be, and one I'm sure he'd be reluctant to leave."

Juliet chuckled. "I can tell you for free that he won't move again. He was anchored here already with his charity, but now there's Alastair too... if you offered it, he'd turn you down without a blink."

"I had a feeling that might be the case," Kim said. She paused, preparing something in her mouth. "*Most* people are a part of our service for life. On occasion, someone will leave us and be removed from our books. Sometimes it's because they violate their own protection so frequently that it becomes impossible for us to keep them safe. Sometimes people just grow tired of running. Sometimes they decide they just can't live a lie any longer, and they'd rather deal with the consequences."

"And sometimes they catch the eye of the Met commissioner," Juliet finished, amused.

Kim gave a small laugh. "Well... *very* rarely, yes. I think you understand what I'm driving towards."

Juliet hummed. "I do. You're wondering whether, going forwards, Jay's protection will still fall to the UKPPS—or if Scotland Yard will be taking on those duties."

"I appreciate you might not be in a position to say, but..." Kim took a breath. "Now Ian's gone, I don't blame Jay for wanting to cut his ties to the UKPPS and be free. I just want to make sure he'll be safe as he heads into the future. We're very proud of how he's changed, and... well, we want the best for him."

If they were here, Juliet thought, her heart glowing. *If you could see them together, just for five minutes.*

"I know you'll want some official confirmation," she said. "If you leave me with your contact details, I'll ask Sir Alastair to get in touch with you and give you his own assurances. For now, between the two of us, you have absolutely nothing to worry about."

Kim's gaze softened. "Really?"

"Really," Juliet murmured. "Sir Alastair is extremely fond of him. Extremely protective. In the wake of the kidnapping, we've made considerable improvements to Alastair's private security. As his partner, all of those measures extend to Jay."

"That's very reassuring to hear."

"We'll be monitoring closely for any future threats, not only in London but also in Manchester. If a problem arises, we'll take immediate steps to neutralise it."

"Thank you," Kim said, her expression more relieved by the moment. "Thank you, I... I appreciate your reassurance. We try not to form attachments to our people. Jay has always been something of an exception, though."

Amused, Juliet retrieved her fork from within her salad. "Isn't he just?" she said. "He's really quite exceptional at being the exception. Never met such a consummate outlier in all my life."

Kim's smile seemed to shine.

"Thank you for your time," she said. "I'll leave you to finish your lunch, but here's my card. If you could pass it along to Sir Alastair, and let him know that I called... it's not urgent, of course. I'll wait until I hear from him to close Jay's file officially. But it sounds like I can get all the paperwork together."

"I'm imagining a big red stamp," Juliet said, twirling her fork. *"Happily ever after,* block capitals across the front. Leave me your details as well, will you? I'll forward you the wedding photos."

Kim looked surprised and delighted, taking another card from inside her coat. "That's on the way, is it?" she asked.

Juliet reached out, taking the card between two fingers.

"Oh, it's coming," she said with a wink. "Just give me another six months."

Chapter 26

Two Years Later

SEVERAL PEOPLE HAD WARNED JAY TO EXPECT IT, AND IT TURNED OUT they were right. No day would ever pass as quickly as your wedding day.

Around half past five, Jay seemed to come back into being. He found himself standing by the sink in an empty ground floor bathroom, pressing his damp palms to either side of his neck. The past five minutes had been the only part of the day where nobody knew where he was. The sound of water rushing from the tap was clearing all the chaos from his head. It felt good just to stand here, to be aware of his own thoughts again.

As he looked at himself in the mirror, his collar undone and his dove-grey satin tie pulled loose, the platinum band around Jay's finger caught his eye.

He grinned to himself, dazed, and shook his head.

They'd all been right that today would be a blur. They'd been right about something else too, something that made it all worth it. Married *did* feel different. It felt incredible. The two of them would wake up tomorrow morning in their suite, look back on today's whirl of happy commotion, and smile—then the really good part could begin.

Drying off his neck with paper towels, Jay let himself enjoy these last few moments of peace. They still had the evening reception ahead of them, their first dance and the cake and everybody drinking. He knew *his* lot would behave themselves, all the people from the Fieldhouse Foundation, but the hordes of politicians and Oxbridge alumni would be another matter. Tidied up, grounded and ready, he helped himself to fancy hand cream and an imperial mint from the bowl. It was his wedding day, after all. He slipped out of the bathroom, tucking the mint between his teeth and his cheek to enjoy at his leisure, and headed back along the corridor.

Arriving in the lobby, he found that the changeover for the reception was well underway, all the Cliveden team busy moving tables and chairs. He wondered at once if he should help. Though he'd spent the last twelve months as a wealthy man's fiancé, his blood and his bones remained as working class as ever. The sight of other people carrying chairs awoke instincts in him that he'd never quite be able to put aside.

Before he could come to a decision, something else caught his eye: a figure hovering beside a nearby pillar, hanging back and watching the staff.

At the sight of his new husband, Jay's heart gave a thump.

Alastair was even more gorgeous than the day they'd met. He'd stripped down to his shirtsleeves and his waistcoat in the afternoon heat, and the muted lavender silk hugged the curve of his back like it loved him. He'd retired now, released from Scotland Yard's grooming guidelines, and he'd voiced more than once that he might try growing a short beard. Even the thought sent Jay's blood into a simmer. It had taken several months for Alastair to learn to use his reading glasses responsibly, not to peer at Jay over the top of them unless he really did want to be fucked across the nearest item of furniture. He still did it, just not when Jay was on the phone to the gas company. Jay had never doubted he would look like an absolute dream on their wedding day.

Only one thing spoiled the view.

Alastair was biting the corner of his thumbnail. He'd developed the habit in the early stages of wedding planning, and continued it ever since. Whenever it was pointed out to him, he dismissed the suggestion with a tut and claimed he had a patch of dry skin. Strangely, this dryness only appeared when he was feeling out of place. Jay had coaxed him into a large glass of Glenfiddich last night, just to make sure he got some sleep. He wondered if another glass now might be wise. They had a lot of guests on the way, a lot of friends. The line between a hectic day and a stressful day could be extremely thin.

Then Jay remembered where they were, and realised he could do a lot better than whisky.

He put his plan into action at once. If they didn't take this chance, they might not get another. He slipped across the lobby, glancing around to make sure Juliet and her laminated wedding timetable weren't on the scene. All eyes were elsewhere, all attention diverted.

Stealing up behind his new husband, Jay caught hold of Alastair's hand.

"Oi," he whispered in Alastair's ear, squeezing his fingers as he jumped. He smelled like the new hair wax he'd bought specially for today. Its scent was crisp and enticing, and Jay had longed to take a breath of it all afternoon. Alastair glanced at him, frowning in confusion. "Come on," Jay said, tugging on his hand. "Quick. Before anybody spots us."

Alastair's expression opened. He didn't ask; he didn't say a word. He slid his fingers between Jay's, willing in an instant to follow. Jay pulled him quickly across the lobby, down a hallway and out through an unlocked staff exit into a courtyard, stumbling over the gravel in their dress shoes.

They raced hand in hand across the lawns, laughing like boys as they checked over their shoulders.

No one saw them go.

Alone beneath the trees, Jay lifted Alastair's hand to his lips.

"Do you think Juliet'll go mental?" he asked, kissing Alastair's wedding ring as they strolled. They'd chosen matching bands, simple and clean, with an engraving hidden inside: *Grow old along with me.* "When she sees we've done a bunk, I mean."

Alastair chuckled. His eyes were bright in the light of the setting sun, happier and more at ease than Jay had seen him all day. "I imagine she's already formed the search party. She'll have men with torches and hounds on our tail any minute now."

"Tell her it was my fault," Jay said, wrapping his arm around Alastair's waist. "You were being good, waiting patiently for the next stage of her fairytale wedding to begin. Then your wicked new husband stole you off into the woods. Slung you over my shoulder and ran. Nothing you could do to stop me."

Humming, Alastair cuddled into his side. "'Husband'."

Jay grinned. He'd thought it too, several times over the course of the day. For months, that word had been like the wedding suits hanging together in their wardrobe—there within reach, but not real just yet.

Now it was real for the rest of their lives.

"Husband," Jay said softly, touching his nose to Alastair's temple. "That alright?"

"Mm. Incredibly alright." Alastair took in a breath, resting himself against Jay as they walked. "This is perfect, sweetheart. Thank you. I didn't realise how much I needed it."

Jay smiled. "It's been a long day," he said. "We've earned a few minutes just for us."

"It's been wonderful. Genuinely. The happiest day I can remember, and we're barely halfway through. But... well, I'll admit it's been..."

"Bloody fast?"

Alastair huffed. "Mm. Fast, and very busy."

Jay kissed the slope of Alastair's shoulder, their footsteps perfectly in sync. They'd walked this path in every season now—seen it in the snow, bare branches all around, no noise whatsoever but the soft and steady crunching of their boots; seen it in the heights of spring, explosions of tiny flowers and bobbing little birds in every tree. Today, on their wedding day, the summer was just tipping into autumn. The leaves were at their best, their colours rich and golden, the grass scorched dry by a hot and sunny August. All the trees seemed to glow in the evening light, decorated specially just for them.

"Feels like we haven't stopped all day," Jay said, brushing his thumb against the curve of Alastair's waist. "Everyone keeps taking you away from me."

"I've felt that, too. I don't think I've seen so little of you in months."

"Mm. Needing you for this, needing you for that. Needing you for photos. Even during the ceremony, it was hard to... you know, with everybody there watching..." Jay pulled a face, hoping that Alastair understood. "Is it wrong that I kept wishing we were on our own?"

"I hope not," Alastair said, amused, "given that I was thinking exactly the same."

Jay grinned in relief.

"I kept worrying I was going to mess up my lines," he admitted. "Say my name when I was supposed to say yours. Or just blurt out some random person's name. Not because I secretly want to marry them or anything, just because I was so bloody nervous. Felt like my mouth wasn't getting any signals from my brain."

Alastair laughed, delighted. "I hope you know that I'd have understood completely."

"Yeah? I'm glad I didn't, but..."

"I spent most of the ceremony worrying about you. You'd gone so pale. Holding onto my hands like you were about to pass out."

"Jesus, Al, I'm sorry."

"Don't be. I've never felt so protective of you in all my life. I almost wanted to shout at them all to avert their eyes and stop making you so self-conscious. Then someone started coughing—"

"Christ, I remember the coughing!"

"But not *properly.* Not one single, simple cough."

"No, they had to try and be quiet about it. Little *huh-chuh-chuhs* every time one of us spoke."

"And the crinkly sweet wrapper?"

"Yes! Who the hell was eating sweets?"

"I think it might have been a cough drop. I certainly *hope* it was a cough drop. If it was anything nice, I'd like to know why the grooms weren't offered one."

"I couldn't even work out who it was," Jay said, laughing. "Then I realised I'd stopped paying attention to the registrar, and... well, I know that bit's meant to be... you know, it's the important bit. The bit that makes it all real. And I felt so guilty, because I couldn't even concentrate. I was just staring at you and wanting to cry."

Smiling, Alastair hugged him around the middle, pressing his cheek to Jay's shoulder.

"It's *legally* important, perhaps," he said. "But as to the happiest moment of our life... well, I'm personally enjoying this one more."

Warmth filled Jay's chest in a wave. He gathered Alastair in and hugged him tighter as they walked, kissing him gently on the head.

"I'm enjoying it too," he said. "I'm glad I stole you. I saw you standing there on your own in the hall, and I realised I wanted you to myself a while. Wanted some time to remember what this day's all about."

Alastair pulled in a happy sigh. "I'm looking forward to waking up in the morning. Sleeping a little later, having breakfast when we want."

Jay's chest ached at the thought. If they didn't leave their room at all, didn't see another human face all day, that would be fine. He would happily spend every hour between dawn and dusk in the window seat, smoking and watching the clouds with his husband.

"Let's make it a quiet day tomorrow," he said. He nudged Alastair's temple with his nose. "Just us."

Alastair smiled, lifting his head to meet the nuzzle. "That sounds idyllic," he said, brushing his lips over Jay's.

Jay kissed him back, helpless to keep himself from smiling. Though the challenge of walking safely soon put an end to the kiss, the smile remained on Jay's face. They settled back into their stride, flushed and grinning; Jay hooked his thumb through Alastair's belt-loop.

"Mad to think we're married," he said. "I didn't know if it'd feel different or not. I think it does, though."

Alastair hummed, wrapping his arm around Jay's lower back. "It's comforting, isn't it? Being a married man. I feel very settled. Very proud and supported."

"I get you. It's nice, thinking the world'll treat us as a married couple."

"Mm. Using our new names at last."

"Ah! I've been practicing. Okay, don't help me. I've got it. I'm going to nail it. Here goes. The Right Honourable Lord Fieldhouse-Harding—"

"The Right Honourable *the* Lord Fieldhouse-Harding," Alastair corrected, biting down into a grin.

Jay rolled his eyes, aghast.

"What?" he demanded. "Why is there just a random *'the'* stuck there? That doesn't even make any... alright, fine. The Right Honourable *the* Lord Fieldhouse-Harding, otherwise known as Baron Fieldhouse-Harding, otherwise known as... my husband."

He kissed Alastair fondly on the head, prompting a pleased glow.

"And the Honourable Jay Fieldhouse-Harding," he added, "otherwise known as me."

Alastair squeezed him around the waist. "Word perfect. Spot on."

"And we're certain that I have to be 'the Honourable'?"

"Yes, dear heart."

"Definitely not allowed to be the *Dis*honourable Jay Fieldhouse-Harding?"

"No, dear heart. It's taken a year to reach an agreement on *any* courtesy title. Besides," Alastair added, leaning contentedly into Jay's side, "I'm afraid you've signed the paperwork now. You're my honourable husband for life, whether you like it or not. And I'll be hiding the marriage certificate when we're home, which means you can't return me without the receipt."

Grinning, Jay nuzzled at the top of Alastair's ear. "Fine. I'll make my peace with being honourable," he teased. "For you."

"Will two weeks in the Seychelles help?"

"It will."

"After a restful few days here, of course."

Late breakfasts, Jay thought, shining inside. *Afternoon walks. Pull your chair out for you at dinner, rub your wedding ring as we talk.*

"Wherever we're resting," he said, "I don't mind, love. So long as you're resting next to me."

Alastair's eyes sparkled in the sunlight.

"And I always will be," he said. He splayed his hand against Jay's lower back, stroking him gently through the fabric of his waistcoat. "Perhaps we should fasten our shoelaces together before we go back. That way we can't be pulled apart anymore."

"Holy shit. Have I mentioned that I love your mind?"

"Might make our first dance somewhat precarious, but..."

"Al, we both know there's a ninety per cent chance that I'm going to end up flat on my arse, whether we're tethered at the ankles or not. At least this way I'll take you down with me."

"And really, isn't that what marriage is all about?"

"Speaking after nearly five hours of wedded bliss," Jay said, "yes. Yes, it is. That's literally all there is to it."

Alastair's laughter rang through the trees. Jay nuzzled closer to him, grinning, nipping the shell of his ear.

"Jay," Alastair said softly, tightening his arm around Jay's waist. "We're here."

Jay looked up.

A familiar fork was appearing in the path ahead. At its junction stood a familiar tree, brighter than a bonfire in the golden light. Few sights in the world ever put Jay in mind of a greater power, but this would always be one of them. This tree was altar, priest, and god at once. Stepping beneath its boughs felt like moving from this world into another.

As he and Alastair settled close against its trunk, a moment came which raised the hairs on Jay's arms. He cupped his hands around Alastair's face, shivering as his husband cupped his too. They looked into each other's eyes, a breath apart as their hearts beat gently beneath their waistcoats. Jay had a feeling that whenever he looked back on their wedding day, it was this part he'd remember first.

Alastair brushed his thumb beneath Jay's lips, following its path with his gaze.

"I, Alastair," he murmured, "take thee, Jay, to be my husband."

Jay's heart heaved. He laid their foreheads together, trembling, then closed his eyes and said the words. "I, Jay... take you, Al, to be my husband."

Alastair's fingers curled gently in his hair, keeping him close. "I'll love you for the rest of my life, Jay. I promise you. I'll honour you. Look after you. Stand next to you without condition."

The words came easily, as natural as breathing.

"Whatever gave me life," Jay said, "it wanted me to spend it with you." His throat tightened; the tears didn't stop him from speaking. "You're my best friend and my hero. And I'll never give you cause to give up on me. Never."

Alastair's eyes began to shine. Overcome, he swallowed and made no sound. He stroked Jay's face with his fingertips instead, shaking a little, gazing at Jay's lips.

Jay smiled, cradling his husband close.

"It's alright," he whispered, resting his lips against the bridge of Alastair's nose. "I know. I love you, too."

How long they stayed holding each other, Jay couldn't be sure. Beneath this tree, time didn't exist as something which passed. It simply existed as it was, a pool instead of a river, and the world and all its people could wait. Their tree glowed gently, holding them here as the insects in its canopy swirled and hummed, the sunshine warm upon their skin. It felt like being blessed.

When the last of their tears had dried, Jay kissed the patches of pink on Alastair's cheeks. "You okay, love?"

Alastair nodded, cuddling closer to him. "I absolutely adore you."

Smiling, Jay ran both his hands up the back of Alastair's waistcoat. "This is where I realised, you know. First time we ever came to Cliveden. We were underneath this tree, and you asked me to stay and have dinner with you. Do you remember?"

Alastair shivered, nodding gently.

Jay's heart was singing with the memories. "I looked into your eyes and I thought... this guy right here is everything. And he's so out of my reach, and so perfect. And it'll cripple me forever when he leaves."

Alastair's fingers scrunched in his hair.

"Never," he whispered. He pushed close, pressing Jay's body up against the bark. "Never, Jay. Never, never."

Their lips came together in a rush.

For all of three seconds, Jay tried to kiss Alastair gently, as sweetly as their wedding day deserved. His husband's arms then grew tight around him, grasping his body through his suit, and he surrendered and kissed Al like he wanted. *We're married,* he thought, burning with joy, and pushed his hands across the heaving of Alastair's chest. Alastair shivered with a moan against his lips. *Oh, fuck. My husband.*

When they finally made their way back through the forest, ruffled and giggling, Alastair's hand snuck into Jay's back pocket.

"Stay close to me for the reception," he said. "Promise me. Don't let anyone else take you away."

Jay sealed it with a kiss, holding his lips to Alastair's cheek. "I won't leave your side, sunshine. Promise."

"Just sit me on your lap all night and feed me cheesecake. If everyone is horrified, it's entirely their own fault for coming."

"Suppose they should know what we're like by now, shouldn't they?"

"They should indeed. They've had two long years to learn. And now that I'm retired, and I no longer have to rely on anyone's professional respect, they can all just cope with the sight of my tongue down your throat."

If Jay had ever laughed this loudly in his life, he didn't remember it.

His husband grinned, stopped him on the path, and snaked both arms around his neck for another kiss.

Attempting to slip back into the hotel unnoticed, they were met by a wall of cheers. As applause and whistles rang through the lobby, Jay flashed them all a guilty grin and tightened his arm around his husband's waist, hoping it wasn't too obvious they'd crept off into the woods for a snog. Most of their guests seemed to be here already, kitted out in their finest and ready to celebrate, everybody holding champagne. Behind the crowd, the Cliveden team were getting ready to open the buffet, arranging the hot plates and polishing baskets of cutlery.

Jay scanned the sea of happy faces, expecting to see Juliet among them, possibly tapping her watch in their direction with a scowl. He couldn't pick her out, though.

Alastair addressed the crowd, holding onto Jay.

"Thank you all," he said, his fingers curling protectively around the buckle on the back of Jay's waistcoat. "We're so glad you could be here. It means the world."

Smiling, Jay placed a proud kiss on his husband's shoulder. *I'm staying close, love. I promise.* As people filtered over to chat, offering handshakes and congratulations, he kept his arm around Alastair's middle. Anyone who wanted a hug could hug them both.

After a few minutes, Connor slipped his way to the front of the queue, unmissable in his sunshine-yellow suit and bearing two glasses of champagne. A lifetime in marketing had given him an unparalleled ability to get away with being cheeky. Nobody blinked as he cut directly to Jay's side.

"For the happy couple," he said, bright-eyed, and handed the first glass to Alastair. "I thought you'd need one. You must be desperate by now. Is it true that it goes by in a flash?"

Jay took the second glass gratefully. "Mate, you would not believe." He gulped back a few mouthfuls of champagne, trying not to remember what this cost per bottle. "*Gahh*—thanks, Connor. Listen, have you seen Juliet? She's not been looking for us, has she?"

"I don't think so," Connor said. "Haven't spotted her in a while, to be honest. Do you want me to see if I can find her?"

"Oh, no. Don't worry. She's probably just having a rest somewhere. Don't blame her."

Alastair hugged Jay gently for his attention. "Darling, have you met Mr Garston? I was just telling Richard about the community art project you're running in November..."

Jay gave Connor an apologetic grin. With an understanding nod and a pat to Jay's arm, Connor slipped off through the crowd, leaving Jay to join in with a familiar routine: greeting some random and apparently important person, smiling like he'd heard so much about them, then following Alastair's lead in conversation and laughing at their jokes until they left. He'd been accompanying Alastair to fancy social events for nearly two years now, and they had the whole performance worked out. He'd already done it about twenty times today.

As this latest random person went on, Jay occupied himself with champagne and stroking his husband's lower back.

They circulated for another twenty minutes or so, saying hello to familiar faces and introducing each other to new ones, always together. Everyone from the Fieldhouse Foundation was here, all overjoyed to see Jay married. Several even shed a few tears as they chatted. Larry had made it, along with Mrs Larry and the little Larries. All four were miniature replicas of their father, even the girls. They were wearing shiny new shoes and clearly under orders of their very best behaviour. As she was presented to them, Mrs Larry actually curtsied. Jay threw his arms around Larry in a bear hug, clapping him between the shoulders.

Larry laughed in his ear, gripping him back. "Congratulations, sir."

Grinning, Jay pulled back to arm's length and held him by the elbows. "Mate, I've told you. You don't have to 'sir' me, even when Al's around. This isn't that kind of household any more."

Larry's eyes flashed with mischief. "Of course, sir. Very good, sir."

"Daddy," whined a small voice from somewhere below. They glanced down to find the smallest of Larry's progeny gazing up at them. She hadn't quite grown into her ears yet. "When we gonna eat? I'm 'ank marvin'."

As a wide-eyed Larry hushed the little girl, and Mrs Larry hurried to apologise, Alastair laughed in delight.

"Not at all," he reassured them, then gave Jay a hopeful smile. "I'm getting hungry too, as it happens. Shall we find out if they're ready to cut the ribbon on the buffet?"

Jay had been daydreaming about chocolate-covered strawberries for the past three hours. If anything, it was a little odd that the buffet hadn't opened yet. He seemed to remember from Juliet's comprehensive wedding notes that they all should be eating by now.

"There's a plan," he said. He scruffled the hair of the smallest Larry. "You hang tight, yeah? We'll go see what we can do."

As they cut across the room towards the buffet, Jay held a hand out with a smile.

Alastair took hold of it, amused. "It's a five second walk, darling."

"So?" Jay said. "That's five seconds we can spend holding hands." He gathered their fingers together, keeping hold of them as they reached a small huddle of the waiting staff. "Is there anything we can do to help, guys? Think a few people are getting peckish."

It was rare for the Cliveden team to show any kind of uncertainty. Only Jay's familiarity with them flagged up the small skip in their smiles, the fractional pause before politeness and reassurance kicked in.

"We're waiting for the final nod from the assistant manager, sir," a red-haired girl with freckles said. "Just to confirm the kitchen has everything ready to go. She should be here at any minute."

Weird, Jay thought. Unexpected delays were unusual at Cliveden. Things generally ran like clockwork. Stealing a glance at Alastair, he found a similar thought on his husband's face—not exactly concern, more a suspicious curiosity.

It vanished from Alastair's expression in an instant, replaced by a gracious smile.

"Thank you," he said to the staff. "And please don't worry. I'm sure everyone can sustain themselves for a little longer."

They nodded politely, grateful for his understanding, and carried on polishing the cutlery.

As Jay and Alastair moved away from the buffet, Alastair seemed to have a destination in mind. The slight pull of his hand steered Jay casually around the outside of the crowd, heading towards an arch which led away from the lobby.

"Are we going somewhere?" Jay asked.

Alastair hummed. "Testing a theory," he said, smiling at a group of Fieldhouse workers as they passed. "This way." He tugged Jay through the arch, across a wood-panelled lounge, then over towards a staff door partly hidden by a curtain.

Suspecting something, Jay hung back a little.

"You're not going to be snippy, are you?" he said. Alastair opened the door. "The kitchen'll have mixed up the gluten-free sandwiches with the gluten ones. Something like that. Mistakes happen."

Alastair cast him an amused look, pulling him through.

"Of course I'm not going to be snippy," he said. "And who knows? Perhaps I'm wrong. But have you noticed something odd about our most recent trips to Cliveden?"

Jay racked his brains. There'd been a considerable number of meetings with the wedding planner, discussing seating plans, testing different kinds of cake, deciding whether peonies and lily of the valley were clichéd or iconic—the answer to which still privately eluded Jay.

"We've been here quite a bit," he said, following Alastair along the staff corridor. "Getting things ready, I mean."

"We have indeed." Alastair flashed him a smile over one shoulder. "And always with Juliet in tow. She's been more than willing to throw her toothbrush into her handbag and join us last minute. I don't think she's missed a single chance to come along."

Jay blinked, lost.

"So she can help with the wedding," he said. "Right? She's been working on this like she's planning an invasion of Russia, Al. She added me to the Asana team within three hours of us getting engaged. It's no wonder she wanted to be here."

"Mm. Though I'll admit I've suspected another reason, too." Alastair laid a finger against his lips, gesturing for Jay to hush, then approached a closed door at the end of the corridor. *Guest Services Assistant Manager,* read the polished wooden plaque. They'd visited this office more than once in the last few months, sometimes just to say hello, and always been very warmly welcomed.

To Jay's surprise, Alastair reached directly for the handle. It wasn't like him to skip a knock. He twisted the brass arm with a squeak and cracked open the door, unleashing the sound of a hastily-stifled moan. There came a gasp, then a clatter as some object hit the ground.

Smiling, Alastair pushed wide the door.

In a flurry of peacock blue satin, Juliet removed herself from the assistant manager's lap. She staggered a little as she got down, smoothed her dress back over her petticoats and swept her ruffled curls back from her face, fanning the flush from her cheeks with a hand. Open-mouthed, Jay turned his astonished attention to the figure still slumped within the chair.

Katie stared back at him, her collar flipped up and her hair ruffled wildly onto end. The bottom half of her face was smeared with Juliet's lipstick.

Alastair hummed, thoroughly unsurprised.

"I don't remember seeing this on the timetable, Juliet," he said. "Or does this come under the broader heading of 'buffet'?"

Jay creased. He couldn't help it. As he bent against the doorframe, trying not to laugh, Juliet cleared her throat and made a valiant attempt at dignity.

"Given that preparations for the reception were proceeding so smoothly," she said, holding her lipstick-blotched chin high, "I thought I'd check and see if there was anything the guest services team needed."

Alastair raised an eyebrow. "Or wanted?" he said.

Jay bit down into his lip, unsure why he loved Katie's wide-eyed look of guilt so much. "The buffet team want to know if the kitchens are ready to go," he told her, smiling. "They're hanging fire for your signal."

Her face flashed with horror. "Oh, *God.*" She grabbed towards a vacant spot on her desk, found it empty, then bent down and retrieved her fallen phone from the floor. "Shit, shit. I'm so sorry. I'll check with them now."

"This was entirely my doing," Juliet said at once. "I distracted her. It's not her fault."

Alastair cast a fond frown in her direction. "If you think we'd be annoyed over such a minor delay, and for such a worthy cause, then you clearly don't know us at all."

With a grin, Jay added his support. "It's good to keep people waiting for food at a wedding," he said. "Gets their appetites up. Fewer leftovers to take home."

Relief relaxed the line of Juliet's shoulders. She drew a breath, her chest heaving beneath its satin sweetheart neckline, and risked an embarrassed smile at them both.

"Katie was helping me to adjust my tights," she said.

Alastair huffed. "Was she?" he said. "She clearly needs more practice at it, given that she's accidentally removed your knickers in the attempt."

Blushing, Juliet snatched a flutter of mint green lace from the back of Katie's chair.

"So it seems," she said, hiding it away within her fist. "How unfortunate."

Katie finished her conversation with the kitchen, put down the receiver, and gave them both a look of deepest apology.

"Everything's ready," she said. "They're going to start moving the food through right now. It's all still hot and nothing's overdone." She got out of her chair with a squeak. "I'll go make sure they're—"

Laughing, Jay put out a hand to stop her. "You'd better have a minute with a mirror first, chick. Your team can carry dishes on their own."

"Agreed," Alastair said, his eyes sparkling. He slipped his arm through Jay's. "Perhaps we should go ahead and ensure everything's in hand, darling. I'm sure Katie and Juliet will join us when they can."

Smiling, Jay wrapped his hand over Alastair's.

"I do believe that's a splendid idea," he teased. He dropped Katie a reassuring wink, enjoying the nervous grin that it caused. "You two finish up with Juliet's tights, and we'll save you a plate of mini quiches."

As Jay led the way back along the corridor, Alastair leant in to kiss his cheek.

"Good for Katie," Jay murmured, holding open the door for him.

Alastair hummed. "Yes. Very good for both of them."

"I didn't know that Juliet—?"

"Oh, yes. Her women are rarer, but often seem more meaningful."

"Well, I hope this one's meaningful. Hope it turns into something."

"Mm, so do I." Smiling, Alastair faked a laboured sigh. "I suppose we'll just have to keep coming to Cliveden, and bringing Juliet along with us. Make sure there's plenty of opportunity for things to develop."

Chuckling, Jay squeezed him around the middle.

"Oh, no," he intoned, and guided Alastair back into the lobby.

To Jay's surprise, they performed their first dance without a stumble. He worried that he'd had too many glasses of champagne to manage it, overshot alcoholic courage and ended up in alcoholic incompetence. But with Alastair held close to him, and the familiar sound of *Come Away with Me* playing across the crowd, it felt like a practice session at home in the lounge. The faces watching from around the dance floor blurred away, leaving the two of them alone with the music.

As Jay realised it was going well, he grinned with relief at his new husband. Alastair's eyes were bright as stars. They reflected all of Jay's happiness back at him, proud and full of love.

We're married, Jay realised again in a rush. *For real. We did it.* It seemed strange that it made him feel so dizzy. They'd been planning this day for months on end, agonising over every little detail, and still it had come as a surprise. This was the first night of the rest of their lives. From this day on, he had a husband and a family, and nothing would take that away.

The dance passed all too quickly, three minutes and eighteen seconds gone by in a flash. Alastair didn't talk until it was over. He simply relaxed and let Jay lead, resting in his arms, looking up into his eyes.

As they finally embraced, surrounded on all sides by applause, Alastair spoke softly in Jay's ear.

"What were you thinking?" he asked. "You looked like you were in rapture."

Jay held onto him, trying to put it into words—trying not to cry.

"Can't believe how far we've come, that's all. Can't believe how much we've..." He pressed his face against Alastair's shoulder. "You're actually mine. For good. I'm so lucky."

Alastair's chest seemed to swell. He brushed his fingers through the back of Jay's hair, holding onto him as the band struck up another song, inviting the other guests onto the floor.

"I'd go through it all again," he said. "All of it, Jay. Even the very worst. So long as I get to hold you on our wedding day."

Jay's throat gripped. He swallowed, rubbing Alastair's shoulders to try and calm himself. "You used to say we can't have everything in life. Do you remember, sunshine?"

Alastair huffed, smoothing his hair. "So I did," he said. "Thank you for correcting me on that."

For a few minutes more, they simply held each other and swayed, letting their happiness sink in.

At last, Alastair murmured, "I think we've earned a few minutes by ourselves, don't you? Shall we find a quiet spot and some dessert?"

Speechless, Jay nodded. He took hold of his husband's hand.

They spent the rest of the night eating cheesecake together in a corner, whispering and laughing as they fed each other spoonfuls.

They spent the rest of their lives side by side—and even in the hardest of times, they were happy.

The End

Acknowledgments

I have a lot of people to thank for *The Sheltering Tree*. I'd like to start with my incredible clan of patrons, who very literally kept the roof over my head as I worked on this book. 2020 was... well, we'll say eventful. I paid bills and fed my family thanks to the kindness of my readers, and sharing updates on the progress of Jay and Alastair kept me sane. I can't possibly express how grateful I am to everyone who reached out a hand to stop us falling.

I'd like to mention the special generosity of the following people:

Adelaide P., Annmarie H., Christine M., Ciara, Cindy L., Claudia C., Elaine S., Emily L., Erin M., Holly B., JoAnne P., Johanna D.C., Kate M.L. Kay & Marissa S.S., Kiley, Laura A., Lea W.B., Lynda Q., Maria E., Marz, Mice, Michelle J., Patty L., Peabodycat, Petra S., Rachel M., Sara S., Sarah P., Scaredy Cat, Star R., Yasmeen H.

In addition, a heartfelt and loving thank you to Colleen and Janelle for the vast amount of hard work, patience and support you've invested in me and in this story. It's been a joy to work with you both; thank you for taking such good care of me. Shout-out to Rachel

Maybury for not only suggesting *The Sheltering Tree* come into existence but expertly promoting it as well. Thank you also to my intrepid squad of first readers—Johanna, Holly, Petra, JoAnne and Billie—who helped to put my fractious mind at ease. And to everyone who read and enjoyed this story in its sapling form: thank you, too. This wouldn't have happened without you.

Of all the trees in the wide and verdant forest of my friends, four in particular have gone out of their way to shelter me this year. I'd like to express my love for Petra Stedman, who hid me in her pocket and fed me crumbs; Ewebie Larkin, deputy commissioner of shenanigans; and Kay and Marissa, who brighten even the rainiest of days.

My final words of thanks, as always, are for Carrie. You're having a bath as I type this, angel. I can hear you listening to show tunes and singing. When you're done, we'll have fishfinger sandwiches and carry on with *Crooked House*. I think Sophia maybe did it. But the great aunt is looking kinda shady, too.

Please don't ever change.

Also by J.R. Lawrie

Three stories sure to warm the heart and captivate the senses. Full of romance, humor, sweetness, and the perfect amount of heat, this collection is perfect for an evening by the fire.

FOR SERVICES RENDERED

Dr. David Christmas has heard every joke in the book when it comes to his name. Weary of the festive season and from his long shifts in the emergency room, David is also tired of his lonely single life. His only hope for Christmas is a glimpse of the shy but gorgeous neighbour who lives above him.

Christmas-loving Julian has nurtured a crush on the grumpy man downstairs for years now. Still hurting from his ex-boyfriend's cruelty, he hasn't yet dared to say hello. When an injury on Christmas Eve puts Julian directly into David's careful hands, a little healing might be on the way.

KIND OF A BIG DEAL

and

THE FARRINGDON CLUB

Up-and-coming comedian Zack Wynn splits his time between the stage and the London pizza restaurant where he works, until life hands him one hell of a Christmas present. Richard Garston is the handsome and clever older man of Zack's dreams, but what exactly is it that Richard *does*?

Soon, Zack learns the truth: Richard's classified role in the British government makes him a much bigger deal than he claimed.

Is Zack ready for the politics and power of Richard's world?

And is Richard's world ready for him?

For news and updates, you can find J.R. Lawrie on Twitter as @jrlawrieauthor or visit jrlawrie.com

About Carnation Books

Carnation Books is a fandom-powered publisher of the best in inclusive fiction. Founded in 2016, Carnation Books is at the forefront of new author discovery. Visit carnationbooks.com to learn more, and to sign up for our story-filled newsletter!